THE

FIRST FALSE STEP.

𝔄 𝔑𝔬𝔳𝔢𝔩.

" When lovely woman stoops to folly,
And finds too late that men betray,
Ah! what can cure her melancholy?
What can charm her cares away?"
GOLDSMITH.

LONDON:
PUBLISHED BY EDWARD LLOYD, 12, SALISBURY-SQUARE,
FLEET-STREET.
—
1846.

THE FIRST FALSE STEP;

OR,

THE PATH OF CRIME.

𝔄 𝔯𝔬𝔪𝔞𝔫𝔠𝔢,

BY THE AUTHOR OF "VARNEY, THE VAMPIRE," "THE RIVALS," "JANE SHORE," ETC.

IN THREE PARTS.

PART I.
INNOCENCE AND TEMPTATION.

CHAPTER I.
THE TAVERN BY THE OLD GUN DOCK.
—THE BOAT ON THE RIVER.—THE
CHASE.—THE CATASTROPHE.

MODERN improvement has swept away an old tavern that stood close to the Gun Dock, on the banks of the Thames. When in existence, it was named the Victory, and within its old walls, patched as they were like some ancient garment, till scarcely a vestige remained of its original material, many a choice spirit has flashed and lived for many a happy hour. Well known and well appreciated were the alcoholic mixtures prepared at the Victory, and the evening was still but young when the small, low, black-looking, sanded parlour was always full of guests.

There were persons who came there as regularly as they rose in the morning, or retired to rest at night, or conducted any other ordinary routine business of the day— persons who could not have lived without the parlour of the old Victory, unless, indeed, they could have managed to transfer their affections to its more flaunting neighbour and rival, the Admiral Benbow.

But now, not a vestige of the old house remains. It is among the things that have been; and never again will that small spot of earth on which it stood support a structure within which so much mirth, jollity, wit, and good feeling, once found a home. But the evening on which we would conduct our readers to the house was one of gloom. There was a new and strange visitor within its walls—a visitor who repressed the laughter— a visitor who smothered the sparkling jest upon the lips of the speaker—a visitor who commanded the shutters to be closed—by whose stern mandate no one spoke in a higher tone than that of ordinary conversation, and who seemed to have enforced the servants of the house to creep gently up and down the old staircases as if they were afraid of awakening some one. Need we say that visitor was Death?

Yes; Death had entered within those jocund doors. The ghastly messenger that beckons humanity from the world, to which it clings with all its faults, to another it knows not of, had taken possession of that mansion which had so long been devoted to mirth and revelry, and, perhaps, in too many cases, to riot and licentiousness. It is strange the effect produced by one frail vestige of humanity, which has surrendered to its Maker that divine essence of it which is immortal, upon living, breathing man. He whom in life they might have treated with contempt, becomes respected in death; he whose voice while living might have been drowned by many others, is treated with respectful silence when no sound can come from his lips.

There were the usual number of guests in the old, blackened, dingy parlour—perhaps there were a few more than usual—for curiosity to hear the how, the when, and the where the death which had taken place in the house had occurred, drew every one who knew anything of the family, or of the old tavern, to the place.

There was plenty of conversation, too, but it was conducted in a subdued manner. The usual evening orators of the parlour were wonderfully quiet; those who were in the habit of speaking much, spoke little; those who had usually spoken but little, said now nothing at all; and a few of the more timid guests, who had occasionally come to hear the great Sir Oracles of the old parlour of the Victory settle the affairs of the nation, gave their orders to the waiter in a whisper, and then crept into odd corners, as if their greatest desire was to get entirely out of the way.

By degrees, however, the conversation became a little more general, and one man, with a commanding frontage, as he knocked the ashes from his pipe, glanced round upon the company, and said,—

"Well, so our old friend Woodward is gone at last; that's the way of the world. Landlords of taverns go the way of all flesh, as well as other folks. We are all grass, my friends—nothing in the world but grass."

"I suppose that accounts for some people being so green," said a youngish man, as he stretched out his legs, and pulled up to his knees a pair of loose horseman's boots of the period, which he wore.

All eyes were turned upon the speaker, who was a stranger to every one in that assembly. The audacious irreverence of the remark he had made appeared to strike everybody, and there was a look of marked displeasure upon the countenances of the elder frequenters of the room.

"Are you aware, sir," said one, with great gravity, and as if he intended every word he uttered to sink deep into the stranger's soul—"are you aware, sir, that, precisely over your head, through that ceiling and the floor above, Mr. Hercules Woodward, the landlord of this house, lies a corpse? I ask you, sir, are you aware of that, young man?"

As this person spoke, everybody looked up at the ceiling above the young man, as if they expected to see the corpse of the late Mr. Woodward make its appearance in some way, and say, "Yes; that's precisely correct; here I am."

"I am aware," said the young man, "that old fat Woodward is gone; but as to his being directly above my head, though it is a piece of news I can't, for my part, see the vast importance of."

He who had reproached the young man was about to speak again; but the gentleman with a commanding frontage waved his hand, and said,—

"Allow me;" then, turning his commanding frontage full upon the young man, he added,—"Young sir, with the long legs and faded waistcoat, I did not make a remark to you, and I have a great mind to ——"

"To do what?" said the young man; and he turned a sinister and ferocious look upon the other.

"Nothing," said the gentleman with the commanding frontage—"nothing whatever."

This was a serious disappointment to the assembled guests; for, although none of them would have liked to have tackled the disagreeable-looking young man themselves, they would have had not the least objection in life to a good row between him and the man with the commanding frontage.

The stranger laughed an odd sort of discordant laugh, and scarcely had it passed his lips, when such a tremendous noise came from the room above, in the shape of a heavy bump upon the floor, that every one simultaneously jumped upon his feet, looking both astonished and terrified.

There was but an instant's pause, and then every echo in the house was awakened by a shriek, which seemed to come from the same apartment.

The young man who had been so near creating a disturbance rushed to the window, and, flinging it open, cried out in a clear, loud voice,—

"Off and away, is it—off and away?"

There was a loud shout in answer to him, but the words were unintelligible to the guests in the parlour; and he sprang from the window, which was but a few feet from the ground, and then disappeared.

Some of the guests in the old parlour ran to the door, and others again crowded to the window, but nothing could be seen of the young stranger; and they were just recovering from the shock they had received, and beginning to ask each other what the noise from above had proceeded from, when Mistress Woodward, the widow of the landlord whose corpse lay in the room above, entered the oaken parlour, wringing her hands and exclaiming,—

"Oh, save her—save her! She's my only child—the only tie I have on earth. Save her, I implore you! Save my Minna, my beautiful child! She will be killed—she will be killed!"

Having uttered these frantic exclamations, she sunk into the arms of several who rushed forward to support her, or she must, in the excess of her emotion, have fallen to the floor.

The sounds of shrieks, and cries of alarm from without the room, were sufficiently indicative that something serious was occurring, and, with one accord, all who were not actively engaged in attending upon Mrs. Woodward rushed out into the porch of the old tavern, filled with alarm and curiosity.

There they found almost the whole establishment assembled within a few paces of the threshold, in attitudes of alarm, and all gazing up at an old gable end of the house, around which ran a low, wooden gallery, which for many years had been unused from its rotten and insecure condition.

When the old Victory tavern was first built, no doubt this sort of gallery or balcony was appended to that part of the house, in order that luxurious topers might there quaff their ale and smoke their pipes, while they, at the same time, commanded a view a good way down the Pool.

That side of the house had originally been but of weather boarding, so that, when that rotted, and the balcony rotted likewise, the structure became insecure.

Mr. Woodward was one of the leave-things-alone sort of men, and when, one day, some years before the events we are now recording, a heavy customer went into the balcony with a pot of ale in one hand and a pipe in the other, and found that it gave such a lurch, that he blessed his stars when he got out of it again, minus the ale, and the pipe, and his hat, Mr. Woodward had merely looked up and said—

"Ah! well—ah!—yes, yes; I have been thinking for these last five years that that wasn't safe, do you know; well, well, we mustn't use it; it's no use trying to build up another, for the side of the house wouldn't hold it. I'll have that pulled down some day."

With most people, things that are to be done some day, are never to be done at all, and so it was with Mr. Woodward's balcony; and there it remained, having an ominous sort of obliquity, and, from that time forward, no one ventured into it.

Its state of insecurity was well known to all the frequenters of the Victory, and hence, when they now beheld standing in it, with her eyes fixed upon the river, the young and beautiful girl, Minna Woodward, the daughter of the deceased landlord, they were horror-stricken, and between wonder at what had induced her to appear there, and fear lest some terrible catastrophe should overtake her, they stood like men completely paralyzed, not knowing what to do to avert the impending danger.

The young girl stood in the balcony with her hands crossed upon her breast, her head was thrown backwards, and her long and beautiful hair reached nearly to her feet; her loose white morning gown enveloped her slender frame: she moved not, she spoke not, but her eyes were fixed upon the stream, as if by some horrible fascination which deprived her of all power to withdraw them.

Her mother had now partially recovered from the state of torpor which had come over her, and, rushing from the house, she flung herself upon her knees, shrieking for that aid for her daughter which no one seemed to know how to render her.

"Save her!—save her, some one!" she cried—"get ladders, and save her—quick! quick!—the additional weight of a child in that balcony would bring it to the ground! Oh! snatch her from destruction, and earn a mother's fondest prayers! she is my child —my only one! You are men, all of you, and can do thus much for the widow and the fatherless! You know, all of you—it is commonly known to all who have been here more than once, that Minna has occasionally walked in her sleep—she is doing so now. God help her! or, sleeping or waking, she will never walk again!"

It was a sweet twilight; the sun was gently sinking, and the west was a flood of golden light: the slant rays, tinged with the glories of a thousand colours, fell upon the form of the beautiful girl, giving her an appearance far more of Heaven than of earth, and seeming as if they were intending to gild with beauty that death which, to the perceptions of all who looked upon her, appeared so certain.

A man at this moment approached with a ladder, but as he neared the balcony, there was a slight but still perceptible movement of the old rafters which still supported it, and he recoiled in dread of the task he had assigned himself.

"Heaven help her!" he said; "I would have saved her if I could, but I have children of my own. I dare not throw away my life, for I have children of my own."

There was a kind of stunned silence now among those who looked upon the figure of the girl; they saw her slowly move her hands, and stretch them out towards the river.

"She will speak now," said one, in a low whisper—"she will speak; and it is said that what is uttered by persons in that state is prophetic, and will surely come to pass."

"There, there," said the girl, in an excited voice, "are two boats upon the river; in the one a woman; in the other, the star of her destiny. Yes, yes, there are two boats upon the river. I see them there in the sweetest sunshine. The tide whirls them down the stream. Ah, now I see his form—he who occupies the one. 'Tis he, 'tis he! He has returned—returned to greet me, and yet shuns me. Heartwell, Heartwell, what have I done? What have I done? There, there! Ah, how he propels the boat through the eddying stream—his face is pale—there is blood upon his lips—he shuns me—he holds up his hand between me and the light of Heaven. And now the other boat—the other boat! It nears him now, and in it sits a pallid, shrinking form—'tis kneeling, and its hands outstretched, clasped amidst the tangled meshes of its hair. Can my eyes deceive me? No, no—that form, that face, they are my own, and as in a glass I now shall see my future fate. He flies me, and I pursue him—I who once flew while he pursued. There—there, he turns his face away. How the boat follows him! Now it whirls round in some encircling eddy; then, again, it shoots onward like a living thing, bearing its trembling burden to the loved one. It is myself—it is myself—an image of my destiny—a picture of that which shall be, when time has worked out Heaven's decrees. Behold—behold the boats near each other—now he pauses—does he relent? Yes, yes; the oars drop from his hands. No longer does he turn his face away in sternness and in wrath; he will speak to her again—to that once loved and long lost one. Heartwell! oh, Heartwell, this is mercy!"

The girl's attitude became more indicative of mental disturbance; she clung to the rails of the balcony with frantic force, and her voice rose to a tone of joy, as she cried,—

"There, there—the boats meet. He no longer shuns her—he will speak to her—now she nears him. She has been kneeling in that long wherry; but see, she rises to her feet, and, as the boats touch each other, she stretches out both her arms to clasp to her heart, for the first and the last time, him whom she loved. His action is the same; he relents, he relents—he bids time roll back to that happy period when both were innocent; he clasps her to his heart, and calls her his own once again. She is happy, and Heaven is merciful, for see, there comes a surge of the waters, the boats separate, and, heart to heart, cheek to cheek, they fall into the stream—like a huge chasm it opens to receive them; they are seen no more, but, side by side, they sleep beneath the surging waters. The dream of fate is past; my heart has read the star of my own destiny. Have mercy, Heaven!"

With a shriek of anguish she dropped upon her knees upon the balcony, and from the shock which she thus gave it, it loosened itself entirely from its frail fastenings, and bearing her with it, came down with a loud crash, sending a cloud of dust on to the small quay, or landing-place, below, and close to the feet of the astonished spectators of this singular scene.

The probability is that, had any person been in that balcony at the time of its fall, in full possession of all their physical energies, they would have come to some serious hurt; but the young girl whom we have thus introduced to the reader, being, as she was, in a state of somnambulism, and so totally unconscious of the danger of her situation, came down so gradually with the balcony, but beyond a shake, she sustained no injury. The fact was, after the first slip it made from its support, there was a slight pause in its fall for about a quarter of a minute's duration before it thoroughly wrenched itself from the old wall and fell entirely. This pause, no doubt, it was that saved Minna Woodward from destruction; but the fall had the effect of at once arousing her from her strange trance, and rendering her conscious of where she was, and the scene around her. The presumption that she must be killed upon the spot was so strong upon the mind of every one, that they all involuntarily recoiled from what they could not help thinking would be the sad spectacle of her remains; but when they heard her voice, which now rose in a frenzied cry for help, while the name of her mother mingled with her supplications, some who had the most presence of mind rushed forward to extricate her from among the ruins of the balcony. Before, however, they could accomplish this, there appeared, to the surprise of them all, a human form, at the door above, which had led into the balcony, but which now had all the appearance of an opening into the house.

These last two or three events, as is always the case when any rapid and serious actions occur, had followed so close upon each other as to occupy much less time in their proceeding than we have been compelled to take in relating them. In fact, the cloud of dust which the fall of the balcony had created, was very far from having dissipated, when there appeared this figure we have mentioned at the now apparently unmeaning-looking opening in the wall. None knew that figure amid the confusion of the moment, but when his voice rose, loud and clear, above all other sounds, and the words "Minna! Minna! tell me that you live!" reached the ears of the beautiful girl, who had gone through so strange an adventure, she herself sprung to her feet amid the ruins of the old wooden structure, and exclaimed, in a voice of joy and hopefulness,—

"I am here, Heartwell!—Heartwell!—David Heartwell, I am here!"

The leap from that ancient doorway down among the ruins was a perilous one, and one which few men, even with a strong impelling motive, would have cared to take; but David Heartwell, the chosen of Minna's fondest affections, was not of the calculating and careful order of human beings; he was more in the habit of doing the daring act first, and thinking of it afterwards, than of pausing on its first impulse. He had a cool head and a stout heart, and was as active and as agile as an eel; he measured the distance for a moment with his eye, and then he took the leap. He alighted in safety close to Minna, and she, with a cry of joy, flung herself into his arms.

CHAPTER II.

THE HONOURABLE BULKLEY HARDING GETS THE COMMAND OF THE EOLUS FRIGATE, AND THINKS IT A BORE.—THE DINNER AT LA ROCHE'S, AND THE BIT OF MISCHIEF CONCOCTED.

DAVID HEARTWELL, whom we have, in the few last paragraphs of our preceding chapter, introduced to our readers, was a lieutenant in the royal navy. It was in the thick of the war then, and young men got their promotion quicker than they could have got them now in these piping times of peace.

A few hours in that stirring period, when the boom of British cannon was awakening very uncomfortable echoes in France, would frequently make an alteration in the rating of a whole ship's company of officers.

The emulation of the lieutenants of the royal navy was of the most remarkable character; they were a class of men upon the verge of a rank in society which made them company for any one.

If they could but procure the couple of epaulets instead of the one, they were made men; and a class of officers who signalised themselves to a greater extent during that long period of war, which demonstrated the fact of British ascendancy to the whole world, could not have been found.

Under these circumstances, it may well be supposed that many of these gallant men found that death which they all held in such contempt, and so thinned their ranks to make way for the senior midshipmen.

Lieutenant Heartwell had been serving on board a vessel which had been taken from the French, and brought into an English port, from which it was commissioned as a cruiser under the British flag.

But unfortunately this ship, although a good one originally, had been so mauled in the taking of it, that its captain, after an eight months' cruise, during which he made several prizes, was glad to get into Portsmouth harbour with four feet water in the hold.

These interesting facts were duly communicated to the admiralty, and the consequence was that the ship was paid off, and the officers given a promise of speedy future favours.

There was a fine new vessel about to be put into commission, called the Eolus, a first-class frigate, with such fittings and appointments that among the initiated there were the most sanguine hopes that, if properly manned and officered, she would have one of the most satisfactory cruises on record.

The captain of the disabled French vessel was immediately appointed to a command, vacant by death, but there was no room in the vessel for David Heartwell, so he was for the time out of commission, and he used all the interest he possessed to get appointed first or second lieutenant to the Eolus.

It was pending these negociations that he took a run up to London, to see his old sweetheart, Minna Woodward, the pretty daughter of the landlord of the old Victory.

It did not often happen in those stirring times, when in nautical phraseology, bullets were scuttling people's nobs, that young sprigs of nobility and fancy lordlings were so eager as they are now, when a captain of the royal navy is quite a drawing-room article, to step over braver and better men's heads into the post of danger.

But there were some exceptions, some enforced exceptions to this rule; these were young men of first-rate connections, but such determined blackguards, that their friends, as if by common consent, found out they could do nothing for them except on board frigates and first-rates.

Perhaps it was with the charitable hope of something or other scuttling their nobs, that they sent them there; and among this number was the Honourable Bulkley Harding, who, although of the best connections, was anything but the best of individuals; he had been to sea before, so there was some excuse for sending him again, and probably his noble relatives—for he had noble relatives—were anxious to continue sending him until the necessity of doing so should no longer exist by his non-return on some occasion. But, like the bad penny, which passed into a proverb, such persons always do return, while better men find an honourable death in the service of their country.

It was not unfrequently the case that, with some extremely capable lieutenants, there would be a captain who owed his elevation entirely to political considerations; consequently, nobody was very much surprised, excepting the Honourable Bulkley Harding himself, when he was gazetted to the Eolus new frigate. He had an uncle, a lord of the Admiralty, which accounted fully for the phenomenon of his appointment.

The Honourable Bulkley, as he was usually called by his intimates, or the Honourable Bulk, was at breakfast at Mivart's, when a note from his uncle briefly announced to him his appointment to the Eolus, and the necessity for his almost immediate departure for Portsmouth.

Seated with him was an exquisite of the name of Puffington Smaley, who was the great friend and confidant of the Honourable Bulk, as he always familiarly called him. This individual had perhaps the smallest quantity of brains which could possibly enable a man to go through life with any degree of ordinary decency, without possessing, of his own, a sixpence in the world. He contrived to go through life indulging in almost every one of its luxuries; and such a state of things he solely achieved by laughing, and crying "capital!" to all the nonsense which was spoken by persons with better filled purses than his own. A more abject, slavish soul than his there could not be. The mere fact that a man should be content to live under such circumstances, said little indeed for his mental powers, or for that feeling of honest independence which, if not one of the highest, is at least one of the most attractive attributes of human nature.

He looked stedfastly at his patron while the letter was being read. The sycophantic creature wished to take his cue from the expression of the other's countenance, and he fancied he saw an appearance of blank dismay.

"Some d——d disagreeable letter, I suppose," he said. "Throw it into the fire, my Honourable Bulk."

"Throw you in the fire," said Sir Bulkley. "Who told you it was a disagreeable letter? I shall lose the marchioness's balls this season."

"Indeed, that's horrible; it's excruciating. Crucify me, if I wouldn't as soon go into the family vault as lose the marchioness's balls; but what's the reason—is the old man dead?"

"No; but that tiresome uncle of mine, fancying I want promotion, when I only want to be left alone, and to have the liberty of—of ——"

"Of getting into debt."

"Psha! I am appointed to the command of the Eolus new frigate of war, and I suppose I must be off to some rascally station, where I shall hear nothing all day but the banging of broadsides."

"Monstrous!—quite monstrous!" said Smaley; "too bad, by Jove!"

"Well, it can't be helped, I suppose. I am in that situation in life that I must take what I get, and seem to be thankful, I suppose. Read that note, Smaley, and just tell me what answer you'd send to it."

He tossed the note over to his companion, who read as follows :—

"Admiralty.

"NEPHEW,—It is not on account of your deserts, but to give you an opportunity of acquiring a better name than you have at present, that I have procured you the appointment of captain to the Eolus, one of the best ships in the service. You may chose any officer you like, of sufficient standing, for your first lieutenant, and you must be at Portsmouth in forty-eight hours.

"Don't let me hear of you again, unless you bring into port a couple of prizes, or have found an honourable grave at the bottom of the ocean.

"Yours, as you deserve,
"HENRY HARDING."

"What do you think of that, Smaley?"

"Well, I'm d——d!" said Smaley; "that uncle of yours is a perfect savage. The bottom of the ocean! Dreadful idea. One might reconcile oneself to be smothered in rose-leaves and sunk in a sea of eau-de-Cologne; but to be disemboweled in the first case by chain shot, and then thrown into some common cold water, is certainly not pleasant at all."

"Well, what answer would you send, then?"

"If you'll allow me to dictate an answer, my dear Sir Buck, I think I can get you out of this dilemma."

"How?"

"I should commence thus—No. 3, Curzon-street, May-fair."

"Well, well."

"You jolly old muff,—If I were half as ugly as you, and had lost my hair beyond the power of the balm of Columbia to restore—if I were as incapable of joining in the fascinating evolutions of the mazy dance, I might go to sea; but as it is, you incomprehensible old muff ——"

"Psha, psha!" said Harding; "don't be an ass."

"That's just what I was coming to, as a conclusion—don't be an ass. I remain, you jolly old muff, yours truly, Bulkley Harding."

"Choose my own lieutenant!" muttered Harding to himself; "there's something in that!"

The door of the apartment was very silently opened, and a footman appeared in a hesitating manner, with a tray in his hand, on which was a card.

"Well, well, what is it?" said Harding.

"If—if you please, sir," stammered the footman, "a gentleman has left this card, sir, and is waiting below."

"What is it?—what is it?—I can't be pestered."

"If you please, sir, I don't know."

"Can't you read, idiot?"

"Yes, sir; but, if you please, there's nothing to read."

The footman advanced and showed Harding the card which was upon the silver salver. It was nothing but a plain blue bit of pasteboard, of a very fine and silky texture. It was perfectly soilless, and bore not the slightest indication of from whom it came.

Harding took it into his hand, and he shook so as he looked at it, that Smaley was positively alarmed.

"Is—is he waiting?" he said.

"Yes, sir," said the footman; "the strange gentleman is waiting below."

Harding paused a moment, and it was evident he did so in order to recover his composure before he ventured to speak.

"You—you will show him," he said, "up here. Thank God I am going to sea: I thought he was dead."

"Who is it?—who is it?" said Smaley.

"What's that to you?" cried Harding fiercely. "I am occupied."

"Oh, don't let me intrude, of course," said Smaley, rising; "mine's a mere passing call, you know; but don't let me intrude upon you, of course, if there's any business. Good morning to you."

"Good morning, good morning."

Smaley was not a little curious to see who the mysterious visitor could be, and as he followed the footman down stairs, he said—

"John, John, who is it?"

"I really don't know, sir. Never saw him before, and I can hardly say, sir, as I have seen him now."

"Why, didn't you say he was down stairs?"

"Yes, sir; but I didn't see his face—at least, 'tis a strange face if I did, for it was all a kind of——"

"What?"

"Blue, sir."

Smaley started back as he repeated the word "blue."

"Did you say blue, John?—perhaps you mean he is Mr. Blue."

"I beg pardon, sir," said John, "he's just in that room, and I must show him up."

Smaley nodded, and winked, and placed his finger by the side of his nose, to signify to John that he was going to do something rather clever, and then he popped behind a pedestal which was in the hall, while John passed into the waiting-room, where the mysterious stranger had been shown.

In a moment, a man enveloped in a cloak emerged from the room; his hat was on, and pulled low over his brows, leaving but the lower part of his face visible: to the surprise and consternation of Smaley, that was as nearly the colour of the blue card that had been brought up into the drawing-room as possible.

In his eagerness to have a good look at him, Smaley gradually projected his head from behind the pedestal, so that his affected concealment of himself was a mere farce.

The mysterious man saw him, and turning abruptly, he placed his face within a quarter of an inch of Smaley's, as he said, in a deep, hollow voice,—

"Shall you know me again?"

"No, no," cried Smaley, "I don't want. God bless me, what a singular face! I beg your pardon, Mr. Blue, I wasn't looking at you. You see, I dropped my pencil-case, and it rolled behind here, you see; so I—I—you understand."

The stranger paid no more attention to Smaley, but walked up the staircase; the drawing-room door opened, and then instantly closed, and John then came timidly down the stairs again.

"Don't you really know who he is?" said Smaley.

"No, sir, I don't; it may be the what-d'-ye-call-'em, for all I know."

"Has he ever been here before?"

"Certainly not, sir."

"Well, I am amazed; but, however, I have a thousand places to call at, so I can't wait any longer. John, if you find out anything about this blue fellow, tell me, and I'll give you half-a-crown at Christmas."

"Very much obliged, sir," said John, as he opened the door to let Smaley out, and then added to himself, "A snigirificant wretch! Half-a-crown at Christmas, indeed! What a liberal idea!"

The mysterious stranger remained half-an-hour with the Honourable Bulkley Harding; what passed at that interview was only known to themselves, and at its expiration the man with the blue face walked down stairs without troubling the servants, and let himself out.

John heard the street-door bang, and ran up stairs; but whoever had banged the door was gone, and the mystery remained as obscure as ever.

Harding's cab had been waiting at the door for half-an-hour, and in a few minutes he came down. His step was unsteady, and his whole nerves seemed shaken. He was very pale, and as he walked across the hall it was evident that a child might have struck him to the earth.

He got into his cab with far from his wonted alacrity. His tiger was astonished at the ease with which he was permitted to get up behind, for it seemed to him that his master had the greatest anxiety in the world to get away without him, and it was only by great tact and experience that he generally succeeded, after letting go the horse's head, in clawing hold of one of the hind springs and getting up.

[See p. 5.

But the wonder of the tiger was still further excited, for, for the first time since he had been in his master's service, the horse's head was turned eastward, and the miry narrow streets of the city were traversed.

"Where are we going?" said the tiger. "I shall have to give him notice if he comes this dodge. This won't suit me. The city be blowed—decidedly low. My eye, here's a go!"

They were now in Thames-street, and one of those stoppages had occurred, which result from some complicated piece of villany got up between a coal-waggon and a carrier's van, and some half-dozen chaise-carts to fill up the interstices.

"Here is a go," said the tiger. "How is we to get our bit of blood out of this?

There'll be a blessed smash somehow or other, and a werry good job too ! for a cab as is once been in the city is no longer the same wehicle."

" Clear the way, there—clear the way, there !" cried the Honourable Bulkley Harding.

" Is there anything else you'd like ?" said one of the attendants upon a coal-waggon ; "cos you've only to say it, you know."

" Where's the police ? where's the police ?" said Harding.

" Ah," said the fellow, " where's the blessed police ? Strikes me, sir, there ought always to be a private watchman here to lift you over."

At this moment there was a slight opening made by one of the chaise-carts mysteriously disappearing down a narrow entry. Harding's nervousness had now turned to passionate recklessness, and the space was certainly too narrow to afford him the least chance to get through, but he touched the spirited horse he drove with the whip, and he dashed forward.

" There he goes again," said the coaley, and crack came the wheel of Harding's cab against one of the heavy double-tired ones of the coal-waggon. Harding's wheel was shattered to pieces, and down went the cab on one side.

It was a piece of good-nature on the part of the coalheaver to hold Harding's horse, but the latter was in no humour to construe it in that light, and he slashed at the man with his whip for really doing him a service.

" Vell," said another of the men who was with the coal-waggon, but who was now, by the sudden movement of the cab forward, completely behind it, " that's gratitude, I sup- pose. You shall have it between you, so here goes."

Taking up the cart whip, he began to lay it about the legs of the tiger, in a manner which made that individual execute the most grotesque dance imaginable on the little square perch behind the cab.

Hanging on by the straps, he kicked and plunged, and roared and shouted, to the great amusement of the bystanders, until at last he could endure it no longer, and loosing his hold, down he came into the mud.

By this time the Honourable Bulkley Harding had become convinced he was in the wrong box. Some constables came up, who stopped further hostilities ; to them he gave his card, and then dashed off at a rapid pace on foot to wherever he might be going, leaving the unfortunate tiger to do the best he could in the uncomfortable circum- stances under which he was placed.

CHAPTER III.

THE VISIT TO THE VICTORY.—THE OPPORTUNE DISCOVERY, AND THE THREAT OF VENGEANCE.

IT did not much matter to the Honourable Bulkley Harding that he was compelled to get out of his cab where he had, for he from the first entertained no notion of taking his cab and tiger the whole of the way with him.

The fact is, he was bent upon an expedition which he had no desire that any one but himself should know anything of, and, in order that we may make that expedition intel- ligible to the reader, it is necessary that we should premise a few circumstances.

The fame of the beauty of Minna Woodward, the daughter of the landlord of the old Victory Tavern, had spread far and wide, and had reached the ears of parties to whom the neighbourhood where so fair a creature had been born and nurtured was a *terra in- cognita*.

One night it had happened that the reported beauty of the landlord's daughter became a theme of conversation among a party of dissolute young men, one of whom was Bulkley Harding.

After repeating one to the other the extravagant encomiums they had heard passed upon her beauty, the subject dropped ; but when the party broke up, at a remarkably early hour, one of them said to Harding,—

" Are you inclined for an expedition through the city, to see this fair creature of whom report speaks so highly ?"

" I am ignorant of the whole locality," said Harding, " and should never find the place."

" And I ; but I know some one *en route* who can not only give us the necessary piece of information, but enable us to make such an alteration in our appearance, that we shall not attract the attention and suspicion which we should otherwise run a good chance of doing."

" Agreed," said Harding ; " it will be a novelty to me, at all events."

The expedition was immediately undertaken ; but as nothing particular occurred at it beyond Harding's seeing and being deeply smitten by Minna, we need not recount to the reader its minute particulars.

While in the house he made some advances to Minna, which were disdainfully repulsed ; and he was then and there informed by a gossiping person, who was in the dingy parlour of the old tavern, that it was well known thereabouts Minna was engaged to a Lieutenant Heartwell, of the Royal Navy.

With all the malice of a petty nature, Harding never forgot the name of Heartwell, but vowed to himself, should ever opportunity and time serve him, he would be revenged upon him for standing in his way, as he considered he did. He never for a moment seemed to consider that Heartwell's attentions might be, as indeed they truly were, of a most honourable nature ; but he only looked upon him as a rival in the affections of a girl whom he would have liked to have won for himself, until after a time familiar charms would have failed to please, and he would have cast her aside to perish, or to lead what life of terror and despair she might.

It so happened that within a short period of this visit to the Victory, he who had accompanied Harding there was killed by a fall from his horse ; but that circumstance rather led Harding still more to dwell in his imagination upon the beauties of Minna Woodward than in any way quenched his passion for her.

A variety of circumstances, however, prevented him from again visiting the Victory ; but whenever he saw some little demirep or fashionable piece of frailty, he could not help contrasting her in his mind with the pure and beautiful Minna Woodward, and unconsciously almost to himself he was nourishing for her a passion which only now wanted a little stimulant to become perfectly gigantic.

We are inclined to believe that something must have passed between Bulkley Harding and the mysterious man with the blue face to have induced him thus suddenly to start for the old Victory Tavern, for the state of mind he was in was by no means a favourable one for the prosecution of intrigue. Certain it was, however, that when he met with the misadventure concerning the cab, he was bound for the old Gun-dock, at Wapping.

Thither, then, will we follow him.

With what had occurred the preceding evening at the old tavern the reader is sufficiently acquainted. Death is in the house, for the corpse of the landlord occupies the room above the old oaken parlour. Minna and her mother are absorbed in grief—a grief which is certainly somewhat lightened by the presence of Lieutenant Heartwell, who had made what haste he could from Portsmouth, and arrived at so opportune a moment to whisper consolation to the beautiful Minna. It must not be supposed that it was very early in the day, although we have mentioned the Honourable Bulkley Harding was taking his breakfast when he was waited upon by the mysterious man with the blue face.

The vitiated habits of the young roue were such as always to produce in him a propensity to turn day into night, and, consequently, it was what sober, serious people call the afternoon when he found himself in the immediate neighbourhood of the old Gundock.

The acquaintance of the young man in whose company Harding had at first visited the Victory, was a fellow in the city, who described himself by the extremely dubious appellation of an agent. He was probably one of those men who are willing to do anything for anybody on a consideration, without being at all scrupulous as regards its morality or its honour. His name was Drake, and to him Harding first went to borrow an overcoat, which should sufficiently conceal his fashionable apparel.

Drake never asked impertinent questions ; it was sufficient for him that his customer was a man with money, and, therefore, there was no likelihood of any troublesome explanations at police offices.

Harding got accommodated at once, and promised to return in the course of an hour. He walked onward, and after making various inquiries by the way, he found himself before the low doorway of the old tavern, which contained, what in his eyes was so rare a treasure, but which he was so far from being the person to appreciate.

He could not help being struck by the air of gloom that was about the place. It was too early for the usual frequenters of the house to show themselves, and moreover the state of affairs within was so well known in the neighbourhood, that people abstained from congregating round the doors with noisy mirth as usual, and not for years had the old house worn so serious an aspect.

" Something must have happened," said Harding to himself, as he crossed the threshold; "something, surely, must have happened, that I know not of; but little care I what it is, provided I can induce the beautiful Minna to be mine."

He had not forgotten that to turn to the right would lead him to the cabin-looking parlour, where he had but once before in his life sat.

There was no one there, but still the room had a comfortable aspect, from the abundance of old, dark, wood carving about it. The floor, too, was clean and sanded, and as Harding flung himself into a seat, he felt pleased at the novel contrast which that place afforded to the gorgeous apartments with which he was familiar.

He rang the bell, with the hope that, as on the occasion of his former visit, it would be answered by Minna; but, to his mortification, a fat, blowsy-looking damsel, with her sleeves tucked-up, and not the cleanest face in the world, came to take his order.

"Did you ring?" she said.

"Yes. Has the landlord's daughter left?"

"Left who?"

"The house—the house."

"Oh! left the house! Perhaps you mean Miss Minna? Why should she leave the house?"

"But has she?"

"What call's she to leave?"

Harding looked despairingly.

"Bring me a bottle of wine," he said, "and answer me yes or no. Is Minna Woodward within?"

"What?"

"I want to know if she's at home, within the house."

"Well, you needn't be in a passion about it, if she is. Are you the undertaker?"

"The what?"

"The undertaker. Old Wood'ard lies to-day in a common shell, I suppose, till the day of his funeral; we don't know what unwholesome people may have been in that!"

Harding scarcely knew in what way to frame a question to this woman which should elicit the answer he wanted.

After a moment's pause, however, he added, as he held some silver he had in his hand towards the woman—

"Perhaps you will understand this universal language. Answer me truly what I shall ask of you, and you shall find me no niggard hand at rewarding you."

The woman took the money immediately, and then she said—

"Well, sir, what is it?"

"It is this," said Harding: "to my eyes, Minna Woodward is a most beautiful creature—I love her!"

"Indeed, sir!"

"Yes; and I would fain make her mine: I have come over here on purpose to speak to her, with the hope that I may find her more kind than cruel. Now, I dare say you can say a good word for any one, and if you will for me, be assured that each one you utter will meet with a silver, or perhaps with a golden, reward.

"Well, that is pleasant!" said the woman. "Of course you love Miss Minna honourably?"

"Oh, of course—of course."

"And you will marry her?"

"Most decidedly!"

"Well, then, that's just as it ought to be, and you'll see if I don't earn the money you have given me."

She left the room, and Harding congratulated himself upon the cleverness with which he had managed the affair.

"Women," he said, "are ever women's worst friends; it is really astonishing how they will betray each other. Let your purpose be what it may, against any one of the sex, and you will find some other who will aid you. I shall surely succeed now, for I have a friend at court—a spy in the enemy's camp."

Harding thought himself very clever, and, as a general thing, his remarks might be wonderfully correct; but there are instances in which the wisest may miscalculate, and as he by no means belonged to that class, it is by no means to be wondered at that he committed an error of judgment.

In about five minutes, the woman returned, and coming up to him she said, in quite an off-handed manner—

"I have done it, sir."

" Yes, yes, you have spoken to her ?"

" I have, so that you can't say but what I have earned my money, sir."

" And what does she say—is she coming ?"

" Oh, dear, no."

" No! what do you mean ?"

" She says she declines having you on account of not knowing you, and being engaged to somebody else before, but she's very much obliged for the kind offer you have made to her."

" D———n!" said Harding; " was there ever such a fool ?"

" Well, it was foolish," said the woman, " considering you didn't know her and she didn't know you."

Harding paced the room passionately.

" Woman," he said, " I am a gentleman."

" Oh, I know that," she said, jinking the money she had in her pocket, " you behaved as sich."

" Susan," cried a stentorian voice at this moment, which might have been heard in a gale of wind.

" Coming," shouted Susan.

" Is that impertinent scoundrel gone ?" added the voice at this moment, which might have been heard in a gale of wind.

" Muster Heartwell, sir, a lieutenant as is. He's a-keeping company with Miss Minna, and he didn't seem to like it at all, but began a foaming, and a frizzing, and a bustin', like our best bottled ale."

" Heartwell—Heartwell ?" said Harding, reflecting for a moment; " a lieutenant in the navy, I presume ?"

" Yes, sir, in the navel."

" What a cursed chance," said Harding, as he immediately slouched on his hat as far over his eyes as he could, and concealed the lower part of his face as much as possible by the collar of the rough great coat he wore. It was well he did so, for the next moment the door of the room was flung open, and the athletic form of young Heartwell appeared in the entrance.

" Now, sir," he said, " you have had your answer, I'll trouble you to leave; there's death in the house, and you may thank your stars for it, or I might adopt some mode of showing you the outside of the door that mightn't be so agreeable."

" This is a public tavern," said Harding, concealing his own voice as much as he possibly could.

" But we'll overrule that little objection," said Heartwell; " are you going? It is not everybody that has a choice given them, but I am a sailor, and foolishly liberal; which would you like best, now, the door or the window ?"

" Heartwell, Heartwell," said Minna, " do not be violent, for my sake; let him go in peace, or stay in peace, as best may please him."

" Why, my darling, what are you afraid of?" said Heartwell; " I should like to have such a fellow as that on shipboard—I'd let him see what was discipline and who was master."

Harding either mustered courage enough naturally, or the presence of Minna inspired him.

" I will not go at any man's bidding," he said, " vapour and bluster as you please; 'tis not the boldest dog that yelps the loudest."

These words put the finishing stroke to the passion of the young sailor. Freeing himself in an instant from the feeble detaining grasp of Minna, he sprung upon Harding, and with a power which probably under circumstances of less excitement he would not have been enabled to exert, he fairly lifted him from the floor, and flung him through the parlour window of the old tavern into the street.

The window was old and rotten, so that a moderate degree of force sufficed to smash it to atoms; and fortunate it was for Harding that he went backwards through it, for by that he saved his face from being cut by the broken glass; but, as it was, he was completely stunned and bewildered for a few moments, and scarcely knew where he was.

" Heartwell, Heartwell," exclaimed Minna, " you know not what will be the consequences of this violence; possibly that man meant not to insult me, and you know not how far a meaner spirit than your own may lead him."

" My dear Minna, you consider this matter too seriously—far too seriously. This scoundrel knows he has got off cheaply, with far less punishment than he deserves; think no more of him, he is no more worthy of your consideration. It does, indeed, grieve me that he should have paled the rose on your cheek ; come, my dear Minna, let me see you smile again, and do not let the consequences of what may occur disturb you."

"With you, Heartwell, I can have no fear. Ah, I know not what I should have done had you not arrived as you did yesterday. I was half distracted by the melancholy bereavement I had suffered. My poor mother's grief rendered me incapable of action ; but now that you are here to advise and direct us, it seems as if the blow of Providence, which has deprived me of a father, has fallen but lightly on my heart."

"My dear Minna, such persons as yourself can only suffer through your affections. You feel that you have still about you those that love you and those whom you love ; therefore is it you own to a serenity that otherwise would not belong to you ; but let us come back to your mother, to my mind she seems duller to-day than yesterday."

With Minna fondly hanging upon his arm he went to the little parlour behind the bar of the old tavern, where they had been conversing when the aggravating message of Harding was brought to them.

The reader will perceive that Susan must have betrayed the confidence that Harding reposed in her. She had taken his money, and remained faithful to those who were best entitled to her good services, and hence, when he congratulated himself upon the facility with which one woman betrayed another, he did not altogether expect that he had got hold of one of the exceptions to the rule, as in truth he had.

It was doubly aggravating to such a man to find, that not only was he foiled in the endeavour to corrupt an honest servant, but made a laughing-stock into the bargain.

All this might have passed off though, tolerably well, but the aggravated assault which had been committed upon him was sufficient to drive him desperate ; and yet it is strange how many very angry men have sufficient wit in their anger to hold off from attempting anything which they suspect to be beyond their power.

In all his rage, and in all his excitement, the Honourable Captain Bulkley Harding did not venture to cross the threshold of the old Victory. He looked volumes of indignation, and his countenance was quite distorted by the violence of his emotions. He shook his clenched fist at the house as he said,—

"My time will come ; love and hate shall yet accomplish something. Minna Woodward, you are far dearer to me now, because you contemn my love ; had you shown yourself a rose easily to be plucked, you would not have suited me, and I should have slighted what I will now make a principal object of my existence. Come what may, and let who may stand in my way, you shall be mine ; and as for you, Heartwell—why, as for you, you shall be the first lieutenant of the Eolus, one of the first frigates in the service, but with the comfortable conviction that your captain is your deadliest enemy ; and yet will I manage matters so that you shall have no cause of complaint. You shall wish yourself dead, and yet dare not wag your tongue against me ; and, Minna Woodward, fancy that at present you can defy me ; fancy that, as you hang upon the arm of your lover, you are safe ; but, oh ! if there be cunning in man, if there be duplicity and treachery in woman, if there be power in gold, I will get you to make that first false step that shall hurry you to destruction. I will win you, I will wear you, but I shall not keep you long,"

With a sudden appearance of more than natural calmness, he turned and left the spot.

CHAPTER IV.

THE CURIOUS GUESTS.—THE EXPLANATION OF THE NOISE IN THE CHAMBER OF DEATH.—THE BLUE FACE AGAIN.

ONE by one, as the evening drew in, the accustomed guests took their seats in the parlour in the old Victory. They did not, however, come in with the boisterous revelry of other times, but one by one they dropped in silently, with a nod of recognition.

The feeling of awe which death had inspired was still upon them. It would be long before the old house resumed its accustomed air of pleasant jocularity. The landlord was missed, and there was no one to supply his place. But there was one topic upon which the guests were most anxious—a topic which one and all wished to have explained, and that was what had caused the mysterious noise over-head in the chamber where the deceased landlord had been lying on the preceding evening.

The reader will recollect, that previous to attention being called to the startling circumstances which had ensued in connection with Minna, a loud rumbling noise had been heard above, which no one had been able to translate or come to any conclusion concerning it; but now each guest that came to the Victory came with a hope of ascertaining something upon that head.

It seemed to be contrary to the visitors to utter any remark until each had his pipe and his flagon before him; but when some five or six were thus provided, the senior of the party gave an extraordinary long whiff, and looking about him, he merely uttered the monosyllable of,—

"Well."

Now there certainly was not much in that, but, strange to say, everybody seemed to know intuitively to what he referred, and one who sat opposite to him, after a grave preliminary shake of the head, remarked,—

"Ah, we live in strange times, and folks don't rest in their shells now. Lord bless you, when I was a boy it was quite different. If a man went dead then, he was just kept comfortably till he began to turn; but now a-days, what with one thing and what with another thing, and what they calls improvements, there's no saying what'll happen."

Somebody was about to make a reply, but the door opened, and a tall, wiry-looking young man walked in and flung himself into a seat.

"A jug of ale—a jug of ale!" he cried. "Quick, quick; for by the South Sea snake, I am thirsty and be d——d!"

There were seven guests in the parlour, and fourteen eyes would have unquestionably glared upon the intruder, had not Job Whittle, the sail maker of the neighbourhood, who was present, possessed but one.

"What are you staring at?" said the stranger.

The thirteen eyes immediately looked slap at the ceiling, and then Job Whittle slowly brought his one eye to bear upon the intruder as he said,—

"My friend, it strikes me you were here last night."

"Well, so were you."

"Yes, yes—ah, but hem—hem—yes, yes."

"Well, booby, what do you make of that?"

"Gracious everything! Mr. Blunt," said a little man, who was the farthest off, to his neighbour, "he calls Job Whittle a booby; Job Whittle, who has been churchwarden twice and beautified the church."

"Ah! ah!" said Job Whittle, "it's all very fine, but I'm here every night, which makes a difference; and when you've cut your wisdom teeth, which you have not yet, you'll learn to respect your elders and your gravers."

"Besides," said another, "there was a noise last night, and when anybody wanted to run out and see what it was, nobody could get out."

"Well?" said the stranger.

"Well—ah—well; the reason they couldn't get out was all owing to you."

"And well?" said the stranger.

"Oh! why—oh! that's it."

"But what do you make of it?"

"Well, I—a—Mr. Whittle, what do you make of it?"

"Oh, we shall see," said Job Whittle, "there's time enough."

"A famous old house this," said the stranger, as he stretched out his leg and dabbed his heel upon the floor, "and there's been some rum customers in it at times. Did you ever hear of Mr. Morgan?"

"What, that keeps the—the—the snuff shop below?"

"Keeps the devil below! I mean Morgan the pirate; damme, he sat in this room once."

"Lor!" said the small man who formerly addressed Mr. Blunt. "Why he was a most ferocious fellow."

"He was, and so was his lieutenant Handford, and he again had an old friend whose name was ——"

"What—what?" said several of the guests.

"Never mind—damme!"

A strange crashing noise came from above. Job Whittle dropped the pipe from his mouth as he exclaimed,—

"There's a row again."

"Well," said the stranger, "and what do you make of it?"

"I don't see," said one, "that we are obliged to make anything of it, but I've no objection to go and see what it is."

"Haven't you?" said the young man, rising; "you must have an equally slight objection then of walking through me, or you may swallow me first if you like."

" But this is very extraordinary," said Job Whittle, " and I must confess ——"

Scarcely were these words out of his mouth when from above there came three distinct taps on the floor.

All looked up except the stranger, and he, as he had done on the preceding evening, dragged up his heavy horseman's boots as he muttered,—

" Done at last! The treasure's down !"

Then rising, he dashed out of the room with vehemence.

There was a silence which lasted nearly five minutes, and then one ventured to say,—

" Old friends, what do you think of that ?"

" Stop a bit," said Job Whittle; " I haven't begun a thinking yet—ring for Susan."

This was an operation that was unnecessary, for with a scream Susan rushed into the apartment, pausing not until she reached the fire-place, ; and, indeed, such was her rapidity of movement and fright, that some present were strongly of opinion that she would have got up the chimney if she had not been held.

Fear is a contagious feeling, and its effects upon the guests in the parlour of the old Victory, and more particularly upon Susan, was such that they rose *en masse* in the most ludicrous attitudes of fright, the conviction that something had occurred or was about to occur being visibly impressed upon the minds of every one of them.

Had there been any hiding-places of ready access no doubt but they would have been with no small degree of avidity seized upon; but there were none, and amid the chaos of broken pipes and upset flagons, each of the guests, no doubt, fancied he held his life upon but a frail tenure.

" Oh! oh! oh!" said Susan; " I never shall forget. I have seen something at last, and it's blue."

" It's what ?" cried several.

" It's blue! it's blue! I was just above the corpse, thinking of nothing."

" Above the corpse!" exclaimed everybody.

" I means in the room above," said Susan, " and I heard a noise, so down I comes— meaning to go to the bar parlour, and speak to missus; but, oh, gracious! as I passed the door—fancy my feelings—I say, fancy my feelings—it opened like a *bum*-shell ; and then, as if the bung had flewed out of a new ale cask, out comes the thingumty ; and I felt as if I stood on my head with my feet to the second floor."

" What a dreadful sight that must have been!" said Job Whittle.

" But who was it—who was it ?" said another.

" As I am a livin' breathin' sinner," said Susan, " and being in a tavern, havin' a natural feelin' as the Lord of Hosts shall have mercy upon me, I seed a sight as was enough to make one *friz*."

" Was it a man—was it a man ?"

" I don't think so. It must have been somebody else as isn't proper to mention— leastways, not now. Did you ever hear, gentlemen, of the ' What-do-you-callum' having a blue face ?"

" Blue," said Job Whittle. " I never did; but I don't see why he shouldn't be blue."

" Nor does me, Mr. Whittle, and all I have got to say is, as somebody came out of master's room as was with a face as blue as nothing."

" A blue face, do you say, Susan ?"

" Yes ; I wish you'd all have seen it; the hair would have stood on an end on all your faces. I sha'n't recover it for one whiles to come, and as for going up and down stairs by myself, it's a thing I wouldn't wenture upon for worlds and worlds of diamonds."

Such sounds of confusion now ensued within the old tavern, that one would have thought at least half a dozen devils were let loose, and were disporting themselves within its walls. There was such a scampering in the room above, and then such a bang of a door, after which it seemed as if something fearfully heavy had rolled from the top to the bottom of the staircase, that the visitors in the parlour stood as if paralyzed, with their teeth chattering like castanets.

Susan sat down on the sanded floor, and executed some feats in the hysteric line, and not one had courage to move from the apartment to ascertain the cause of the tumult. We will, however, with the privilege belonging to us as historians and careful collectors of facts, proceed to state what those circumstances were which produced such terror among those of whom we have been speaking.

Although the chamber of death was not so immediately above the little room, called the bar parlour, as it was the ancient cabined apartment into which Susan had rushed with such frantic fears, yet, in consequence of the general stillness of the house, the sounds which came from that solemn room did not fail to reach the ears of Minna and her mother.

Lieutenant Heartwell happened not to be in the bar parlour at the moment, but he

[See page 20

returned almost immediately, and he could not fail to see by their countenances that something alarming had happened during his temporary absence.

It was Minna who spoke in answer to his inquiring look.

" Oh, David—David," she said, " we have again heard a noise from my poor father's room.   Surely it cannot be accident again."

" Indeed," said Heartwell; " it is possible that a similar accident to that which accounted for the tumult last night might happen, but it is not likely."

" Yes, yes," said Mrs. Woodward; " I know you have all tried to convince me that the confusion of last night arose from the breaking of one of the tressles that supported the coffin of my poor husband; but I did not think so.   I cannot, with truth, say I thought so."

"But are you certain," said Heartwell, "that imagination has not deceived you this time, and that there has really been a noise from the room above?"

"Quite—quite certain. We both heard it."

"Without the permission of you both," said Heartwell, "I would not intrude into that apartment; but if you have no objection to my doing so, I will go to it at once, and ascertain if any change has taken place in its arrangements?"

As he spoke, he took a candle, and moved two steps towards the door. It was at that moment that, from the room in which the corpse lay, there proceeded the three solemn knocks upon the floor which had produced so alarming an effect in the parlour.

"There, there," exclaimed Minna; "there again. What can all this mean?"

"Heaven help us!" said Mrs. Woodward, as she wrung her hands.

"Hush! be calm," said Heartwell; "rest safely here, and I will bring you an accurate account of whatever has occurred. There can be no possible occasion for apprehension."

Minna sprung forward, and clung to Heartwell.

"No, no, do not go," she said. "What hope have we now but in you? We cannot tell, you cannot tell either, but this is some decoy for your destruction. You know, Heartwell, you have made an enemy to-day."

"Minna, Minna, these are the counsels of fear," said Heartwell, "and therefore I may not listen to them. Let me go, I beg of you. There can be no danger. I will be back again in a moment or two; but the reality of these things should always be ascertained at the outset, so that the imagination be left no time to dress them in false colours."

He gently, but firmly, disengaged himself from Minna's grasp, and then with a quick step he left the little room, to proceed upon his errand of discovery, as to what had caused the mysterious sound from a room in which one might suppose the profoundest stillness ought to reign.

He had scarcely got half way up the staircase, when he met Susan in her hasty downward progress, and such was the impetus with which she came, that she dashed the candle from his hand, and nearly threw him down as she passed him, exclaiming,—

"Blue, blue, blue—all blue."

This would have been enough to bewilder most men, and it had rather a stunning effect upon Heartwell for a moment.

"Is she mad?" he exclaimed; "but, however, I'll not go back for a light."

There burnt a lamp on the staircase, with a dim and a sickly lustre, but it was so ingeniously put into a nook, that it gave very little light anywhere else but in the nook. There were, however, some faint reflected beams upon the staircase, and, guided by them, taking three steps at once, Heartwell sprang up.

Before, however, he got up to the top of the flight, he became aware that some one was descending, but whoever it was turned abruptly, and fled upwards.

The probability is, that the intruder in that domestic portion of the house thought that whoever it was that was coming up the staircase intended to pass on to the second-floor, and that the chamber in which the corpse lay would not be visited.

But this was a mistake as regarded Lieutenant Heartwell; he was close upon the heels of the fugitive, and they dashed into the room in which the corpse of the late Mr. Woodward lay, so nearly together, that it would have been difficult to say which was first.

Heartwell was a powerful young man, and one not likely often to meet his match; but now he seemed to be pretty equally pitted against some one, for they both rolled on the floor together, and it seemed a very doubtful case as to which would have the mastery.

Men of courage, and accustomed to personal contests, never make more noise than necessary over it, and in this case neither Heartwell nor the stranger uttered a word, reserving all their breath for the struggle in which they were engaged.

Heartwell had his antagonist by the throat, while that antagonist had such a clutch of him by both sides of his collar, that he could not shake him off.

Under such circumstances as these, a great deal is done in a very short space of time, and probably, at ordinary speed, one could not have counted twenty before Heartwell and the intruder, in the course of their struggles, reached the landing outside the door, and then rolled, still fast in each other's grasp, down the staircase into the passage below.

It was this which had so alarmed the guests in the parlour, and well calculated it was to do so.

Of course the sounds of such a tumult could not fail to reach the ears of Minna and her mother. Although the latter was too terrified to move, anxiety for her lover's safety armed the former with courage, and she sprang into the passage with a light, calling upon him loudly by name.

Accident, rather than any personal prowess, during the fall down the staircase, was likely to produce its results ; and it so happened that Heartwell's head came with a disagreeable bump on the last step, producing sufficient temporary confusion in his ideas to enable his opponent to shake him off and spring to his feet.

It was only for a moment though, and then Heartwell rose and rushed after him. The stranger then spoke for the first time, as he turned about at the door of the tavern.

" You will have it," he said ; and he drew a pistol from his pocket.

Simultaneously with the shriek that burst from Minna's lips came the loud report of the pistol, as it was discharged full in the face of Heartwell.

The young lieutenant reeled a pace or two, and fell flat on his back.

Minna had just time to see that the face of the murderer was a bright blue colour, before the light she carried fell from her relaxing hold, and she dropped insensible on the threshold of the bar-parlour.

CHAPTER V.

THE HONOURABLE LADY CLARE'S MANSION.—THE HUNDRED POUNDS.—ARISTO-
CRATIC SCRUPLES.—THE PLOT.

LADY CLARE was a lady of fashion: she was a tall woman, with a Roman looking cast of countenance, and as thoroughly heartless as any fashionable woman could aspire to be. Her manner and style of conversation were sharp and rude, which frightened many people into an opinion that she was a very clever woman.

But, with the million, rudeness is often mistaken for repartee, and emphasis will pass for wisdom.

People were afraid of Lady Clare, with a few exceptions, and some of those laughed at her, while others took pains, as Sir Peter Laurie would say, to put her down.

There are a great many ladies of fashion, who, without any ostensible means of their own, entertained an opinion which Lady Clare had, that society at large, in some way or another, is bound to support them, and that not on the pauper scale, but handsomely, and at a swingeing rate ; they must have a carriage, footmen, an own maid, a box at the opera, and other little indulgences ; and where these things come from they care not, so that they do come.

Certainly it is a melancholy thing, when, through the carelessness and extravagancies of some family, any of the female members are left so totally unprovided for ; but when such is the case, we cannot see that these noble paupers are entitled to more consideration than the poorest inmates of a workhouse.

But, in this blessed land of equal rights and privileges, what are called the higher classes of society will be supported somehow. The pension list is swelled to provide them with a maintenance ; or, by hook or by crook, or by one way, or by some way, or in any way, anything else to the contrary, in any wise notwithstanding, as the lawyer would say, they will have it.

Notions of morality and social virtue have always to us seemed to occupy a medium position in society, and to decrease as we go above or below—that is to say, we consider kings, and queens, and princes, and lords and ladies, to be somewhat, in their ideas of right and wrong, on a par with those, perchance, whose iniquities arise from their brutal ignorance and their necessities.

It is in that class of society where are to be found fair amounts of intelligence and education, and where people are much dependent upon the social estimation in which they are held, that we may expect to find social virtues.

Most certainly we do not look for such qualities in the fashionable Lady Clare, nor do we precisely hold her up as an example of the whole of her class.

The question of how Lady Clare lived, was frequently asked by the uninitiated, but never answered. She did manage to live, and live well too, and the mystery remained unsolved, except to a very few.

That few, however, knew full well how it was accomplished, and while they despised the woman, they paid her liberally for her services.

She was, in fact, an assistant in intrigues. She was always willing, for a consideration, that her house should be made the scene of any clandestine meeting ; she was always willing, likewise, for a consideration, to undertake the delicate task of being the go-between in *liaisons*, and by such means was it that she frequently got handsomely paid by both parties,—by the one for her services, and by the other for her silence.

But Lady Clare had an aristocratic and refined air about her which was quite charming. Of course, it would never have done for any one to go to Lady Clare, and say,—

"My lady, I have set my heart upon a seduction, and here are a hundred pounds as a retaining fee." Oh, dear, no! she was above that. A barrister will unblushingly accept of a few pounds to aid in any iniquity; to endeavour to make right appear wrong, and wrong appear right—vice assume the majestic aspect of virtue, and virtue assume the damning countenance of vice. This, we say, will barristers—who think themselves too good to dine with a writer for the public press—cheerfully do. But not so Lady Clare; she took Hamlet's advice, and assumed a virtue, if she had it not.

If those who were initiated into her mode of doing business wished for her services, a sum of money, so obviously lost at cards that there could be no mistake about the intention to do so, was the retaining fee; and after that her ladyship was always expecting to hear what she was expected to do.

That there are such women among the aristocracy let no one doubt. These demoralizing facts are too well established to admit of dispute; and, indeed, it would be contrary to human nature to suppose that because a particular class of society happen to be more protected from the consequences of crime than any other, that those vices which so closely border upon legal criminality should be scarcer among them. Common observation teaches us that it is not so; and, on the contrary, where circumstances preclude the necessity for that activity of intellect which is necessary to so many to enable them to jostle through the world, the passions will usually usurp the place, and run to riot and extravagance.

This is what makes the monarchs of England so eminently sensual as they are. Idleness has begot in them vice, and to keep at bay their great enemy, *ennui*, they must have recourse to illicit enjoyments.

Harding knew well the Lady Clare; he had been frequently to her house, and he was far from being ignorant of the very questionable manner in which she lived. And this is the way such men conduct such intrigues, relying not upon any powers of their own, bringing no mind to the task, but seeking rather to betray than persuade.

Lady Clare was at home, as her card signified, every Friday—that is to say, those possessing the *entree* to her house might walk in and out on the evening of that day at their pleasure. This was known, of course, to Bulkley Harding, and as it was a Friday on which he paid his ill-omened visit to the Victory, he congratulated himself that he so soon had it in his power to engage Lady Clare in his service.

At nine o'clock, which was the earliest hour at which he could decently present himself, he made his appearance, and took the first opportunity of engaging Lady Clare at cards. She was not slow to perceive that there was something more than met the eye in Harding's mind, and that he had come with some more particular object than merely to pass a few hours. This supposition was confirmed, when, in the most marked manner, he lost a no less sum than one hundred pounds.

She darted at him a look of intelligence, as, with no small amount of satisfaction, she pocketed the note which he handed to her.

"By-the-bye," he said, "Lady Clare, as I am here, I may as well amuse you with the relation of a little adventure that has befallen me."

"I shall listen with the greatest pleasure," she replied.

"Nay, but you will smile when I tell you that I have found a divinity at Wapping."

"At where?" exclaimed Lady Clare.

"At Wapping—the gun dock, at Wapping; through the city."

Lady Clare arched her eyebrows, as she said, with great nonchalance,—

"I never heard of the place; there's the great gun in the park, and the great bomb; but as for a gun dock, I never heard of such a place."

"I could hardly have supposed," said Harding, in a low tone, "that, even had you been aware of the existence of such places, you would have pleaded guilty to the fact; however, I assure you I am extremely serious on this head, and desire most earnestly your co-operation."

Lady Clare nodded, as much as to say, "I perfectly understand you;" and then she added,—

"I must own I feel a degree of interest in what you are saying, and should like much to see this divinity of—what's the name of the place you mention?"

"Wapping."

"Ay, Wapping. Is she maid, wife, or widow?"

"A maid, of peerless charms; and her proper address is, the Victory Tavern, Gundock, Wapping. She is intelligent as well as handsome. I cannot help thinking, even your ladyship's refined taste would find nothing to complain of in the bearing of the girl. Indeed, I had almost dared to hope, that by some means your ladyship might have found an opportunity to see her, that you might indeed have invited her here, and that I might have had the pleasure of meeting her."

"There may be difficulties."

"I shall be very happy to play a hand at cards with your ladyship occasionally."

"I will think of it."

"But pray be brief. That troublesome uncle of mine, who is in the Admiralty, has appointed me to a frigate. I must show myself at Portsmouth, but I hope to find, when I get there, that affairs are not in so forward a state as to enforce my presence; in which case I shall be here next Friday evening. May I hope that by then you will have made acquaintance with her whom I mentioned to you?"

"And if you should not be able to come?"

"I will come, you may depend. I cannot be forced on board, and, under a plea of serious illness, I can probably manage to detain the vessel a short time. If, however, the orders for her sailing be so imperative that she must leave port, I will let her go under the command of the first lieutenant, and follow to meet her where I can."

"I never knew you," said Lady Clare, "so urgent on any affair as this."

"Probably not. Hitherto I have had but one passion to goad me on, now I have two."

"Oh, indeed! then there is rivalry in the case, as well as admiration?"

"There is—hate and love alike impel me; and hence I am more urgent than I should be. I have, Lady Clare, set my heart upon the prosecution of this affair. I am assured, too, there is a mystery about the girl. I have been assured by one on whom I think I can rely, that she is not exactly what she seems."

"Indeed! Why do you shudder when you mention that one who has so assured you?"

"Did I shudder?"

"You did, most perceptibly."

Harding cast an uneasy glance round the room, and then he said,—

"Lady Clare, I cannot tell if I am suffering from a mind diseased or not, but the fact is, I have been now for two years haunted."

"What?"

"Haunted—I say haunted, Lady Clare."

"You speak in riddles; pray explain yourself."

"I don't know what impels me to tell you, but I feel a wish to do so. Listen."

"I will, with interest; for you have awakened my curiosity."

"It shall be amply gratified. About two years since, Lady Clara, I don't mind confessing to you that I had been, for a period of six hours, in one of the fashionable gaming-houses in the metropolis. I had lost a considerable sum; and, as I lost, I drank deeply. Wine, however, had no effect upon me. The state of irritation I got into defied its powers; and, finally, when I lost all I had, I rushed precipitately from the house. I found that it was the grey light of morning, and that the streets were nearly empty. I had not a sixpence in my possession, and therefore was compelled to walk, which I did at a brisk pace, cursing my evil fortune as I went. I had not proceeded far when I became conscious that some one was following me, adapting his pace to mine. In the frame of mind I was then in, such a circumstance was most annoying—I could no bear it—I was ready to quarrel with the whole world. I turned abruptly, and ——"

"Ah, Lady Clare," cried an elderly exquisite, as he sauntered up to the table, "it is really too bad for Harding to monopolise you entirely—I can't possibly permit it."

"Really, Sir Lumley," said Harding, "your interruption is very ill-timed."

"And unwelcome," said Lady Clare.

"Ha! ha! ha!" laughed the other; "very like, very like. I know you ladies go on the rule of contrary. If there's any secrets going on, I ought to know all about it— everybody trust me with secrets."

"Then I don't admire everybody's discretion," said Lady Clare.

Harding rose, as he muttered to himself,—

"It's infernally strange, but, somehow or another, I never can get that story told to anybody. Lady Clare, you will remember—you will see or hear from me by next Friday."

"But, Harding," said Lady Clare, "I should like to hear ——"

"You shall—you shall—another time. Adieu. I shall have enough to do to get to Portsmouth in time. Post horses must do that for me; and, likewise, I have to see my uncle before I start."

He left the house.

Sir Bulkley Harding paused not in the neighbourhood of Lady Clare; indeed, he was in a mood of mind that would scarcely have permitted of inaction. A rapid pace was that best calculated to keep pace with his thoughts—the motions of his mind, and these were scarce so pleasing as they might have been.

The interruption he had just endured from the ancient exquisite, seemed to him to be something of a character with what he had endured before; but it was exceedingly provoking. There was, however, no help, and Sir Bulkley Harding thought over the various matters that had to be done in so short a space of time.

"Events," he muttered, "are crowding on each other; indeed, the time I have to stay is so short, that I know not how to act, or what to do first. There's my uncle, I must see him and thank him for doing that which I had rather he had been broiling under the equator, than have done. He told me not to go near him; but I can understand that my thanks will not be unwelcome, neither will a check be so from him. I will, therefore, hasten; but 'tis too late now—to-night, after eleven. Oh, no—no; too late to-night; the old admiral is of the old school, and I can see him in the morning—the morning let it be—it would have been better to have done it at once, but the morning."

Having made up his mind as to the next step to be pursued, he immediately returned to his club, where he sought to pass the evening; but he felt uneasy and unsettled; and, besides, he saw no one that appeared to interest him. He was, in fact, unsettled, and he strolled about, and gave orders for post-horses and carriage to be ready at a moment's notice next morning, to carry him to Portsmouth with all the speed money and horses could perform.

The next morning Sir Bulkley arose at an earlier hour than he could well remember ever having risen, determined to see his uncle as soon as he could do so. He wished to see him alone, for he thought that he was fully equal to the task of seeking to impose upon his relative's feelings and good sense by the appearance of joy and reverence for his person. Upon inquiring for his uncle, he was soon shown into the apartment where he was seated before a warm fire, reading the gazette.

"Humph!" said the old man, who, notwithstanding his station, was too honest to play the hypocrite, and seem glad that his nephew was come. "Well, what brings you here, nephew?"

"I should have thought that could hardly have been a subject of inquiry, after the letter I received from you, in which you announced the promotion you have so kindly exerted yourself to obtain for me."

"Ha!" said the admiral, drily, for he believed in his heart that Sir Bulkley would much sooner have remained in town.

"I come to say how many thanks I owe you for this act of kindness and friendship on your part, uncle. Believe me, it will never be effaced from my memory while I live, and should it happen that I do not return, all I ask of you is, you will not deem me ungrateful."

"I believe you anything," said the admiral; "in that case, nephew, when you get alongside a Frenchman, as I hope to God you may—and though you are a scamp, still you are a Harding—but if you get alongside of a Frenchman, giving broadside for broadside, think of gratitude then. Give 'em another cheer, and another broadside, and say, that's your way of acting gratefully towards your own countrymen."

"Never fear, uncle, for me. I haven't had the years at sea you have had, and have not had the opportunities of becoming such a sailor as you are."

"And don't want."

"You have mistaken me."

"Ah, yes, I have, I dare say; uncommonly likely that old Admiral Harding would be mistaken in his estimate of any man. No, no, nephew; you know enough of London to spoil you, and to make a better man than you have any chance of becoming a worse than need be. Go along about your business—go aboard your ship, though I know you'd a great deal rather have stayed here living upon society, wasting your manhood, frequenting hells, and amusing yourself with intrigue."

"Indeed, my revered uncle ——"

"Oh, be d——d!" said the admiral, testily; "I—I—I hate a hypocrite."

"Nay, you are harsh—exceedingly harsh. A sailor is said to be generous—you are so; but do not refuse to hear me out, and I can assure you I have come here on purpose to thank you in this instance for your friendship. I shall go down to Portsmouth by post-horses almost immediately."

"You ought to have gone last night."

"I waited but for this interview—the opportunity of not only thanking you for the favour itself, but for the very handsome permission which accompanies it, and makes the boon more valuable than it was otherwise."

"What do you mean?"

"I allude to the permission to choose my own first lieutenant. I cannot do otherwise than say this is handsome; it adds an additional motive for gratitude."

"Indeed. And you will make use of the permission to name as your first officer some infernal rip—a scapegrace like yourself—one of your boon companions; a fashionable man, who is a better judge of wine and women than he is of sailors and the trim of his vessel."

"You wrong me, uncle."

"And who is this worthy to be?"

"Lieutenant David Heartwell."

"Lieutenant Heartwell!" said the admiral, in surprise.

"Yes, uncle."

"Why, he has not long returned with some prizes, and his vessel was put out of commission; he is a brave man and a good officer. He was very highly spoken of—very highly, indeed; he will be a great assistance to you."

"Yes; I thought I should be acting more in conformity with your wishes in thus acting."

"Well, well, that certainly does seem well; I must commend you for this."

"I am happy to hear you say so; he will be ready, I dare say, soon to go upon his duties, for I am really tired of town, and shall be glad to have an opportunity of shewing you, uncle, that for once you have made a mistake in judging harshly of me; time, you know, will teach us many things, and I hope to prove better than you hoped."

"Well, well, I must own this is a sign of amendment. Well, nephew, I wish you all the success in life; plenty of that, and an abundance of broadsides."

"There is nothing that I desire more than that, uncle; I have resolved to begin a new career, and one, too, I hope that you will approve of; but let me assure you I have not been so bad as you seem to imagine."

"Say no more on that head," said the admiral, "if you wish me to believe in your amendment, because the denial of the past will not aid it. I am glad, however, of all this, and I have some hope that you will do something now that will not disgrace our name."

"I will not; and now, uncle, I shall, within half an hour, take a post-chaise to Portsmouth, and shew myself on board the vessel; but I fear it may be some days before I shall be able to sail."

"Some days—some days?" said the admiral; "why, what is to hinder you from going immediately on board?"

"I have a very severe cold settling on my lungs; it is very slight at present, but the journey will, no doubt, render it worse. However, there is no help for that, and all that I hope is, it will not be absolutely necessary to sail for a few days, till I have so far recovered that I may be able to discharge my duty creditably."

"I hope so, too, nephew; and in saying I have hope, I say more than ever I felt before; but I recommend you to hasten down to Portsmouth, and if ill health should detain you, you must do the best you can; but do not let the vessel sail without you."

"I will not, if I can be carried on board with any hope of success; but this is anticipating the worst, which, with care, will scarce happen."

"No, no."

"And now, uncle, let me once more thank you for the kindness you have shown me in this appointment. It is what I earnestly desired, and for which I feel I owe you a deep debt of gratitude."

"I am well pleased to hear it," said the admiral; "it's a good sign to hear you have grace enough left for any such feeling. Nephew Bulkley, I wish you honour and success."

"Thank you, uncle; and now there is one more subject upon which I wish to speak to you."

"What is it?" said the admiral, looking hard at his nephew.

"It is this, uncle. I have left it to the last, as being the least pleasant to me. I have been out of commission long now, and my purse is dry."

"You do not want much at sea."

"No, no; but there are some things that are necessary, and I cannot go to sea with credit without them. Besides, there is one or two things I should like to see settled before I go."

" And I must give you the means, I suppose—that is what it will come to. Give me my desk, Bulkley, will you, and I'll give you a check."

Sir Bulkley Harding rose and brought the small desk his uncle had pointed to, and placed it before him. The old admiral pulled out of a drawer in it a check-book, and wrote out a check for the amount of two hundred pounds.

" There," he said, as he handed Harding the check, " there ; may it prosper you as you deserve. Now hasten to Portsmouth, and don't let me hear from you, save and except you have occasion to send home a prize, or to write a dispatch home that you have beaten an enemy."

" I assure you, uncle, that I will do my best, and I hope it will be attended with success, that I may show you I am sincere."

" It must be attended with success ; the ship is a good one, a first-rate vessel—the men are good, and you have chosen a brave and excellent officer as your first lieutenant. You cannot fail under such circumstances, and as long as you do your duty, you never need fear the result. Farewell, nephew, a pleasant voyage, and a successful one."

" Farewell, uncle ; thank you for past favours, and may I be fortunate enough to win your good opinion in what I shall do. I shall endeavour to gain it, if I succeed not."

He then was cordially shaken hands with by his uncle, who really believed in all the appearances of amendment he saw.

Harding, as he walked down the stairs, thrust his tongue into his cheek, and then felt for the check, and, finding it right, he walked out of the house, and made immediately towards the quarter where his uncle's bankers were.

Having presented the check, and received in cash the amount, he turned from the house, muttering to himself as he went,—

" Now, then, I'm for Portsmouth as quickly as horse and man can carry me."

The next place he sought was the club, whence he sent for the post-horses. After a few adieus to some of the individuals who frequented the club, he stepped into the carriage, and dashed away for the port.

He was soon carried away beyond the reach of London sounds, and now that he had got into the quiet country road he had some time for reflection, for here he was unlikely to meet with any interruption whatever.

" She must be mine—yes, yes, she must be mine! and in a very few hours I shall be traversing this road on my return. I have everything in train, and I must succeed. This Heartwell, too, he will be forthwith gazetted by my uncle, and he, too, will be coming down. I must leave the ship before he comes aboard; I would not see him until the ship is on the point of weighing anchor, and then he cannot decline the commission, and he shall wish his right arm off before he ever saw me ; but that has yet to be done.

" Then, the ship—all I hope is, the Eolus will not be ready ; neither captain nor first lieutenant have been aboard. They surely cannot have advanced very far in filling her with stores and fitting her for sea ; but, should that be the case, she shall sail without me before I would give up this project that I have I must, I will have her. Love and hate impel me—I will be avenged for the insult I have received, and such a vengeance shall fall upon him that he shall indeed regret the life he lives, the breath he breathes —every pulsation of his heart shall bear a pang of sorrow with it, such as he never dreamed of."

Thus, nursing his evil feelings within himself, the Honourable Bulkley Harding was whirled along rapidly by the post-chaise. Town after town was passed, posting-house after posting-house was stopped at for relays of horses ; not a soul did Sir Bulkley hold any communion with, but he sat back in his post-chaise while the horses were being changed.

At one place, indeed, he got out for refreshments—what they called dinner, but not what Sir Bulkley had been in the habit of calling by that name.

The ride had sharpened his appetite. He had a great desire for some food, and accordingly he stopped at the next hotel that promised anything at all likely to afford accommodation such as he desired.

He was shown into a private room, and then was served with some cold poultry—some that had been touched at a previous meal. This was, at first, a source of irritation, and he complained loudly of it to the waiter. This worthy assured him that it had not been handled.

" Good God ! do you mean to say, by way of recommendation, that these legs and wings haven't been pulled about by somebody's greasy hands ?"

" No, sir, they have not, I assure you. They are beautiful and tender as ——"

"There, take them away!" roared Sir Bulkley. "Take them away, and bring me some ham, or something of the sort. I can eat bread, but not that."

The waiter removed the dishes, and went down stairs, complaining that they had a very dainty customer who couldn't eat a bit of a chicken. For his part, he couldn't

think what he had been in the habit of eating—something made up at a doctor's, he supposed.

Some ham was taken up, and off that Sir Bulkley contrived to make his meal.

This refection over—after having drank some wine, he again stepped into the post-chaise, and away he was again hurried rapidly over the road. Nothing impeded him—the roads were dry and hard, and in good condition. This was fortunate; and as he was known, and paid liberally, good horses were put on, and they dashed along the roads.

Night came on, and he had yet to get to Portsmouth; nay, it was two good hours' journey yet.

"Drive on like hell!" he said to the post-boy. "Never mind horse flesh—whip and spur—whip and spur—drive on there!"

"Yes, sir," replied the post-boy; and then his whip would crack in the night air, the horses would wince and start forward until they were dappled with foam, and reeking with sweat. Their smoking sides were dripping with the moisture the speed had caused.

"Drive on—drive on! a golden reward will be your consolation."

"Hurrah!" said the driver, as he reached the top of the hill. "Hurrah! now for a fair road—no grass will grow under their feet."

This was true. The horses were urged along, and flew over the ground; and thus they continued till the lights of Portsmouth were seen in the distance. It was not long ere they entered the town itself.

It was late—the hour of ten had chimed, and the far greater number of the inhabitants of that sea-port town had gone to their beds, but yet there were some about; the hotels were open, and to the first naval hotel in the place the post-chaise dashed up, and pulled up to the door.

Immediately several of the officials came out, and the door was opened, and the Honourable Bulkley Harding stepped out. He threw a guinea to each of the postilions, and then entered the hotel.

Here, indeed, he met with every accommodation that his luxurious disposition desired, and he seated himself in a splendidly furnished private apartment.

"Is the proprietor within?" he inquired of the waiter.

"Yes, sir."

"Tell him Sir Bulkley Harding wishes to speak to him."

"Yes, sir."

With a low bow the waiter retired and delivered his message; when, a few minutes afterwards, the proprietor of the establishment entered.

"Are you the proprietor?" he inquired.

"I am, sir, at your service."

"Is the Eolus off here?"

"She is, sir."

"Do you know anything of her?—how soon is she likely to proceed to sea?"

"I don't know anything about her, save that there is neither captain nor first lieutenant aboard, and have, therefore, no opportunity of learning."

"Thank you; I remain here until to-morrow, until I go on board."

"The Eolus, Sir Bulkley?"

"Yes; I am her captain. After going on board, I shall return to town. Let me have post-horses as soon as I may require them."

"Assuredly, Sir Bulkley."

"And now some good wine, supper, and the Gazette."

"Certainly, Sir Bulkley, most certainly." Bowing low, the proprietor retired, leaving Sir Bulkley to his own reflections and meditations.

"Well," he muttered, "here I am, thus far. I would I could learn the state of the Eolus—I would that something might delay her—surely her armament cannot be delayed. She is new, and one of the finest vessels in the service. Let me see; she will sail down the Channel of course; delays may take place. It would be giving Heartwell a chance, and yet he must sail without me, if the orders are peremptory, sooner than I would miss being present at Lady Clare's. Minna she will get by some means,—she has plenty of devices to lure the bird from its perch—yes, yes—that I cannot doubt. She would have some plan to rid me of—but no, nothing could do that but death; and yet I thought that he had rid me of him ere this."

*　　　*　　　*　　　*　　　*　　　*　　　*

The next morning, the Honourable Bulkley Harding sent a message to the second in command, stating that he would be on board the vessel in an hour, and desired that the gig should be sent for him.

The captain's gig was immediately sent by the second in command, and received the person of the Honourable Bulk, and then he gave the word to push off for the vessel.

This was not long accomplishing, for she lay not far out; and in a short time he was received with the usual ceremonies by Mr. Herries, the second lieutenant, the third in command, now the first, until the first lieutenant, or the captain, should be on board; and now for the time the latter was in command of the vessel, and gave orders for hoisting his flag.

"Mr. Herries," he said, addressing the second lieutenant, "I feel much indisposed."

"I regret to hear it, Sir Bulkley," said the lieutenant.

" And so do I, because I shall be compelled to be ashore possibly for some days."

" Yes, Sir Bulkley."

" What condition is the ship in—I mean as regards her complement and her stores?"

" Neither are completed yet."

" Indeed !"

" No, Sir Bulkley."

" Then it will be some days before she can possibly be got ready to sail ?"

" I think so."

" How long do you think it will be before she can be ready to weigh anchor?"

" Certainly a week, Sir Bulkley—perhaps ten days, or it might be a fortnight."

This was welcome intelligence to Sir Bulkley, and he continued silent several minutes, considering in his own mind what had best be done.

" Well," he at length said, " there will be nothing for me to do yet. Are we to have our stores from this place?"

" As I understand, Sir Bulkley," replied Herries, " we are to have them here. A small corvette is to be sent to us here from Chatham, but in case it does not arrive, we shall touch there for them."

" Indeed ! Well, then, I could as easily join you there, as here."

" Certainly, Sir Bulkley."

" Well, I will think of that. Let them man the gig again."

The word was passed, and the crew of the gig was soon in their places. When this had been accomplished, Sir Bulkley Harding was conducted over the ship by the second lieutenant, and he could not but be well pleased that he had such a vessel as this under his command.

" You have a fine vessel, Sir Bulkley," said the lieutenant. " A finer I never saw."

" Yes ; she will do some service."

" I hope so, sir ; the men are ready and willing to lie alongside the French whenever they can get a good opportunity."

" That they will have before long, I doubt not ; but see the vessel is kept trim."

Mr. Herries attended Captain Sir Bulkley Harding over the side of the vessel, and the word was given to shove off.

Sir Bulkley Harding was, in fact, the captain of the Eolus, and had taken possession of the ship ; but he had merely remained on board some two or three hours, and then he quitted her, intending to return on board to take the command as soon as his intrigue had been completed.

This was one way of serving himself and his country too, but that was the fact, and he no sooner put his foot on shore than he hurried back to the hotel.

" Fortune," he muttered, " is so far kind, that she has given me ample time ; I doubt not but she will continue to be so. She is capricious ; but at the same time she loves to favour those whom she has once favoured."

" Fortunes, like misfortunes, never come alone," he thought, " and if she will but hold now in the same track, I will soon win and wear the flower I long to pluck, if Lady Clare will but be true, and true I have no doubt she will be,—it is to her interest to be so. But now for London—ay, for London, where so many pleasures are to be found ; there is no other place in the world like it ; and yet, let me succeed, as I must and will succeed, I shall then go to sea without regret, were it only to prosecute my plans of revenge upon this Heartwell. Yes, David Heartwell, I am thy evil genius. You shall lose all you love, and even the love of life ; but you shall not lose life itself. Oh, no, no ; I will care of you and prevent that."

CHAPTER VII.

LADY CLARE'S VISIT TO THE VICTORY.—THE SUCCESS OF HER RUSE.

LADY CLARE had a decided genius for intrigues ; she was the presiding goddess, who kindly lent her aid to those who were her devotees, and helped them to those delights they sought. She was fertile in schemes and plots ; and seldom was it, indeed, that the fish, once hooked, was by her ladyship lost.

The affair in which the Honourable Bulkley Harding had engaged her was an intricate and difficult one, and, therefore, showed her audacity and ingenuity on the occasion, which were, indeed, never wanting.

She ordered out her carriage, and her two tall footmen behind, dressed in gorgeous liveries, whose long staves were loaded with silver, and her coachman with an unexceptionably full-bottomed and curled wig. It was quite a dashing and remarkable affair—one that was very sure to attract attention.

These servants of her ladyship pretty well understood what they were going about—it was impossible, utterly impossible, that any two London flunkies and a fat coachman could be long ignorant of the fact. They knew as much as her ladyship—perhaps more. However, London flunkies are particularly wide-awake people, and never think of seeing what they haven't any necessity to see, except in a private way.

" Well, Tummas," said one, " what's the dodge to-day—where are we going to ?"

" I'm d——d if I can tell; but it's east, I believe—isn't it, coachee?"

" Yes."

" Ah! the city lies that way, does it not—that cust low place, where they do so much trade ?"

" Yees; there's nothin' there but money and goods—so I'm told; and nothing fit for a gentleman to see, taste, or smell. It's infamous."

" If she's going to stop, we had better drive back west the while, else my lungs will never stand such d——d pestiferous air."

At this moment, Lady Clare was seen descending the steps, and one of the tall footmen, with pattern calves and legs, immediately opened the carriage-door, and her ladyship stepped in. The footman touched his hat, and receiving some instructions from her ladyship, closed the door, climbed to the side of his fellow, and the carriage rolled away.

When they had cleared the city, by her ladyship's orders,—who, by-the-bye, was not so ignorant of the whereabouts of Wapping as she would have wished Harding to believe, —the coachman drove direct to that interesting locality, and then one of the footmen got down to inquire respecting the situation of the old Victory. The house was well known, and in a few minutes Lady Clare found herself but a short distance from the house.

Suddenly she pulled the check-string, and the coachman hastily drew up, and a footman was at the door in an instant to know her commands.

" I feel very unwell," said her ladyship. " I have a giddiness. I think I will leave the carriage; the open air may revive me."

The footman opened the door, and proffered his arm, for the purpose of assisting her ladyship to descend the steps. She had hardly, however, touched the ground, when a vertigo appeared to seize her, and she apparently fainted in the arms of the footman.

Minna Woodward (for Lady Clare had stopped the carriage immediately in front of the Victory) and David Heartwell were both attracted to the window by the noise made by the servants at this unforeseen circumstance, and they both instantly went out to offer any assistance Lady Clare might require.

Her ladyship was led into the little bar parlour, and after some moments signs of returning animation were observable, and then she was able to speak.

" What has happened?" she exclaimed; " tell me what has happened? Has any one been hurt? Let me have the consolation of knowing that no injury has been done to any one, and then I shall care not for myself."

" Madam," said Heartwell, " you may make yourself easy upon that score, no accident ever has happened. From what we can hear, you were taken unwell in your carriage and brought in here, where, let me assure you, you shall receive every attention."

Most admirably did Lady Clare put on the confused look of a person gradually recovering consciousness, after the total lapse of memory, caused by fainting.

" And to whom," she said, as she glanced around her, " am I indebted for so much kindness? Alas! I see I am surrounded by the young. Learn from me, although it be on the impulse of a moment, that rank and wealth give not happiness. You see in me one who, by the force of circumstances, although surrounded by the glittering insignia of rank and station, and ample means, is more touched by a simple kindness than probably you would be yourselves."

There was nothing that any one could quarrel with in this speech, as regarded its sentiment, but still the tone of it seemed to say, poor and low people, don't envy me, although I am rich and high, but make yourself contented, for we have all our troubles.

This was too much like the usual cant of the rich towards the poor to please Heartwell; and, moreover, holding the station he did, let her be whom she might, he had a right to consider himself to the full her equal.

" Madam," he said, " I am greatly pleased to find that the attention we have been enabled to bestow upon you has resulted in your recovery. I am Lieutenant Heartwell of the royal navy."

" Oh, I beg your pardon," said Lady Clare; " I really thought you were the waiter."

"The waiter, madam!" said Heartwell.

"My dear sir, you need not be offended; if I had met you in the private apartments of St. James's, I might just as absurdly have mistaken you for a prince of the blood—really, I hope you are not offended."

"It is impossible," said Heartwell, "for a lady to offend a gentleman."

"What a sweet romantic old house," said Lady Clare. "Until we see such places as these, we can scarcely believe in the existence of them. I should like much to ramble over such an ancient building."

"To all its rooms but one," said Mrs. Woodward, "you are welcome;" and then she turned aside to hide her emotion.

"All but one!" exclaimed Lady Clare. "Have I then unconsciously touched some chord of tender sympathy? Alas! I would not willingly have done so. I may be careless, thoughtless almost to a fault, but I am not unfeeling; that, when you know me better, you will find."

Lady Clare was a good actress for an amateur; and she tolerably well succeeded by this speech in dispelling the effect to her prejudice, which her vivacity concerning Heartwell had produced.

"There is death in the house, madam," said Heartwell, "and that is the reason you see the faces here wearing an unusual gloom."

She looked up into Heartwell's face, with the appearance of great sincerity, as she said,—

"Sir, you have frankly told me who you are, and it therefore behoves me to return your confidence; there is my card, and believe me that you have made a friend in one who never makes a friendship in vain."

There was the charm of high breeding in her manner; for that may, and does often, exist along with the most heartless profligacy. The young imagination, however, of Minna Woodward, who had not yet spoken to Lady Clare, was more taken probably by her specious manners than that of any one else; and now her ladyship thought it high time to commence operations, by devoting her attention to that quarter. Turning, therefore, to Minna, she said,—

"My dear child, perhaps I ought not to say so, but I cannot help the exclamation, of —how beautiful you are! May you be as happy as I am sure, from the ingenuousness of your countenance, you deserve to be, and may you make the happiness of some one who can fully appreciate you."

Heartwell was pleased, and as his hand quickly sought that of his betrothed, he said, in those low tones which love alone can modulate the tone to—

"Yes, my Minna is beautiful, and she shall be happy."

"I understand," said Lady Clare, "your hearts are already united. Will you give me leave to call you friends? I must see you both at my house. I lead a homely life, but reside in the midst of that society which, to the young, is ever so fascinating. Now, my dear Minna, I am sure we shall be great friends; and when sated with the glitter of what is called high life, wearied of its monotony, and displeased with its frivolity, I shall feel that I can come here and be happy, because all around me seems sincerity."

To the young and romantic imagination of such a being as Minna Woodward, could there be anything more alluring than such a state of things? Here were at once the impenetrable folds of a curtain which had divided her from a state of society, concerning which she had heard and read much, torn asunder. With all the advantages of being merely a spectator, she would be enabled to enjoy all the magic of those scenes to which a lady of title, who really wished to befriend her, could introduce her.

And how delightful would it then be to relate to Heartwell all that she had heard and all that she had seen! To come back from the glittering saloons of aristocratic wealth to that humble home, which was endeared to her by so many of her happiest recollections, would always be delightful from the very contrast.

Nor did she for one brief moment dream that such scenes could win her heart from peace and happiness. Oh, no! Heartwell was too dear to her for that, and what earthly power could wean her from his arms?

She looked at the moment all the pleasure that she felt as some of the results of the proposition which Lady Clare had made dawned upon her mind.

Her ladyship saw at once that she had fascinated her victim; she seemed to feel that she had done enough for once; and rising, with one of those fascinating smiles, which were to her a matter of practice, she thought it best to take as charming an adieu as possible, rather than push the matter further at that interview, which might have brought her friendship to the verge of suspicion.

Before, however, another word could be spoken on either side, the servant-maid, whom we have already occasionally introduced to our readers, came abruptly into the bar-parlour with a large official-looking packet in her hand, on which were printed the words—" On his majesty's service."

The packet was addressed to Heartwell, and bore the Admiralty seal.

" In commission again !" he cried, joyfully. " I am appointed to a ship."

" Oh, no, no," said Minna, and she clung to him. " I thought that you were safe here, and that they knew not where you were."

" Nay, nay, Minna. General orders forced me to report myself to the Admiralty within four-and-twenty hours of my residence at any particular place. I have had the happiness of being here beyond that period of time, and therefore it is that this official communication has so promptly reached me."

" But Heartwell, Heartwell ——"

" Oh, I shall be afloat again on the dark blue waters; again shall I tread the deck of a gallant vessel. The din of conflict will again make music to my ears; again shall—— My Minna—and had I for one brief moment forgotten thee! oh, forgive such treason to my love. If I rejoice that once again my country calls me to fight her battles on the bosom of the deep, it is that I may win such a name in her annals as it shall be your pride to hear uttered. It is, my Minna, that I may become more worthy of you; it is the thought of you that will animate me in the hour of conflict; and when the world talks of you as the betrothed of David Heartwell, your cheeks shall glow with the pleasure of the thought that I am worthy of you."

" Worthy—more than worthy!" now sobbed Minna. " What, oh, what is this you call fame and glory, to the joy of pure affection! Heartwell, it is an error of the imagination; oh, stay with us!"

" I cannot, Minna—I dare not. See here—read the communication; is it not a flattering one? is it not one that should please you?"

" No—no—no!"

" Nay, dearest, your eyes are dimmed with tears, and you cannot see the words; I will read them to you,—

" Sir—Highly appreciating your recent services, their lordships have thought proper to appoint you forthwith first lieutenant to the new frigate Eolus, now lying at Portsmouth, whither, within eight-and-forty hours after the receipt hereof, you are expected to proceed.   " I am, sir, your most obedient servant,
                                        " J. Leftwich, Secretary."

" There, Minna, you hear—the Eolus, a new vessel that not an officer in the navy would not pant to be on board of. This is promotion—promotion unsolicited, too, for I have no friends at court. I have fought my way step by step up the ladder of promotion, not the ladder of fame. We are safe to have a most successful cruise, and when next I look upon your sweet eyes, I shall hold a captain's commission, and, perchance, the war may cease."

" Perchance not," said Minna.

" Of course we cannot tell; but should it not, I shall return at times to tell you how I love you still."

" Perhaps never," said Minna; " but we will speak of this another time, Heartwell. Recollect we have a visiter here."

" But not an unfriendly one," said Lady Clare. " Believe me when I assure you I have not heard unmoved that which has passed. I cannot stay now to express my feelings—they lie too deep for utterance. Farewell, and may Heaven above guard you!"

Heartwell handed her to her carriage, and a feeling of satisfaction came across his mind at the thought that, in his absence, Minna and her mother would have such a friend as Lady Clare—one rich and powerful enough to shield them from harm, and to interpose between them and any act of oppression that might be attempted to be perpetrated against them.

He lingered a moment as he saw the carriage drive off with its fair occupant; and then a sudden sensation came across his heart of doubt, and he said in a low tone to himself,—

" Is this woman's assumption of feeling genuine?"

But Heartwell was of far too generous a character to take up light grounds of suspicion. He blamed himself for entertaining them a moment, and yet it was with a slow step and a reflecting brow that he re-entered the bar-parlour of the old Gun Tavern.

CHAPTER VIII.

THE PARTING OF THE LOVERS.—MINNA'S TEARS.—THE PROPHETIC GREETING.

IT is night. A soft moonlight rests upon the gently agitated waters of the Thames. There is a projecting window from one of the rooms of the old Gun Tavern; it opens upon hinges, and the lattice is thrown back. Within a few paces of it stand two forms, and truly might we say with Byron,—

"Both were young, and one was beautiful."

Motionless they seemed as two marble statues, and as the rays of the soft moonlight fell upon them they looked something more than mortal, and as if the pure affection for each other which had found a home within their breasts, had lifted them above humanity.

Those figures consisted of a tall and well-proportioned man; the curling dark hair, as his head was slightly bent, had fallen over his brows, and with his left arm he encircled the slender form of the fond, trusting being to whom he was the world and all the joy that it could give her.

She was pale, because grief was sitting heavily at her heart; but she was not so pale as the jealous moonbeams would have made her. Her face was pillowed upon his breast for many minutes. They did not speak—they did not move. It was the parting hour of Minna Woodward and her lover.

"And there they stood as if entranced—
The world forgetting—by the world forgot."

Time passed unheeded; they needed not language to express the feelings which each heart could translate so well to each other. No protestations of affection were necessary between them, they seemed as if they could have stood locked in that gentle, that pure embrace, until the break of dawn.

The accessories, too, of the scene were all such as to harmonise well with the feelings of those twin hearts—for well may we call them such. There was the quiet river, giving such an air of repose even to the very houses that throng along its banks—that repose which a mass of water always gives to any scene. It was rather an undulation of its whole surface than a ripple, which gave a slightly dancing aspect to the moonbeams; then, too, it happened to be an hour, although it was an early one, at which the busy scenes the river's bank usually exhibited were stilled, for it was shortly after sunset, when active, out-of-doors labours had ceased, and a period of rest had arrived.

The sky was cloudless, and so, wanting its apparent motion from fleecy vapours, the moon appeared stationary in the deep blue vault, as though it had paused to look down upon those two young beings, who, in the freshness of existence, loved each other with a holiness of feeling more than mortal.

Never perhaps had that ancient window exhibited such a scene to the quiet eye of night: the hands that had fashioned it had long since mouldered to decay, but it was worth the making, that, at some period of its history, it should hold, as it were, in a frame, so sweet a living picture.

For about a quarter of an hour that silence was maintained, and then, by Heartwell, was it broken, as in a softened and subdued voice he said,—

"My darling Minna, never before when I have left you have you so much seemed to dread my absence. Wherefore now, sweet girl, when under better auspices by far than ever yet I parted from you, I go to seek my fortunes on the waves, do you look so sad?"

"I am sad, Heartwell. Very, very sad."

"Nay, dearest, is not this the third time we have stood by this old window, on the eve of my departure?"

"It is, Heartwell; and there are many who believe a third chance fatal."

"My Minna, are you of that many? this is obvious superstition."

"It is, and yet ——"

"Nay, nay, banish such fears. Leave superstition and its thousand hideous fancies to those who waste a lifetime on the deep, and may well be excused for nourishing strange thoughts of the strange sights they see, and the strange sounds they hear; and so, Minna, if I, a sailor, am free from these feelings, surely you may well be so."

"Do you not believe in presentiments, Heartwell?"

"No, except they accrue upon evidence clear and definite of that which is to come."

"Of course, Heartwell, your spirit is bolder and more daring than mine. I am but a weak and timid girl, and so cannot but confess my fears that—that ——"

"That what, Minna?"

"That we may never meet again."

"Nay, while to combat the possibility that we may never meet again would be absurd, the probability is strongly in our favour."

"But you are rushing into danger, Heartwell."

"I am; but from the nettle, danger, we pluck the blossom, safety."

"A well-turned sentence of the poet's, but a weak argument to one who loves."

"Nay, smile, my Minna, and let me dream that I saw joy, and not sorrow, on your face, when last I looked upon it."

"I cannot smile. You know that I have more than common cause of grief at present."

"True, true—you have not now a father; but remember, Minna, that we have often agreed in saying, that death was not so much a sadness, as the end of sadness; a rational grief for those whom we have loved, and who have left us, well becomes the best of us; but beyond that all should be serenity and hope."

"I know that you are right, Heartwell; but when did philosophy ever yet successfully combat with the feelings?"

"Well, well, Minna, we will talk of something happier."

"Call you your departure a happier theme?"

"No, we will not speak of that, but of my return. Keep that in view, and so cheat the mind in the reflection on the weary interval. Days will soon accumulate to weeks, and weeks to months, and so when a few brief months are passed away, we shall again meet, perhaps to part no more."

"I will be happy in that thought."

"Now, Minna, you speak more like yourself, and I can leave you with a lighter heart. You will hear of me, although I cannot of you, and you shall hear with pride of him who loves you. For my sake, you will be very careful of yourself. You will make what kind and judicious friends you can, but still not hastily."

"Yes, yes, Heartwell."

"Your mother does not seem, since your poor father's death, so capable of throwing a protecting arm around you as she was, so that much now will depend upon yourself, and your own native energy of spirit."

"I will think of you, and so arm myself for anything."

"Do so, Minna, and, 'mid the roar of the waves, and the din of the conflict, your name shall be my talisman."

"Do you see that boat?" said Minna, as she pointed to a small, black-looking wherry, that was floating idly down the stream.

"Yes; surely its occupant is lazy, or he might urge his little bark well on with the current."

"He seems approaching here."

"We will retire from the window; idle curiosity may prompt him, and we cannot object to his coming in this direction, since there is a landing-place."

They retired a pace or two from the window, but Minna seemed disinclined to get further, and so in silence for some few minutes they watched the progress of the boat upon the river. The stream was running down, and had he who was seated in the wherry done no more than keep the head of his boat to the stream, he would have floated quietly down past the old Gun tavern. But that he did not do, for as he neared, it was evident he was pulling with one oar quite against the stream, so that the boat came broadside towards the tavern. In its progress, too, it had to pass through the long stream of moonlight that fell upon the waters, and then they saw clearly in it, the outline of the figure of a man who was entirely in black, and whose face seemed hidden by some mask, or dark medium, placed before it.

"Who can that be?" said Minna.

"I cannot tell," replied Heartwell; "he's a strange-looking fellow, and we really have no right to inquire; the river is a highway."

"And yet ——"

"What would you say, Minna?—he seems coming here for a purpose? If you think so, I'll ask him."

Heartwell stepped forward to the window, Minna still hanging to his arm, and in a loud, clear voice, he said,—

"Hilloa! halt, there! Are you coming to the tavern? The landing-place is a little higher up."

The boat was now very nearly opposite to the window, and suddenly the man who occupied it shipped the oar he had been using, and deliberately stood up in the very centre of the frail wherry.

His figure was tall and thin, and it was now evident that something was over his face.

[See page 29.

He spoke in a voice which, in consequence of the stillness around, had a solemn and strange effect.

" Beware !" he said. " Beware—beware of the *first false step !*"

Without another word, he sank into the bottom of the boat, and it glided past the window, being almost in a moment lost to view in the deep shadow of some barges that were close at hand.

CHAPTER IX.

THE SECOND WARNING.—THE FUNERAL IN OLD STEPNEY CHURCHYARD.—THE MYSTERIOUS MOURNER.

HEARTWELL has left, and Minna's heart is desolate. She feels now that she has double cause of grief. The loss of two whom she has loved presses heavily upon her spirits. Her father dead, and her lover far away, were two contingencies but ill calculated to impart to her countenance the hue of health, or the aspect of happiness.

Of course, all hope of seeing Heartwell again was not obliterated, but still was there something terrific in the contemplation of the many fearful chances with which such a life as his was sure to abound.

"If he should not return," she would say to herself, "what would become of me? I can see that my mother's health is failing fast. We are alone in the world. We are almost the last of our race. Should the news of Heartwell's death ever reach my ears, Heaven grant that it may have the power to still the beating of my heart for ever."

It was not to be wondered at that these feelings of gloom should much increase, as the morning approached when the remains of Mr. Woodward were to be consigned to their last resting-place.

After that day of gloom and misery, it was likely enough that somewhat of her serenity would return, but until that last and sad ceremony was over such a result could not be expected.

On the morning appointed for the funeral, her state of agitation was extreme; but, when she saw her mother, she found upon her face such a look of concentrated woe, that she almost lost a consideration of her own suffering in the attempt she made to give her consolation. There seemed, likewise, to be something upon her mother's mind, in addition to the grief which might naturally be supposed to fill it at such a juncture.

So impressed was Minna with this conviction, that she took occasion to ask her if such was not the case.

"My dear," said Mrs. Woodward, "you know as well as I that we have ample reason to believe the chamber of death in which your poor father has lain has not been free from intrusion. You know the old bureau, of which he always kept the key?"

"Yes—yes."

"It is that, then, which appears to me to have been the object of some depredator; 'tis very strange, Minna, but it certainly has been broken open. What has been taken from it, it is impossible for me to say, for I knew not its contents."

"Do not regret, then, the loss of that which we cannot appreciate."

"Yes—yes; but there is a secret."

"A secret, mother?"

"Hush!—hush!—I should not have said so much. Oh, how I shall now blame myself —Minna, forget it!"

"I wish, mother," said Minna, "that you had said nothing, or that you would say more."

"No—no—no. I cannot—I dare not. It is not a secret that will make you happier —far from it. It is one better buried in oblivion: you may believe me fully when I say so much. Forget, Minna, the chance word that may have arrested your curiosity."

"Mother," said Minna, "I have never yet disputed your commands—I will not do so now. We hold not memory in our grasp, to retain or cast it from us as we please; but I will not again mention this subject, if you interdict it; and now, dear mother, let it rest. Duties of a higher—of a different nature, call upon us now. Oh! that this day were past."

Mrs. Woodward's feelings were too poignant for utterance, and she could make no reply; a deep sigh, more resembling a sob, escaped her. The day on which a funeral takes place is one of extreme solemnity. It is then the parting of the living from the dead is seen and felt. This becomes so plain and palpable to the feelings, that grief take on this day a new form, and becomes more violent.

It is then that death becomes more apparent, and the loss more clearly defined; the loveliness of the living more lovely, and the absence of those who have gone becomes more perceptible. It is strange, but grief bursts out anew, and the greatest exertion of will and fortitude are often unable to effect calmness sufficient to go through the trying scene of the funeral.

Both Mrs. Woodward and Minna felt the necessity separately of endeavouring to comfort and console each other, and were resolved to do so, if it were possible; but it was not, as they afterwards found.

The first great shock to their feelings was the act of screwing down the body. Mrs. Woodward was carried away in an almost fainting state from the room, and the very men whose office renders them used to such scenes, and therefore not easy to be moved on such occasions, when they saw the grief of the beautiful Minna Woodward, felt that there was yet that which they had so seldom looked upon, that they could scarce even hide those emotions of grief which they felt.

Minna took a parting glance at her dead father's features, and, kissing his forehead, she sobbed, and staggered from the room.

The body was then screwed down, and the mutes were placed at the door; and every mark of respect that could be paid to the dead was observed by the neighbours and frequenters of the old Gun Tavern.

The mourning habiliments which Minna and her mother that day assumed were a new source of grief; for again did the cause of this change of attire come freshly and more forcibly upon them. Again a fresh burst of grief, and the wound in their hearts was once more torn open, and bled afresh.

"Oh, mother, mother!" exclaimed Minna, involuntarily, as she put on her mourning—"Oh, mother! I would that I had died before I had seen this day!"

"Hush, Minna! hush! not from you ought such a wish to come, but from me; the old and seared must die; for you life has yet charms; you have yet to feel all the pleasures and sorrows of life."

"The sorrows are greater, mother; and what amount of pleasures can ever compensate for moments like these?"

"If we had the choice, Minna, the case might be different; but as it is, we have not. This last act we are called upon to perform towards one whose life has been almost our own, has great grief and sorrow attached to it, and yet I would not forego for worlds the duty I have to perform, greatly as it grieves me. We have spent many years of happiness together, Minna, and that makes my present grief the more poignant; yet I could not say I would we had never met. I should be ungrateful for the past, and unhopeful of the future."

"I hope, mother," said Minna, with a deep sigh, "I may have reason to say as much, should it ever become my melancholy duty to do as you have now to do."

"God grant me strength to go through with it," said Mrs. Woodward fervently.

"Amen!" ejaculated Minna.

Their conversation was interrupted by the arrival of one or two mourners, who had been invited upon the strength of old friendship, rather than from any relationship they had held to the deceased.

The moment had arrived when the gloomy and sorrowing procession was formed, Minna Woodward and her mother acting as chief mourners; and thus they left the old Gun Tavern, to follow the late owner to his last home,—to the last spot of earth he would ever occupy.

The day was a dreary one; it was dull, and the heavens overcast; there was nothing extraordinary in it, but to the mourners all seemed to be gloomy and mournful, save the faces they met with.

It was a mournful and sad spectacle, to those who knew the deceased man, to see this last act of homage that the living can pay to the dead; but the thousands whom they met, looked upon it as merely a common occurrence, one they had seen so often, that they did not take much notice of it; in fact, curiosity alone to see what sort of features the mourners had, prompted them to see or endeavour to see their faces, or look at them at all.

They were narrow and crowded thoroughfares which they had to pass through, to reach Old Stepney Church, and a densely populated neighbourhood—a populace whose thoughts and feelings were not of the most refined character, and yet they made way for the solemn and sad procession.

Stepney church was reached, and the tolling of the bell struck loudly and solemnly on their ears, as they passed through the iron gates up to the church porch.

The grave was reached; the clergyman, bare-headed, and clothed in white, read impressively the service for the dead; all was still, save his sonorous voice; the pulsation of a heart could be heard, so solemn and still was the occasion that had brought them there. Minna and her mother stood side by side, absorbed in grief, and their tears fell silently, even as the clergyman spoke.

Among the mourners was one man whom no one knew. He was unknown to all, but there he stood by the side of Minna, regarding her, rather than the body. He was tall and thin, but no vestige of his features could be seen; he sedulously and carefully concealed them by the cloak which he wore, and the handkerchief he held up to his mouth. That he was tall was evident; and that he was thin might be seen when he occasionally drew the cloak he wore more closely together as the wind blew.

However, no notice was taken of the stranger, who stood there, motionless as a statue, while the service was being performed.

The body was lowered into its appointed place, and Minna stooped down, from some indescribable emotion, to take a last look at the coffin, as the earth was being thrown into the grave on it.

The stranger bent forward at the same moment, and uttered andibly in her ear, as he did so :—

"Beware, beware of the *First False Step !*"

Minna uttered a slight scream, and, with an effort to rise, she fainted, and fell insensible by the side of her father's grave.

Immediate assistance was offered, and her restoration effected ; but the stranger was gone. No one had seen him go ; they had not become aware he was gone until they looked for him.

This incident interrupted the return of the parties to their home. Minna was terrified, and taken home in a coach. The warning that had been uttered in her ear was so ominous to her, because she had heard the very words spoken by a man—and she supposed he must be the same—in a boat, as she stood in the window with her lover, on the eve of their parting.

CHAPTER X.

LADY CLARE'S SECOND VISIT.—THE THIRD WARNING.—THE FETE.

SIR BULKLEY HARDING, we have said, left Portsmouth to return to London, which he did without delay ; but there was a little incident occurred on the road, which might have had other consequences, and it was not without its effect upon a mind constituted as was Sir Bulkley Harding's.

He had stopped at an inn on the road, while his horses were being changed, to partake of some slight repast, before he again set out for London.

It so happened that Lieutenant Heartwell was that very day proceeding to Portsmouth as Sir Bulkley was coming from the same place. It was night, and Heartwell had stopped for the same purpose as Harding, only the latter took the stage.

When Heartwell entered the inn, Sir Bulkley was about to leave it, and they were face to face in the hall.

Heartwell was somewhat surprised to see the man he had so unceremoniously thrust out of the old Gun Tavern, and that, too, through the window, dressed in the garb of a gentleman, and he looked a second time in his face, to be sure that he had not mistaken him.

David Heartwell would not have acted as he had done, had he known who and what Sir Bulkley was ; but, as he did not, the change somewhat surprised him.

Sir Bulkley, too, saw, and distinctly recognized him, and he now felt himself to be placed in such a situation, that he could not allow such an evident recognition to pass without a word, though he had rather not have met him there at all ; but it was not in Harding's nature, to allow any opportunity to pass in which he could exert malevolence, or ill-will ; though the object were unknown and the effect for the time unfelt, he could enjoy the secret triumph.

"So," said Sir Bulkley, as the other reached him, "so you have quitted possession of the old Gun dock."

"Well," said Heartwell.

"I thought, you had taken such a liking to the place, you intended to keep it all to yourself. Have you come to do the same here ?"

This was said in a kind of sneering tone, that grated upon the feelings of Heartwell, who constrained himself to reply,

"I shall, if I have the same reason to do so, and use the same means."

"You will repent this."

"I do not at present see how. But you must be other than what you appear to be, else you would not be skulking about in different disguises, with apparently no better object in view, than the brave one of insulting a young lady. I would I had more time at disposal, and you should repent having seen me a second time, but beware how I cross you again."

"Ay, beware," said Harding, "beware, indeed; I pray you to remember your own prayer."

"When I do aught that ill becomes a gentleman, I may."

"Once more," said Harding, with increased bitterness and wrath, "beware, for I am not crossed in vain."

Heartwell was about to make a yet more angry reply, but Harding walked through the hall and stepped into his post-chaise and drove off before he could recover himself.

" Who is that man?" inquired Heartwell, of a waiter—" and what is he?"

" Don't know, sir."

" Do you know his name?"

" No, sir."

" Have you seen him before?"

" Can't say I have, sir, he has only stopped here to change horses."

" Perhaps he may be known to some one about the house—will you inquire for me—I have a particular reason for knowing?"

" Yes, sir, I will sir," said the waiter; and Heartwell walked into the common room.

Here he waited for some time, until, in fact, the waiter returned, whom he had commissioned to gain intelligence.

" Have you learned anything?" he inquired as the waiter came up.

" No, sir."

" Not known, eh?"

" No, sir, nobody knows him here."

" It is very strange," muttered Heartwell, thoughtfully. " I hope that no danger lurks around my beautiful Minna."

* * * * * * * *

Sir Bulkley Harding hurried on to town, well pleased, that whatever had passed, all tended towards the one object he had in view. The time it gave him to pass in London was all he desired; and he was anxious to reach Lady Clare's, to be certain what progress had been made with regard to the affair he had interested her in, and how she had succeeded with Minna Woodward.

He knew Heartwell was out of the way, and that was another object gained, as well as a satisfaction; for he knew he was on his way to take his command, as first lieutenant, on board the Colus.

It was evening again ere he got to Lady Clare, who was glad to see him, and greeted him with a welcome, saying,—

" I am glad to see you again, Sir Bulkley. You have spent no more time than the journey occupied."

" Very little more, my lady, I believe; but how have you succeeded in the little affair in which I feel so deeply interested? Have you seen Minna Woodward?"

" Yes, I have seen the party you mention; I have been to the house. Oh, what an odious old tumble-down place. Why, who is there that could believe in the existence of such places?—they are quite antedeluvian. And, oh, what a vile neighbourhood!"

" It is not the casket, but the jewel that I speak of," said Harding;—" the east is not the west, we know, and the two quarters of the town are inhabited differently."

" I never knew that till yesterday," said Lady Clare; " but I contrived to find the old Gun Tavern and its inmates, and saw Minna Woodward, and must say that for the class she is very beautiful."

" Very beautiful!" repeated Harding, involuntarily. " Such as one might in vain look for elsewhere. But proceed."

" I entered the tavern, and saw the girl, as well as some irascible seaman. I forget his name—a lieutenant, I believe. Do you know him, Sir Bulkley?—he is of your profession, at least so he took the pains to inform me."

" Yes," said Harding, wincing; " I have seen him; his name is Heartwell; he is a lieutenant."

" Ah, something of the sort, I believe. But, Sir Bulkley, I think you will take nothing by the affair; your pains will be wasted."

" Indeed!" said Harding. " I think if I have your ladyship's good offices I shall succeed. However, let me have your assistance, and I can see no serious impediment."

" But I do," said Lady Clare.

" What!" said Sir Bulkley. " Her notions will be so dazzled that time will do wonders."

" And that you have not got."

" I have a fortnight in London. There was no necessity for my going to Portsmouth— certainly none to keep me there, so there can be no impediment."

" But this Heartwell is a far more serious rival than you can imagine, Sir Bulkley; the girl's affections are as thoroughly set upon him as his on her, from what I could see."

" But he is out of the way now, and she will forget him."

" Pardon me, Sir Bulkley; you know I don't think much of romance, especially that of love, but this is a serious and settled case, and the absence of Heartwell by no means alters the case, except she is now more easily attacked; but I say again you will not succeed."

"Will your ladyship persevere and see her again? If I could see her here—if I could obtain an interview with her, much might be done. Let me entreat your ladyship to see her again. I—I will stop at nothing, and my gratitude to your ladyship shall be definite and tangible. Heartwell, you see, is by this time at Portsmouth."

"Yes, yes, I was present when the commission was sent him to the Eolus."

"Yes, yes—my vessel."

"I see, Sir Bulkley—love and revenge are both alive in your bosom."

"They are, as I told your ladyship before. I have now two passions that urge me on, and they are irresistible."

"Well, well," said Lady Clare, with a yawn, "I will visit these people again, and see what can be done with them. There was death in the house when last I was there."

"Your ladyship may find the obstacles less important than you imagine."

"I am not usually mistaken," said Lady Clare; and then some other guests entered the apartment, and Sir Bulkley took his leave.

A few days afterwards, Lady Clare determined upon another visit to the old Gun Tavern, and upon this occasion found Minna alone.

It was to the immense dismay of the coachman and the two footmen, with long wands, that they found themselves once more driven towards the city, by the irresistible command of their mistress.

True it was they protested most strongly and urgently against such a disposition of their time and attendance between themselves, and resolved they would not stand it, and, in fact, they must resign, if they were subject to this kind of degrading annoyance any more.

However, they found they were at the old Gun Tavern, and yet Lady Clare had not fainted this time, but got out quickly, and entered the house to the amazement of the lacqueys.

"I'm d—d," said one, "if her ladyship hasn't taken a queer taste."

"A taste of this fashion," said the other, telegraphing the action of drinking out of a bottle.

"She can get better at home than here."

"Oh, bless you, they never pay duty here; it's all genuine, and no mistake; but, perhaps, she's doing a little business, here."

"Perhaps so, and yet it is decidedly low and vulgar—she must be a poor-minded wretch. I would not exchange taste with her."

"It would be a disgrace."

"Beyond redemption."

"D——e."

In the meanwhile Lady Clare advanced to the little bar-parlour, where Minna Woodward and her mother were seated. Sorrow had scarcely become sadness, yet it was somewhat of a more active quality; and Minna saw with pain that her mother's health was daily becoming worse and worse, until her fears were directed in a channel she feared to think of.

She thought the time might possibly come when she would be motherless as well as fatherless, and that earlier than she dare think of or imagine.

"I have come," said Lady Clare, assuming a charming air, combined with frankness and condescension, "I have come to thank you for the attention you have bestowed upon me. I am one who never promises in vain, or forgets a favour."

"Do not think of the trifling act of duty, for such it really was," said Minna.

"But it is not every one who does it; and, morever, I cannot permit any one to do me a favour, and then think meanly of me, by imagining I can forget it."

"We are well assured that you would not," said Mrs. Woodward. "Will you please to take a seat, my lady?"

"Thank you, I will. I have come to ask you a favour," said Lady Clare.

"Indeed, my lady, we shall be but too happy to oblige your ladyship in anything we can, if you will but let us know how we can do so."

"You remember I was present when a gentleman, your friend, received orders to go to Portsmouth, to join his ship?"

"Lieutenant Heartwell."

"The same. Well, as your father is dead, and he is now gone, I determined, in my own mind, to become your protector till his return; this is but an act of friendship, which, I promise, shall be more gratifying to myself than even to you."

"Your ladyship's kindness is great, and I scarce know how to express my thanks for such a favour; and yet I know not how to accept of it, since my mother is my protectress, in the absence of those we mourn."

"She is, and yet I flatter myself I can take upon myself that character also without destroying that connection, which it would be improper to sever. That is not my object; I merely wish you to come to my house on a visit, and see it; you will see much that will amuse you, and, I need scarcely add," she said, glancing her eyes round the room, "that will astonish you too."

"You are very good, my lady; but," said Mrs. Woodward, "these sights will do my poor Minna no good."

"But it will habituate her to those things which the chances of life may place in her power: her lover is a sailor."

Minna looked at Lady Clare, as she uttered these words, with a look that at once told that artful woman she had ensnared her young heart by that speech; and, moreover, Minna could not banish from her mind the possibility that she would one day, and that day might not be far hence, become motherless.

Heartwell, too, had noticed the apparent break in her mother's health. Not that Minna saw this with a calculating eye, or even an approach to caution or prudence; but hers was the watchfulness of love, that made her tremble with apprehension of a second bereavement; and hence the offer of protection when coupled with the inuendo respecting Lieutenant Heartwell, had all the charms that could make it acceptable to her mind.

"Mother," said Minna, "Lady Clare is very kind,—very kind indeed; but I will not leave you; that would be far too great a sacrifice for any pleasure or benefit."

"So it would—so it would," said the Lady Clare, "and it is not what I desire; but you will not refuse me my first invitation: it will extend to but a short time. I have a few intimate friends in a mere homely way; I wish to show you some few persons as an introduction; say you'll come."

Minna hesitated, and her mother appeared reluctant and undecided.

"The carriage is at the door, and it shall bring you back. Surely, Mrs. Woodward, you do not think that any motive but pure kindness and a desire for your daughter's welfare, would induce me to make such a request more than once. I would ask no one else."

"No, my lady," said Mrs. Woodward, as she found she was compelled to speak. "I have no such thought, and if Minna decides to go, she has my permission."

Minna made no remark; she seemed to be in doubt about something.

"You hear what your mother says, Minna," said Lady Clare; "if you are unwilling, of course I cannot urge you."

"I thank you," said Minna; "I will accept of your kind offer with thanks. I will go with you, but I must return very soon to my mother again."

"Certainly—certainly, whenever you please, my dear; and now, if you have made up your mind, we will go immediately, for I have lost some time in coming here."

Minna, seeing that her mother made no objection to the arrangement, instantly left the room, and made a hasty disposition of her dress for riding, and then returned to the bar-parlour.

Lady Clare, in the meantime, had held a short conversation with Mrs. Woodward, during which she pointed out the benefits likely to arise from this introduction; and that good lady truly believed in the disinterested professions of the Lady Clare.

"Mrs. Woodward," said Lady Clare, as she turned round condescendingly, "if any harm be offered to Minna, you blame me; and when I say that, you may imagine the care I will take of her. Adieu."

Lady Clare sailed out, and Susan opened the door, and she opened her eyes and her mouth as she looked upon the person of a "real" lady,—a titled lady.

"Good-bye, dearest mother," said Minna, "good-bye; and be sure I will not stay. I could not do so."

"Go, my child; it may be for your benefit. You may some time or other need friends; and why should I prevent your doing so? Good-bye, my dear—good-bye!"

Minna followed Lady Clare, and entered the carriage with her ladyship.

It was getting dark, or a little after sunset, and the lamps in the street were just about being lit, and yet there was light enough for useful purposes. They could see all around them; and Lady Clare took care to employ Minna in some conversation, so that she was pleased enough with the novelty of her situation, which was indeed as new as pleasing. There was a window at the back of the carriage—a small, oval window—which enables those inside to see out, and any one outside to see in, when the bit of cloth that is usually nailed over it is lifted up. Suddenly this window was smashed in. The laides started, and Minna and Lady Clare both uttered a scream.

Minna sat opposite, with her back towards the horses, and she saw the window darkened for a moment, and the same voice she had heard so mysteriously before, again uttered those ominous words,—

"Beware of the *first false step!*"

Minna screamed.

"Stop the carriage," said Lady Clare.

For a moment all was confusion and dismay, in the midst of which Minna entreated to be let out.

"Let out, Miss Woodward! You surely cannot think that this alarm is any pleasant joke belonging to my carriage. I dare say I have suffered more from fright than even you."

"Yes, my lady; but those words—I ——"

"Never mind what the silly people of this neighbourhood may say. Had it been westward, such an insult upon a lady would have instantly been resented, and the offender secured. I assure you it is more the fault of the diabolically low neighbourhood in which we are, than aught over which I have cognizance."

"I am far from blaming your ladyship. I am sure you knew not of it; but there are terrors of the mind which are not weakened by reason, and such are those that I feel. I would that I were at home—that I had not come."

"You will be at what I hope you will for the future consider your home," replied Lady Clare, "in a very short time."

Thus Lady Clare sought, between kindness and authority, or assumption, to quell the rising fears of Minna Woodward, who certainly could not but think that some friend had taken the trouble to warn her for the third time.

"It cannot be for any evil purpose I am warned, surely? If evil were intended or wished, they would not surely allow me to continue in any course likely to bring evil. But what am I about now? Surely I cannot be in bad hands. This Lady Clare is too sincere and frank—she is too kind—and is, certainly, too much the lady of fortune and rank, to be even liable to suspicion."

While Minna Woodward was thus endeavouring to combat her own fears, and account for the motive of the warning she had received, Lady Clare had been engaged in whiling the time away with animated descriptions of balls, parties, and routes, until at length she suddenly exclaimed,—

"Oh, they are coming!"

"Who are coming, your ladyship?"

"My guests. I have just a few friends whom I wish you to see;" and as she spoke the carriage dashed up to the door of a large house, the knocker of which was in continual requisition. The street was filled with carriages, and the house was completely illuminated.

Minna looked through the windows of the carriage in mute astonishment. Such things she had heard and read of, but never saw before; the number of guests were prodigious.

"Are all these people coming to your house, my lady?" she said, in a doubtful tone.

"Yes, all," said Lady Clare, in an indifferent tone, as if it were an usual circumstance.

"You have a large party, then, and I have come at an inconvenient hour, at least one in which I cannot very well mingle; for your ladyship knows that I am known to none of them."

"Yes, Minna, that is very well, so far as you are concerned; but you are my guest, and you will receive the same attention as any one else, who does not happen to be known perhaps more; but many of these people are unknown to each other, though known to me perfectly well."

Minna was silent. The glare of the lamps and the liveries and dresses, certainly, even from the carriage windows, seemed to her the work of enchantment, or of some dream.

The carriage stopped, and Lady Clare alighted, followed by Minna Woodward. She entered her house, in which the latter beheld a sight that well might engage her. The rooms were rapidly filling with guests, and Minna could see the saloons, as she passed, were filled with well-dressed persons.

Minna could not but feel that some sort of treachery had been practised towards her by Lady Clare. Most unquestionably she had been asked to visit her ladyship with the presumption that it was to be in the most quiet and domesticated way, and now to find

that she was to be inveigled into the glittering entanglement of a fashionable rout, was certainly far from being pleasant to the feelings of her whom we are pleased to call our heroine.

But still the circumstances by which she was surrounded were of that nature, that it was difficult for her to show any degree of resentment from apparently so puerile and insufficient a cause; for, after all, to the majority of minds, it would seem like kindness on the part of Lady Clare, to introduce Minna Woodward into such a scene of magnificence, without harassing her with preparations; and Minna was young, too, and human. We do not hope to claim for her an absolute indemnity from all earthly weaknesses; it was natural that her spirits should be elated by the strains of exquisite music that met her ears; it was natural that she should pant for some sort of personal insight into those scenes of aristocracy, wealth, and importance which, to the perceptions of the young who have not had an opportunity of mingling in those gay and glittering scenes, have always a romantic charm.

How few minds are there, likewise, who, on the immediate spur of the moment, will do or say the right thing precisely in the right place. Minna had shrunk from an encounter with Lady Clare's guests, but she had not refused absolutely to become one among them.

She had hinted at her own incapacity, as she imagined, to mingle with such a throng, and yet now she found herself, with feelings more of curiosity than timidity, gazing around her, upon a scene common enough to all but herself, but which, from its novelty, was to her most exquisitely enchanting.

Lady Clare was a good tactician; she knew that to dazzle her victim at once presented the best possible hope for the future; she wished to entrance the very senses of Minna with delight—she wished her to draw such a comparison between the home she had left and that superb mansion she was now in, as should bring with it a distaste for the former commensurate with her admiration of the latter; and thus she hoped to wean her from humble virtue to glittering iniquity, as if the gilding of those rare saloons could compensate for that sunshine of the heart, that, until that night, had never departed from the heart of Minna Woodward.

The cares of existence may, for a time, cloud the brow—sickness may lay its icy hand upon the heart—grief for those who are taken from us may bring the ready tear to such eyes as Minna's; but still, in her heart of hearts, a consciousness of right, of innocence, of spotless purity and virtue, would present to her consolations, such as none not so situated could hope for.

In the darkest hour of tribulation, to those who have not cast from them that majesty of principle which has triumphed over all temptation, dreams of joy can never be unknown.

And did Minna forget that warning voice? did it not recur to her again and again? and did she not, more than once, faintly translate it to mean, that her even consenting for one moment to seek that abode of luxury and selfishness, was, of itself, a first false step. It was so, and yet not one of serious moment, although, possibly dangerous in its results. It not unfrequently happens that innocence overmatches itself. Minna should not have accompanied Lady Clare at all. She should have felt, as well she might, that by doing so, she was establishing dangerous contracts in her mind, making it far more difficult for her to be contented as she was, because she was acquiring a more intimate knowledge of what, had destiny befriended her, she might have been.

Like a personification of some evil principle, did Lady Clare watch the young and innocent girl whom she was luring to destruction. She saw the earnest gaze of admiration Minna cast upon the almost regal adornments of those apartments; she saw her gaze with awe and enthusiasm upon the rare specimens of the sculptor's art, looking only not like life, by being more exquisitely beautiful; she saw the colour mount to her cheeks, as aspirations of ambition crowded about her heart; then she chose her moment, and, bending to her ear, she whispered—

"Minna Woodward, compare this to a dirty public-house at Wapping. The odours of sweet flowers fill this place with delicious perfumes; the stench of tobacco clings to you from your own home. Politeness, grace, beauty, and intelligence here, are things of course. Do you find them at the Gun tavern? I say again, compare this house with that you have left."

Minna shuddered; she was making the mental comparison. Like an arch-fiend, possessed of power to read her heart, Lady Clare had but put into words its aspirations.

"I ought not to have ventured here," said Minna.

"Not venture here, and wherefore? You have youth and beauty. Do a hundred wax lights add a wrinkle to your brow? Do those gorgeous colours, reflected by the crimson hangings, rob you of any hue of health or beauty? Do those strains of music awaken unpleasant sensations? No, Minna Woodward—no! It is for you, and such as you, that such scenes as these are created."

"Not for me—not for me," said Minna, sadly.

"Have you a reason?"

"I have. Born in a lowly state—yet happy, because affection blessed my earliest years—I panted not for those I knew not. My humble home, in which I passed my earlier life, had ever to me a thousand household charms about it. The palace-like glitter of such a place as this, has often, I will grant, in description, warmed my imagination; but, like the fleeting interest I have felt in some sweet fairy tale, the hope to realize the visions of the fancy has passed away. I am sorry I came here."

"A most foolish sorrow, Minna; of all the false philosophy and follies the human mind is capable of, that which teaches us to tremble at innocent enjoyment, for fear that they should not last for ever, is the most pernicious."

"Nay, it is not quite that feeling, Lady Clare."

"But I'm sure it is; and, however, such as you, Minna, may disguise it to your own mind; it is, in truth, from such a narrow piece of bigotry, you draw your sad conclusion; shake it off—enjoy the moment. Will you join the dance?"

"No, no: my dress is all unsuited."

"True—true. Come with me; we have ample accommodation here, and you shall soon take your place among that throng in the inner saloon, with nothing singular in your appearance except your superior beauty to all those present."

Minna shrank back. There was something to her mind uncommonly uncomfortable in hearing praises of her beauty from a woman. From the lips of Heartwell, whom she loved, she could hear such commendations for an age unwearied; but from Lady Clare they came harshly and artificially across her senses. But still she hesitated; the mental struggle was a severe one—reason and determination seemed to triumph for a moment.

"Lady Clare, Lady Clare," she said, "I cannot remain here."

"You cannot?"

"Place the determination in what phraseology you please—fancy me foolish, ungrateful, if you will—but let me go."

"What is there to fear?"

"Everything—everything. The spirit of my recently-dead father seems to beckon me away. Oh! it is sacrilege to his memory to have come to such a scene as this."

"And do you fancy," said Lady Clare, with an appearance of solemnity—"do you fancy, Minna, that ever the spirit of your dead parent could feel aught but pleasure in your pleasure?"

"This is false reasoning," said Minna. "Let me go—let me go."

"Will you make a scene?"

"A scene!"

"Yes; here in my house. Would that be right—would it be grateful?—would it accord with your commonest notion of propriety? I have warm and strong affections. I little thought, Minna, that you would have turned upon me thus. I feel as if I could scream, and summon all those guests around us in a moment, making you the centre of attraction; and you would drive me to such an extremity, and to such distress of mind, rather than remain my guest for one brief hour."

Minna was a little alarmed.

"If—if," she said, "it were only for an hour ——"

"Who can make it more, except with your consent? You can go now, if you will—go now; we make no prisoners here. But think again; fortune may yet place you on a giddier pinnacle than this; and would you, then, shrink, because she heaped her favours upon you? Nay, Minna, do not mistake the timidity of rusticity for philosophy—a common error, child—a very common error. Come to my chamber."

"And I shall go in an hour?" said Minna.

"Ay, or earlier, if you will. Who is to say you nay? Here is a large house full of people—people of rank and standing—people who have reputation—people who scorn a dishonourable action. Why, in these aristocratic regions, the very age of chivalry returns. Come—come this way—this way."

Through a door opening on to a brilliantly lighted staircase, the walls of which were covered with specimens of the choicest art, the Lady Clare led the still reluctant but half-bewildered Minna. Ascending with her then a short flight of stairs, she took her into an elaborately-finished chamber—such a chamber as Minna, in her dreams even, had never pictured; and feeling now that the eyes of none of her ladyship's portly guests were upon her, she breathed more freely; and as there was really much to admire, she began almost to be ashamed of her former fears, and to regret that she had spoken so freely to Lady Clare about her wish to go.

Some rapid changes in her dress, effected by her ladyship's French maid, and the addition of some costly ornaments to her hair, neck, and arms, produced a wonderful revolution in the personal appearance of Minna.

When she was led to a glass, she started with surprise, for she scarcely knew herself. It was Lady Clare's policy that she should get but that one bewildering glance at her own adorned charms; and then, scarcely knowing whither she was being led, in a few more minutes Minna was in the ball-room, under the blaze of light from countless candles; and surrounded by a throng attired in such glittering costume, that her eyes were dazzled with the sight.

"If any one asks you to dance," said Lady Clare, "for Heaven's sake, refuse not!"

"But—but—I know so few dances."

"Exactly, exactly! All the better."

"Can that be possible? I may be asked to dance a measure I never heard of!"

"It's highly fashionable to know nothing," whispered Lady Clare. "Gracious Heavens! You would not commit the dreadful vulgarity of knowing either the step or the figure you stood up to dance to?"

With these words, which certainly rather astonished Minna, her ladyship glided from her; and in another moment, attired in the extreme of fashion, and certainly presenting a tolerably elegant appearance, the Honourable Bulkley Harding stepped up to Minna.

"If disengaged," he said, "may I request the honour of your hand for the ensuing dance?"

Minna shrank back. There was something about the tone and manner of the man which seemed to come upon her with a dim kind of remembrance. It is no uncommon phenomenon of the mind to have a kind of sentiment of having met a person somewhere, without being able to trace in the memory any distinct circumstances connected with him or her. All that we are assured of on those occasions is, whether the circumstances under which we have met the parties be of an agreeable or of a disagreeable tendency.

To Minna, the sound of the Honourable Bulkley Harding's voice brought with it a feeling associated with some kind of misfortune; and yet she knew not why. Truthfulness compelled her to admit that she had no engagement for the dance, and it was with trembling accents that she said,—

"I must decline, from non-acquaintance with the dance."

"Nay, you will see as you go on," was the reply; "you perceive the set is formed, and we are in place—fear nothing! Eyes that love you are upon you."

"That love me?"

"Yes; and therefore you can be as happy as you will."

"But tell me—tell me ——"

"At the next pause I will."

The music had struck up a few bars, and obeying the impulse her companion gave her, Minna found herself carried through a dance, of which she was as completely ignorant as any person possibly could be.

The giddy exercise, and the exciting whirl of some of its positions, did much to destroy the calmer reflections of Minna; when the dance was ended, she did not refuse to partake of some refreshment from a side table.

Then, with eager curiosity, she sought to ascertain the meaning of the rather obscure words which had been uttered by her partner.

"You spoke," she said, "of the eyes of those who loved me being upon me."

"I did, indeed; and in so speaking I uttered no more than sober truthfulness permitted me."

"Yes, yes. I'm very glad; and perhaps this accounts for Lady Clare being so anxious to get me here."

"Fully," said the stranger; for a stranger he was in name to Minna Woodward.

"I think I begin to understand; of course an officer in the royal navy is company for any one."

"Most decidedly."

"He could take his place among the highest and the noblest; besides, there is a native dignity about him, which even majesty itself might well wear. Oh, now, tell me, is this a friendly, pleasant, little plot?"

"Can I keep the amiable secret from you? It is, indeed."

"Then if I had left, I should have lost ——"

"The exquisite pleasure of remaining."

"Yes, yes; but where are those eyes that love me?"

"Where are they?—close at hand."

Minna turned completely round.

"I do not see Heartwell," she said.

"See who, sweet piece of perfection?"

"Heartwell,—Lieutenant Heartwell. You said the eyes of one who loved me were upon me. I do not see those eyes."

"Because you won't, look in my face, my angelic creature. Can you doubt that your charms have produced a flame in my breast which will be undying? Can you, for a moment, suppose that I could look unmoved on such beauty?"

"Sir!"

"I love—nay, to say I love you, is to say little—I adore you. I live but in the basking light from your eyes."

"Unhand me, sir. I cannot and will not endure this insolence."

"Insolence! blame that Heaven which made you beautiful, and gave me capacity to admire its handicraft."

He had got a firm clutch of her wrist, and now Minna felt, that to get away from so ardent a lover, would create just what Lady Clare would call a scene, a circumstance she wished to avoid as much as possible. It was, therefore, with tremulous accents of entreaty, that she said to him,—

"Sir, if you are the gentleman, which your presence here and your appearance bespeak you, you will allow me at once to leave you."

"Nay, nay; is this kind?"

"If it were it would be what it is not intended, sir."

"Is this generous?"

"Sir, is it just? Another moment and I'll cry for help. I will not be detained thus against my will to parley with a stranger upon such a subject."

"Minna," whispered Lady Clare, "how can you be so foolish, this is but a jest."

"A jest, madam?"

"Yes, surely; one of these pieces of badinage, that are common to society. Really, Minna, your own natural, good, sound intellect, ought to have told you better than that. This gentleman is a nephew of mine, and, after that, surely you can acquit him of having any but the most respectful feelings towards you."

"I never jest with strangers," said Minna.

"But you will forgive me," said Harding, "on my assurance that I meant no offence? on my solemn word of honour, that I thought you fully understood me, and went with me in the little war of words."

"It matters not," said Minna, "I can return home."

"Not yet, not yet," said Lady Clare. "I will enable you to stay longer than you meant, by placing my carriage at your disposal, for your return. You are heated now with dancing; take a seat, and when you are rested, even then you will find how early it is, and what folly it would be to think of going."

She led Minna to a couch where there were several ladies, and, finding a seat for her in one corner, she left her, promising to return in a few moments.

Minna had scarcely time to give a passing reflection to what had occurred, when some one from behind said to her, in a deep and serious voice,—

"If I'm wrong, I can but be laughed at for my pains; but I cannot help thinking that you are really a stranger here?"

There was a friendliness in the tone that was irresistibly attractive, and Minna turned and looked in the face of the speaker.

CHAPTER XI.

THE ADMONITION.—THE TUMULT AT THE BALL.

HE who had so addressed Minna Woodward, was a man past the prime of life. How he'd got into such an assembly as that, was a mystery; for Lady Clare was uncommonly precise as to whom she admitted; she had no objection to any amount of prodigality, extravagance, or vice, but she had a most wonderful objection to any spies in the camp. Probably this person had got in by assuming a vice, if he had it not, but most certainly he appeared to be a very different character from that of Lady Clare's other guests.

Young persons go far more by physiognomy than those of maturer age; they have not yet learned to mistrust their own perceptions, and the fallaciousness of first appearances has not been strongly forced upon their observation by experience.

Hence, Minna, after the gaze of a second or two into the face of him who now addressed her, felt as if she could have abandoned at once all reserve in speaking to him.

"I am, sir," she said, "a stranger here."

"Then why did you not continue so?" he said, quietly and earnestly. "What false feelings brought you here?"

"I came here at the solicitation of Lady Clare."

"No doubt of that; but you look too innocent for such a place; let me advise you, to go home as quickly as you can; do not ask me to be more explicit, but ask your own heart if you like the company you see around you. If you're innocent—pardon me for appending the doubt to it—you will be gone."

Lady Clare at this moment made her appearance. She seemed to have some sort of suspicion, probably from Minna's looks, that the stranger had been giving her a caution.   She was so angry, that she looked redder than the paint entitled her to look.

"Sir," she said, " I forget who introduced you."

" Oh, madam," said the stranger; "I asked for Sir Bulkley Harding at the door, and was at once allowed to pass in unmolested.   A sure proof of what high esteem your lacqueys hold him in."

" Are you a friend of his?"

" I hope so."

" You hope so, sir! you speak ambiguously; perhaps, sir, if I were to find the honourable Bulkley Harding in these rooms, and bring him to you, he might not be so anxious to claim your acquaintance."

" Oh, yes he would, madam."

" Then, sir, if I may trespass so far upon your patience, as to ask you to remain where you are, till I seek that gentleman, I shall be much favoured."

" Oh! certainly, madam, I've not the slightest intention of moving for some time, yet."

" Apropos," exclaimed Lady Clare, " here comes Sir Bulkley Harding," and, as she spoke, that individual lounged up to the couch, no doubt attracted by seeing Minna seated on it.   " Sir Bulkley," added Lady Clare, " pray introduce me to this gentleman, if he be a friend of yours, of course, as such, he's abundantly welcome."

Harding advanced to within a few paces of the couch, and then he gave a start of surprise, and a look of consternation, both of which were by far too well done to be assumed.

" You know him?" exclaimed Lady Clare.

" He knows you," said Minna.

" We know each other," said the stranger.

" Confusion!" muttered Harding;—" my uncle, the First Lord of the Admiralty."

" Yes," said the stranger, who, indeed, was no other than his uncle; " I have a reminiscence of appointing you to a ship at Portsmouth some days ago."

" Yes, uncle; but—but a ——"

" Instead of being in your vessel, you're in London; while the din of war is assailing every harbour on our coasts."

" I came, uncle, to make needful preparations for my departure, of which you will recollect I informed you by letter.   I have things to purchase, things to pack up, and bills to settle."

" Is this a naval accoutrement shop, a packing warehouse, or an attorney's office? Harding, this will not do; I received a note that I should find you here to-night, and that your name would be my passport to these apartments.   Beware, sir!   If you're in London four-and-twenty hours longer, your commission shall be superseded."

" Uncle," said Harding, " I shall of course obey you.   It is not a hard condition, for I intended to be off to-night."

" Which makes you bite your lips and look angry.   You have deceived me more than once.   Beware! I say; you may deceive me once too often."

" Allow me, my lord," said Lady Clare, " to express the great pleasure I have in your lordship's company."

" Madam," said the uncle, " the pleasure is not mutual, I regret to say."

" The fact is," said Lady Clare, " the honour of a visit from you ——"

" Is not very likely to be repeated."

The old man seemed to have forgotten Minna, or, if not, he probably considered that he had said quite enough to her, and that if she did not choose to take the warning he had given her, it was no business of his.   He did not even bestow upon her a parting glance; but with an appearance of indignation which, no doubt, he found it extremely difficult to conceal or to prevent, burst out into some passionate ebullition, and walked from the room.

It must not be supposed that this little altercation had entirely escaped the notice of Lady Clare's guests; slowly but cunningly they had gathered round, and when they saw that which promised to be a pretty quarrel enough in the commencement was going to subside so quietly, they seemed to consider themselves as dreadfully ill used.

" Why, Harding," said one fop of a fellow, " it seems to me that the old fellow thinks you're a coward."

" It's better, sir," said Harding, " to be thought a coward than to be one in reality."

" Ay, he means you, Deddington; he means you are going to put up with that."

" No; upon my soul, no; I'll kick any one from here to Coventry who attempts to cast any reflection upon my courage."

" Will you get out of my way?" said Harding, who, in proportion as he was obliged to

suppress any ebullition of anger with his uncle, seemed furious with everybody else ;—
" will you, I say, sir, get out of my way ?"

"Oh, dear, no; not upon compulsion," said Deddington ;—" couldn't think of it."

It was a ludicrous act, and Harding might certainly have adopted a more dignified
course, but probably he acted impulsively ;—he seized the nose of Deddington with so
ferocious a nip that he twisted him nearly off his feet ; and then, as if the act of violence
he had committed had deprived him of all self-command, he sent the throng of coxcombs
who had assembled to jeer him flying in all directions.

As might be supposed, such a state of things as this produced no small amount of confusion among the guests of Lady Clare, who were before amused at the altercation between
the uncle and nephew, and considered that an agreeable variation of the amusements
of the evening ; what had now occurred, and the prospect of a serious riot, seemed to be
most especially pleasant to all but those who were immediately engaged in it. These
latter were certainly too great sufferers by the serious attack which had been made upon
them to see the joke so vividly as did those who were merely spectators.

Bulkley Harding, bad as was his cause, was not without his supporters ; some hastily
sided with him ; while others took the parts of those whom he had assaulted, so that
Lady Clare had the satisfaction, if satisfaction it could be called, of finding her guests
divided into two factions in her own drawing-rooms.

This was a kind of thing which her ladyship by no means considered desirable ; the
flimsy veil of propriety which she had hitherto managed to hang over her assemblies
would, by such a means, be rather too hastily torn aside ; so, in the most heroic manner,
she flung herself into the centre of the fray with the hope of staying its further progress.

Perhaps if she had allowed it to be fought out upon the spot, it would have been better
for the various parties concerned, and less actual mischief might have resulted ; because
so many combatants would have been engaged, that individual quarrelling afterwards
would have been almost ridiculous.

"Gentlemen, gentlemen," she cried, "will you remember where you are ? This is my
house, and you are my guests ; is it, then, proper or gentlemanly that you should make
this place a scene of strife ? I beg of you to have more consideration for me, if you have
none for yourselves."

This admonition produced a pause, and then Bulkley Harding said,—

" This affair will keep. I know those who have insulted me, and they shall yet discover that it is not to be done with impunity."

As he spoke he fixed his eyes upon a young man named Herbert, who was a major in
the army. Having great family interest, he attained that rank long before his deserts
would have given it to him. The look which Bulkley Harding had cast upon him could
not be mistaken ; it was one of defiance and promised strife. As such it was at once
translated by Major Herbert, who, walking close up to Harding, whispered to him,—

" You know where to find me at any time."

" I do," said Harding, " and it is a knowledge I shall avail myself of."

Major Herbert made a slight inclination of his head and then turned away, as if the
affair were completely arranged.

Lady Clare, however, was too old a tactitian, and had seen too much of society not to
be full aware of what was intended ; and she became engaged in a mental calculation
with regard to which of the young men she could least spare ; if, indeed, she could spare
either of them. That a duel was intended she had, of course, no manner of doubt, and
that it was in her power to prevent it by getting magisterial interference, she of course
knew well enough ; but that was the last course she would ever have thought of adopting,
for the young scions of aristocracy who crowded her soirees would have felt themselves
greviously hurt at the fact that a quarrel, commenced in her saloons, could not be allowed
to take its even and regular course. It would have been a decided infraction of that do-
what-you-like sort of feeling with which every one visited her, and well she knew that
she would be treading upon dangerous ground if she interfered with that eccentric and
curious system of honour which prompted these young men, on any and the slightest occasion, to risk their lives with each other : and yet, somehow or another, never to interpose to save them from committing the most flagrant outrage on feeling and morality,
was decidedly wrong.

Our readers may readily conceive how terrified poor Minna Woodward was at this
untoward event ; how devoutly she wished herself back at the old Gun tavern, far removed from the contaminating influence of that glittering scene which had already taken
by far too strong a hold upon her young imagination.

Oh ! how devoutly she wished for Heartwell ! How she longed for but the most transient glance of that honest, open countenance which bespoke the soul of honour; but that was not the scene to find such a one as he. Never by his presence were these polluted saloons graced; as far removed as virtue is from vice was David Heartwell in character, temper, habits, and disposition from the parties who formed for the most part the guests of the detestable Lady Clare.

We call this woman detestable because vice assumed in her one of its ugliest aspects. A human intellect may be weaned from its better judgment, and stoop to vice and criminality, while yet there may remain sufficient traits of what might have been to induce us to pity, while, at the same time, our judgments force us to condemn; but this woman, whose character we wish to hold up to our readers as one most fearfully bad, was one worse than criminal, for she was the systematic cause of vice and criminality in others; the base pander was she to evil passions; a woman, take her for all in all, whom we hope, rather than believe, there are but few specimens of.

The anxiety of Minna to be gone increased each moment; she knew not the hour, but she thought it must be late, for there were no means in those splendid apartments of noticing the progress of time. Alas, Minna Woodward, where now was that apparent decision of character which had promised in thee better results? Would he, David Heartwell, the gallant, and the true, have believed for one moment that such a being as you would hesitate when you feel that you see the right path before you? but that giddy whirling dance, and the insidious draught, in the shape of refreshment, that had immediately followed it, had exercised a most baneful influence on Minna; she was not quite herself, and, although her anxiety now to leave that place was really great, she had scarcely strength of mind enough left to combat any specious argument that might be used to induce her to remain.

Instead of, after determining that she wished to go at once, making an effort to leave the house and get some conveyance homeward, she meekly implored the Lady Clare to allow her to depart.

"Let me go," she said, "now; I wish to go—the hour is late; my absence will create uneasiness at home. I thank you for your courtesy; I do not hesitate, it is not from any feeling, or wish to be persuaded to remain, that I speak; but, I must, believe me, I must get home."

"Why, you are as bad as Cinderella," said Lady Clare, "who felt herself compelled to leave at a particular hour."

"No," said Minna; "no; she yielded to the temptation and remained; that I cannot, may not do. I implore you to let me go."

"Will you make me a solemn promise—so solemn, that no force of circumstances can induce you to break it, that you will visit me again?"

"No—no! I dare not—I cannot. Why would you drag me from that obscurity in which I was happy? The glimpse I have had of this mode of life, is amply sufficient. I shall never pant for it again."

"Indeed; you have a strange taste, Miss Woodward."

"Call it what you will—taste or no taste, Lady Clare; by habit, thought, feeling and understanding, I am totally unfit to become one of your guests. Believe me, I do not say this to be flattered into a contrary opinion; it is a strong conviction, not likely soon to leave me. I will believe that, in bringing me here, your motive was a good and kindly one; and now, having said thus much, even if I have your censure for what you may call my folly, I implore you to let me go at once."

"Oh, certainly," said Lady Clare, suddenly; "if such are really your feelings, Heaven forbid that I should desire you to stay. Will you not make to me the solemn promise I require of you, to come to me again?"

"No—no! I cannot. Do not ask me."

"Then this is to be your first visit here, and your last. I will not ask you, Minna Woodward, if that is grateful or kind of you, because you know that such conduct will not admit of such expressions. I regret the chance that threw you in my way; if we must part, though, let us part in peace."

"I have no other feeling," said Minna; "perhaps I am wrong, perhaps I am mistaken; pity my ignorance, if you like, Lady Clare, and my want of ambition, and my want of taste, but again, I say, that this style of life has for me no charms."

"You shall go," said Lady Clare; "we may meet again under different circumstances. I promised you that when you did leave, you should reach your home as expeditiously as possible; my carriage shall, therefore, be placed at your disposal. Remain here for a few moments, while I make that arrangement. You need speak to any one unless you like; I shall be with you soon again."

See page 47.

The Lady Clare, with a peculiar expression upon her face, sought Bulkley Harding,' who yet lingered in the rooms, not liking to leave, although he had the full conviction on his mind that now, since his uncle knew of his presence in town, every moment was precious to him. She led him into a small apartment adjoining the principal saloons, and there they remained in close consultation for the space of about five minutes, after which Harding, without again entering the room, left the house by a back staircase, and Lady Clare, with a look that might have sat well on the arch-fiend dimself, again sought Minna Woodward.

To Minna, the few minutes' delay appeared an age of anxiety; for now that she had come to a full explanation with Lady Clare, and felt that the acquaintanceship was completely broken up, she naturally wished to leave the house as soon as possible. She certainly had not expected so ready an acquiescence in her leaving as her ladyship had at last accorded to her; and she felt at the moment some few compunctions of spirit; and a kind of feeling as if, after all, she had not behaved quite so well to Lady Clare as she ought to have done, always supposing the motives of her ladyship in introducing her to her house to be of a pure and immaculate character.

Lady Clare was not slow to detect this feeling in Minna when she returned, and had she not detected it, the apologetic manner in which Minna spoke would have been amply sufficient to shew it to her. Her ladyship accordingly almost assumed an air of hauteur, as she said,—

"Heaven forbid, Miss Woodward, that you should remain here one moment against your own inclination; the carriage is at the door, and I have already directed the servants where to take you—farewell!"

"Farewell!" said Minna; "and such thanks, Lady Clare, as I can give you, pray accept; I can say no more."

"No more is requisite—we part friends, that is sufficient."

Minna descended the staircase with a feeling of regret, struggling, at the same time, with one of pleasure, that she was about to leave that scene which had been to her anything but one of enjoyment. Such was her state of mental agitation, that she totally forgot she was attired in some of the finery belonging to Lady Clare, and that a part of her own simple and unadorned costume was left in her ladyship's dressing-room.

She had ornaments, too, in her hair, glittering things which looked of price, but which were in reality nearly worthless.

Then, in the hall, there was the blaze of lights, the throng of richly liveried servants, some belonging to the house and some to the guests. The passing and repassing of many persons, the confused hum of conversation of many voices, while from without came the clamour occasioned by the disputes for precedency between the drivers of the different carriages, for the street was full of vehicles, and there was more than the ordinary bustle contingent upon such a state of things.

All this to poor Minna, unused as she was to so much bustle and excitement, seemed perfectly bewildering, and in no degree tended to restore her to calmness and thoughtfulness. Some one touched her arm, saying,—

"This way to the carriage, this way to the carriage—the carriage waits."

There was a confused rush of persons, and scarcely knowing where she went, she found herself handed up the thickly carpeted steps of a carriage, and with a feeling of thankfulness that she was out of the glare and the bustle of that crowded hall, she sunk back upon its well-stuffed cushions with a sigh of relief.

"Home—home!" she said. "I shall be home at last. Once again, after this one terrible episode of my existence, I shall look upon my mother's face in the quiet of my happy home. I can tell all to Heartwell when I see him, and confess to him how foolish it was to be allured by this Lady Clare into visiting her, and intermingling with a throng of persons who to my mind now appear so utterly heartless and uncongenial. We will talk it over pleasantly together, this glimpse of what is called high life, that I have had—quite a sufficient glimpse to teach me its worthlessness and to make me happier than I was before."

In the midst of these reflections, Minna began to wonder much what the time was. She fancied she heard rain beating against the carriage windows, and upon more accurately observing them, she became convinced that such was the case.

She heard the wind, too, howling, and fancied, too, that it blew with a sufficient power to shake the vehicle to and fro. This, however, was probably nothing but imagination, although, to tell the truth, it had become a blustrous night, and as unlike what might have been augured from the early promise of the day as anything could well be.

But Minna comforted herself with the words,—

"I shall soon be home—I shall soon be home!"

The carriage proceeded rapidly, and yet, when at length it stopped with a sudden jerk, she could hardly believe it possible that the distance between the tavern at the Gun Dock and the mansion of Lady Clare had been traversed.

But still it must be so, those well-hung carriages glided on so smoothly, bowling over the ground with greater speed than they appeared to make. The carriage had stopped, and therefore she must be at home.

"I have some courtesy, at all events," she thought, "to thank Lady Clare for, and I will write to her, doing so, which shall be the end of our connection. I wish never to see her again; but she shall not think me utterly unmindful of an intended kindness."

The door was opened and the steps let down with a pompous clatter; the night was pretty dark, and rain was falling. Minna could scarcely see the arm that was held forth to assist her in alighting from the carriage, but she never doubted for a moment where she was, and at once springing from the vehicle, she entered the door of a house, which was immediately closed behind her.

It was then, for the first moment, that the horrible supposition crossed her mind of having been decoyed somewhere, and that she was not at home.

She was in a spacious hall of what must be a large house. It was very dimly lighted; but before she had even time to utter an exclamation, she was seized by two persons, and hurried up a staircase with such precipitation that, had she not used her feet quickly, she must have fallen. A landing-place was crossed, a door was opened, and she was almost thrown into an apartment which, to her first perceptions, was in total darkness.

These events succeeded each other with such fearful rapidity, occupying not less time in acting than we have been compelled to take in recording them, that Minna not only had no time to think, but, being so hurried forward in the very first flush of her amazement and dismay, she had not been able to gather breath to speak.

It was not until she heard the door of the apartment into which she had been thrust close upon her, that she found power to scream.

She terrified herself, then, with the shriek she uttered, if no one else; but it was the first impulse of her agonized feelings. Then all was still for a few moments as the very grave.

Where she was remained a mystery profound and inexplicable. She feared to move a step lest it should be into danger. A feeling of intense wonder came over her at her own simplicity, in allowing herself to be so easily inveigled into such a trap. Was it a jest, or some piece of terrific, earnest piece of villany? The name of him to whom all her thoughts tended rushed to her lips, and, with frantic accents, she cried,—

"Heartwell! Heartwell! David Heartwell, save me! oh, save me! 'tis Minna calls you. Imprudent but not guilty, Minna Woodward. Heartwell, Heartwell! oh, where are you now?"

She sank on her kness, and with clasped hands, remained some minutes in an agony of painful thought. All was still; had she been in one of the most desolate of nature's wastes, the silence around her could not have been more intense and profound. Feelings of awe and wonder now began to mingle with the first sensations of alarm. She trembled still, but she looked up, and kneeling as she was, strove to pierce the gloom around her.

There was surely some dim light in that apartment which her eyes had now become accustomed to, or else it had made its faint appearance since she had entered it; for now she could see something of the place in which she was.

She looked in vain for the source from whence the dim light came; she could not find it, but by its mysterious influence she was enabled to make some observations upon the place in which she was. And now she rose to her feet, looking timidly around her.

It was a spacious room, and from what she could discern, it was furnished in an elaborate and costly style; she could see that there were immense looking glasses upon the walls, and rich hangings dependant from them. Here and there some bright piece of gilding, which had caught a little light, shone out like a gem amid the darkness.

The carpet she trod upon felt like many folds of richest velvet; there was an air of luxurious refinement about the very atmosphere which impressed her with the notion of the wealth that was congregated there.

"Where am I?" she said; "oh, where am I?"

But this time she spoke low, for the wrapt stillness of the place had its effect upon her in effectually subduing any louder expression of her apprehensions.

There was no echo in that well-furnished apartment to the sound of her own voice, and after she had spoken, all was calm and noiseless as before.

There was a luxurious warmth, too, in the place, which she could not account for. For a brief moment she pressed her hand upon her bosom, and murmured faintly,—

"Is it a dream? is it a dream?"

Well indeed might Minna Woodward ask herself such a question, for so strange, varied, and unaccountable were the circumstances in which she had been involved, that they seemed to transcend all sober reality.

It seemed the next thing to an impossibility, that in but a few hours so many events should have crowded themselves, and such ample food for reflection have been stored up in her heart. Yet there she was, with all the evidences and feelings of existence about her; her perceptions were clear, there was nothing of the tangled and oddly assorted nature of a dream in what she saw about her. Dim as was the light that fell upon surrounding objects, so far as she did see them they were clear and defined. It could be no dream; she had most certainly and incontestibly been betrayed into a strange house, but whether to accuse Lady Clare in her own mind of the act or not she could not tell.

In fact, in the hurried state of mind she was in, and among the many causes for fear which her imagination conjured up, she became in such a fever of spirits that calm reflection was almost completely out of the question.

And now, her senses being almost preternaturally acute in consequence of her alarm, she fancied she heard a light footstep near to her, but although she strained her eyes in the direction of the sound, she could see nothing.

Her agitation ·became extreme, the death-like repose of the place had a terrifying effect; and as she observed by the dim and uncertain light that came from she knew not where a couch close at hand, she gladly sat down upon it, with a feeling of relief at the welcome rest which it afforded to her.

Now again, she felt convinced that some one was not far off, and amid the profound stillness of that place she thought she could even hear the suppressed breathing of some person in her immediate vicinity.

"Speak! speak!" she cried; "tell me, for the love of Heaven, what is the meaning of all this, and wherefore I am brought here? there is some mistake; excuse it any way, so that I am again permitted to seek my home."

Her own voice had completely died away, and all was profoundly still again, before the least notice was taken of this appeal; then in a low voice some one spoke; and so gently were the words uttered, that, although they brought no comfort in themselves, nor gave any hope of her immediate deliverance, yet they were not such as to create in her mind any new alarm, but rather, perhaps, stimulate the curiosity they were intended to arouse.

"Minna Woodward," said the voice, "feel no alarm; you are safe from all harm, for you are protected by those who love you. This night is a crisis in your destiny; meet it boldly, and you will be happy."

She turned her head anxiously whence the voice proceeded, as she replied immediately—

"No friend would detain me here against my will; there needs no mystery in the performance of kindly actions. Let me seek my home."

"Yes," said the voice, "you shall now have the home, to which your beauty so justly entitles you,—such a home, as such as you will grace,—a home, replete with all the luxuries of life. Minna Woodward, a new existence is open before; you can now cast off the old associations which have held your mind in thraldom; and the freest wing you can give to imaginative power, will not enable it to reach a flight beyond those luxuries which shall be freely placed at your disposal. Your whole life shall be one long summer's day of delight. Care, even by name, shall be discarded from you. You shall know nothing, dream of nothing, but joy. Minna Woodward, you will not stand in the way of such a glorious destiny?"

Minna clasped her hands; she could have shrieked at that moment, as the dreadful truth came across her mind, that she was betrayed. The voice of the speaker had increased in loudness; it was really assuming the libertine, who, under the most specious pretexts, was seeking to ensnare his victim.

Bewildered, terrified, and confounded, Minna felt a sudden tremor seize her, and for a moment she fancied consciousness was about to leave her; but by one of those powerful efforts of mind, which so frequently overcome sensations of bodily indisposition, she shook off the feeling, and rallying all her energies, she rushed in the direction of the door. It was fast; and with the bitterness of anguish, she tottered back to the couch whence she had so recently risen.

In another instant, she was perfectly confused and dazzled by the sudden accession of light to the apartment; as if by enchantment, it became brilliantly illuminated, so brilliant indeed, that it was painful to the eyes, and she could not look upon the dazzling scene around her.

In truth, it was a dazzling scene; for whether they were of a meretricious character or not, certainly, in that magnificent apartment, there seemed collected every kind of decoration which could enchant the senses.

The air, too, was filled with the odour of delicious perfumes; and everything that could possibly be thought of, seemed to be devised for the purpose of getting up as strong a contrast as possible, between the imagination and the judgment.

And scarcely had Minna a moment in which to recover from the sudden and dazzling effect of all this brilliancy, ere she felt her hand taken by some one, and with a shriek of surprise, she saw a human form kneeling at her feet.

It needed but a second glance to show who it was. It was he, who at Lady Clare's had so pertenaciously followed her from room to room, and concerning whom so great a contention had arisen—Bulkley Harding. It was he, who now, with an aspect of romance and sensibility, which really formed no part of his disposition, knelt at the feet of the beautiful Minna Woodward, in the hope of luring her to destruction. And not for long did he now allow her to remain in doubt, concerning the reality of her situation. With an impassioned mode of speech, perchance half real and half assumed, he immediately commenced addressing her.

"Minna Woodward," he said, "I have you. The length of time I have loved you, dates from that moment when first I looked on such a paragon of beauty; that love has deepened to a resistless passion, maddening and overwhelming, and will make you mine, or perish. You cannot dream of the extent of the feeling, the reality of which no language can convey. I love—I adore you. Look around you, Minna Woodward, at this scene, to which you have been abroad. It is tame, spiritless, and common, in comparison to those to which I shall introduce you. You shall not have time to think or to dream of the past; a halo of delight shall surround you, and you will become, dear Minna, mine only."

Thunder-stricken, indignant, and alarmed, Minna Woodward was for some moments incapable of replying to this most audacious speech.

She was not one who could indulge in invective, such would have been most completely foreign to her nature; and yet, if one word more than another could have expressed the indignation which she felt at being enforced to become the listener to such an appeal, she would have used it; and now, while terror struggled with despair, she would have risen, but that the retaining grasp of her hand, which Harding held, prevented her, and she called,—

"Help! help! help! Oh, Heartwell, Heartwell, where are you now?"

"It is enough," said Harding, and he arose to his feet. "Tell me, oh, tell me, Minna Woodward, do you love another?"

"Hope sprang up in her breast, and it was almost with a feeling of compassion for the hopeless love which she fancied she saw depicted in his countenance when she said,—

"And will you accept that as an answer to this wild declaration which you have made?"

"I must—I must," he gasped, with well-acted sincerity; "but, Minna Woodward, hear me once again."

"No, no, no."

"Nay, but for a moment."

"'Tis madness!"

"Perchance it is; and yet, Minna Woodward, I would make you mine by the holiest of ties that can bind heart to heart—in the sight of Heaven, Minna, I will make you mine; I ask for no passion, without principle to guide it. As my wife, Minna Woodward, my honoured wife, it would be my pride and pleasure to see around you every charm existence could portray. Believe me, best and dearest, I harboured no unworthy thoughts concerning you. You refuse me, and I am desolate,"

"Was it not unworthy," said Minna, "to lure me to this house, instead of to my home? Was that consistent with that nice sense of honour you so much boast of?"

"Oh, I was mad!" said Harding; "I was mad! I hoped to move you to some pity, if not to love; I had a thought that when you knew the passion that consumed me, you might tell yourself how in vain it would be to look for another who would love you as I love you. I did not wish to lure you from a humbler station by telling you that I was wealthy, and that the blood of nobility flowed in my veins; that I might, if I so chose, find a match among the proudest. I did not wish to lead your young imaginations from the path you chose, by telling you of the blaze and magnificence in which you should live, or by describing to you how your mother's latter days would pass amid luxurious comforts, gilding her old age with a serene joy, nor did I wish to paint to you how you could scatter gifts around you, bringing down upon your heads the blessing of a thousand hearts. No, no; I only wished to tell you that I loved you."

"And I have answered," said Minna, "I love another. Assuming, perhaps, wrongfully, that your affection is as honourable and sincere as you would paint it, I feel that I owe to you such a confession. I love another."

"And his name ——"

"It matters not. Let the fact suffice I love another, and can never be yours."

"Be it so; I will not press you to disclose the name of him who stands between me and my dearest happiness. You love another, and that is enough."

"And now I may depart in peace?"

"Not yet; you have the climax yet to see of a domestic tragedy."

"A tragedy! What mean you?"

"When I told you, Minna Woodward, that my love for you was not merely a part of my existence, but life itself, I spoke no more than truthful feeling fully warranted.

You cannot love me, but the proof that I adore you, even to the full amount of devotion, you have yet to see."

"I cannot comprehend this wild discourse," said Minna; "already I feel that I have listened to by far too much. The night must be already far spent; Heaven knows, it has been a night of confusion and terror to me. Let me leave, I pray you; I pray you to let me leave. The thoughts of you now will be those of some consideration, forgiving the means by which I have been compelled to listen to this declaration; I shall think of you— I shall think of you with a kindly feeling. Do not, I pray you, tempt me to contrary reflections. As you are a gentleman, a man of honour, one who values the world's opinions and Heaven's justness, I now implore you no longer to keep me imprisoned here, but to let me go, as well as to provide me with some means of reaching home as quick as possible."

"Yes, yes!" said Harding, assuming a wildness of manner, and clasping his hands emphatically. "Yes, it must, it shall be so, Minna Woodward; when I am no more give a sigh to my memory, but do not accuse yourself of being innocently the cause of that deep despair, which has tempted me to my destruction. I shall die to-night."

"Die!"

"Yes; you shall have a convincing, although a terrible proof of my sincerity; from my lifeless body you shall take the key of that door. No one will impede your progress from the house, for now we are here alone; forget me then, and be happy with him whose fortunate destiny has enabled him to win the heart I would gladly have called mine."

All that had hitherto passed was as nothing in comparison to the gush of terror that came over her as these words were uttered. She felt that she was in the presence of a madman, one who might not, for aught she knew, scruple to fulfill his threat, and commit some desperate act of suicide, even in her very presence.

On the impulse of the moment, she clang to his arm.

"No, no, no!" she cried; "for the love of Heaven be calm. If you have one real spark of that feeling which you say has driven you to this dreadful resolution, it should suffice to turn you from it. True affection is ever self-sacrificing. Am I to be convinced that you love me, by driving me frantic in enacting such a scene of horror before me?"

"Despair! despair!" cried Harding. "I am as some desperate gamester, who has set his very life upon a throw, and now all is lost—lost—lost! Death is before me with a grim aspect—he beckons me to the grave—with this mortal coil I will shake off the yearnings of affection. I come—I come, grim visitant! I come—I come!"

He made a frantic rush to a small ebony cabinet which was in the room. The reflection that, probably, he had within it the means of inflicting upon himself some frightful death, terrified Minna beyond all calculation.

Shrieking with dismay, she sprang after him. She clang to him, and, struggling in each other's grasp, they reached the cabinet, the door of which he flung open.

CHAPTER XII.

TREACHERY, AND THE FATE OF MINNA.—THE DREADFUL MORNING.

THE interior of the cabinet was more extensive than its outward appearance would have warranted any one in supposing, and it seemed to be filled with a number of articles of the most incongruous and oddly assorted character.

There were books, bottles, articles for the toilet, and a number of other matters of the most opposite description; among which were firearms of a curious and costly character.

When Minna observed that there were means of destruction in the cabinet, she became, in the height of her alarm, convinced that it was for the purpose of finding with one of them the means of self-destruction, that Harding had so suddenly rushed to that miscellaneous repository.

Her terror became excessive. To her, whose whole life had passed amid the quiet scenes of domestic affection, the idea of becoming the enforced witness of a fearful deed of blood, was most excruciatingly terrific. She forgot, at the moment, all the dictates of prudence. If she did doubt the sincerity of the presumed dreadful intention of her despairing lover, that doubt was not sufficient to induce her to run the fearful risk of seeing him madly do the deed he threatened with so much apparent despairing determination to perform.

That they were alone in that house, she now too fully believed, for it was with no weak voice she had before called for help, so that now to attempt to procure assistance would be madness.

"Hold! hold! For the love of Heaven hold!" she cried, as she saw Harding lay his hand upon the richly surmounted hilt of a pistol. "Dare you for one moment dream of yourself taking that life which should be left to Heaven's disposal; one moment's reflection must and will disarm you of the wish to commit so desperate an act."

"I only know," he said, "that your heart is another's. Sufficient for me is the concentrated agony of that thought."

"You shall not do the deed you meditate!"

"Shall not?"

"I say you shall not. You dare not. You pause even now. I again say you dare not!"

Harding made a pretence of being much overcome by some sudden revulsions of feeling, and, leaning against the cabinet, he said in a low voice,—

"Oh, Minna, Minna! say that you will yet love me. Can you doubt a passion, which, in its excess, would have taken me from this world for ever? Say that you will strive to love me."

"Thank Heaven!" exclaimed Minna.

"Wherefore, this sudden thanksgiving?"

"Your reason has returned, your murderous intention has passed away. You no longer can contemplate that dreadful deed, which would have hurled you to perdition. I thank Heaven with all my heart and soul for that."

"And you have saved me."

"No, no."

"Yes, Minna Woodward; but for your presence, I should have done that deed, which time, nor the bitterest reflection, could have recalled. You are my better angel."

"Not to me," said Minna, "be any commendation. The hand of Heaven has saved you for better purposes."

"I will hope so. If you bid me, I will indeed strive to think so. But Minna, can you ever forgive the wild ungovernable passion that impelled me to take so desperate a step as this night I have taken, to enter your presence for a time, to hear me tell you how I loved you?"

"Yes, yes. Let me go now in peace."

"Is this possible? Can you indeed forgive such an outrage, Minna Woodward?"

"I do, I do. Live to think with better and holier thoughts of this night's proceedings, I pray you. Allow me now to seek my home. Let this night be a lesson to you, as well as to me."

"I breathe again! I breathe again! Oh! Minna, if I thought really that from your heart you would forgive me, and find for me some excuse——"

"Be satisfied," said Minna. "I would not say I forgive, if the feeling were foreign to my nature."

"Still I cannot convince myself. Yet, Minna, if, before you go, you would drink one cup of wine, and append to it what sentiment you please; I shall, indeed, think that, although you may not forget the cruel selfishness that brought you here against your will, you really do forgive it."

Even as he spoke, he took from the cabinet a decanter, in which was, to all appearance, some wine; but Minna exclaimed, as she moved towards the door, which she was in an agony to see unfastened,

"No, no, no—I cannot!"

"Then," said Harding, "I am convinced that sincerity was not in your words of forgiveness. Madness comes again. I ought not to live, since I have nothing to live for that can invest life with a single charm."

As he spoke these words, he placed the decanter of wine and a glass upon the table, and once more seized from the cabinet a pistol.

Despairingly, Minna rushed forward and laid her hand upon his arm.

"Madness, indeed," she said, "has come again. Will you, if I take some of this wine, make me a solemn promise, that you will then allow me instantly to depart to my home?"

"I will—I do."

"On your sacred word?"

"On my honour."

" Then give me the glass.   I do forgive you if you can forgive yourself."

With an affectation of great agitation of manner, which completely disarmed poor un-suspicious Minna, he poured out a glass of the wine, which he handed to her.

" You forgive me," he said ; " but this last time it has been with a qualification which renders the forgiveness of little avail."

" Indeed !"

" Yes, I cannot forgive myself."

" Then, I will forgive you freely," said Minna.

" Thanks, thanks—a thousand thanks, dearest Minna ! Oh, how much do I owe to you."

" No more, no more—I cannot hear such language."

" You shall be conveyed home with speed, the moment you have finished your wine. You may trust me now.   I am not the mad, desperate man I was.   I am now convinced that you cannot love me ; and I love you too well to inflict upon you another pang."

In her anxiety to be gone, Minna was not slow in drinking the wine ; she took about two-third's of the glass-full, and then placed it on the table.

" Now," she said ; " fulfil your promise?"

" I will," replied Harding, and he touched a bell.

In an instant, the door was opened, and a tall, hard-featured woman appeared.

Harding pointed triumphantly to Minna, as he said,—

" 'Tis done !"

The woman stepped up to her, and had she not held her up, poor Minna must have fallen to the floor.   Every object in that magnificent apartment seemed to her to be whirling round in a wild career of the maddest confusion ; her brain felt as if liquid fire were poured upon it.   She tried to shriek, but an indistinct murmur only came from her lips.   Insensibility rapidly ensued, and she sank upon the arm of that fiend-like woman, who had answered the summons of Harding.

The drugged wine had done its dreadful duty.   The victim was in the power of the destroyer.   Oh, Harding, Harding ! can you ever again look up to the blue vault of heaven, and hope to be forgiven ?   Can you flatter yourself even that a day of dreadful retribution will not come at last?

*   *   *   *   *   *   *   *   *

It is morning. The soft beautiful light of day is lingering, to steal in through the mas-sive and rich hangings of a costly chamber.   There are mirrors on its walls, and every appliance of taste and luxury might there have been found.   A man steals slowly from the room—a guilty wretch. His eye shuns the daylight ; for it seems as if God was look-ing into his heart.   He is attired in a loose dressing-gown, and he slinks into another apartment, where, with draughts of wine, he seeks to still the whisperings of that con-science, which is not quite dead, even within such a heart as his.

This man is Bulkley Harding. He has met the woman on the staircase—that wo-man who answered his summons, after poor Minna had so unconsciously partaken of the drugged wine.   They converse in whispers together for a few moments ; and she pro-ceeds up stairs, while Harding, as we have stated, takes himself to the wine-cup for sup-port, and consolation from his own thoughts.   And now we will follow that—we can scarcely bring ourselves to call her woman, to the chambers which Harding has just left, and to which she proceeds with all the calmness and indifference in the world.

She draws aside the heavy window-curtains, and admits light into the apartment. The morning's rays fall upon the costly bed, and upon the face of one who seems to sleep ; but it is the sleep of insensibility.   The breathing is slow and laboured, while occasionally low moans come from the lips.   It is Minna Woodward !   For a moment or two the woman looked upon the wreck which ungoverned passion had made, and then she muttered,—

" Oh ! she'll soon get back her good looks, I'll be bound.   Much ado about nothing ! She certainly is a nice-looking girl.   Ah, I hate them all.   I suppose, now, for a day or two, we shall have nothing but fainting and crying.   Rubbish !"

She took from a capacious pocket a small phial of a stone-coloured liquid, and uncork-ing it, she placed the neck of the bottle between the lips of Minna, and steadily poured its whole contents into her mouth.

" You'll soon be all right now," she muttered, " I'll be bound.   I'm sure you are not worth all the trouble and expense you have been, and all the trouble and expense you will be.   There's no accounting for tastes, however, I suppose.   The men are all fools, to my mind, to be running continually after a parcel of girls.   I have no patience with them—none in the world."

Minna soon began to give evidences of the power of the antidote which she had

swallowed, for she shifted her position, and opened her eyes, fixing them upon the face of the woman with such a gaze of pitying supplication, that it would have melted any heart but so obdurate a one as hers to see it.   She, however, was not of the melting order of human beings, and all poor Minna got, in reply to her speaking glances, was—

"Well what now?   What are you staring at?"

"You are not my mother?" said Minna, faintly; and she passed her hand across her brow as she spoke.

"Your mother!   That's a good joke."

Minna shuddered, and turned ghastly pale.

"Who will kill me?" she said, "who will kill me?   Oh! what kind hand will take my life?"

"Rubbish!" said the woman.   "How can you talk such nonsense?   Come, come! we don't want any scenes here."

We cannot bring ourselves to recount the conversation that ensued now between Minna and this woman.   With difficulty the wretched girl was prevented from laying violent hands upon herself, and finally, in a state of absolute exhaustion, she fainted. The woman took a huge pinch of snuff from a tin box she had in her pocket, and then, with all the *sang froid* in the world, she said,—

"Ah! that's over—the worst I call it; she'll be better now. She'll most likely have a good cry when she comes to herself again, and that'll do her a world of good. Well, if there is anything I hate more than another, it is people making a fuss about their fine feelings. Bother their feelings! I've got no feelings, and never had any, and don't intend. Well, well! Harding has been very liberal about this affair, and it pays well; that's a comfort."

So saying, she took no further notice of Minna, but left her to recover from her insensibility, or not, as nature chose; but she had no intention of leaving her to do, perhaps, some desperate deed when she should come to her senses, for in the course of a few minutes a servant wench, with all the appearance about her of being one of the worst specimens of her class, took her station by the bed-side to watch Minna, when she should recover, and prevent her from attempting either escape or self-destruction, both of which were much to be feared.

CHAPTER XIII.

THE FEARS OF HARDING.—THE PROPOSAL TO MINNA.

THE woman who enacted so prominent a part in that house, as to prove that she was its infamous mistress, went direct to the room where Harding was indulging himself, with potations both deep and strong, in order to give him a report of the state of his beautiful victim.

After having first helped herself to some wine, she said,—

"Well, she's fainted away."

Harding changed colour, as he said,—

"You do not think there is any danger, I hope?"

"Danger!"

"Yes, yes. Have her well watched. I have my fears that she will yet attempt some desperate act."

"Well, she's about as likely a one as ever I saw to do so."

"You think so?"

"Yes, I does."

"I—I half repent ——"

"Oh! you do, do you? Why, what's come over you? Repent, indeed! You had better go and say your prayers next!"

"No, no, no; don't talk to me of prayers, woman. I don't want such things mentioned; but I tell you I have serious fears now about the result of this affair."

"Well, all I can say is, you should have had them before."

"That cannot now be helped. When she recovers, tell her that I will marry her."

"Very good."

"Describe my state of mind as bordering upon distraction, and tell her that I will not leave the house until I have made her my wife. Assure her of that, and it may, at all events, quiet her, and make her not meditate anything desperate. You can tell her that I can get a special license, and marry her here. All that can be easily managed. My man Robert has played the parson before to-day, as you well know; and, indeed, I am always of opinion that it's the best way of getting over all scruples."

"Perhaps it is, and perhaps it ain't. Why didn't you do so at first?"

"In this case it was impossible."

"Well, of course you know best. I'll propose it to her, and if she will listen to reason at all, of course she'll say yes, and be made an honest woman of. Bless me! what dreadful prejudices there is in society, when you comes to think!"

The lady kept helping herself liberally to the champagne which Harding had before him, as she spoke, but it produced no more effect upon her than if it had been cast into a waste-butt. Her rubicund visage quite sufficiently proclaimed how accustomed she was to deep potations; and it was not until Harding, with an oath, told her to bring another bottle, since she had emptied the one he had, that she rose to go.

"Very good," she said; "I'll tell her, of course, that you'll marry her; and what a fortunate woman she ought to think herself! By-the-bye, does she know your real name?"

"She does," said Harding. "I was introduced to her by my real name and designation at Lady Clare's; but that matters not, since the marriage will be but a mockery, and indeed it will give far greater safety to the proceeding."

" Oh, very good," said the woman, with the same indifferent and careless tone ; " as I remark, you know best. I'll tell her, and as for you putting yourself in a fidget about such a matter, it's just about one of the silliest things in the world to do. I should have thought your experience would have taught you better."

" Well, well, say no more—say no more—let the matter rest with that understanding ; I must leave within a very few hours, but I don't want to leave a riot behind me, such as might ensue if I did not settle this affair ; be, therefore, as expeditious as you can, and in the meantime, send Robert to me. I suppose he's in the house ?"

" You may depend upon that, and drinking, as usual."

" You know that in that particular," said Harding, " I am at the mercy of the whole of you ; and most unquestionably you should not be the one to complain of Robert."

" Yes, I ought," she said, with a laugh, as she left the room ; " for I drink champagne and he ale."

When she was gone Harding rose and paced to and fro, for many minutes, in silence.

" I do repent me," he said, " that ever I engaged in this most desperate affair ; the shadow of some coming evil seems to oppress my soul. I am certain, now—would that I had been so before—that something extremely serious will be the result of this passionate adventure. How I shall now dread any glance of Lieutenant Heartwell ; it will seem to me as if my very countenance will reveal to him the truth of this night's proceedings : sooner or later he must know all, and then—how implacable, how terrific an enemy I have made for myself. I repent me, yet—no—have I so soon forgot the indignity that was heaped upon my head at the old tavern, when, taking advantage of his brutal strength, he flung me from the window !—have I so soon forgotten that, or the promise I then gave myself of vengeance ? No ! had I all that has been done to do over again, it should be done. I may have given myself an occasional passing pang, but I have the satisfaction of feeling that I have destroyed his happiness for ever, and will persevere ; Minna Woodward, in all her beauty, shall be mine and mine only. The agony of reflection that now oppresses her will pass away, and although she may find herself mated with the man she hates, instead of the man she loves, pride will now induce her to conceal the bitterness of her feelings, and the secret of her dishonour, known only to so few, is not likely to pass her own lips ; by that means I am safe from Heartwell. She cannot well explain to him how, or under what circumstances, she believes herself to be my wife. By heavens, it would be a rare treat to see them meet ; a treat which I shall have sooner or later. Who's there ?"

" It's only me, sir," said Harding's man, Robert ; " I understood you wanted me, sir."

" Oh, aye, certainly—Robert, come in and close the door. Do you remember the last time you appeared in canonicals ?"

" Yes, sir, I should think so ; I married you to that little dark-haired girl, you know, her you took away from the lawyer's."

" You did, Robert. I wonder what has become of her ?"

" Bless me, sir, don't you know ; I thought everybody knew that."

" Indeed I do not, Robert ; have you heard any news of her ?"

" Lor, yes, sir, to be sure ; she drowned herself."

" Drowned !"

" Yes, sir, that was the end of it ; nobody knew who she was, but I happened to be about the place, and saw her. It was off Southwark bridge she went, and there was an end of her. A nice-looking little piece of goods she was, sir, when first we knew her."

" Peace ! peace !" said Harding ; " why did you tell me this ?"

" Why did I tell you, sir ? why, I thought you wanted to know as a matter of curiosity."

" Enough ! enough, enough ! say no more."

" Why, you know, sir, she had no occasion to drown herself unless she liked."

" Certainly, Robert ; certainly not. I believe you remember I was very liberal ?"

" You was, sir ; you gave her a five pound note, sir, and told her to make it last as long as she could ; that was a year-and-a-half, sir, before she made a hole in the Thames ; so between you and I, sir, I really think she made it go a long way."

" You scoundrel, how dare you speak to me in such a strain ; leave the room, sir, and provide yourself somewhere with a clerical costume ; and, hark ye, I am serious in this affair, and must have it conducted with all due caution and discrimination. No quivering or nonsensical pantomimic tricks, that may breed suspicion. I say be careful, or you will find that a contrary course will be very much to your cost."

" Be careful, sir ! I always was careful ; I haven't been with you all these years not to have learnt a thing or two."

Robert left the room, while his master eyed him, as he went out, with a savage scowl.

"The rascal," he said; "nothing pleases him so much as the finding out of some uncomfortable fact to throw in my teeth; and yet he is useful to me, and has a rough and ready talent in his way, which has got me out of many a serious dilemma; I cannot well part with him. Besides, the inevitable consequences of employing these scoundrels are, that, in a short time, they know too much. To make them useful one must be confidential, and so it is that men of likelihood and mark become in time the very tools with which they have hewn their way to the accomplishment of their purposes."

With pain we again enter that chamber where lay the unconscious Minna Woodward; happier, far happier would it have been for her had she never again awakened to the consciousness of existence, and that that trance of death in which she lay were death itself.

But this was not to be; her destiny was not yet fulfilled; yet was she to enact a busy part in life; and although a blight would be for ever on her soul, and all thoughts, feelings, and aspirations, must be completely changed, still would we bespeak for her the kindly sympathies of those who knew her in her beauty and gladness; and we trust that throughout all chances and changes they will keep in mind that happy and innocent girl who on the terrace of the old Gun Tavern conversed with her lover on the dreamy future.

The woman who had the control of the arrangements in that dreadful house dismissed her who watched by the bed-side of Minna; and then, as she had received her instructions what to propose to the wretched girl when she should be in a condition to hear it, she set about endeavouring by every means in her power to restore her to consciousness. This, by the aid of stimulants, was effected, and once again Minna looked up into that face where could not be found the faintest trace of feeling.

"Well," said the woman, "what do you mean to do?"

"Die," said Minna.

"Oh, stuff, not yet awhile, I'll be bound. I tell you what it is, the only reparation Sir Bulkley Harding can offer you is to marry you, and that he is willing to do at once. I am sure it is very liberal of him. He's sent for a special license now, and I believe there'll be a parson in the house."

Minna placed her hands over her face and sobbed bitterly. After a time, she spoke in a voice of great anguish, saying,—

"No, no, no! this is some new delusion—some heartless mockery. If you have one pitying sensation in your breast, give me the means of death."

"A delusion do you call it—being married a delusion? I dare say there's hundreds of thousands of people who wish it; but it's rather too real; I tell you he means it, and let what will come of the affair, you had better be an unwilling wife than something worse. Who can reproach you when you are married, too, to a gentleman? It is possible you may not like him quite so well as you may like somebody else; but where's the odds? The beauty of being married is, you may consult your own inclination afterwards. So don't be a fool, but think yourself amazingly well off. Your husband will have to support you, and then you're as comfortable as a queen. Everybody's not so lucky; there's lots of young women who would jump out of their skins for half the chance."

It is probable that poor Minna heard nothing of all this, for she was busy with her own thoughts; thoughts which came at all events, as regarded the most essential particular, to the same conclusion, that the heartless creature who addressed her wished her to arrive at. With startling firmness she said, suddenly,—

"Be it so; I will be his wife. I wish once more to look upon my mother's face; it shall be as a wife, and then welcome death."

"Ah, you'll alter your mind about that," said the woman; "so you had better get ready as soon as you can, and come down stairs. You'll find all your clothes here, and the finery you wore at the ball, so that you won't be bad off for a wedding costume; upon my word, you are lucky—a most fortunate female. Lady Harding, to be sure, you'll be; a nice idea. Well, it's better to be born lucky than rich, at any time."

Minna made her no answer; but, when she was alone, she arose, and kneeling by the bed-side, she prayed long and fervently; she prayed that she might never again look upon the face of Heartwell, but that he would feel sufficient indignation at her supposed capricious conduct, to cast her from his heart for ever, and without regret; for her mother, too, she prayed; and, then, with imploring earnestness, she sought forgiveness for a crime she meditated, and the dim shadow of which was already darkening her soul.

That crime was suicide.

Yes; she, the young, the beautiful, the intelligent, she whom we have already pre-

sented to the reader in all the spring of life, and rich in endowments, she, standing as i
were but as yet upon the very threshold of existence, contemplated suicide.

Oh, that there should be found any human heart capable of dragging down to such an
abyss of wretchedness, one of Heaven's best and fairest creations! For more than a quarter
of an hour she poured forth her incoherent supplications to the throne of mercy; she
fancied, then, that she was calmer and better able to go through the scene that awaited
her, and attiring herself, then, in the faded finery of the evening before, she moved from
the room, looking more like a spectre than a living being.

Her countenance was of a death-like paleness, and still there was a confusion in her
mind, which made her more than once pause to ask herself if, indeed, all the horrors of
the last four-and-twenty hours could be real.

She was well watched; for, she had not proceeded down above four stairs, when she
was joined by the woman, who gave herself credit to Harding, for having induced her to
consent to the marriage.

"There now," she said, "you are quite another thing—just step this way, and you'll
find all prepared. What is there to fret about, now? just nothing; and I shall have to
call you my lady, in another ten minutes—think of that."

Minna shrank from the contaminating touch of this woman as she would have done
that of some loathsome reptile; the very sight of her was a shuddering horror. She made
her no answer, but, following her wheresoever she chose to lead, with a kind of gloomy
resignation that was frightful to behold, they reached a smaller room upon the ground
floor. There was but one window in this room, and through the interstices of a Venetian
blind, which was let down to its entire length, but a faint light came into the apartment.

No doubt this was purposely done, for fear Minna should look a little too scruti-
nizingly at the sham clergyman, who, perhaps, would not have been able to bear a very
close examination, notwithstanding his possession of an amount of effrontery of a most
extraordinary character.

Minna was left alone in the room for some seconds, but not for a sufficiently long time
to enable her to make any observations of the place, or to indulge in any reflections of
her own. Through another doorway came Harding; a consciousness of guilt even oppressed him sufficiently to prevent him from looking in the face of that wan and pale
victim of his baseness.

Not a word passed between them, for, close upon his heels came Robert, looking as de-
mure and devout as any evangelical parson could, for the life of him. This rascal could
act his part very well; he took, indeed, rather a pride in the performance, and producing
a veritable prayer-book from his pocket, he said, solemnly,—

"Being authorised by special licence, obtained from the proper authorities, to solem-
nize a marriage between Minna Woodward, spinster, and Bulkley Harding, bachelor, at
any time, and in any place, the same parties may choose, I have no hesitation in at
once proceeding to the exercise of my sacred functions. I should wish some witnesses
present."

"They are here, your reverence," said Harding, as the woman and the maid-servant
entered the room.

"That will do," said Robert, solemnly. "I shall now proceed; and I trust that you
will make a virtuous and exemplary husband to that young lady."

"D—n you!" muttered Harding, as he gave Robert a kick with his heel.

"What did you remark, sir?" said Robert.

"That we are quite ready, your reverence," added Harding. "Curse you, be quick!"
he appended in a whisper.

"Don't hurry the church," said Robert, "or you'll come under the ban of ecclesias-
tical censure."

He then opened the book, and in the most edifying manner read the marriage ceremony.
Harding then took a ring from his finger, which, although not a plain gold one, answered
the purpose sufficiently well, and he pronounced the mock vows with an assumption of
ease that sat very ill upon him.

Poor Minna's voice was scarcely audible, and when the brief ceremony was concluded,
and she believed herself to be the wife of the man who had destroyed her peace of mind
for ever, she turned towards him, and was evidently about to speak; but he interrupted
her by saying, with much respect,—

"Lady Harding, we shall be alone immediately, and any observations you may have to
make, I shall be most delighted to hear."

This was a sufficient signal to those who played the subordinate parts in that most
sacrilegious farce, to leave the room, and they accordingly did so.

CHAPTER XIV.

THE STRANGE INTERVIEW.—MINNA'S DENUNCIATION OF HER DESTROYER.—HARDING'S
FEARS AND THE ESCAPE.

THEY were alone—alone for some few brief minutes, before either spoke. Minna could not sufficiently command her feelings to give utterance to the thoughts that were swelling at her heart; and as for Harding, he wished, before he uttered a word, to ascertain what Minna herself might say in her particular state of feeling, so that he might govern his own observations accordingly. And she did speak first. She was not waiting for him to commence; for, in truth, she cared not if he spoke at all. It was she who wished, before she left that place, to say something to him which she hoped he never could forget.

A deep sense of the wrong which had been done her nerved her, and in a low, but clear voice, she commenced,—

"Sir, you have achieved a great triumph. Being a clever, calculating villain, you have succeeded in deceiving a poor and ignorant girl, unacquainted with the world and its ways; one, sir, who not only never heard of such unexampled baseness, but who never in imagination could have conceived it possible. This, then, is your victory—the triumph of guilt over innocence; and now, sir, you may glory in it, and among that dissolute few, who may court such society as yours, you may make a boast of the ruin you have made. It will get you, doubtless, the ready laugh and the unblushing jest. Let there be no drawback to the barbarous joy you may feel in my destruction. The tragedy, sir, shall be complete, it shall not want a catastrophe—one which you can tell well, and which you can dress up, if it may so please you, in the colours of romance; and while the boast of that poor triumph lasts you, and while you can jest upon it, do so. We shall never meet again."

Twice or thrice Harding had tried to interrupt her, but his voice faltered, and his limbs trembled; the flush of conscious guilt was on his cheek, and he cowered and shrank before that young girl, as though she had been some avenging spirit sent from heaven. He did summon courage enough to gasp out,—

"Minna, Minna, you know not what you do! you are angry—maddened. Better thoughts will come to you."

"God of heaven!" exclaimed Minna; "think you ever better thoughts will come to you? Nay, you shall hear me—you cannot stir. I speak with a prophetic warning. Let that which I have to say sink deep into your very soul."

"No, no, no," cried Harding; "I can hear no more, and wish to hear no more. Girl, you are mad, and know not what you say."

"I may be mad, and Heaven knows I have cause; and yet you shall listen to me as yet, perchance, with the prophetic voice of madness, I shall speak to you; for ofttimes it would appear that to those whom Heaven has smitten with the loss of reason, there is given a prophetic power unknown to soberer judgments. Therefore, mad though I may be, I speak to you, Harding, of that which is to come, with a warning voice; and I tell you that a day of retribution will arrive—a day of bitter and terrific retribution—and then you will think upon me and the words which now come from my lips. Sooner or later, Harding—the lapse of time will matter not—there will come a period when despair will seize upon your very soul—when the heart you have broken, though it be mute, will plead fearfully against you when you crave for that mercy to which you feel you are not entitled; and when amid the despair that shall seize upon you, you will in vain seek relief from those pangs of conscience which cannot but be yours."

"Nay, this is midsummer frenzy. I tell you, girl, I will hear no more; say what you like, prate of these matters as you will, I care not."

"I have said all that I wish to say—my speech is done. Heaven help you, and forgive you!"

"Have you done?" said Harding, who now seemed upon the point of giving way to passion. "You will please to recollect who I am, as well as what I am. To please you, and to induce you to feel more at home with yourself, I have become your husband—that is a fact which seems to have escaped your memory; but, you will recollect, with the title, if it so please me, I can enforce a husband's rights. Beware, I say, that you do not push this romantic spirit of obstinacy too far, perchance you will yet find you are trespassing upon a patience not, at the best of times, of great endurance."

"I have no desire to trespass further, even upon you, personally," said Minna. "Farewell!"

"Hold! hold! where are you about to go?"

Minna was deaf to his cries; and, with a sudden energy which no one would have given her credit for, she rushed from the room in which that mock ceremony had taken place—a ceremony, however, which she fully believed in the reality of—and gaining the street door before any of the parties in the house could have the least suspicion of what she intended to do, she at once rushed precipitately from that ill-omened mansion into the street.

Harding pursued her as quickly as possible; but by the time he reached the door, she was nowhere to be found. Pursuit, therefore, was madness, since he knew not in which direction to go; and stunned and mortified by the manner in which she had left, he stood irresolutely in the passage until he was joined by the woman of the house.

"She is gone!" he cried; "she has escaped."

"Escaped! You were with her yourself—how came you to let her go?"

"On my soul, I know not. After upbraiding me bitterly, she suddenly left the place before I could recover from my astonishment. I suppose I shall now have this affair bruited all over the town. Confusion seize her! but I must take my chances. I have not a moment's time now to throw away; send some one directly to order me a carriage and post horses. I must to Portsmouth at once; for well I know the implacable character of my uncle; should he discover that I am in London beyond the four-and-twenty hours he mentioned, it would be my irretrievable ruin."

These words really alarmed the woman, for she had by no means done with Harding yet as a customer; and if he were irretrievably ruined, as a matter of course he would cease to be a desirable one. Robert was immediately dispatched in all haste to procure the post-chaise, and in less than half an hour from that time, Harding, without any further preparation for his journey, was proceeding as fast as post horses could carry him, towards Portsmouth.

And thus ended that night and morning of so fearful and extraordinary a character— a night and morning to Minna Woodward, which were to exercise their baneful influence over her as long as she existed—a night and morning which were to be for ever subjects calculated to engender remorse, even in the breast of such a man as Bulkley Harding, callous as he appeared to be, and dead to all the best of human sympathies.

CHAPTER XV.

HEARTWELL'S PROGRESS.—THE GALE AT SEA, AND THE SAILOR'S DREAM.—MIDNIGHT ON THE OCEAN.

GLADLY, and with a feeling of exquisite relief, do we turn from the vice and profligacy of such a man as Harding, and from painful reflections on the most unmerited sufferings of poor Minna Woodward, to follow the more cheering, the more noble, and the more heart-delighting progress of our friend Heartwell, in whom we feel so great an interest, and whose welfare we have no doubt will be equally dear to our readers.

Gallant Heartwell! long may you remain in happy ignorance of those secrets which will make you feel most desolate!—long, long may it be before you again touch the shore, but to learn those dreadful tidings that will be more than sufficient to drive your soul to madness, and make you contemplate some desperate act which will involve you and all you love, perchance, in one common destruction.

But to our narrative: Heartwell reached his destination full of radiant hope—such hope that a gallant heart like his was entitled to feel; and who could possibly be more entitled than such a man as Heartwell, to feel emotions of happiness and felicitation? Armed was he in his country's cause; his deeds of gallantry and daring were the themes of conversation to all who knew him; he was one of those bold spirits of which a century produces but a few, and who are equally esteemed for personal prowess and bravery, as they will be of the ability to command.

As Harding had arranged, Heartwell, when he arrived at Portsmouth, found that he was to take immediate command of the vessel, and bring her round the coast, stopping at various places for the purpose of permitting him (Harding) putting off to join her.

Such a duty as this is at all times a troublesome one, but still it was one which a lieutenant all times is bound to perform for his captain, if so directed; and little suspecting who that captain was, and what circumstances they were that detained him ashore. Poor Heartwell bent all his mind to his profession, and with the greatest care and assiduity directed his energies to the service of his country, and the pleasure of that man who on shore was undermining his every prospect of earthly happiness.

The ship was as gallant a one as ever stemmed the waters; the crew were all picked men; and, to take the Eolus frigate all in all, there never went out of port a vessel more admirably adapted to support the honour and glory of old England.

It was a hazy and dusky night when the Eolus, taking advantage of a light breeze that gently filled her flowing sails, sailed majestically amid the cheers of thousands of spectators out of Portsmouth harbour. It was well known to all that her service was of the boldest and most hazardous description; she was to hover round the principal ports of the enemy, occasionally to make a dangerous recognizance, to pick up what prizes she could, lodge them in some British port, and then as quickly as possible resume her hazardous service.

The sun, on that evening, sank fiery red, and there was a strange bank of black clouds in the far off horizon, presenting in its slightly indented outline all the appearance of some stern battlemented wall, breaking the clear outline of the upper sky. Heartwell stood on the quarter-deck of his gallant vessel with his arms clasped behind him, and he gazed long and earnestly upon that south-western sky, which was glowing with the ruddy hues of sunset. Heartwell had been too long upon the ocean not to understand it well in most of its moods, and as he looked upon the portentous aspect of the weather, he suspected that one of those channel squalls, which prove frequently more disastrous to shipping than the wildest storm upon the most extensive ocean, would not be long before it showed itself. He was not one, however, to be lightly intimidated by the strife of the elements, although, under the circumstances, a much heavier responsibility rested upon his shoulders than he ought to have stood under; he well knew that if any untoward accident occurred he should be blamed, while any amount of success in watching a gale, or in beating an enemy, would, to all intents and purposes, be appropriated by the captain.

But this did not deter him from performing his duties to his country—that was a paramount consideration; and when he saw that the darkness was increasing, and that the mysterious looking bank of clouds was rising slowly but surely from the horizon, and must soon envelope the whole sky in gloom, he beckoned to the second in command, a bluff and weather-beaten officer, and pointing to the south-west, he said,—

"What think you of the weather? To my mind, some precautions against a sudden accession to the light breeze that now fans our decks, would not be amiss."

"Why, to my thinking," replied the other, "looking at all things, we are as many miles as we can be now too near in-shore. If there ain't a gale to-night, I'll never trust the looks of a sun-set again."

"It is my own impression," said Heartwell; "with this light breeze we can run out. I shall be much mistaken, if it lasts us long."

Far off, upon the surface of the sea, there was a suspicious-looking curl of foam, not natural to the mighty element under ordinary circumstances; the light wind, too, which Heartwell had just mentioned, and which blew rather from the shore than towards it, was evidently not so steady as it had been, but seemed on the increase, for it came only in fitful gusts now and then; while, in the intervals, the small quantity of canvass which the vessel carried, hung idly to the masts, and she reeled heavily in the trough of the sea.

These were a combination of circumstances, always suspicious to the eye of a seaman; and although the nautical saying of "after a calm comes a storm," might seem to convey nothing but an evident truism, yet experience has taught those who have led a long life upon the deep, that nothing is more suspicious and indicative of some coming elemental strife, as a calm of the nature which seemed now to exist in the channel.

The crew of that gallant vessel had been picked, as well for good seamanship as well known and undaunted courage; and possibly now there was not a man among them, who did not anticipate the orders Lieutenant Heartwell gave.

These were to get out to sea as quick as possible; and with that wonderful precision and energy of movement, which in our vessels of war ever excite such admiration, the course of the stately fabric was altered, as if by magic; and from running along the coast, almost within gun-shot distance, the Eolus turned seaward, and taking advantage of every puff of wind to expedite her progress, she went through the surge of waters for more than hour, at considerable speed.

By this time the sun had completely sunk, and the black mass of clouds had nearly climbed up to the meridian of the heavens, when the wind suddenly dropped completely, and the ship no longer made any perceptible progress through the waste of waters.

The second lieutenant walked up to Heartwell, and pointing to a black cloud which now enveloped a third of the sky, he said—

"It's beginning to get lighter in the horizon, and as sure as this is the Eolus frigate, and we've got to do the best we can with her to-night, there will come a squall from under the tail of that cloud, direct in-shore."

"I expect as much," said Heartwell. "We must be prepared. The wind has completely left us. Have in every bit of canvass. Keep her head to the squall, if possible, and we may ride it out."

"I have my fears," said the other. "The Eolus is built for sailing, and sits but lightly on the water; if a squall took us broadside, I don't like very well to think what might happen."

"We must be prepared," said Heartwell; "if the squall come at all, it will come from about two points there to the southward."

In less than five minutes, every stitch of canvass was taken in; and now it was only by the opposition of the wash of the sea, that with difficulty the vessel's head could be at all kept in the required direction.

The progress she made was insignificant; and yet it was ascertained, most probably from having got into an under current, she was making a slow and devious progress to the southward.

"Well, that's satisfactory, at any rate," said the second lieutenant. "We are getting on, if it be slow. I wouldn't be the captain of this vessel, and not on board of her to-night, for a couple of prizes."

"Do you know anything of our captain?" said Heartwell.

Lieutenant Lacy, for such was the name of the second in command, made a most horrible wry face, as he replied,—

"I never saw him but once, and I haven't heard much of him. What I have heard I don't much like, so perhaps the least said is soonest mended."

"Certainly," said Heartwell, "we have our duty to perform to our country under all circumstances. Our captain may certainly make it much pleasanter or much un-pleasanter."

"Remarkably true that, Mr. Heartwell."

"And yet," added Heartwell, "I cannot think it possible that an incompetent man would have for one moment been appointed to a vessel like this."

"I don't know," said Lacy; "he may be a seaman or he may not, but there's one very suspicious circumstance, and that is, that he is a family connexion of a lord of the Admiralty; and another very suspicious circumstance is, that they have made you his first lieutenant."

"I can imagine," said Heartwell, "that the first of these occurrences might possibly awaken a suspicion that political influences have more to do than competency with the appointment; but as to making me his first lieutenant, I do not see how that can be made anything suspicious."

"Don't you? then I do."

"In what way?"

"Why, you are to be his dry nurse, to be sure; he'll be down below, most probably, when anything is to be done, and you'll be expected to pretend that he has told you beforehand what to do while you are doing it all yourself."

"Without arrogating to myself," said Heartwell, "any personal praise, I must confess I have seen this principle of dry nursing, as you call it, carried out to some extent in the navy."

"Oh, well, never mind," said Lacy, "it comes to much the same in the end."

"And, by Heavens!" said Heartwell, "here comes the squall."

The termination of the black cloud was plainly visible; a strange lurid kind of light shot from under it across the surface of the ocean, and then the water afar off presented an appearance of the most violent commotion. A rushing noise succeeded, and Heartwell had just time to cry out, in a loud, clear voice,—

"Hold on all, for your lives!" when the ship appeared to be almost lifted out of the sea, and so terrific a gale of wind swept over her, that the tall masts bent like reeds, and several men were swept from the deck into the sea, along with a great number of iron articles, some of them, too, of a weighty character, which the gale carried over the vessel's side.

For about the space of two minutes this frightful storm of wind continued, and then one of the masts gave way, toppling over the deck, bringing with it a mass of cordage and smaller spars.

Having accomplished this amount of mischief, the gale ceased as suddenly as it began; the ship righted, and all was as still and calm as before.

"Clear away," shouted Heartwell, "clear away!"

Fifty men immediately sprang forward, and the splintered piece of mast was secured, so as to prevent it doing more mischief.

"The squall's over," said Lacy, "now for the hurricane, and if that don't last all night, I'm a Dutchman."

He was right enough in predicting that the hurricane was about to commence, for scarcely had the wreck occasioned by the broken masts been cleared, and an order to launch a boat in order at all events to make an effort to save the men who had been washed overboard half executed, when the hurricane began in earnest, and the thoughts of such a thing, in the now tempestuous sea, had to be abandoned.

The wind for a time then, although blowing freely, was inconstant, for it varied repeatedly in the point from whence it came, ranging from the south-east to as far to the south-west.

By great skill and management, the vessel was enabled pretty well to run along the coast without making much way to leeward, so that there was a prospect of getting tolerably clear of danger while the storm continued at its present height.

The night now became pitchy dark, three of the best hands in the ship were lashed to the helm, and nothing more could be done now than to keep off from the shore as much as possible, and wish for daylight.

Heartwell had remained upon deck for many hours, his clothing was saturated with sea-water, and he had not tasted refreshments since mid-day; under these circumstances, leaving the command of the deck to Lieutenant Lacy, he proceeded to his own cabin, when, after making some necessary changes in his apparel, he flung himself upon a couch to catch a few moments' repose, for not only was he aware that the skill and energy of Lieutenant Lacy was fully equal to any emergency, but he knew that as a thing of course he would be called if anything uncommon threatened to occur.

Exhausted nature speedily sunk into a brief repose; but the mind's energies had been too strongly called upon to allow of its being profound or lasting, and he sprung to his feet again, with the fear that he had been long slumbering from his duty, when, in reality, not half an hour had elapsed since he had trod the deck.

The lamp that swung from the cabin ceiling cast but a dim lustre around it, as it swung to and fro with the heaving of the vessel through the surging sea.

After one hurried glance around him, he hastened upon deck, and there he found that, although the wind that blew was quite entitled to be called a hurricane, it was certainly not so terrific as it had been.

"Mr. Lacy," he said, "I shall keep the deck. Let me beg that you will turn in and rest. What's the time?"

"Midnight," said Lacy. "You have had a very short relief. An hour is enough for me at any time; I will be up again at the end of that period."

"Nay, make it two, if you please. I am sure I cannot sleep to-night."

Lieutenant Lacy went down below, leaving Heartwell on the quarter-deck alone. After a time he sat down, so as to screen himself from the wind, and fixing his eyes upon the leaden-coloured sky, a feeling of greater inclination to repose now came over him than he had before felt when surrounded by all the appliances for rest in his own cabin.

And yet he could not be said to sleep. Indeed, he fancied that he had all his faculties about him, and he swayed to and fro with a dreamy kind of consciousness that he was adapting himself to the motion of the vessel.

His thoughts then wandered to the shore, and to the old Gun Tavern at Wapping, where he had left all that he loved. He thought of that ancient window, looking on the Thames, at which he had stood with the beautiful Minna Woodward—when, without reproach he had held her to his beating heart, and whispered to her how dear she was to him. In fancy he could see her sweet, winning face, and those soft, lustrous eyes, into the clear depths of which he had so often looked entranced.

All these were thoughts of happiness, and although now far from her, her image was not the less distinct in his heart's inmost shrine. He loved her with a love surely beyond precedent. To him she was the star of destiny, the impulse to honourable deeds, the wreath of fame, and around her were concentrated all the hopes and all the aspirations of that gallant heart.

Unconsciously to himself, he pronounced her name, and then, as if its utterance had been an invocation, he felt the warm blood go back to his heart with a frightful gush, as, within a few paces of him, he thought he saw her clearly and distinctly, as if she had at that moment risen from the deep.

"Heartwell, Heartwell, save me!" said the vision.

He sprang to his feet with a cry of alarm. The appearance had vanished, and he stood like one entranced, with the cold drops of mental agony streaming from his brow.

CHAPTER XVI.

THE APPEARANCE OF AN ENEMY.—THE ENGAGEMENT, AND ITS RESULTS.— THE CAPTURE.

THE cry of Heartwell was heard by several of the crew who were near at hand, and they rushed to the spot where he stood, to ascertain what was the cause of the alarming sound they had heard, and one of the gun-room officers stepped forward, and touching his hat, said, in a deferential voice,—

"Has anything happened, sir? We thought we heard a cry of alarm."

For a moment or two Heartwell could not reply; he was completely spellbound, and seemed like one in a dream, and it was not until the question was repeated, that he could make any answer to it.

"No—no," he said—"nothing. You saw nothing?" he added, looking round him yet in doubt.

"No, sir; we saw nothing," was the reply; "but we heard a cry, and thought something had happened."

"No, no—nothing," said Heartwell. "Go to your quarters."

The men obeyed, much wondering what had been the occasion of the cry they had heard. Heartwell was left alone, and he paced to and fro some minutes, endeavouring to recall his senses to himself.

It was many minutes ere he could compose himself sufficiently even to think. Some confusion seemed to reign in his mind, and when he could think calmly, he said,—

"It must have been a dream; and yet, how terrible and real did it seem! Did I sleep? Surely I must, and my thoughts wandered where my heart is. It must be so. But why I should have uttered that terrible cry I cannot think; but I thought Minna cried for aid; yes, cried for aid. Minna Woodward. Psha!" he said, trying to dispel the effects of the vision: "it must have been the excitement produced by the storm and memory mingled together, that has caused this trick to be put upon me—a wild trick of the imagination, which the hurricane that is blowing ought to dispel, and chase away. And yet —and yet I cannot forget those words—that look. God of Heaven! if—but, no, no—she is safe—safe with her mother, at the old Gun-dock."

He increased his pace on the quarter-deck, as though he would shut out other thoughts —as though he feared that unwelcome and distorted imaginings would crowd upon, and make him, stout-hearted and brave as he was, as weak as a child.

"It cannot be otherwise," he muttered. "She must be—she is safe."

He continued to pace the deck, stopping now and then to listen to the wash of the waves, and the creaking and straining of masts and cordage. The wind still blew a hurricane, but, at the same time, it had not increased; but still it raged at a fearful rate across the channel. The Eolus, however, yet sped merrily on, without a stitch of canvass, going at a fearful rate, tossed on the ocean, and sailing lightly and beautifully, like the storm-bird on the white-crested waves.

"She does, indeed, sail beautifully," muttered Heartwell to himself, as he felt the ship's motion to be free and unrestrained. There were no heavy, laboured motions, such as are often found in less skilfully constructed vessels. "He must, indeed, be a poor seaman, who cannot make something of the Eolus, too. If the enemy be not cowardly dogs, we must come to close quarters, and prizes ought to be plentiful, and good work cut out for us all."

By this time Lieutenant Lacy came up from below, to resume authority on deck, and Heartwell now feeling that he, too, required rest, called to him, saying,—

"As you have returned, Mr. Lacy, I will myself now turn in. We have been going merrily enough before the gale, and the shore is yet distant."

"And the wind seems to have decreased a little," said Lacy.

"I am of that opinion too," answered Heartwell. "In the morning we shall be better able to tell what we are to do."

"Yes; daylight is the only thing we can now desire, and that will not be very long before it begins to make its appearance in the east; and then the wind may shift, relieving us of storm and of darkness."

"Most true," said Heartwell; and he turned while he was speaking, and went below.

Heartwell threw himself upon a couch, and his thoughts wandered back to the scenes he had been so very lately a partaker of, at the old Gun Tavern. There was contained his heart's best treasure—his beautiful Minna Woodward.

He thought he could see her hanging on his arm as she used to do while he was there. He thought he could hear her lips pronounce his name, but it was in an altered tone. He started; but sleep crept insensibly over him, and he fell into a profound sleep, in which all was forgotten.

The fatigue he had endured, both of body and mind, now disposed him to sleep soundly, and it would have required an effort to arouse him; and he slept on, little dreaming of the catastrophe that was being, or had been enacted at London. He was in blissful ignorance of all that had been done; and surely, in his case, it might well be said,—"If ignorance is bliss, 'tis folly to be wise."

Oh! could the gallant heart, that beat so true, always remain in such ignorance, fighting his country's battles, and performing those deeds of heroism and devotion, for which his only reward was the approving knowledge that he had done his duty nobly; but, alas! there was no earthly reward for him, and he had fought and bled for many, to find no happiness as his reward for the toil and danger he had successfully braved.

Heartwell had slept some hours, and when he awoke he gazed around him, and endeavoured to recall the past. The motion of the vessel, and the lamp that remained suspended, soon convinced him that he was at sea, and throwing off at once the drowsiness that yet clung about him, he arose and went on deck to ascertain how matters stood. Lieutenant Lacy was at that moment giving some orders to the men, and when he saw Heartwell, he said,—

"I think this hurricane is leaving us; the wind shifts and is inconstant; besides, yonder is the sign of coming daylight."

"So I perceive, Mr. Lacy," said Heartwell. "It has been a rough encounter for the Eolus; there are others, I fear, who have not ridden it out so well as we."

"Indeed, I think not, sir; those who had not the good fortune to get out to sea, or took early enough precautions, have, ere this, found out the depths of the channel."

"I fear so."

"Everything, however, is right with us during the night, and we are fairly out at sea now."

"I am glad of it. We may meet with something to do before the morning is over, for this gale has come from their side of the channel."

"I have more than once thought of that," said Lacy, "and it will be welcome intelligence to the men when they are ordered to clear the decks."

Lieutenant Lacy now left the deck, and proceeded to his cabin to finish his night's repose, which, as a seaman, he was well satisfied if he obtained it by instalments.

The morning now broke, and the sun's rays were seen to gild the eastern horizon, like a few golden threads. The heaving of the sea and the foam of the billows now hiding and now exhibiting the rising sun to the view of the seamen, and spray looking more white, and now and then the rays would dance upon the waters, and strike the eye in all its glitter and beauty. The wind now changed, and they stood fairly amid channels, rather inclining to the French coast.

Their duty now became less arduous, and the whole of the crew had been relieved in turn, and breakfast had been served out to them, when there was a cry from the man who kept the look-out that made the crew strain their eyes to descry the object.

"A sail—a sail!" was the cry.

"A sail," said Heartwell, and he looked in the direction pointed out, when he took the glass and made a careful examination of the stranger.

After a few minutes so employed he handed the glass to Lieutenant Lacy, saying, as he did so,—

"Tell me what you think of her? She is, I believe, a Frenchman, and carries eighteen or twenty more guns than we, and she is attended, too, by a corvette."

Lacy took an accurate survey of the strange vessel, and when he had done so he shut up the glass, saying,—

"To my mind she is a French sixty-four at least, and a corvette in company, and she stands well out."

"She does so," said Heartwell; "and in half-an-hour we shall be in a better position to judge of her intentions, and her armament, or I am mistaken."

"She is not likely to run away, I think," said Lacy.

"If she do she will give us a chase," added Heartwell.

"You mean to fight, Mr. Heartwell?" said the old sailor, with a look of satisfaction at his superior in command.

"Certainly; there is no cause for our declining the fight; the superiority they have is not a sufficient odds for an excuse to run away."

"No, we have done as much before; and with such a crew as that which is aboard the Eolus much may be done."

"We will bear down upon them, Mr. Lacy, and try our fortune; if we succeed in capturing the Frenchman and his companion, as I have no doubt we shall, I expect it will be one good deed, and the first the Eolus has been engaged in."

"It is her maiden engagement," said Lacy; "and we shall see how she behaves herself. I would the mast had not toppled over as it did last night."

"That has been, in some measure, remedied," said Heartwell; "but there are enough left to answer our purpose. The wind veers and is changeable; but it blows stiffly. Now we shall have a chance."

"Yes, we sail well, and shall have the advantage of that," said Lacy; "but see, the Frenchman does not alter his course; he seems to stand out for us."

"He does; and he will suffer for his temerity," said Heartwell.

The two lieutenants separated and proceeded to their duties. Heartwell gave out his orders with promptitude and precision, while the men, confident in his skill and judgment, and their own courage and prowess, obeyed with alacrity and good will.

The order to clear the decks for action was received almost with a cheer, and men here and there were preparing to doff their clothes to have more freedom of action in their limbs when the moment of strife should come.

The deck was cleared, and arm-chests were placed at different places, while muskets, boarding-pikes, and cutlasses were strewn about ready for immediate use.

The men stood at their guns—every man was prepared, and every ear strained to catch the commands of Lieutenant Heartwell. The shot lay in pyramids by the guns, and powder had been served out; every gun was well loaded, and placed in position.

The two vessels neared each other; the Frenchman stood towards them, coming very slowly, followed at some short distance by the corvette. Evidently the intention of the latter was to creep up and do what mischief it could, when the Eolus was too much engaged with the sixty-four, her companion.

The Frenchman had the advantage in weight and guns, and in the number of men, by a full fourth, besides the corvette, which could have maintained a running fight on its own account.

There was a pause on both sides of some time as they neared each other, and each minute seemed an hour, while they all, with breathless suspense, watched every movement that was made.

Heartwell addressed the sailors in some few pithy sentences, such words as such men love to hear; and he breathed a spirit and courage into them, that was well expressed by the hearty cheers when they heard the order given for all hands to quarters.

The drum beat the tattoo, and a glass of grog was served out, and was received with much pleasure, not for the effects it produced, but because they pledge each other; and it may be the last glass they may drink with many a shipmate, who now stood side by side.

They were now scarcely a mile apart, and there was a breathless silence observed throughout the ship.

The mode in which Lieutenant Heartwell intended to fight can be better explained by the conversation that took place between him and Lieutenant Lacy; but we may as well say that the two French vessels were coming from the French shore, or rather along it, the sixty-four a-head of the corvette some quarter of a mile, while Heartwell had steered the Eolus to meet the Frenchman upon his larboard quarter. Things were in this state when Lieutenant Lacy came to Heartwell as the latter beckoned to him.

"Mr. Lacy," he said, "I need hardly say to you that the chances of war may place me in a position that better men have occupied—the command may devolve upon —— "

"I understand," said Lacy; "there's no knowing what may happen to you or me."

"Neither need I say fight her to the last; for you are too old and experienced an officer, and too brave a man to do otherwise."

"No; I will do so."

"Exactly; now see how the two vessels are sailing."

"I do."

"Then I shall sail between them, and place the corvette hors-de-combat as quickly as possible, so that I may not be interrupted during our fight with the other."

"Exactly, Mr. Heartwell; I comprehend your plan, and a good one it certainly is, and will be, I think, successful."

"We are close in upon the sixty-four," said Heartwell, "and shall have a salute, no doubt."

He was perfectly right. In a few moments more they came upon the larboard quarter of the Frenchman, who saluted them with a whole broadside and a deafening cheer.

The Eolus, however, replied not; every man stood at his quarters, stern, and awaiting calmly the word that should give them the opportunity to reply. They strained their eyes, and gazed up aloft to see what mischief had been done, but, beyond a few ropes, nothing had been hurt.

"Their guns," said Heartwell, "might have been better served, but then it is a first broadside."

"So it is," said Lacy, "but when they do hit anything, it is a chance shot, and that must happen now and then."

They now passed the stern of the Frenchman, and Heartwell gave the word to fire, in a loud clear tone.

It was then the sailors returned the shout of the Frenchman with such a clear, hearty cheer, that it was carried far over the blue waters. Then, and almost simultaneously, a broad sheet of flame flashed from the larboard side of the Eolus, and a well-directed broadside was pounced into the stern of the Frenchman, much to his amazement, for the commander did not seem to have comprehended Heartwell's manœuvres. Indeed, he seemed to imagine that the Eolus had declined the combat, and was sheering off, intending to make an attack upon the corvette alone, without saluting them.

The effect of this broadside was strikingly different from that of the enemy; for, though they had more guns and heavier mettle, and had a broader mark, yet their shot scarcely took any effect beyond cutting a few ropes and causing a few splinters, while the Eolus's broadside went clean in the Frenchman's stern; and had it not been that he stood higher out of the water than the former, his decks would have been completely raked; as it was, great damage was done, and many men killed and wounded; and, it was afterwards seen, the machinery connected with the wheel was injured, and prevented him from wearing round; indeed, for a short time, he had no command over the vessel at all.

The Eolus still sailed on, but slightly altering her course, so as to come down starboard to starboard with the corvette, who had endeavoured to manœuvre to get out of the way, but the wind was so decidedly in favour of the Eolus, that escape was impossible, and the captain of the corvette apparently made up his mind for the worst, and seemed to depend upon the aid of the larger vessel, and the chapter of accidents; however, he determined to have the first fire, but, like his comrades', it was ineffective, and, in return, he received such a rattling broadside from the Eolus, that the deck was strewed with dead and dying, while it was splintered in every direction.

It seemed as though the English shot and picked out every valuable part; and then again, before they could recover from the effects of this, a second broadside was poured in.

This was a fatal one to the corvette, for it sunk her. She had several wounds below water-mark, and the ocean poured in from several shot-holes so rapidly as to defy any hope of stopping it out, and she speedily began to settle in the water, while the crew took to their boats as best they could.

Heartwell, now the smoke had cleared off, turned his attention to the larger vessel, of which the commander seemed to think that the Eolus would escape, and had contrived to wear his vessel round, and was bearing down upon it.

Heartwell saw him coming, and determined to wait for him. The French commander appeared to have the hope of being able to practise the same manœuvre that had been used towards him, and so come across the stern of the Eolus and rake her; either from want of skill, or defective machinery, he could not accomplish what he intended; for, at the critical moment, Heartwell just altered his course so as to place it out of his power to rake him.

The broadside was given, but they were at too great a distance, and too ill-directed to take any effect; and as he now came down upon the Eolus, Heartwell had the advantage of the wind.

"Full of blunders, as usual," said Lacy; "these Frenchmen don't seem to understand the use of their vessels, but want them to move about in a hurry, and then they lose every chance, and give us plenty; but here he comes, and now for some steady work for us."

"Yes," remarked Heartwell, "we now come to close quarters."

This was the truth, for the French vessel now approached broadside to broadside, and began firing as she advanced.

"Steady," cried Heartwell, "be steady, men, and don't throw away your shot, but take a cool and deliberate aim; let every shot tell upon some part or other, and the victory will soon be yours."

A hearty cheer was the response that was given to his words, and the men again awaited calmly the approach of the Frenchman; and he now came, enveloped in clouds of his own smoke. He fired at random, and it was a great doubt if the gunners could tell where they were firing, especially as there were no flashes from the Eolus, to show them her whereabouts.

Heartwell stood watching the enemy, and the progress he was making towards her; and when he was satisfied with her position, he again gave out the word to let loose the tide of destruction. The vessels now gradually neared each other, and the firing was steady and incessant on both sides; flash after flash was seen, and peal after peal of the deafening roar of the cannon were heard in rapid succession.

The word of command could scarce be heard, save by the aid of the speaking trumpet, and the vapour that enveloped each vessel seemed completely to hide them from each other's view.

The concussion in the air, caused by the heavy and constant firing, produced a calm around them, and the sails hung idly to the masts.

Heartwell walked over the length of the vessel, to see with his own eyes the extent of the damage his vessel had received, and the amount of loss he had sustained.

In both cases he found it to be much less than, from the superior force and power of the Frenchman, might easily have been expected.

"Well, Mr. Lacy," said Heartwell, "he holds out; but he hasn't done us much damage, that I can perceive."

"Very little, considering," said Lacy; "and what is done, is fortunately of a reparable character, and does not even now impede the working of the ship."

"I think we are approaching nearer to each other," said Heartwell, as he looked up at the enemy's masts.

"Yes, we are," returned Lacy; "and there," he added, "there goes one of his masts; come, that's well done."

For a few moments, the fire of the enemy seemed to slacken, and confusion seemed to reign for a time. The Eolus, however, kept up the fire, and the two vessels were fast drifting together, and a few more minutes would bring them together.

Heartwell ordered a good look-out to be kept, and to lash the vessels together, to prevent separation, and then all hands were ordered to be in readiness to board.

"Now, Mr. Lacy," said Heartwell, "we will board in two parties from the deck, and you will command one while I lead the other."

"From what point," inquired Lacy, "shall we board?"

"That must depend upon circumstances; but from the most accessible place that can be found; and when on the enemy's deck, we shall join, and drive them all below, and the ship is ours."

"I see," said Lacy; "and here we are, then, for now are we yard-arm and yard-arm."

"Then lash them together," exclaimed Heartwell, "all hands upon deck."

The men, however, had not waited for this order, but had commenced lashing the vessels, so as to bring them alongside.

During all this time, the vessels continued to fire at each other with undiminished fury. The Frenchman had cut away his wounded mast, and now resumed the fight. The closeness of the two vessels caused their broadsides to tell upon each other with destructive effects, and the decks were streaming with blood, and the vessels were splintered all over.

The Frenchman had several of his guns useless, for in more instances than one he had several of his port-holes knocked into one, and the guns could not be worked.

The word was given, and with a loud cheer the boarding parties rushed towards the enemy, who crowded their own decks, for well did they knew that the English would board them now they came to close quarters.

It was altogether a hand to hand contest now, and the daring courage of the British now showed conspicuously, and their resolution and strength was put to the test, for the decks were crowded with men, beyond the complement even of a sixty-four.

The state of the vessel, however, told the Eolus's men that the French had suffered very severely indeed; their deck was wet with blood, and many dead bodies lay in different places; indeed, from the number of men they had presented the almost certain mark, and they lay in heaps.

They now, however, outnumbered the crew of the Eolus; and yet, the hardy tars hesitated not a moment; and full of confidence, and high courage, they rushed to the attack with such a hearty soul-inspiring shout, that certainly to many of the enemy was a death knell; and so some of them seemed to think it.

Heartwell was the first to jump on the enemy's deck, which he accomplished by climbing up to the bulwarks, and then jumping down. He was quickly followed by his crew, and within a minute or two, they executed the same act of daring at the other end of the ship.

The affray now became too hot, and too close, to last very long, when even there was a direct collision—a charge or rush of the British—then the enemy gave way; but they ran to any elevated position from which they could fire down upon the British, without exposing themselves to the determined rush of the English sailors.

This annoyance caused the Eolus some loss; and then Heartwell directed Lieutenant Lacy to station marksmen in different places, and to charge up aloft against them.

In these manœuvres the second-lieutenant was greatly assisted by the top-men of the Eolus, who, seeing how matters stood, whenever they could get a view of them, they fired at them, and this diverted their attention, and enabled those below to approach with greater safety; but the two vessels becoming so closely engaged, the masts and rigging of the one became mixed with the other, and they had the hardihood to climb along, until they had reached the enemy's yards, and then drove them away; so they were soon placed between two fires, and were bravely conquered.

During this, the strife continued below, and the enemy were gradually driven below, from one point to another; till, after a desperate resistance, and an enormous loss on their side, they surrendered!

The order to stay the firing was given, and the Frenchman's flags hauled down; at that moment, the victors gave three hearty cheers for the victory they had so nobly achieved.

Heartwell had himself disarmed the captain of his sword in single fight, and he was always where the combat raged thickest and boldest, hand to hand, he never shrank from any odds.

The crew were brave and chosen men, and led by such a man as Heartwell, they were positively invulnerable; they were irresistible, and so they proved themselves.

And now the smoke cleared off, they had a better view of their prize. It was a fine vessel, though damaged in places; yet it was not of such serious character as to cause any apprehensions for its safety, or its ultimate service and value.

It was a proud moment for Heartwell, standing as he did among his own crew, and a great portion of the enemy's, hailed as the victorious commander of a victorious crew! Full fairly had he earned his laurels; for never had commander more freely faced an enemy; and where help was needed, there was he; his voice and example were contagious and an unerring signal for the retirement of the enemy, who could not withstand the conduct of the men when he led them.

Nor was Lacy wanting on this occasion, he did his part like a brave man, and an able officer; and none can tell the feeling, with which men grasp each other's hands, after such deadly encounter as that in which they had been engaged.

"Allow me to congratulate you, Mr. Heartwell," said Lacy, as he joined him on the deck of the French vessel.

"We have achieved a glorious result to-day, Mr. Lacy," returned Heartwell, holding out his hand, at the same time returned the hearty pressure of his second in command.

"Will you go to Plymouth with this?"

"Yes, we shall; and then we shall be relieved of our charge and our wounded."

"Exactly; I guessed as much."

"You, Mr. Lacy, I must beg will take possession of this ship, and secure the prisoners in a proper manner; you shall have as strong a body of men as I can give you."

To this arrangement Lacy was well pleased to accede; it was a post he coveted, and one, as he was to be accompanied by the Eolus, he lost nothing that he might have partaken in had he been on board.

With what feelings of pride and triumph did Heartwell hoist his white sails, and steer for Plymouth harbour, that being the nearest port he could run into.

The odds at which he fought had been great. Not a vestige of the vessel he had sunk remained, save some of the men who had been saved floating about on some spars and boards.

The weather now appeared mild and genial, the day was bright and clear, and the wind was light; and many were the thoughts of pride and glory the men indulged in, as they sailed easily along towards Portsmouth harbour.

"Minna," said Heartwell to himself, as he paced the deck thoughtfully, and watching the progress of his prize, as well as admiring its build—"Minna will hear of me as I wish to be heard of—as a victor in my country's cause."

Heartwell had received more than one wound in the affair; but they were light, and involved no trouble, or laid him up. He could perform his duty just as well as though they were not.

The night came on again, but it was a very different one from that which had preceded it. There were light winds and a calmer ocean, and the two vessels crowded all sail; yet they had received damages which crippled them, and prevented them making such sail as they otherwise could have made.

The night passed quietly enough, and the two vessels sailed in company. There was no attempt to retake the vessel by the Frenchmen ahead; indeed it was not thought of, the Eolus being so close at land.

The morning broke, and when the sun had been some few hours old, Plymouth harbour appeared in sight. This was a welcome sight to many.

The guns of the arsenal and battery fired a salute, and the whole town turned out to see the entrance of the Eolus and her prize, and many a church bell was rung in honour of the victory.

The vessels now entered the harbour, while proper authorities were sent for to receive the prisoners and the charge of the prize; and then some necessary repairs would have to be made before proceeding to sea again, but that would occupy but a few days.

CHAPTER XVII.

MINNA AT HOME.—THE DREADFUL EXPLANATION.—THE WARNING VOICE AGAIN,
AND THE MYSTERIOUS STRANGER.

ALAS! what a dreadful morning was that to poor Minna Woodward which dawned after that night of suffering and woe. We need not describe how, with frantic haste, she sought her home; how, guided almost by an instinct, rather than reflection, she found her way to that once happy abode of innocence and peace.

Oh! of what a different character now was the agony of sorrow that oppressed her, compared to the description of sorrow she had felt even at her poor father's death; with what a bitterness of anguish she now blamed herself for a seeming want of affection for him and his memory.

Now that she could, with less of passion and more of grief, review what had occurred, she deeply wondered that for one moment the wish to obtrude upon that class of society of which she had now so horrible an experience, should have arisen in her mind with sufficient intensity to induce her to yield so readily to the invitation of that dreadful Lady Clare, and to become a visitor at her more than questionable house.

To think of the proceedings of that fearful night was madness; and even a passing reflection upon them was almost enough to tempt Minna to the commission of some fearful deed hazarding her soul's safety.

She did reach home, she knew not how, and by the morning light, pale, haggard, and oppressed, and with such an expression of unutterable woe on her face, that those who had known her in her happiness might well fail to recognize her now. She crept rather than walked within that doorway which had so long sheltered her.

She shuddered to think of whom might be the first person she might meet. She knew not herself the look of anguish that pervaded her countenance; she could not guess how fearfully miserable she appeared, and it was only with a start of surprise that an old servant, who had known her from earliest childhood, gave, that she began to guess, indeed, that she was strangely altered.

"Where is my mother?" she said, and her very voice sounded like a funeral dirge— "where is my mother?"

"Oh, Miss Minna!" said the old servant, "how dreadfully ill you look. Your mother's gone to lay down a little, and she has been so anxious about you."

"I will go to her," said Minna.

Slowly and sadly she ascended the stairs of that abode, which was so dissimilar to the splendid mansions she had so recently left; but which, to her mind, would ever be associated with so much terrific recollection.

Mrs. Woodward was sleepy; she had sat up waiting the return of Minna, until exhaustion had compelled her to seek repose.

Minna approached the bed, and drawing on one side the curtain which shaded her mother's face, she sat down there in an arm-chair, which she recollected from her earliest childhood, to await her awakening. She felt thankful that she had yet some time given her for reflection, notwithstanding its painful, nay, its almost agonizing character; and she was enabled to arrange in her mind what she ought to say to her mother, with regard to what had occurred.

"I will not keep from her," she said, "the fearful secret. She shall know all; and, thank Heaven that I can add to it the information, that I am a wife. Yes, yes; the vows have been breathed, although they bind me to one whom I have so much more reason to hate than love. I am his wife, and I will bear his name. He cannot cheat me now of that melancholy wretched consolation; and oh, Heartwell! when I think of thee! But that is weakness."

The very pronunciation of the name of Heartwell seemed almost to drive her distracted; forgetting that her mother slept, and that she wished her yet to sleep, she uttered a sound of despair, and Mrs. Woodward opened her eyes.

"Minna, Minna!" she said, "have you come home at last?" and then she trembled at the look of terrific despair which she saw upon her face.

"My child, my child!" she said; "you have something dreadful to tell me. Speak, Minna! oh, speak, and do not let me dread aught that may be worse than the truth."

"Mother!" she said, and she seemed to be gasping for breath as she spoke. "Mother, I have something dreadful to tell you. Do not, oh! do not speak to me; but hear all, and then condemn me if you will; it may, perchance, be mercy so to do."

A painful consciousness that Minna would not speak in such a strain, unless she had something more than ordinary to communicate, terrified poor Mrs. Woodward fearfully, as she exclaimed,—

"Minna, Minna! another moment of suspense will kill me."

"You shall not endure it," said Minna; "you shall know all, without disguise to thee, and to thee only dare I be so communicative.   Listen!"

With such a wrapt attention as some poor criminal might be supposed to bestow upon the frightful particulars of some impending and terrific doom, did Mrs. Woodward listen now to that narrative of terror which came from Minna's lips.

We would not, because we cannot hope to do so fully, attempt to set down, with anything like the force with which they were spoken, the words of bitterness and anguish in which the beautiful Minna detailed the fearful occurrences of the preceding night. With a sad attention which showed a despairing consciousness that the tale must have a very sad end, did the mother listen to her child's discourse; but when Minna spoke to her of her marriage, of that ceremony so roughly and so rudely performed, but from which she derived a wretched consolation, Mrs. Woodward wrung her hands, and in the impulse of the moment, she exclaimed,—

"Minna, Minna! you are deceived.   I feel a consciousness that that marriage was ——"

Minna clasped her hands with frightful energy as she exclaimed,—

"Was what? was what?"

"A mockery."

"Death—death!" cred Minna, springing to her feet, as if with an intention of immediately leaving the chamber.   She grasped her throat convulsively—blood came from her mouth, and she sank insensible to the floor.

All was alarm and consternation—never had such a world of terror been concentrated in that old tavern.   Everything else was forgotten in the presumed danger which Minna was in.

Medical aid was immediately procured, and it was at once announced upon that authority that a small blood vessel had given away upon the lungs, which, although not necessarily fatal, was still dangerous, except the greatest care and attention was bestowed upon the sufferer.

Here, then, was a new circumstance, which at once stopped further inquiry, prevented any steps being taken by the mother, until she ascertained that her child was out of danger.   She could scarcely think of leaving Minna's bed-side for one moment, and all other thoughts and feelings were merged in the great question of would she live or would she die.

Thus, then, many days wore on, during which the gallant Heartwell was fighting the battles of his country, and during which, to do him common justice, Captain Bulkeley was making vain efforts to reach his ship.

That the storm which had come on had rendered it imperative for the Eolus to put out to sea, was a proposition he could not dispute, and, therefore, was it, although torn by vexation, and terrified that he should hear something extremely unpleasant, as regarding the infamous treachery he had been guilty of towards Minna, his state of mind was anything but a pleasurable one.

Fourteen days passed away, and then Minna was pronounced out of danger by her medical attendant, and it was considered expedient to resort to means for the recovering again of her strength and general state of health.

During all this time she had remained in a state of dreamy unconsciousness of surrounding objects, her thoughts had been a chaos of conflicting emotions.   She knew of nothing tangible for a brief moment, but what was mingled with all the wild visions of fancy, and with a thousand other objects.

Happy confusion! happy intellectual bewilderment! and so far happy indisposition that at least for some time had stilled the pangs of thought.

But with returning health of body came returning mental vigour; then the past began to assume its proper shape, and, on the fifteenth day, weakened, oppressed, and exhausted, Minna awoke to a full consciousness of her absolute wretchedness.

The agony of grief that came over her was terrific and alarming.   Those words of her mother that the marriage was a mockery, immediately they were uttered, had seemed to come upon her with astounding truthfulness.   She doubted them not for one moment; and now that reflection had come again, she wondered at the simplicity and ignorance that had induced her to become an actor in the farce.

She made an effort which she had not strength to carry out.   It was to rise and leave the house, to go she knew not whither; but physical weakness constrained her to give up the hasty impulse, although the thought had not departed from her mind.

The horror of having the finger of scorn pointed at her by those who knew her, but not sufficiently well to believe the real story of her wrongs, incessantly haunted her. That was a state of things she could not endure. She was strong enough now to feel all the bitterness of her situation, but not strong enough to rise superior to it, and to look with contempt upon the opinions of those who, if they judged her ill, would judge her harshly and wrongfully.

And now she was wonderfully quiet, she spoke little—a bad sign, for it showed that dark and fearful thoughts were heavy at her heart, and yet there were but two tangible ideas present to her imagination, and they both required the means of their accomplishment to be considered.

The one was that she should leave her house, and get among strangers who knew her not, and the other was to have one last interview with Heartwell, to tell him that now she was unworthy of him, and that she never could be his. To implore him not to judge her harshly, to pity rather than condemn her; or, if he could, to banish her from his thoughts, as if no such person had ever possessed them.

The means by which these two results were to be brought about, she could not even dream of. How she was to reach Heartwell was a mystery. And how she was to live, if she voluntarily left her home, she had no means whatever in conjecturing.

It was at this juncture, and late in the evening, while Mrs. Woodward was sitting by the bedside of Minna, and endeavouring to cheer her heart with better counsel, that word was brought to her that a stranger wished to speak with her, and moving noiselessly from the room, for she was not sure but Minna slept, as she had not answered her for some time, she went softly down stairs, and entered the bar parlour, when a tall, youngish-looking man, well attired, stood awaiting her coming.

CHAPTER XVIII.

THE DISTRESSING INTIMATION.—THE DISAPPEARANCE OF MINNA.

UPON a second glance at the stranger, who had demanded to see her, Mrs. Woodward had a slight impression that his features were not altogether strange to her, but it was so slight that she found it impossible to follow it up, or to remember in the least when and where she had seen him.

Under such circumstances, it is in ninety-nine cases out of a hundred in vain to attempt to follow up the slight clue which memory has given; thought only the more perplexes the dimness of recollection, and until some accident touches on the right chord of memory, it is in vain to hope for a satisfying result.

The young stranger seemed to be perfectly willing to allow Mrs. Woodward as much time as she pleased for the purpose of endeavouring to recollect him, for he spoke not, but endured her gaze unflinchingly, and it was not until she turned her head aside, and he saw by the expression of her countenance how unavailing had been the effort to remember him, that he spoke.

"You have seen me," he said, "but you do not know nor will you yet for a time. I have done all I could to save from destruction one whom I know to be dear to you; but it was in vain. Allured by the false glitter of a mode of life new and strange to her, she has fallen into the snare laid for her destrucption."

"You speak," said Mrs. Woodward, "upon a subject, your knowledge concerning which may be greater than my own, but nevertheless, you will not be surprised at my shrinking to hold such communication with a stranger."

"Nay, madam, I come to give you advice and counsel; let such be welcome on their own merits, whether coming from friend or foe, stranger or intimate. Know you the man who has wrought you so much woe?"

"Yes; Captain Bulkley Harding."

"'Tis he; the marriage, to the recollection of which doubtless your unhappy child still clings, I need scarcely tell you was a mockery."

"Alas! my fears told me as much."

"It is so; and in your present aspect of affairs, what hope have you of being able to obtain even a shadow of justice for your child?"

"None! none! none!"

" Mrs. Woodward, did you chance to know accurately the whole of the contents of that ancient bureau in your late husband's chamber ?"

Mrs. Woodward staggered back a pace or two, and sank into a chair. Astonishment and alarm were depicted upon her countenance, and it was some moments before she could say, faintly,—

" Yes, yes ; tell me who you are, and more than that, what is the extent of your information upon a subject, I am convinced, from the few words you have uttered, you are not wholly ignorant."

" You may speak freely and confidently to me. I know all, and while I can scarcely blame you, I still can enter into the feelings which could induce you to keep a secret so long and so well preserved, and the divulging of which now would bring great censure upon you for the lateness of the act, as well as perhaps depriving you of the society of one who has become dear to you from habit and reflection."

" Yes, yes," exclaimed Mrs. Woodward ; " it is so."

" And yet a sense of right and wrong is surely not dead within you ; it is only lately that I have known enough to enable me to act with the certainty that I am right : but now that I can do so, you would surely be the last to bid me pause."

" I cannot ; I have always felt that I cannot stand in the way of a disclosure of certain facts, when any one should step forward to do so. If you are in a position to proclaim facts, only some of which are known to me, I will aid you. Heaven knows how much I wish that four-and-twenty hours ago you had come here, and then perhaps you might have saved her of whom we are speaking, from the dreadful fate which has been her's."

" I knew it not sufficiently accurately, although I had very strong suspicions. I have been betrayed by one I trusted. He has paid the penalty of so doing, and I can do no more. I could not awaken expectations which might have proved futile : the subject was too serious a one to tamper with. I did my best to save Minna from the destruction which has fallen upon her. She has now her revenge in her own hands. Her destroyer shall be at her mercy."

" Oh ! reveal to me," said Mrs. Woodward, " all you know. You can guess at my affection for Minna, although you may not know its full extent ; and I will take fitting time and opportunity to tell her all that you may communicate."

" No," said the stranger ; " to herself must I relate that which no one but I can communicate to her, and prove. I must see her, and she shall hear a tale which may speak some consolation to her heart, in her affliction. Does she most weep or rave for vengeance ?"

" Her disposition is too gentle to visit even upon the head of him who has worst injured her, much suffering. She looks to Heaven, rather, for consolation in her affliction, than to earth for vengeance. You will not move her to any desperate act, which promises revenge."

" I may not ; but I will move her to an act which will promise her justice, Mrs. Woodward. I swear it—Bulkley Harding, her seducer, shall wed her yet."

" Convince her of that ; for already does the feeling possess her, that the marriage she fancied she solemnized with him was a delusion. Convince her, then, that such a reparation may ensue, and you will be entitled to her gratitude."

" Will you let me see her, then ? It is not that I doubt the discretion with which you would make the communication to her, but I have documents to show her, which I have sworn to myself I will never allow to go out of my posssession, even for a moment ; and, believe me, that in refusing to place them in your hands as confirmatory testimony of what I could disclose, it is not that I distrust you, Mrs. Woodward, individually, but in pursuance of my general resolution not to do so".

" I am satisfied," said Mrs. Woodward, " and you shall see her ; perchance you are able to add so much to that which I know, as may produce a result which, although I once dreaded, I, now that I am left alone by the death of my husband, long for ; and, oh ! if you can but carry out and achieve that which you once promised, namely—that she should become really the wife of that bad man, who has inflicted so much misery upon her, I may have, in time, to acquit myself of some of the blame which lies so heavy at my heart ; for I feel that I ought to have prevented her leaving my house in the society of that Lady Clare, whose conduct was, unquestionably, more than suspicious."

" Nay ; doubtless you acted for the best ; but every moment is of consequence ; let me see her, I beseech you. I have a claim to see her, which you know not of, but which soon, now, you will understand."

" I will go," said Mrs. Woodward, " and prepare her for your visit, with all the haste I may."

Mrs. Woodward hastily left the room, in order to seek the chamber of Minna; and while she was gone, the stranger paced to and fro in the apartment with evident impatience. He seemed, if one might judge from his manner, to have a presentiment of some sort of evil, and, occasionally, he paused to listen if any sound disturbed the unusual stillness of the house.

Somehow or another, since the death and burial of old Woodward, the Gun tavern had fallen off greatly; its old habitual customers, finding that a kind of restraint was upon them, while the body of the landlord remained unburied, had gone temporarily elsewhere to spend their evenings, so that those who had, apparently, filled the reception rooms of the house, were chiefly persons whom curiosity had drawn thither, and when they found that there were no more alarms, and that nothing of an adventurous character was occurring within those ancient walls, they left again, and it was evident that the business of the Gun tavern had, in the death of its landlord, received a mortal blow.

The stillness, however, which reigned within the place, was suddenly interrupted by such a cry of despair, that the stranger staggered, and would have fallen, on the first impulse of his surprise, had he not reached the wall, and leaned against it for support.

It was but for a moment, though, that he was thus unmanned, for, uttering a hasty exclamation of dread, he rushed from the bar parlour, and feeling convinced that the sound of distress came from above, he bounded up the narrow dark staircase with amazing speed, and rushed into the first chamber which presented itself to him. It was that of Minna, and for a moment he believed it untenanted, but a second glance showed him the prostrate form of Mrs. Woodward upon the floor, apparently in a state of insensibility. Before, however, he could raise her, the servants, as well as several alarmed guests who happened to be in the house, made their way into the room.

She was at once raised and placed in a chair, when it was observed that she had a scrap of paper tightly clutched in one of her hands. The stranger took possession of it, and advancing to the light he found that the following words were written upon it :—

"Farewell for ever!—MINNA WOODWARD."

This was sufficiently explanatory of the cry of despair which had came from Mrs. Woodward. The mysterious stranger stood for a few moments like one panic-stricken, and then without speaking to any one, or indeed making the least remark, he turned and abruptly left the house.

CHAPTER XIX.

THE FATE OF MINNA.—THE DREADFUL ATTEMPT.

IT now becomes our melancholy duty to detail in what manner Minna left the home of her infancy, and what were her ideas and impressions concerning the future in so doing.

The step was about as ill-advised and indiscreet a one as she could possibly have taken, and her best friends would have used force before they would have permitted her to take it, but unhappily she had the opportunity of committing an act of great desperation—and she did it.

There was nothing particular in her state of mind, when Mrs. Woodward last left her, which could have induced any one to believe she immediately meditated anything so rash; and, indeed, it was not until she found herself alone that the full amount of wretchedness and disgrace came across her mind with such resistless force, that she felt herself capable of any act, however desperate.

"What will," she exclaimed, "what can become of me? The dread of again looking upon the face of Heartwell will for ever haunt me. One glance from his eyes will kill me; and if I live now, I shall surely encounter such a glance. How can I ever plead my justification? how clothe in language fit for me to utter, and he to hear? I cannot hope to do so. I am now as a thing accursed; to look upon the past is madness, and the future —desolation."

She covered her face with her hands, and remained for many minutes in a state which could scarcely be called one of reflection, inasmuch as it was far more like a delirium of the imagination, in which a thousand thoughts and fancies chased each other through her brain with a frightful rapidity; and then came the fearful thought, that in death alone would she ever find that repose she had lost in life.

Such a feeling as that was more than likely to grow gigantic under the circumstances; and it did so; for in a few moments more it became the sole prevading thought of her mind. She hastily sprang from her bed, and attiring herself in such articles of clothing as came nighest to her hand, she was, in an incredibly short space of time, ready for the streets.

Fearful, then, of interruption, she only allowed herself time to write in pencil the few words on the scrap of paper which had been taken from the hand of Mrs. Woodward by the stranger.

From the moment she had been left alone, to that in which she crossed the threshold of the room, ten minutes could not have elapsed. No one met her, and she passed the door of the back parlour, hearing, as she did so, the murmured sound of conversation within. She paused not a moment, but along the long narrow passage she took her way into the street, uninterrupted by any living soul.

One last sad glance she took at the old house, and then, with a shudder, she turned away, and, with rapid steps, took that road which would soonest lead her out of sight of that building which was once so nearly associated with all her happiest thoughts.

Settled plan of action she had none; grim and terrific, the dreadful thoughts of suicide held possession of her intellect. The how and the when it was to be performed were still subjects to be thought of when she should be at sufficient distance from home, to feel that her awful intention could not be marred by the jealous interference of those who loved her.

How far she had proceeded she could not tell; her notions of time and space were sadly deranged; but feeling that she had attained, at all events, a sufficient distance from home, she paused to look around her as she cowered down beneath an ancient archway leading to some stables.

Here she paused and looked around her with a feeling of dread, lest she should be questioned by any of the passers by. It was a lonely spot, and she felt conscious that if noticed, she might have her intention marred by some one who would see her distress. She turned her head and gazed down the gateway to see if any one were about, but there was nothing stirring—nobody was near at hand—all was still and quiet down below there. She suddenly determined to walk down, and see if there were no place where she could hide and obtain time to think, without any distracting fears that momentarily she might be disturbed.

Creeping cautiously, as though she meditated doing some evil deed, she walked down the deserted gateway.

At the bottom, she found some empty building. She entered it, for it was partially open; it had some means to keep an intruder out, and in one corner she found some straw that had long lain there; and upon this she threw herself, in an agony of grief, for here she could weep unseen and unheard.

Here it was that the same thought of death came over her that had before visited her. How was it to be accomplished, that was the great inquiry that now agitated her mind.

How long she remained in this place she knew not; time passed unnoticed by her, but there she sat in one corner of the deserted and crumbling building; her face buried in her hands, thinking upon the one dreadful subject that now entirely took possession of her mind to the exclusion of all others, and that one was suicide.

"Yes, yes," she muttered, "it must be so—it must be. It is the only means of obtaining that peaceful serenity that I now so much covet. The river—yes, the peaceful, smiling river—that I have so often seen rippling in the dancing sunbeams, as it ran its course past my poor father's house; yes, the peaceful, smiling river, that I have seen glancing in the moon's beams when I have leaned on the arm of Heartwell. Oh, God! I cannot bear the thought of it—it maddens me!"

She arose to her feet, and tottered to the opening at which she entered and emerged beneath the desolate archway.

All was dark and quiet; no sound reached her ears; the dull light of the lamps shone obscurely; the sound of the watch she could hear at a distance. She listened, but they were too indistinct to catch; she paused, however, to listen if they came nearer, which they did.

The slow step of the watch she could distinctly hear as he neared the place; the wind blew down the archway, but she heeded it not; however, she moved away from the spot she stood in, crouched down behind a projecting buttress to conceal herself from the guardian of the night.

There was but little need of that, for that drowsy individual stalked along in all the majesty of a great white coat and lantern, giving a terrible thump on the stones every now and then with his baton or stick.

"Past twelve o'clock, and a cloudy night!" sang out this worthy in sonorous, but drawling accents.

Minna listened to the sounds with an anxiety it is difficult to conceive; she feared to be found; but what a relief was it when she heard the sounds gradually dying away in the distance.

Again did she creep out from her hiding-place, and peer up the archway; and then she once more emerged into the open street. She gazed around her, but she saw no cause for immediate fear or interruption, and she fled through the streets.

She met no one, but, had she done so, there can be no doubt but she would have attracted attention, if, indeed, she had not been stopped.

See page 87.

Her look was wild, her step irresolute, and her purpose apparently undefined, for she wandered through many streets, apparently without any object—she had missed her way, and knew not which way to go to reach the river.

"Yes, yes, the river," she muttered—"the river—it must be the river."

These words were upon her lips as she moved on along the streets, and, at length, she did come near the river. She caught a glimpse of it from the end of a street, at the further end of which she now entered.

A shudder ran through her frame, but she urged herself onwards, despite the feeling that struggled in her breast against the deed she was about to commit.

It was the struggle of the mind against the instincts of nature. She was young—very young, to leave a world upon which she had scarcely passed more than the threshold, and in which she had had such bright prospects, such happiness in store; but how soon were the hopes she had formed blasted most cruelly!

Yes, she was young to embrace that death which the ordinary course of nature would no doubt place at a great distance.

"Yes, yes," she again murmured; "may God forgive me; I cannot live happily or in honour, and I will embrace the sad alternative of death."

She hurried on towards the river, and soon arrived at a wharfing.

The sound of the water washing against the barges and other small craft that were moving about was enough to make a sterner and more courageous heart fail: not so Minna; her mind was made up to one point — to the performance of one deed she was resolved; and, without a moment's hesitation, she jumped upon the barges that were moored alongside, and rapidly walked to the last of them that floated far out into the stream.

Here she paused for a moment, and then, uttering a short prayer, craving mercy for the deed she was about to enact, and calling a benediction down upon the head of him who was far away, and whom she yet loved, she plunged into the stream.

A sudden plash was the only sound that was returned, and then all was still. A moment afterwards she rose to the surface; her clothes were buoyant and filled with air, and she floated.

"Where did you see her?" said a voice on the barges she had just quitted.

"She was here a moment ago," replied a woman; "she made a splash."

"Then she's gone to the bottom. I thought she looked wild."

"Yes, something's wrong; the young girl's beau, I suppose, has been false, and she's now tired of life."

"I'll wager anything to nothing she'd be glad to get out again—eh, gal, eh?"

"Well, I shouldn't wonder; but more fool she to take a cold bath at such an hour. See—what's that?"

"What's what?"

"There, yonder—floating."

"Oh, I'm cussed if I know."

"But it is a woman; there, by the moorings of that barge."

"Why, it looks like a porpoise, or a clothes-basket."

"It's the girl we saw come down this street and jump off here."

"Do you think so?"

"Think! are you a man? go and save the poor wretch; we may teach her to live and enjoy life."

The man who was with the woman crept along the barges until he came to the one against which the body of Minna Woodward was drifting against the moorings, which were secured somewhat low, so that as the stream drifted by, the body of Minna was thrown against it, and was thus held for some minutes, while the man crept round to it, and lowered himself by the chain.

He seized her by the hair and dragged her by that to the side of the vessel, and thus detained her until he had got safely on to the barge. Then, by means of a boat-hook, he contrived to heave her up, and bring her on to the barge.

This was not done without some struggles on the part of Minna; but her struggles were faint, and not directed against anything or for any object; they were the undirected efforts of nature—she was all but insensible.

In this state the man bore her in his arms, dripping with water, towards the spot where his companion stood.

"Is she living?" inquired the female, whose occupation was easily seen in her demeanour and her dress.

"Yes, I believe so; she's plaguey wet. I haven't had so much water down me, unmixed, I don't know how long."

"You fool, she's come from a wet place; what, besides water, did you expect from the river?"

"Certainly not a woman."

"She's a mermaid; bring her along to the house, we can have her taken care of there, and something may come of it. I dare say old Master Whileback can make some use of her."

"Yes, yes—come on; we have been out now too long."

"I shall be out as long as I please."

"Come on."

These last words of the man were uttered in a loud, brutish tone, which seemed to be understood by his wretched companion, who obeyed in silence.

The two went up one street and down another for some time; and, between them, they bore Minna along at a tolerable pace, as if she were walking.

They met with no interruption, and arrived at the door of a house, over which burned a red light. They tapped at the door, which was opened cautiously, with a chain up, and a man peeped out.

"Who have you got?" he said, in a surly tone, and hesitating manner.

"Open the door, will you, and stow your jaw for a time. Do you want to have the Charleys down upon us?"

This allusion to the guardians of the night had the effect of inducing this Cerberus to open the portals of the mansion, and they hurried the unfortunate Minna along the passage.

When the man saw the state the poor girl was in, he made a sudden present of his eyes and limbs to a certain region, and then said,—

"Well, I never saw such a rum start as that; what the devil do you mean by doing such water-cart business? I'm blessed if they ain't got the daughter of old father Thames there, and there's the swells up stairs. Such a night, too, as this—what a pity! they'll spoil all. Cursed fools they are, to be sure. I'd have kept 'em outside, only there would have been a shindy."

The man and woman who bore Minna along between them, hurried her into a side room, in which there was a bed and a fire, and placed her on a chair.

"Send in Bet," said the woman; "we can manage her."

The man left the apartment, and, in a few moments more, the woman denominated Bet—a piece of female propriety of the Saracen's head pattern—came bouncing into the room with the exclamation of,—

"Well, blow me tight, Ben says you got a water-witch with you."

"Call her what you will, but lend us a hand to get these things off—we can put some others on."

"Well, what if we do?" said the woman; "what's to come of it?"

"Why, she's young, and will help to fill the room; they want new faces—they can't always be looking on the same; they get tired, and will go away to some other ken."

The two women now set about undressing Minna; they tore off the wet things that she had on, and replaced them with others of a more tawdry description; but they were dry. They were but ill-calculated to suit the taste of such a one as Minna Woodward, but they were calculated for the place she was then in.

All this while Minna had but a glimmering consciousness of something going on; she could scarcely be called insensible, and yet she was hardly above it; she was passive; she knew her attempt was abortive, but she did not know how it had been rendered so.

"Where am I?" she murmured, when they had nearly dressed her.

"Ah, where are you, indeed; where you wouldn't have been if you had gone to the bottom of the river."

"Was she in the water, then?"

"Didn't you see her clothes?"

"Yes; but I mean did she throw herself in?" inquired the brazen-faced female.

"She did—she meant it; but Ben and I had followed her a short way, and then, before we could get up with her to see who or what she was, she turned down towards the river; we followed, and heard her go splash in the water, but Ben got her out."

"Ah, I see; she's been gammoned by somebody, and they don't want her any more."

"That's it; but come, I think she will do now; we'll take her in the kitchen, and there she can have something warm."

"Yes, she will soon get round—in time enough to walk into the room."

"That is what I want, before those swells go; it will be a mean   attracting them again—she's pretty."

"Yes, but little."

"They like these kickshaw girls best, and that's all we have to look to. Come along, we must take her down."

These two amiables led her out of the room unresistingly, quite unconscious of who or what they were, or what was their object. Poor Minna Woodward had fallen, indeed, into bad hands; these were the lowest and most degraded beings who pander to the vice of the vicious of the great city, and who know neither pity nor remorse; and their sole object in saving her was, that she appeared likely to answer their purposes.

They carried her into a large kitchen where was a fire like a furnace, before which were a variety of implements, and much cooking appeared to be carried on before it.

A variety of odours arose; the steams of roast and boiled, the mixture of liquors and wine.

Minna was placed in a seat near the fire, and some provisions were forced down her. She ate, but she knew not why; all was mazy and indistinct to her senses; and, after that, she had been compelled to swallow some brandy-and-water.

The joint effects of these matters were, that Minna found herself half stupified and sleepy. The water she had been in, the cold wet clothes she had had on her, were so different from the heat of the apartment, that her senses were completely overpowered, and she was unable to sit with safety in her chair.

"Let her have half-an-hour's sleep up stairs," said one, "and, by that time, they will be ready."

Accordingly, thus directed, some of the females present took her between them, and assisted her to walk up stairs to another bed-room on the second floor.

"Here," said one, shaking Minna, "you will be safe for half or three quarters of an hour; I shall wake you up in that time."

Minna, with the help of these people, was placed in a bed, and a sheet thrown over her. She was soon asleep.

Her slumber was short, and the effects of the combined causes were soon dispelled, and then she awoke to a sense of her wretched situation.

She had scarcely began to reflect, ere she heard some persons approach the room and enter it; she was completely hidden by the sheet that was thrown over her by the female.

"We are alone here," said one voice.

"Yes," replied the other, holding a light up, and glancing round the room; "yes; we're alone here, and can speak freely."

"That's what I want. Do you know that cove with the mourning ring?"

"I think I do; he's got a striped blue satin stock on."

"The same."

"Seems to have plenty of money."

"He has plenty of money," was the reply, in an emphatic tone; "he has plenty of money, but he takes care of it."

"Have you seen his purse?" inquired the other.

"Yes; he must have more than two hundred guineas in it."

"So much?"

"Yes, quite; besides that, I saw a roll of notes that are worth something. Why, he had a small fortune about him, such as we don't meet every day."

"We do not, indeed."

"Well, then, are we to let this go by, and not have it?"

"Not if we can get it."

"But how can we get it?"

"How?"

"That's the question; cutting his throat would be making such a mess; it would bring suspicion. Besides, there would be too much noise."

"So there would; but we might overpower him and smother him."

"Stun him first."

"Yes—yes."

"Well, that is easily done; but not in the room, because there are several strangers; and the best thing we can do is to do it as quietly as possible. Get him out of the room somehow or other first quietly."

"Well, well, arrange as you will; we divide the spoil?"

"Of course we do."

"That is agreed upon," said one of the voices.

"Yes, quite; we will manage it between ourselves; but now let's return to the saloon, or we may be missed."

The two left the room, and disappeared altogether.

Poor Minna never before heard of anything half so dreadful. Murder was to be committed; she, too, in the house in which it was to be committed. What were her feelings? She, the confidant of murderers!—unwillingly so, but yet she was the possessor of their secret.

What could she do? She could not save the person who was to be murdered, for where was he? She had not seen him. True it was, she had heard enough to understand who was meant, if she saw him; but how to see him was the question. She knew not how to frame an answer.

See him she must; and yet what could she do where all were so much stronger than she? It would be impossible to do anything by force, and any other means seemed equally hopeless.

Her thoughts were suddenly interrupted by the entrance of some one, who approached the bed with a candle, and threw off the sheet.

"Come, are you awake yet? You've had rest enough, I think. Are you any better yet?"

"I am better," said Minna, sadly; "and should ere this have been better, had it not so happened that I was dragged from my grave."

"Ay, that's always the way. But no matter; you will soon know how to enjoy yourself, without any fear of the future. You'll soon get a living and thank nobody. I see you've been afraid of starving, and all that sort of thing. Lord love you, we never dream of such things. Come, get up."

Minna obeyed the injunctions given her, and rose up.

"Ah! you are a likely lass enough. Who knows but you may please some gentleman or other. You'll be a made woman now. Never fret and stew yourself; we are all merry here."

"Where am I to go?" Minna inquired of her.

"Into the saloon."

"What place is that?"

"Oh, there are many people there—many of us; and there are some gentlemen there with loads of money."

Minna said nothing. She was passive; she felt she was in desperate hands, and scarcely cared what became of herself; and, besides, she had a great object in view—to save some unfortunate person from a dreadful death. She therefore determined to go.

"You will do very well; so come along, and take no notice of what is said or done, because things often happen by accident that are not meant."

Minna followed her conductress into a large room, that appeared to be fitted up as a gambling-room. Billiards, and card-tables, and seats were to be seen in different places. There were side-tables, where there was wine and other refreshments in profusion.

The place was fitted up voluptuously, or in a manner that was intended to be so; but there was, indeed, a contrast between this place and that of Lady Clare's. The difference was great and striking, but the aim and object of both were the same.

It did not take Minna many minutes to distinguish the person she had heard described. He was among the most heedless of the group of gamblers, and had the air of a man used to society, and cared not for money.

He had just taken up a sum of money he had won, and put it into his pocket, as he turned his gaze round the room at the females who were present, when his eye suddenly encountered the features of Minna.

Upon her his eyes rested with an evident look of surprise and interest. She could not but cast her eyes down with shame at her own situation.

"Ha! what have we here?" he exclaimed, suddenly leaving the table, and coming towards her—"what pretty nymph have we here?"

As he spoke he took her hand, and attempted to kiss her lips; but she shrunk back with terror, which caused him some mirth, and he said,—

"Well, come, you are an actress too. I did not expect that; but we shall be better acquainted before long."

"If you will allow me to speak a word to you unheard by others," said Minna, speaking low in his ear, "I can tell you something that concerns your safety."

He took no notice of the request; but after a little while he led her aside, of which no notice was taken, and then said,—

"Speak softly, and tell me what it is you have to say, my pretty dear."

"Your life is in danger."

"My life?"

"Yes; you will be murdered for the gold and notes you have about you. Be as quick and as quiet as you can, and get out of the house, or your life is forfeited."

"And you—will you remain after this? Will you come too?"

"If I was sure they would only kill me, I would not care; but, as it is, I fear my fate would be a dreadful one."

"Then, come along; I will go now."

He turned round, and was about to leave the room, when he was met by a blow from a man who had listened to all that had taken place. The gentleman staggered, but he recovered himself sufficiently to fell the man to the earth.

" Take care of yourselves, and follow me," he said to some of the strangers whom he knew, or who had entered in his company.

The lights were all extinguished in an instant ; but he had seized Minna by the waist, and with her had reached the door.

There was a desperate struggle, and heavy blows were given and taken, and many were struck at random, and struck those they were not intended to strike.

After a desperate fray of some minutes, the individual succeeded in winning his way down the stairs, and had nearly reached the door ; but was met by the porter with a bludgeon.   Here the light over the door gave them an opportunity to see who was friend or foe, and he had certainly been killed, but for Minna, who seized the porter's arm, and in another moment the man lay prostrate, and his weapon in the hands of her preserver.

A few moments more, and they stood in the street, the fresh air of the morning fanning their heated brows ; and then, after a pause, the gentleman hurried off some distance from the spot.

CHAPTER XX.

CAPTAIN HARDING IN HIS SHIP.—THE TAUNT.—THE CHALLENGE.

THE very last man in this world which one would have supposed Captain Harding at all anxious to see, was, undoubtedly, Lieutenant Heartwell ; but yet he no sooner, to a certain extent, got over the first feelings of positive alarm that had come over him upon his reflecting concerning the amount of misery he had necessarily brought upon Minna Woodward, than his own implacable feelings of revenge against Heartwell returned in full force ; and he congratulated himself upon the opportunity that would soon be his, of wringing the heart of the man who had compelled him to submit to the indignity of an act of personal violence he, Harding, could never forget.

That unlucky occasion on which he had been by Heartwell so summarily and so effectually projected from the window of the old Gun Tavern, was one which never could by any possibility be effaced from his memory.

Doubtless, on those occasions when Harding felt that he could have acted a better as well as a wiser part in not involving himself in the desperate villany which had been enacted towards poor Minna, it was when, for a few brief moments, he forgot the bitter and demoniac feelings that possessed him at the time when the strong grasp of the justly incensed Heartwell was upon his throat, and he felt how vain it was to attempt any resistance against one who was so much his superior in physical power.

When, however, this occurrence did cross his mind, he always indulged in the most bitter invectives against Heartwell, and quite reconciled himself to any act of atrocity which should eventually promise him an ample revenge.

"What have I," he would mutter, " placed him in the position he now occupies for ? Why have I made him the envy of many, by letting him occupy a station courted by all, but that, by so temporarily exalting him, I may make his ruin the more certain and the more complete, as well as accompanying it with an amount of mental anguish which I know he will feel to its uttermost."

So far as regarded the means which Harding had taken to accomplish such a result as this, he was acting with the greatest foresight, for on all occasions the discipline of the navy had been of the strictest character ; and now that war was raging, and the thunder of hostile cannons not unfrequently resounded on our very coasts, a captain of a ship of war was invested with an amount of authority which set all calculation at defiance.

Indeed, the only thing wrong that any one holding a command could possibly do, was to fail in beating the enemy ; and that, to do but the commonest justice to our navy, was a thing rarely indeed omitted to be done, and that most effectually, too.

Under these circumstances, therefore, Captain Harding, once on board his own vessel, could, if he chose, be the ruin of any one of his officers.

That the peculiar position in which he could place Heartwell, by letting him know something of the injury which had been done to him, would tempt the latter to the commission of some act of desperation, easily construed to be one of the most flagrant breaches of discipline, might be as fairly calculated upon as if, by some prescience, the action had been seen accurately in time to come.

A challenge—a blow—even such words as might be considered subversive of discipline, would be quite sufficient to ruin Lieutenant Heartwell in a profession he was in every respect so highly qualified to adorn, and to lend a lustre to by his brilliant achievements.

And was it in human nature that he should not be tempted to an exhibition of feeling? Was it likely that, with the remotest hint upon the subject of the dreadful fate of Minna, he should be able to consider with calmness upon the relative positions of himself and Harding?

No; all would be forgotten, but the fact that he, Harding, had destroyed his, Heartwell's, happiness for ever, and that revenge, or rather justice, against the evil-doer could be had.

Then he would do some deed, which, no doubt, Harding would find an amply sufficient excuse for effecting his destruction.

It would almost seem that a less artificial mode could have been adopted by Harding of effecting this object had he chosen; and, unscrupulous as he was as to how he effected his ends, he might, unquestionably, have succeeded in achieving a revenge against Heartwell, sufficient even to satisfy himself, with less trouble and personal difficulty than his persecution of him was likely to cost on board the Eolus frigate. But then we must recollect that, at the moment when Harding was casting about for some means of accomplishing his purposes, the opportunity of destroying Heartwell in this way had almost been placed in his very hands.

And not only was this the case but, by the appointment of Heartwell to be the first lieutenant, he had laid up a good opinion of himself and his discretion in his uncle's breast, which was not likely to be easily eradicated.

When, therefore, a man's revenge and his interests pull in the same direction, there can be but little difficulty in predicting the course he will pursue; and hence was it that Harding never for a moment regretted that he had made up his mind to place Heartwell in such a position? His whole anxiety now was to regain his ship; and although for a time the news of what had occurred, and of the achievements of the very man whom he wished to ruin, were to him subjects of bitter reflection; yet, by the time he reached the seaport where, from information he had received, he found he could join the Eolus, his worst feelings had again resumed their sway; and, with a full recollection of the personal indignity he had suffered from the hands of Heartwell, he panted for his revenge.

We will pass over the preliminaries which heralded the advent of Harding's appearance on the deck of his own vessel.

The Eolus was some few miles at sea; and he reached it on board a small sailing-yatch, which he engaged for the purpose.

His uniform proclaimed his rank; and he was likewise remembered by some of the crew, who had seen him come on board at Portsmouth, so that in a few moments, with all the customary honours, he stood upon the quarter-deck in full command.

Lieutenant Heartwell, who had hastily slipped on his uniform coat, now approached him; and these two young men confronted each other, for the first time, both in their proper characters.

As Heartwell looked in the face of his captain, a dreamy sort of reminiscence came over him, that, although apparently so, it was not really for the first time. When, however, or under what circumstances, he had beheld him, he found it impossible to hazard a conjecture. Nothing was more unlikely that he should associate the Honourable Bulkley Harding, captain of his Majesty's ship Eolus, with the impertinent ruffian he had been compelled to expel by force of arms from the Ship Tavern at Wapping. And yet, the more he looked, the more he felt convinced that they had met before; and along with that conviction, he felt that the circumstances under which they had met were not of an agreeable character; beyond that fact, however, memory would not carry him; and, with a sense of great discomfort, he in vain tried to chase through his brain some event, which he ever seemed to be upon the point of over taking, but never was likely to do so.

There was a strange sneering kind of expression, too, upon the face of Harding, an expression which, if he had met with it upon the face of any one in private society, would fully have justified him in turning upon his heel and treating with marked indifference that individual.

But now he was very differently situated—Harding was his commanding officer, and as such could command an outward deference and show of respect from him, whatever might be his real feelings.

"I shall be extremely happy to report to you at once, sir, the proceedings of the vessel previous to your joining her."

"When you please," said Harding. "I hope I shall find everything to my satisfaction."

There was not so much in these words themselves, as in the manner in which they were spoken, which made them offensive, and but that he recollected the relative position in which he stood to his captain, an rejoinder feeling would have come from Heartwell's lips; as it was, however, he merely bowed and stood aside, waiting for orders.

The ship was put under weigh, and Harding retired to his cabin to open some sealed instructions he had received relative to the cruize upon which the vessel was to be engaged.

From that day Heartwell's troubles began, and it would be as tiring, perhaps, to the patience of the reader as it was to his, to retail all the petty annoyances to which Captain Harding found occasion to subject him; in fact, it would appear that so far as Harding was concerned, the faults of Heartwell might have been summed up under two heads—there was nothing right he said, and nothing right he did.

And yet Captain Harding was so scrupulously, yet so sneeringly polite; and if he said anything of an ungentlemanly character, he took care it should be said when no witnesses were by to hear it.

All this went on until it was quite evident to Heartwell that Harding wished to goad him to some act of insubordination which should give him an excuse for founding an accusation against him of a character to ruin his professional prospects.

A captain who feels so disposed towards any of his officers seldom fails, among the officers of a vessel, to find some one ready enough to assist him by becoming his confederate.

It was in the surgeon of the vessel that Harding found a cringing sycophant, who, he felt certain would be quite ready, at any time, to swear to anything or do anything.

This man, who, from disrepute on shore, had been compelled to gain his living in his professional capacity afloat, soon saw that a hatred of the most violent character subsisted between the captain and the first lieutenant, and he had no difficulty in making up his mind which party it was most desirable for him to side with.

And Harding, although he made no positive confidence with this man, yet let him see that he esteemed his services, and that he was always welcome to the chief cabin with any tale to the prejudice of Heartwell.

Still the difficulty was to get Heartwell to do anything which should give Harding an opportunity of reporting him, and after some time spent in a series of petty aggravations, he determined upon making an effort of a more serious nature.

Affecting a cordiality as new as it was deceitful, he invited Heartwell to dinner in his own cabin, the only other guest being the surgeon, who, without there being any actual understanding, felt there was an implied one, to the effect that he was to be there as a spy upon everything that was said or done, and just to recollect so much of it as was convenient for Captain Harding's purposes afterwards.

Most gladly would Heartwell have escaped the infliction of this dinner, but it was an usual thing in the service for the captain so to invite his officers, and there was no such thing as getting out of it.

At the appointed hour, in full dress, he appeared at the captain's table, where he was received with a lofty kind of freezing courtesy, which, while it promised that the dinner could not be a very pleasant one, still was much preferred by Heartwell to the mock good friendship with which the invitation had been given.

The dinner passed off well enough, and the conversation took a general turn, concerning the service and the state and prospects of the war; but after the cloth was removed, and wine placed upon the table, Captain Harding shewed a disposition to become much more familiar, and raising a glass of the generous liquor to his lips, he said,—

"I will give you a toast, Mr. Heartwell."

"I have no doubt I shall drink it with pleasure," said Heartwell, as he filled his glass.

"Of course, you will; it is as old as the hills, and as respectable. 'Sweethearts and wives.'"

"With all my heart, Captain Harding; although I do not rejoice in the latter article, I will drink the toast."

"But you do not repudiate the former?"

There was a slight accession of colour on the cheek of the young man as he thus found himself almost cajoled into an admission that he was not fancy free, and after a slight pause, he said,—

"That is a subject, sir, that concerns a man so much individually, that I think he had better keep it to himself."

"Nay, Lieutenant Heartwell, I have no such scruples," said the captain; "I have sweathearts by the score, although, like you, no wife; and the only regret I felt at taking a command at this juncture, was that I had to leave on shore one of the most tempting pieces of feminine humanity that ever mortal eyes looked upon."

See page 90.

"Indeed, sir," said Heartwell, coldly, for there was an air of libertinism in Harding's manner, which he was far from liking.

"Yes," continued Harding; "I am not particular as to station or locality, I have run down my game in all situations, and under all circumstances."

"These things are matters of taste," said Heartwell, calmly.

"True, they are; and as long as one exercises a judicious taste, one is entitled to all the credit of being an excellent connoisseur."

"How remarkably true," said the surgeon.

"It is ; but now, Heartwell, let's have your toast."

"Freely," said Heartwell, 'Honour in War as in Love ;' in my opinion, the man is a greater coward who betrays a woman than he who betrays his country."

" Indeed !" said Harding ; " you ought to have been the ship's chaplain instead of her first lieutenant ; but, however, every one to his taste, and since we have drunk your evangelical toast, here's another."

" Really, gentlemen," said the surgeon, " this is very pleasant ; you are amazingly good company, both of you. I drink your toast with great pleasure, Captain Harding, and so I do yours, Lieutenant Heartwell."

The glasses were filled, and Harding said, in a clear voice,—

"Here's to the beauty of Wapping."

"And who may she be ?" said Heartwell, deliberately.

" Minna Woodward, only daughter of some people who keep a dirty hole, called the Ship Tavern."

" Minna Woodward, sir ?"

" Yes ; you stare as if you knew her."

" I do know her, Captain Harding."

" I thought you did, by your looks ; and what do you think of her ? Does she not merit all the eulogium I can bestow upon her ? Saw you ever her equal ? Is she not perfectly peerless in her charms."

" It is not for me, Captain Harding," said Heartwell, gravely ; " to detract from praises of Minna Woodward ; I know the family."

" Oh d——n the family, that's always the worst of it. One can't know a pretty girl but what one must be introduced to the family."

" Very good, very good," said the doctor ; " upon my soul that's very good. D——n the family. Ah, to be sure, that is the worst of it. What have you got to say to that, Lieutenant Heartwell ?"

" Nothing further," said Heartwell, " but to request that this subject may be dropped ; or, that if Minna Woodward's name must be mentioned, that it be mentioned with respect."

" Well, that's cool," said Harding, " at any rate ; I mustn't speak of a pretty girl, I suppose, for fear of offending your notions of propriety. D——n all saints, say I, I don't want any on board the Eolus."

" Sir," said Harding, " it seems that upon this, as well as upon every other subject, we are doomed to disagree."

" Agree or disagree, as you please," said Harding ; " I rather think I shall please myself in saying what I like in my own cabin ; and I here declare, that Minna Woodward is the prettiest girl I know, and that I had more trouble to tear myself from her delightful society than from any other tie which bound me to shore."

" From her society, did you say, sir ?"

" Yes, I did. The night previous to my departure from London, was made short by being pressed in her arms."

" Liar !" exclaimed Heartwell, as he sprang to his feet, and made a catch at Harding's throat, which gave the table at which they sat such a tilt, that the whole of its contents were shovelled into his lap.

The doctor called loudly for assistance, and in a few moments several officers rushed in, and separated them.

" Enough," said Captain Harding. " Mr. Roberts, you have been a witness to the courtesy with which I treated Lieutenant Heartwell, as well as to the gross outrage he has committed upon me. Lieutenant Heartwell, you may consider yourself under arrest, and keep your cabin."

" Captain Harding," said Heartwell, " for some reasons best known to yourself, from the first moment you set foot on board this vessel, you have subjected me to a series of annoyances and persecutions, which I have been forced to meet with such patience and fortitude as I could command ; that you invited me here to-day to insult me, and to drive me past the bounds of all ordinary patience, I feel thoroughly convinced ; and what may be your detestable motive, in thus plotting and planning for my destruction, I cannot guess ; but that you are a villain of the blackest dye, I feel assured ; and I here defy you to your teeth, and brand you as the defamer of innocence, and the subverter of the truth."

" This is well, gentlemen," said Harding, turning to the officers ; " the most charitable supposition is, that Lieutenant Heartwell is mad. Remove him. In the course of a week, or less, probably, I expect to join the combined fleet, and a court-martial shall then decide upon his conduct."

Heartwell was removed in custody of a file of marines to his cabin, at the door of which a sentinel was duly posted; and, as well may be supposed, the greatest excitement prevailed throughout the vessel, in consequence of the extraordinary circumstances that had taken place in the captain's cabin, and concerning which all sorts of extraordinary rumours found currency.

Heartwell was a great favourite with the crew, as such a manly and successful officer as he was sure to be; but the powerful habits of discipline on board ships of war kept down all murmuring, save in whispering among themselves; so that, to all appearance, Harding had fully succeeded in crushing one whose only crime had been that he had stepped forward to the rescue of innocence and virtue.

And what shall we say of the state of mind to which Heartwell was reduced? How shall we attempt to depict the various wild surmises which found a place in his now excited imagination! Over and over again, he asked himself how it could be possible that Captain Harding should know how accessible he was to be wounded through the name of Minna Woodward.

This to him was an unfathomable mystery; but, oh! if he could have imagined but for one moment that what Captain Harding had stated was substantially correct, what agony would have been his! At least, he was spared that much; for there came not across his mind a doubt of the purity and excellence of his much-loved Minna.

CHAPTER XXI.
MINNA'S NEW HOME.——THE DOWNWARD PATH.

"And who are you?" said Minna's companion to her, when they were clear from the desperate house in which they had first met, and breathing the purer and cooler air of the streets.

"Do not ask me," she said; "I am an outcast—a wanderer."

"But you have done me essential service, and I would fain know to whom I am indebted."

"Nay, it matters not. Do you think I could see a fellow-creature perish, without making an effort for his preservation? I have done for you what I would have done for any one; so do not fancy that I am entitled to extraordinary thanks. It has been a duty of the commonest description."

"But you talk of being an outcast and a wanderer. Do you think that I have no feelings of common gratitude, that would induce me to endeavour to save you from such a state?"

"You know not to whom you speak," said Minna; "I am beneath your sympathy. One so fallen as I am may well be excused from giving to herself a once honourable name and description."

"But what is to become of you?"

"I know not."

"Have you no resource?"

"Oh! yes, yes—I have a resource."

"And what is it?"

"In death—that death which I hope soon will come to take me from a world which can have no possible charms for me. I long for it; and but that I feel the Almighty has signified his displeasure against those who would unbidden seek his presence, I should willingly—most willingly—seek a refuge for myself from all misery beneath the river's rolling tide."

The stranger did not speak for some minutes, and then he said, in an expostulating tone,—

"You are young and you are beautiful. I need not affect to misunderstand you. You have become the victim of some one who has reduced you to your present condition. I will not, if you urgently wish the contrary, press you to tell me who you are; but I offer you freely and frankly a refuge. I am myself peculiarly situated, and can offer you a home, if you will accept it."

Minna scarcely knew what she said, or what she was pledging herself to, when, after about half an hour's more conversation, she accompanied the stranger, who paused before a respectable-looking house, the door of which he opened with a key he took from his pocket.

"Come in," he said, "without fear; there is no one here to interrupt you, or to say anything to you. I do not as yet feel myself authorised, upon our very short acquaintance, in detailing to you the mode in which I live. You will find here, however, every comfort and some luxuries; the only thing is you must wait upon yourself."

" Most willingly," said Minna. " Can I be sufficiently thankful ?"

She found that the house was handsomely furnished, and it seemed to be most mysterious that no person was visible except her guide, and after a time he left her in an apartment by herself, after pointing out to her some provisions in a bureau, and telling her she might rest in perfect security.

Wearied and exhausted by recent events, Minna soon sunk into a profound sleep, nor did she awake until the bright sunshine was streaming into the apartment, and falling upon her face.

It was strange how complete had been the mental transformation which had been taking place in Minna—a kind of reckless disregard of the future had found a home in her heart. She had even no plans, no hopes, no wishes; the utter impossibility of again occupying the place in society which once she held, prostrated every energy. She had fallen, and she seemed now to consider her existence a kind of pilgrimage towards the tomb, the circumstances or the sufferings connected with which it was not worth while making an effort to alter or alleviate.

She was heart-stricken, and beaten down completely by that blow of fate ; and probably now she did not commit suicide, more because she lacked the energy to do so, than for the reason which she assigned to the man who had taken her under his protection.

It was singular, too, but every hour which she remained away from home increased her dread and horror of returning to it.

It seemed as if every sympathetic tie which had once bound her to that place was lost, and any fate seemed preferable to that of living an object of pity or of shame in her father's house.

It was false reasoning—frightfully false reasoning. And now what Minna wanted was some friend full of disinterestedness, and capable, by high mental power, of exercising an influence over her which should enable her to see her real position. Such a friend, which, alas! she had not, would have awakened her to the fact, that, although she had been betrayed and injured, yet there was no necessity for her discarding all hopes of serenity, if not of happiness, and that, although she had committed the first false step of becoming infatuated with the allurements of Lady Clare's glittering mansion, she had by no means sunk so low as to forfeit the respect of the good and the virtuous ; but, alas! there was no one to tell her this—she had nothing but the whisperings of her own fancy to appeal to. She could only tell herself that she had fallen, that she was degraded, that she could never again look upon her young companions, or associate with the dear friends of her happy youth. And this was a feeling that was likely to grow upon her, respecting which a short time would probably render indisputable.

Alas! Minna Woodward, we dread, with a feeling of bitterness and anguish, the toil of tracing the frightful downward path you are doomed to tread. But, think as we may, it must be done ; and let who may be involved in these frightful proceedings, which shall herald your own destruction, we have a duty to perform in chronicling events which we see pictured forth in the future; may they serve as a warning rather than an example to the young and the beautiful.

A week has elapsed, and Minna is in her new home. It is needless to say in what capacity. As the mistress of the man whose life she had saved, she took yet another step downwards in that path of iniquity which appeared to be so broad and open for her.

And yet the mystery of how this man lived remained to her as profound as ever ; she had promised him that she would make no effort to discover it, and that she would never descend lower in the house than its parlour. She had likewise solemnly engaged that whatever she should hear in the way of opening and shutting of doors, or the movement of feet, should not induce her to move from one particular room while those sounds proceeded, and she had religiously kept her word.

Probably it was with somewhat of surprise to the ostensible master of the house that she had so kept her word ; and it might be that became the principal reason why he at length thought proper to place an amount of confidence in her which suddenly, and without her solicitation, he now did.

She had told him, as a matter of course, who and what she was, so that he was enabled to address her by her proper name ; and now, as they sat together in social and friendly intercourse, he said to her,—

" Minna Woodward, you have kept your word so well with me, and trusted me so implicitly, that I cannot but, in return, repose in you the utmost confidence."

"I hope that I deserve your confidence," said Minna; "and yet, I beg you to with-hold it if you have the shadow of a doubt that I do so."

"I have no doubt whatever; and you will understand when I do inform you of my real situation, that it was more kind to keep you in the dark regarding it, than thoroughly to awaken you to its dangers."

"Indeed," said Minna; "you alarm me."

"But yet, by keeping your own counsel, I hope that the danger of your position will be but a nominal one. You must have perceived that nothing is wanting here to constitute a life of luxury and enjoyment; you must see that there is money enough for all purposes; and now I tell you frankly, Minna, that the way in which all that is accomplished is by the doubtful dishonesty of cheating the government."

"I really do not understand you," said Minna; "how can you cheat the government?"

"I requested you when first you came here, you will recollect, not to venture below the precincts of the basement floor of the house."

"You did."

"Nor to heed any sounds you might hear, whatever their nature, proceeding from the lower regions."

"Most certainly; and I have obeyed your injunctions to the very letter."

"Have you ever heard of any such sounds?"

"I have, frequently."

"And what did they resemble?"

"That I can scarcely tell; it seemed to me as if a number of men were at work in some singular way; and occasionally strange hissing sounds, and the rushing of water, have come upon my ears."

"You are quite right; and I tell you at once, and frankly, that one of the most extensive systems of illicit distillation of spirits is carried on beneath this house that London and its exigences ever called into existence."

"Indeed."

"Yes; for more than two years now, unsuspected by the authorities, large sums have been made in this way. The concern belongs to me; my confederates have been faithful; my machinery perfect, and my sales rapid; my profits immense; and now, Minna Woodward, I have trusted you with the secret which will enable you any day you like to make me the inmate of a prison."

"Would to Heaven, then," said Minna, "you had not trusted it to me; and yet, I know not why I say so, for it is as safe in my keeping as it could possibly be in yours; and perhaps, now that I know it, should any circumstances of danger arise, I shall be the better able to act with advantage and effect for you."

"Nay, now, mark me; let what will happen, keep yourself free from a suspicion of knowing what is really going on. With the greatest difficulty I have induced my confederates to believe that you may be safely and entirely trusted, and, therefore, now you will not be so dull as you have been in this house, because you will be able to come down stairs and watch the really interesting process of our illicit manufacture of spirits."

"If I may do so," said Minna, "without bringing trouble or dissatisfaction upon you, I shall be glad."

"You will not bring the least; on the contrary, your presence, occasionally, will, I am certain, have a cheering and beneficial effect upon us all. There are rough fellows amongst us—men who require the influence of some feminine spirit to keep them in curb, and if you will not disdain the office, will do me much pleasure by merely showing yourself occasionally amongst them."

"Most assuredly I will. Heaven knows I owe you much. I have, at least, had peace since I have been here, and no reproaches, many of which would, assuredly, have been showered upon me elsewhere."

"Hark!" said the man, as a bell suddenly sounded in the lower part of the house. "They're commencing operations, and that is a signal for me—you can accompany me at once."

Minna trembled a little, as she hung upon her companion's arm, and descended to the passage of the house.

"Come, come!" he said, "do not be alarmed—there is nothing to fear. The process of distillation is one of the simplest of chemical operations, and there is nothing at all dangerous or disagreeable connected with it. You will be much amused as well as edified."

"I do not doubt but I shall."

She hung on his arm and they descended the staircase leading to the kitchen, and during their progress, he whispered to her—

" It was only after much anxious search that this house was found. It has most extensive vaults, which suits our purpose well, and by the precautions we take, not the least notion can pervade the neighbourhood of what is going on in them. Luckily, there is a public-house at the back, so that if even any one detects the scent of spirits, it is attributed to that establishment, and no one dreams, for a moment, that it comes from here."

As they descended, Minna heard a confused hum of occupation, and occasionally a fitful glare of light shot across her path ; but how astonished was she when she really got below, to find herself in an extensive subterranean vault, dimly lighted to be sure, but yet sufficiently to enable her to see its extent, and that it was filled with apparatus of different descriptions, whilst some dozen or more men were bustling about, and the air was pregnant with the odour of spirits.

" This is quite a new scene to me," she said. " And do you mean to tell me that you make spirituous compounds here ?"

" Yes, certainly ; a very large quantity of raw spirits is manufactured on these premises. I am, ostensibly, the proprietor of a distillery a short distance from this place, between which and this house we have a short underground communication, so that everything is managed very nicely."

" And yet I tremble for your safety. What would be the probable consequence of a discovery ?"

" The loss of everything, and immense pecuniary liabilities, which would involve me in prison for life !"

" And can you risk such consequences for the sake of gain merely ?"

" Why, the fact is, a few years of it is a tempting little fortune, and, you know, as regards the morality of the thing, it's not likely to lay heavily upon our conscience. Do you see that immense vat ?"

" Yes ; it reaches to within a few feet of the ceiling !"

" It does ; and holds a thousand gallons of spirit! We have five such here, as you perceive."

" I do, indeed! You carry on your system largely !"

" If you please, sir," said a man coming up to him at that moment, " Arrowsmith, the new man, seems rather skulking from his work. We don't like him, sir."

" Oh! nonsense—nonsense ! I can assure you, and you may assure your companions, likewise, that I have brought him here most advisedly. The recommendations I had with him were indisputable, and there can be no doubt of his good faith. Perhaps he's tired— show him a little indulgence."

" As you please, sir. Here he comes to speak for himself."

As he spoke, a man came slowly up, putting on his coat.

" I've had enough of this, Mr. Monks," he said, addressing Minna's protector.

" What do you mean ?"

The fellow seemed a little intoxicated—probably he was, or he would have been more cautious ; but he assumed a swaggering gait, and rolled his head from side to side, as if he were the monarch of all he surveyed, and could just do what he pleased.

" You're driving a good trade here," he said. " It's all very fine ; but the knowing ones will be down upon you some day. Now just look at me. How precious green you must be, Mr. Monks ; you ought to know every metropolitan exciseman by sight. How do you feel now ? Ten o'clock by G—! and they'll be here directly. You're sold, old fellow. Take it easy."

" An exciseman !" said Monks, stepping back.

These words sounded like magic in that subterranean abode. The confederates of Monks rushed forward at the sound, and, even as they did so, a sharp, shrill whistle was heard from the street.

" There they are," said the half-drunken fool, who had made his way among such desperate men.

He tried to place a whistle to his own lips, but it was dashed from his hands ; and then, while Minna, in the greatest alarm, clung to Monks, he said,—

" Throw him into one of the vats."

" No, no, no !" said Minna. " Would you murder him ?"

" Hush, hush !" whispered Monks. " They know what I mean. No. 5 is empty, and he can't get out. It will give all of us time to escape. Of course, this is a contingency calculated upon sooner or later, and, as far as possible, provided for."

The men seized upon the unfortunate exciseman, who uttered a yell of terror, and then shouted,—

" Murder—murder! help! You're not going to murder me, surely? I'm an exciseman, and only doing my duty. Let me go. Help—help—murder!"

His cries were useless. He was lifted up by two stalwart fellows by a leg and an arm each, and, after being canted to and fro for several seconds, he was tilted into one of the vats.

" Now," said Monks, " you all know where to go, and what to do. Come along, Minna, this way."

" Please, sir," said one of the men, " before you go, just for satisfaction's sake, which was the empty vat?"

" Number five."

" D—d if I didn't think I heard a splash. He's in number four."

" What?"

" Number four, as sure as eggs is eggs, sir. He did slip in uncommonly quick, in consequence of its being so full, I suppose. Well, I am blowed!"

" Then we're all ruined!" said Monks. " This is too serious. I never thought of adding murder to the affair; and what will become of us now, Heaven only knows!"

There was such a tremendous knocking at the door at this moment, that it was evident if such blows were long continued, it must be broken down.

" Put out the lights," said Monks, vehemently. " Harkye, my men! this is a most unfortunate night's work. We shall never get any one to believe but that we murdered this man designedly. I will meet you all, you know where; and may Heaven desert me, if I desert any one of you!"

The lights in the subterranean vaults were all extinguished, and at the same moment the street door of the house was burst from its hinges, and the trampling of feet was heard in the passage and rooms above.

CHAPTER XXII.

THE ESCAPE.—MINNA'S TERROR.—THE FUGITIVES, AND THE HOUSE AT BATTERSEA.

THE sudden extinguishing of the lights left the place in such a state of absolute gloom, that for some moments it was impossible to distinguish any one object from another; and had Minna been left to her own resources, with her entire ignorance of the locality, there can be no doubt that she would have fallen into some great danger, or probably met with death itself.

As it was, however, the powerful arm of her protector grasped her round the waist, and she felt herself now hurried on with a speed which, had she wished, she could not have controlled, and which her physical powers prevented her in any way assisting.

" Courage, courage!" whispered Monk. " Rely wholly upon me, and be assured you will be safe. Nothing can harm you, for we have resources yet, known only to ourselves."

" Oh! but the death of that man—the dreadful death!"

" I deplore it; but it cannot be helped now; he was mad to bring himself into such danger."

" His death was no accident."

" I fear not; but what can I do? You know I'm utterly helpless now; once in that vat no human power could save him. Think no more of him I pray you; he has his own imprudence to thank for the catastrophe, frightful as it is. Come on—come on!"

They traversed a variety of intricate passages, and Minna was wondering whither they could possibly lead, when suddenly a gleam of lamplight seemed to come from a narrow opening in the roof.

" Where are we?" she said. " Where are we?"

" A whole street off from the subterranean vault. Yonder is a grating, which I have the means of moving, and which will allow us to emerge into an open thoroughfare; there I trust we shall be comparatively safe, at least, we shall have no occasion to proceed with the speed we have hitherto done, which, doubtless, fatigues you."

" No, no! think of yourself—think of yourself. What do you propose to do?"

" Why, to tell the truth, I hardly know now; the death of that fellow has thoroughly altered the aspect of everything; but for that most unlucky circumstance, I had everything well arranged; but now I really fear there will be great trouble, for there is not one among us now, who might not purchase immunity for himself by impeaching his companions."

" Oh! then do not meet them."

" Do you feel sufficient interest for me, Minna Woodward, to induce you to utter those words from your heart ?"

" Alas !" said Minna ; " my heart, as you well know, has been blighted, more fearfully blighted, than as if my best affections were in the grave ; but, although my constant prayers to Heaven are, that I may never meet with him who first won my tenderest affections, yet I cannot be insensible to feelings of gratitude. You have not betrayed me. I can accuse you of nothing—not even of an unkind word or look. Do not fancy me, then, dead to all human feeling, as not to feel an interest in your welfare."

" I will not, Minna ; and if this should be the last moment of our meeting, I will say that some of the happiest hours I have known, have been spent in your company. It may be necessary that I may be compelled to seek my safety in a foreign land. I did think that if such a necessity did arise, of going alone ; but I will not do so if you will bear me company in my involuntary exile."

" Oh! gladly, gladly !"

" Then that is arranged. Say no more, Minna, of it, but pause here a moment while I remove the grating that keeps us now from light and liberty."

This was speedily accomplished, for it had been loosened before from below, in such a manner that but a small amount of force was requisite for such a result ; and then, having scrambled through himself into the street, he assisted Minna to do so, and they were, comparatively, at liberty, and free from the consequences of the unexpected crime which had been committed in the vault devoted to the purposes of illicit distillation.

Scarcely had this much been accomplished and they began to breathe a little more freely, when a man pounced upon them both, and seizing Monks by the collar, exclaimed,—

" You're my prisoner. Where did you come from, that you thought you escaped so easy ?"

" From a wrestling county," said Monks, " where I was considered an adept. Where did you ?"

Even as he spoke, he gave the man such a tremendous fall that he rebounded again from the pavingstones on which he was thrown, and then lay perfectly insensible before them.

All this had been done so rapidly, that Minna had scarcely time to utter an exclamation of terror before it was over, and then, in such a state of agitation, that but for the support of Monks she must have fallen, she clung to his arm, exclaiming,—

" Oh! this is terrible—this is terrible! Where will the events of this night end ?"

" Hush! be calm—the worst is past—the worst must be past, and now, indeed, we are in safety—believe me, indeed it is so. Walk if you can, not quickly, but firmly ; now—now—come on !"

" I will strive," said Minna, " for your sake as well as for my own."

There was no further opposition to their progress, and they traversed several streets, each moment increasing the distance between them and the illicit distillery, until the assurance of safety began to lend fresh strength to Minna, and fresh cheerfulness to her companion.

That he was morally guiltless of the death of the exciseman she felt certain, whatever might be the case as regarded his confederates, who might not have been near so scrupulous as he was in taking a life, and who really might, with malice aforethought, have thrown the unhappy object of their resentment into No. 4, instead of No. 5.

But be this as it might, there could be no question of the legal responsibility of Monks for the act, and the great danger that was likely to fall upon him as a consequence of it.

Minna could not but perceive, by the expression of the countenance of her companion, occasional glimpses of which she got as they now and then passed a gas-lamp, that he was more anxious about the consequences of the night's proceedings than he chose to confess to her ; and this observation, as a matter of course, tended to give her a vast amount of disquietude.

After a time she adverted to what he had himself alluded to—namely, the propriety and expediency of leaving England entirely, and finding both safety and comfort in another country.

" You will never," she said, " be happy in England."

" I fear not, Minna," he replied.

" Or safe."

" No ; nor safe."

" Then you will, as soon as it shall become possible so to do, carry out your intention of leaving."

" Yes.   But this murder of the exciseman—for a murder it will be called—increases the risk and the difficulty most tremendously.   No foreign government would give up a man merely accused of an infringement of the laws of excise ; but when a charge of murder can be associated with his name, I fear that such would be quite sufficient to induce them to betray me to my enemies."

" But in America, for example, you would surely be in comparative safety ?"

" Yes, if I could bring my mind to go there.   If I were really guilty of murder, I should not for a moment hesitate to find a refuge in America ; but the very going there would be a kind of confession of guilt which I do not feel inclined to make."

See page 111.

" It is so.   I have heard such an opinion expressed by many persons before."

" Well, well, Minna, do not vex yourself about me.   Where I am now conducting is, I believe, a place where we may consider ourselves perfectly safe."

" Where is that ?"

" Some distance up the river I have a friend, in whose house we shall be perfectly secure until the first flush of pursuit has worn away, and I am able with some degree of confidence to venture abroad."

" And you are certain you can trust this friend ?"

" Oh, as certain as that I can trust you."

" Thank Heaven !   Then you may indeed trust him !"

" I know it.   This way, Minna, this way.   Down this street we shall be able to take a boat, for it conducts us to a stairs on the banks of the river, and an hour more will, I have no doubt, see us in perfect safety under the roof of my friend, who is one of the most hospitable of men.   Indeed, I have bound him to me by those benefits which sink deep into grateful hearts, and are never forgotten.   He has known misfortune, and I have even saved him from those worst blows of fate, which might otherwise have completely destroyed him."

" Then he is bound to you by ties of gratitude as well as esteem."

" He is, certainly; although I do not like to place a merely grateful interpretation upon his kindness, inasmuch as I believe I should receive it, had it not been in my power ever to do him a service."

Thus speaking warmly and enthusiastically in favour of his friend, Monks led Minna to the steps by the river side, and arousing a slumbering boy, who was reposing and forgetting all his cares at the bottom of a wherry which was there moored, Monks desired to be taken up the river.

The boy, when once fairly awakened, to do him justice, was not long in making his preparations, and in less than five minutes he was pulling the boat steadily up the stream.

CHAPTER XXIII.

THE KIND RECEPTION.—THE SUPPER AND THE BETRAYAL.

THE air blew cold and keen upon the river, so that Minna was glad to cover up her head and face in her shawl more closely than she had even done before, to escape the severity of the cold.

Oh, how she thanked Heaven that it was up the stream and not down it where Monks purposed and expected to find a temporary refuge from his pursuers.

She might have had the agony, and a great agony it would have been, of passing her old house—that ancient house so familiar to her eyes under all aspects—that shade of her infancy—her happy girlhood, which she never wished to look upon again.

She had since leaving it ever considered that the sight of the old Ship Tavern would be terrible to her.   There might be some changes about it which would be indicative of death, perchance, having again made a home within its ancient walls.   Her mother— yes, she thought of her, although she had not yet ventured upon any inquiry concerning her.   And wherefore had she not?   Alas ! we must not hastily condemn Minna for a seeming apathy which is really strikingly at variance with fact.

If she had loved Mrs. Woodward less than she did, she would have been careful to inquire concerning her ; but it was a dread—an awful, shrinking dread of hearing some sad news that kept her back, and made her strangely strive to convince herself that all was well, and that, perhaps, some little indignation at the manner of her leaving home, might help her mother to forget her.

" Let her think of me as she will," Minna often thought, " so that she does not grieve for me over much.   Oh! if I could but believe that anger against me was sufficiently strong to obliterate every trace of regret, I should be much happier."

This was a very defective style of reasoning, but still from one situated as Minna Woodward was, perhaps it was extremely natural.   At all events, if we condemn it in consequence of viewing it by the light of reason, we cannot but give her credit for an abundant amount of feeling.

" Minna," said Monks, " I suppose the very sight of the river puts you in mind of home ?"

Oh, how that word home, simple in its utterance from any lips, and yet containing such a world of meaning, grated upon the ears of Minna ; she had not heard it now for many a day—she had not dared to mention it to herself, and it was in a strange and an altered voice, evidently struggling with emotion, that she replied—

" It does, indeed."

" Pardon me, Minna," he whispered, " but 1 feel that by a mere inadvertent remark I have touched upon a chord in your mind which vibrates painfully."

" Nay, nay ; it should not do so."

" But it does."

" That I cannot deny, but yet I blame myself for allowing it.   It was a sudden rush of associations, connected with the word home, which came across me, and imparted a tone to my answer, which it should not have had."

"Those feelings are the most natural which can be imagined, but I hope to live to make you feel all the domestic enjoyments of a new home, and to enable you to form the new ties and associations, that shall go far towards making you forget the past."

"You have already done much. You have been to me invariably kind. May Heaven bless and reward you for it. But for you I should now have been no more."

"I rejoice to have saved you."

"And I—and I."

"You see, Minna, that in the worst circumstances we should never despair, for we never know what Heaven may have in store for us. You saved my life, and it would seem that, but for me, you would yourself have rushed to death as a refuge from miseries which you saw no end to, and which were too cruel to bear."

"It was so, indeed."

"How strange, then, has been our acquaintanceship. How singular that we should both have had it our power, by a combination of circumstances, to save the life of the other."

"There must have been some destiny in that."

"Assuredly."

"Then I will hope for greater happiness still."

"Do so, and believe that it may be yours; and now, Minna, I here, in the name of Heaven, solemnly promise you, that, if I escape from my present embarrassing circumstances, and we both get in safety to some country, and that there is no hot pursuit after us, I will make you, according to the laws and usages of that country, my wedded wife."

Tears started to Minna's eyes, as she said,—

"Ought I to expect so much?"

"Yes. And you deserve as much. Think of it, now, as a solemn and voluntary promise, made by me to you. A promise made as the result of reflection, Minna, and not upon any sudden impulse of tenderness towards you."

This conversation was carried on in so low a tone of voice, that it was quite impossible the boy, who was managing the boat, could hear any of it, especially unfamiliar as he was with the voices of his customers.

Now, however, he interrupted them, by suddenly saying,—

"Where would you like to land?"

"At the stairs, by Vauxhall," said Monks.

They were a very short distance from that point, and soon they landed. Monks rewarded the boy liberally, and then he and Minna took their way down a narrow turning to the right, which, if continued to be pursued, would have taken them on to that large, flat, uninteresting part of the country, known as the Battersea-fields and marshes.

But he went not so far as that, for he paused soon at a house, the garden belonging to which was next to a street, and enclosed by a brick wall. The house seemed to be one of some pretensions, and, had it been in a fashionable and agreeable part of the town, would have been of considerable value. No doubt, however, as it was, it remained a memento of some builder's want of tact or calculation, in building an expensive house in such a neighbourhood, which could not command an adequate rental.

"Is this your friend's house?" said Minna.

"It is; and, although from without it has rather a sombre and gloomy appearance, such, I assure you, is not its aspect from within. My friend is a choice friend, and not one who shrinks from the innocent and intellectual enjoyments of this life, from a fear of abridging his pleasures in that which is to come, as your religious people do."

"You are much prepossessed in favour of this gentleman."

"I am, indeed; but then he deserves the prepossession."

Monks rang a bell, which hung at the gate, and, scarcely had the sound of it died away, than footsteps were heard upon the gravel walk within the garden, and the flickering light from a lantern was visible. It was a man; and, the moment he approached sufficiently near to observe who were his visitors, he exclaimed,—

"Ah! my friend Monks!"

"Yes," said Monks. "Open the gate. 'Tis I, and a friend of mine. Let us in, quickly."

The gate was opened, and then Monks's friend held him by the arm, and, in an anxious whisper, said,—

"Good God! nothing has gone amiss, I hope?"

"Yes; everything."

"A discovery?"

" A complete one."

" Alas! alas! I have always, as you know, had my apprehensions that such a thing would ensue, my dear Monks; but I hoped it was yet far distant.   But come in—come. Who have you with you?"

" The young friend I have mentioned to you before as sharing my fortune as well as possessing my best affections."

" Oh, certainly; she is most welcome."

Monks's friend preceded him and Minna to the house, and, in a few minutes he conducted them into a very handsome apartment, where he himself lighted an Argand lamp, as he said,—

" You know, Monks, that all the little luxuries I can pretend to have, ought to be fully at your disposal; because, without your aid, counsel, and true friendship, I should really have had none of them."

" Oh, pho, pho !" said Monks, " say nothing of that.   We come here, now, to ask a far greater favour of you than any I have ever been able to bestow, namely, succour from the law pursuit."

" And you shall have it."

" I knew you would say that before I came.   You see, Minna, that here you may lay aside all care, and feel completely safe.   My friend, here, has hiding-places in his house, purposely contrived between us, when no danger threatened, in case the clouds of misfortune should lour upon me; so that if, which it is very far from being at all probable, any one should find out, or even suspect that I had found a refuge in this house, and it were to be attacked and searched from top to bottom, no one would find me in it, so securely am I well aware, I could be hidden."

" This is extremely pleasing to me," said Minna.   " I do, indeed, much rejoice, that, in the season of prosperity and peace, you have had so much forethought.   I feared that the blow of fortune which had fallen upon you had found you more unprepared."

" By no means; and now we will have some supper."

" A good thought," said Monks's friend, " only it ought to have come from me.   Remain here in perfect security and comfort, while I order some for you.   When I come back, you can tell me at large the particulars of what has occurred, to give me the pleasure of your company."

When Minna and Monks were once more alone, the former, as she laid her hand upon his arm, said,—

" Will you pardon me for what I am about to say ?"

" Nay, Minna, I do not think you would say anything that I should find it difficult to pardon.   Speak freely to me as you have ever done."

" Then how comes it that your frend was up so late as this ?"

" Up so late ?"

" Yes.   You know that this is an hour when most people are in their beds, and yet you find him up and ready to receive you."

" To be sure.   Yes, it is strange, but I did not think of it before, somehow, and will ask him.   You do not, surely, suspect?"

" Nay, my feeling does not, and I feel it ought not, to amount to anything like a suspicion."

" And yet ——"

" Yet I hope and trust this friend, of whom you think so much, is true and faithful."

" Do not doubt him, Minna."

" I will not."

" He comes; and I will now ask him the natural question which you have suggested."

The master of the house now made his appearance; and, when he was fairly in the room, Monks said,—

" By-the-bye, how is it that we were so fortunate as to find you up at so unseasonable an hour as this ?"

" Oh, you may well wonder, Monks; but the fact is, we are all up here, and intended to be up all night."

" Indeed !"

" Yes, we are brewing.   You know that I am a great ale drinker, and an admirer of that beverage in all its purity; and, when we have a regular brewing, I never will go to bed until I am certain that all's right."

Monks glanced at Minna with a smile, as much as to say, " There, you see, how simple an explanation puts at end to all your suspicions."

" A supper is preparing for you," added the friend, " which, perhaps, if we take the hour into our calculation, ought rather to be called a breakfast; and now, while it is being got ready, tell me what has really happened to you and your coadjutors."

"I will," said Monks; "and you will have the pain of hearing that something has occurred of a character of which you had no idea."

"You alarm me."

"And not without reason.   Listen!"

Monks then related to him circumstantially all that had happened in the vault, and with which the reader is already sufficiently acquainted; including the death of the exciseman in the vat, to which he had been consigned either by mistake or design.

"And what is your opinion," said his friend, "regarding this most unfortunate affair?"

"As how?"

"Do you really think the matter accidental, or that the passions of your friends were sufficiently excited actually to induce them to take the man's life designedly?"

"I am lost in conjecture," replied Monks; "and, to tell the truth, there is so much to be said on both propositions that I cannot come to a conclusion on either side."

"I should think you were anxious yourself to know?"

"I am so anxious that, when I see those who have for so long worked with me in that subterranean abode, I shall make a point of ascertaining, beyond the shadow of a doubt, the real truth upon the subject."

"Think you they will tell you?"

"If they do not deny the charge of murder, in a manner to convince me of their sincerity, I shall never look upon them again.   The laws of a government I may violate, but I am not one who has ever wilfully set himself up against the ordinances of Heaven."

"And when do you suppose that your emissaries will give you an opportunity of asking them such a question?"

"Before many hours are over.   One by one they will come here, so as to avoid suspicion, in order to get from me that pecuniary assistance which, in such an emergency as the present, I have always promised them, and to which at my hands they are so peculiarly, I think, entitled, after the large and good service they have done me."

"You are too good to them."

"Not at all."

"Well, well, you shall not be kept any longer without your supper."

He walked to the door, and, as he did so, Minna, who somehow from the first appeared to have entertained anything but a favourable opinion of him, saw that he trembled so excessively as scarcely to be able to command strength to walk.

"Look at your friend," she whispered to Monks.

"Why—why?"

"Something ails him.   He trembles!"

"No, no!" cried the fellow, as he made a rush to the door, which he flung suddenly wide open—"no, no!   Who says I tremble?   It's not true!   Why should I?   Now for it—now for it!   Here you are!   Quick—quick—quick!"

CHAPTER XXIV.

THE ARREST OF MONKS. — THE OFFER TO MINNA, AND HER REJECTION OF IT. — THE REFUGE.

MONKS, upon hearing these words from his friend, sprang from the chair on which he had been sitting, and uttered a sudden and violent exclamation of surprise; but, before he could make any movement at all calculated to ensure his own safety, or to give him even a chance of escape from that house where he had felt he was betrayed, two men rushed into the room and laid hands upon him.

"You are our prisoner," said one; "resistance is useless."

Monks seemed now, for a few moments, to be perfectly petrified, and the officers—for such, indeed, they were—took that opportunity, while he was so perfectly passive, to place a pair of handcuffs upon him, so that, whatever revulsion of feeling might take place when he recovered himself, he could do nothing towards effecting his own liberty, or revenging himself upon the false friend who had betrayed him.

It was a curious scene now which that room presented. Minna had uttered one shriek, and then she stood motionless as a statue, with her hands clasped, and her face as pale as marble.

The officers each had hold of Monks, while the man, who had in so rascally a manner betrayed him, stood close by the door, rubbing his hands together, and trying to look calm, while the heavy perspiration stood upon his brow, and he shook so that any one would have thought him suffering from ague.

After a pause, Monks turned his eyes slowly upon him, and they met, for a moment, those of the despicable wretch who had acted the part of Judas towards him. It was only for a moment though, for the betrayer could not summon effrontery enough to look for longer upon the face of the man whom he had so deeply injured.

"Well," said Monks, camly and sternly, "I know that I shall be made a severe example of by the laws I have offended, but I would not change places now with you to be the world's master."

"Why, why," gasped the fellow to the officers—"why don't you take him away at once? I don't want him here. Take him away, I say; you have your prisoner. Now remove him."

"Really, you are in a monstrous hurry," said one of the officers; "but we are not. However, we don't want to wait here. Do we, Smith?"

"I should think not," said the other; "we are getting too thirsty."

"Ah! to be sure."

"Why did you not say so before?" said the scoundrel. "You shall have what you like here to drink."

"What! drink with you? I should think not. Why, what the devil do you take us for, that you imagine we would drink with an informer, or such as you are? No, no; it's our business to take people who have gone against the law; but we don't hold out a friendly hand to them first—not we."

"Bravo, Bill," said the other. "It would be *pison* if we took anything here. Come along."

"There," said Monks; "such is the reward of the traitor—the contempt of all men. Officers, I will go with you quietly, were it but for the sentiments you have just uttered regarding that man. Let me beg of you to remove these handcuffs, and I give you my sacred promise, in the name of Heaven, that I will make no attempt to escape from you."

Without a word, the officers removed the manacles from the wrists of Monks, and whilst they were doing so, the rascally master of the house, in a voice of fear, exclaimed,—

"Mind what you are about. It will be your fault, you know, if he does any mischief, or commits any assaults. Keep him off me—keep him off. Look how he eyes me."

"Well, he can't kill you with looking at you, can he?"

"No; but—but he meditates some mischief."

Monks made one step in advance towards the fellow, which at once filled him with such an amount of alarm, that he rushed from the room with a precipitation which could not have been greater had his life depended upon his doing so.

"You don't intend to interfere with him?" said one of the officers to Monks.

"Certainly not."

"That's right. You know we should be forced to interfere. He has sold you to the excise for a large sum of money."

"No doubt—no doubt."

"Who is this lady?"

"She is with me—in fact, my wife."

"You will let me accompany him?" said Minna, as she clung to the arm of Monks. "I will willingly share his prison with him."

"We cannot, madam. Our warrant will not enable us to interfere with you. You are free."

"Make use of that freedom, Minna," said Monks, "by at once leaving this detestable house. You will have no sort of difficulty in communicating with me now. Leave here on the instant; there is money for you. Go at once; and if anywhere hereabouts you see a friend of mine, you can say what has happened."

Minna understood by this hint that Monks wished her to warn his comrades not to come to the house; and as he handed her a considerable sum of money, she conjectured that he intended her to render them the pecuniary assistance which he had announced his own intention of doing.

"All that is useless," remarked one of the officers. "We understand it. This house is well watched, and everbody not known who comes to it will be arrested. We don't want to interfere with you, madam; but you had much better go away at once, and keep away."

"Go then, Minna," said Monks, despairingly; "go."

The officers removed Monks to the door; and when Minna for a brief moment was alone in the room, there came into it, from another door which she had not observed, Monks's pretended friend. He advanced close to Minna with such a stealthy step, that she knew not of his presence until he had actually had the assurance to place his arm round her waist.

With a shudder of horror she shrunk from the pollution of his touch; but he again came close to her, saying,—

"My dear creature, I love you—upon my soul, I do. Don't think for one moment of leaving here. Monks is as completely done for as any man can possibly be. He will rot in prison. Remain with me. I will move from here to any more cheerful part of the town you may fancy."

He had spoken thus much before Minna could find breath to answer him; but when she did so, it was with a vehemence of horror that made him shrink back, and no doubt cordially wish he had left his proposal to himself.

"Wretch!" she exclaimed, "death in its worst shape would not present the loathsome appearance to my eyes that you do. Monks—Monks! Help! help; oh, help!"

The door, which had only just been closed upon the retreating forms of the officers and Monks, was flung open again, and they all seemed to see at a glance what was the matter.

"Villain!" exclaimed Monks, as he dashed forward.

The rascal, however, had calculated all his chances, no doubt, beforehand, and he had a means of escape in the doorway at the other end of the room, through which he had come.

Through this door, then, he made his way; but Monks was after him so quickly, that he had not time to fasten it on the other side, which doubtless he had intended to do, thinking that, by so doing, there would be a sufficient pause to enable the officers to interfere.

In both of these calculations, if such, indeed, they were, he was grievously disappointed, for the door easily gave way before Monks, and the officers did not seem at all inclined to trouble themselves in the matter.

"Bill," said one.

"Here you are."

"This ain't no business of ours."

"I should say not."

"Very good."

Minna sunk upon a chair nearly in a fainting condition, while up a narrow flight of stairs Monks pursued his late dear friend, who, finding that the man whom he had such abundant cause to dread was so close upon his heels, fled with the most frantic speed, and shouted for help and mercy, as if a legion of devils had been at his heels.

The officers took the matter as coolly as possible. They had seen at a glance what was the cause of provocation, and, although they would have felt it to be their duty to protect the informer against the violence of Monks, had it been attempted to be called into exercise merely on the ground of the information that had been laid against him, they did not at all consider themselves called upon to save a scoundrel from the consequences of insulting a woman.

That was quite another affair, and they both devoutly wished and hoped that Monks would give his dear friend a thrashing that he would remember the longest day he had to live.

Such a result appeared to be extremely probable. There must be some limit to the chase, and although the pursued made a most desperate attempt to rush into a room sufficiently before Monk reached it, to get its door firmly fastened, he failed in doing so, and as there was no other outlet to that apartment, he was now fairly and completely at bay.

Monks said nothing. There was no necessity to utter one word upon the subject; but doubling his fists, he, in the true English fashion, proceeded to execute a vengeance upon the scoundrel who had not only betrayed him, but insulted Minna, which was likely to do him some good in the way of a warning for the remainder of his existence, if any warning could have an effect upon so unmanly and atrocious a hound as was that false friend.

A very few minutes sufficed to produce a great amount of confusion among the various features of the fellow's face, and he fell insensible at the feet of Monks, who then turned and left the man, proceeding leisurely down the staircase, to where he had left the officers.

It was astonishing what an exhilarating effect the punishment he had bestowed upon his betrayer, had upon Monks. He felt now quite a different man. All that suppressed indignation which had made his heart appear to swell within him, as if it would have burst, had gone, and he was as calm and collected now as any one could possibly be under arrest for such serious matters as those in which he was involved.

Minna flew to him when she saw him again appear. She had feared that the villain whom he had pursued might have used some weapon against the incensed Monks, and she was rejoiced to see him again in safety.

" You are not hurt?" she asked, anxiously.

" Not at all, Minna," he replied. " All is well."

" I hope," whispered one of the officers to him, " you have been moderate?"

" I have. My fists were my only weapons."

" Good."

" I am much beholden to you both."

" Oh, don't mention it."

" I am now perfectly ready to accompany you."

" Come on, then."

" Minna, leave here. Let me see you safe from this house. I have avenged the wrong which has been done you."

Minna hung upon the arm of Monks, and the whole party left the house immediately. Monks took an opportunity to whisper to her, as they passed down the garden,—

" You will do what you can, Minna, to save my former comrades from the snare which has been prepared for them here?"

" I will—I will!"

" There are some among them who, putting altogether aside the fact that they have been employed in defrauding the revenue, are as honourable-minded men, in all affairs of private life, as could possibly be found."

" I do not doubt it."

" You will come and see me?"

" Oh, yes—yes."

" Farewell, then—farewell! Leave us at the gate."

" I will."

The gate was reached. Monks shook hands with Minna, who could scarcely speak for the tears that filled her eyes, and then they separated.

She was extremely anxious to carry out the wishes of Monks, as regarded warning the men not to come to that house; but when she came to ask herself how she was to do so, the difficulties of the task appeared to her to be almost insurmountable.

She did not know them by sight sufficiently to be able to warn them; nor was it likely they should, from the transient observation they had been able to bestow upon her, during her first visit to the vaults, be able to recognize her as one who had been trusted by Monks.

She recollected, too, what the officers had said, namely, that the house was carefully watched, and, although she saw no one, she doubted not but that such was the fact, and, on that account, for her to remain within sight of it, with the hope of doing any good to the comrades of Monks, would have been absurd.

She accordingly trusted to chance, and, as well as she could recollect it, walked slowly in the direction of the landing-place by Vauxhall, by the same route which Monks had led her.

This certainly was, it seemed to her, the only chance there existed of being able to carry out Monks' wishes, and, as the event turned out, she was right; for after she had got out of sight of the house where so serious a misfortune had occurred, she met a man whose face was not altogether strange to her, and who looked at her, too, as if he had a dim recollection of having seen her somewhere.

She paused, in order to give him an opportunity, if he chose, of addressing her, and he embraced it by saying, with great deference and respect,—

" Madam, I hope I am not mistaken; if I am, you will pardon me; but I fancy I have seen you with a friend of mine recently."

" What is his name?"

" Monks."

" You are right. I now remember you. Are you one of those whom he trusted?"

" I am; and to convince you that such is the case, I may name to you that when we last met, there were five large vats."

" Enough, enough! I rejoice to have met you. Monks is arrested."

" Arrested?"

" Yes. He charged me, if I could possibly do so, to warn you and your comrades against going to the house where he was to meet you. He has been betrayed there."

" You astonish me. I have been sent alone by my fellows, because they knew they could trust me, and they thought it safer for only one to come than the whole."

" Had I not, fortunately, met with you, you would have been a prisoner the moment you set foot within the precincts of that house."

" Good Heaven! and Monks, I know, trusted that man so implicitly that he would, I am sure, have quarrelled with any one who had hinted a doubt of him."

" He would indeed."

" What is to be done ?"

" You must yourself decide. All I can say to you is, that I am the bearer of money given to me to meet your necessities, which I will at once and freely hand to you."

" I rejoice to hear you say so, for more reasons than one."

" Do you so ?"

" Yes; for to tell you the truth, several of my comrades—although, let me assure you, that I myself by no means participated in such a feeling—have entertained an opinion that our recent misfortune was to be attributed to the trust that Monks put in you."

" That is a cruel delusion," said Minna Woodward ; " for nothing could be further from the truth. It has been a most grievous thing to me, to think that the dispersion of your company should occur on that night, of all others, when I was first trusted with the secret of your meetings; but, believe me, that the concurrence of those circumstances together was purely accidental."

" No one can doubt it now ; for what would have been easier than for you, now that you are completely free from any controul, in consequence of the arrest of Mr. Monks, than to have omitted warning me of the danger that threatened us, and likewise have gone away with the money that has been intrusted to you."

" I certainly might have done so."

" You might ; and your good faith as regards those particulars ought to be and shall be sufficient to convince the most sceptical, that not to you for one moment is to be attributed the suspicions that have come over us. Allow me, if you please, to be your conductor to where the rest of our little band is waiting, and then you shall yourself relieve their necessities, and convince them of your good faith."

" I will do so," said Minna ; " it will be a great pleasure to me to remove from myself the stigma of having betrayed those who were trusted by him, to whom I feel myself under such deep obligations."

She accepted the arm of her companion, and declaring, in answer to a question of his, that she was well able to walk swiftly, he conducted her at a rapid pace toward Vauxhall.

Minna was exceedingly anxious to get housed somewhere, for notwithstanding the speed that she made she was extremely tired; and, moreover, her dress was ill adapted for the streets, and extremely likely to attract observation when the morning should have sufficiently dawned for the chance passengers to observe how she was attired.

She had not long to wait, for her companion halted at a house in which were bills signifying that it was to let. After glancing cautiously around him for a few moments, he tapped gently at the door, which was immediately opened from within.

" Come in," said a voice; " you've not been long gone. Ha! who is this you have with you?"

" One, whom I will convince you can be trusted," said the man.

" Why, this is she," said he who had opened the door, " whom we have reason to believe betrayed us."

" You have no reason to believe any such thing," said Minna's companion ; " and I shall be able to convince you that you do this lady a great injustice by supposing for a moment such a thing to be possible. It is not so, give me leave to assure you."

" Well, come in ; I'm willing to believe that you are right ; at all events we can trust you if we cannot trust her."

" Alas !" said Minna, " it is very sad to be suspected of treachery when you know yourself to be entirely innocent of it."

" Nay, think nothing of it; they will be but too glad to apologise to you for entertaining such unworthy suspicions; there is but one really troublesome fellow among us who is likely to give you any trouble."

" Be it so; be it so."

The man conducted her into a large room in the empty house, in which were five or six persons assembled; their faces generally wore an appearance of alarm, and no one could fail to see from their aspect that something had happened to induce in them a great amount of nervousness and apprehension.

Several of them seemed upon the point of speaking the moment Minna appeared, but her conductor silenced them by holding up his hand authoritatively, and saying,—

" Stop, stop ; before you give utterance to any sentiment upon this occasion, hear me. You suspect this lady, all of you most wrongfully, of betraying you; let me assure you that such is not the case. She is still trusted by Mr. Monks, and to convince you that she is so trusted by him, she now brings you, as I understand, a considerable sum of money to relieve your immediate necessities. After this, my friends, can you by any possibility suspect her of being untrue to the trust which had been reposed in her."

" Besides," said Minna, stepping forward, " although I blush to use such an argument, if I had all the inclination in the world to betray you I had not the time to do so. Why, it was but a short half-hour before the general alarm took place in the subterranean vault that I was first introduced to its secrets, and most certainly before I knew of the existence of such a place, the man who so indiscreetly avowed who and what he was, and met with death as a consequence of his temerity, was there."

Those arguments seemed to silence them, and being joined by several other of their comrades, some of whom uttered rough excuses to Minna for entertaining any suspicion of her at all; but one, who, no doubt, was the troublesome character who had been mentioned to her, said, in a doubtful tone of voice,—

"At all events, friends, it would be just as well to have the money which this young lady is to bring to us; whether she be true or not there can be no mistake about that; let us see the cash."

This speech evidently gave general satisfaction, and Minna placed her hand in her bosom to produce the heavy purse which had been handed to her by Monks.

"Oh! what a sudden terror seized her when she found that it was gone: a strange choking sensation came over her, and she trembled from head to foot. Hurriedly she searched for the gold and notes, but it was hopelessly; she felt that all was gone, and there she stood, without the means of justifying herself, deprived of the strongest argument she would have been able to adduce of her faith and honesty, and surrounded by men who were likely now to be perfectly infuriated at their disappointment.

"What shuffling is this?" said he who had spoken about the money. "You see she don't produce it."

"It is lost—it is lost!" said Minna, "and I am wretched."

"A fine tale for us. This is a scheme, my friends, for which we are to be betrayed in the same manner that Mr. Monks has been. Death—death to the traitress!"

"Hold! for Heaven's sake, hold!" cried Minna's companion. "Are you men, that you thus advance with an aspect of hostility against a woman?"

"Woman or no woman," cried he who had spoken, "we have too much at stake to listen to any nonsense."

"Would you murder me?" said Minna.

"Call it what you will," said the fellow, "the same hands that threw an excise officer into a vat of ardent spirits are not likely to scruple at anything that will ensure their safety, because the tears of a woman may stand in the way."

"You're wrong," said Minna's companion, "very wrong; and you will find that something more than the tears of a woman stand in the way of the execution of such a bloodthirsty piece of villany as that which you contemplate. I am so convinced of the innocence of this lady, that I tell you frankly, comrades, only through me shall you reach her to inflict upon her an injury."

"No, no," cried Minna; "if there must be a victim to the lawless rage of these men, let it be me; and it will be a sufficient consolation to me, even in the pangs of death, to feel that there was one who believed me guiltless of what had been attributed to me. The sin be upon the heads of those who would immolate me at the shrine of their own passions. I tell you all—I declare to you all, that I am innocent—entirely innocent of that that I am accused, and now sacrifice me if you will."

"No; this shall not be," cried he who had so firmly taken her part hitherto; "I say it shall not be. Nothing of so monstrous a character shall take place here."

"Down with them both," cried he who, in so bloodthirsty a spirit, seemed inclined to execute a summary vengeance upon poor Minna; "down with them both. What are they to us?"

"Then, self-defence," cried the man, "will urge me to do the best that I can."

He sprang to the window as he spoke, and flung it wide open. The day was breaking, and a rush of cool sweet air came into the apartment, as well as a flood of light, which had before been prevented from gaining admission in consequence of the panes of glass being completely begrimed with the dirt of many years' standing.

"Now," he cried, "make but the least attempt to injure that lady, and I will call so loudly for assistance, that some passengers in the street must hear me. Then, where will be your chance of safety?"

"Down with him—down with him!" cried several, and they stepped forward a pace or two towards him.

"He is himself a traitor to our cause," cried the ruffian who had created so much of the mischief; "we will have his life and her's too."

"Call for help—call for help, for Heaven's sake!" cried Minna, as she sprang forward, and cowered down by the window close to which her protector stood.

"Wait yet a moment," he said. "You talk of life, and you may do so, but it will require an amount of moral courage on the part of some of you which I do not think you possess. I can sell my single life but at the price of two of yours. Come on, now, whichever of you feel inclined to sacrifice themselves for the remainder."

He drew, as he spoke, a pair of pistols from his breast, and with one in each hand, he calmly awaited the advance of those who had so lately been his coadjutors; but who, from thinking and reflecting men, had, by the great danger of their position, been converted into positive fiends.

He reasoned correctly indeed, when he supposed that no two out of the number would be fool-hardy enough to sacrifice themselves for the remainder, there was a general pause of irresolution; they all held back, and Minna breathed freely again, for she hoped that there was safety, both for herself and for him, who had so gallantly risked so much in her defence.

"Now," he said, " I'm willing to make terms with you, old friends—but friends no longer; from this moment we have done with each other; and it is evident that no sort of pleasant companionship can ever again exist between us. I will leave you; but you have nothing to fear from me. For my own peace of mind and calmness of spirit, I would not betray you; offer me no obstruction, but let me leave this house at once with this lady, as freely as I entered it. Stand back."

Mechanically they gave way before him, and while Minna crept close to him, and under the very shadow of his arms, he moved towards the door of the apartment without interruption.

"When you get to this stair-head," he said, "fly. Stop not till you gain the street, and I will soon join you."

The stair-head was gained, and Minna obeyed his injunction. He followed her quickly; it was a winding staircase, and when he had got a short distance down, some of his comrades crowded above, as if to watch his departure. He could not see what they were about, and suddenly Minna heard a heavy fall, and a deep groan—something had been thrown from above, which had fallen upon his head, and crushed him to the floor. She could not tell what it was; but a feeling of certainty came over her that he was killed.

To rush into the street and shriek for aid, was now the work of a moment. Those misguided men had done their worst, and she no longer had any terms to keep with them.

"Help! help!" she shouted. "Murder! murder!" and her voice reached far and wide. Doors and windows were flung open; and chance passengers in the immediate neighbourhood hurried in alarm towards the direction from whence arose those frantic sounds.

CHAPTER XXV.

AGONIZING REFLECTIONS OF HEARTWELL.—THE STORM.

WE must leave Minna Woodward for a while, in order now to turn our attention to the disastrous condition of poor Heartwell, who, it will be remembered, had, after having had his feelings so greatly outraged by Captain Harding, committed himself so far as to be guilty of a breach of discipline, that threatened for him the most disastrous consequences.

Our readers may imagine, far better than we can at all attempt to describe, the agony of outraged feeling that came over him when he found himself a prisoner in his own cabin, and left to the sad company of his own reflections.

In vain he asked himself how it was possible that Captain Harding could at all become acquainted with the fact of his acquaintanceship with Minna, and the warm interest he took in her fate; and yet that, in something connected with Minna, he had found the key to all the petty annoyances he had received from his captain, he now no longer doubted; and he felt as convinced as if he had been repeatedly assured of it by Harding himself, that the mention of Minna's name at the dinner-table was very far from being an accidental circumstance.

He paced the narrow confines of his cabin with a bewildered head and a throbbing brain. At one moment he accused himself of great rashness in acting as he had done in the captain's cabin, while, at another, he only wondered that he had not killed him upon the spot, for the vile calumny he had cast upon one who, he, Heartwell, believed to be purity itself.

And what, he asked himself, was to be the result of all this?—a court of inquiry into his conduct, which must result in his dismissal from the service with ignominy—and for what?—because, like any honourable man, he had taken the part of an innocent and unoffending girl, against the ribald sarcasms of a libertine.

"And this, oh heavens!" he cried; "this is the result of the good fortune upon which I so much prided myself when I received the appointment to this dreadful ship

Minna—Minna! can I again approach you with love, when I shall be forced to tell you in the same breath, that I am a disgraced man, and thought no longer worthy to serve my king and country ?"

And then he was confined to the narrow dimension of the cabin, with nothing to withdraw his mind from the circumstances of deep depression in which he was placed, and Heaven only knew how long that confinement would last. It might be weeks, or it might be months, for his release was out of the question, until a court of inquiry had been held upon his conduct.

And then he asked himself what would be his defence when charged with the high breach of discipline, of which he had been guilty. What could he say in extenuation of his conduct?

Invited to the table of his captain, and wine placed before him ; the conversation, taking a lively turn, and because a publican's daughter—in the not very classic neighbourhood of Wapping—is mentioned with disrespect, he is to get furious and commit so stupendous a breach of all laws and regulations appertaining to the service, that it would seem almost impossible any officer could so far forget himself as to be guilty of.

And this was the simple story, a story he could not deny.

These thoughts were maddening ; and as day after day now passed in bringing with them no extenuation of his sufferings, no company, for the officers were forbidden to visit him, and even the sentinel, who kept watch and ward over him, upon pain of the most serious consequences, was ordered not to answer the most common-place question, no wonder that he became nearly maddened, and that towards sunset on the fifth day, when he felt, from the labouring motion of the vessel, and the bustle over head, that rough weather had ensued, he was pleased, and could almost have wished that that gallant vessel should plunge to the bottom of the sea, carrying him and all his enemies to eternity.

" A storm, a storm," he cried, "is brewing !—Heaven grant it may come."

He heard the wind howling among the rigging ; he heard the trampling of feet and the creaking of cordage in the blocks. A heavy swell caused the vessel at one moment to sink into the trough of the sea, while at another she rose upon the crest of some mountain wave, as if upheld by some unseen hands.

The wind increased until it blew a furious gale. He heard the hoarse shouts of the seamen to each other, and the loud tones of the officers through the speaking trumpets, which they were compelled to use in giving their orders to those aloft.

Occasionally, too, with a the sharp report, like that of a discharged musket, a rope would give way, and some of the standing rigging would come down, producing a momentary confusion on board the vessel till all was righted again.

But the tempest, by far, had not reached its height ; the gale became a hurricane, the waves rolled mountains high, and the shouts and confusion that reigned around beggared all description.

Oh! that was a fearful night—a fearful night for all on board that vessel! a night of such terror that it seemed it would never end, and as if the winds and the waves had conspired together effectually to produce the destruction of that gallant vessel, and all who had trusted to her for safety from all the perils of the deep.

It was perfectly maddening to such a spirit as Heartwell's to be shut up within the narrow confines of that cabin, and to hear this mortal struggle between man and the elements of nature. He could have sprung upon death, and, like the spirit of the storm, breasted the fury of the ocean's strife. He shouted, he shrieked to be allowed to lend his aid, if it were but for one brief hour, in assisting those who were battling with the wind and the waves.

But it was all in vain—his cabin door was made fast. From the increased noise and confusion upon deck, he knew that the storm was gaining upon the ship ; he felt that the gallant vessel laboured through the sea, and, from the orders he heard given, he knew the imminent danger in which they were.

And now there is a momentary lull in the tempest ; the wind was gathering strength for one mighty effort, and all knew that such was the case, as, with breathless anxiety, they held on to save themselves from the squall that they knew assuredly would return with accumulated fury.

Oh, that terrific calm! It had no soothing effect upon the minds of those brave sailors, too well they knew its treachery.

And now, from afar off, they heard a low wailing sound ; it seemed more like the moan of some mortal spirit in its agony than the wind careering over the surface of the deep—and yet such it was.

From a hundred miles away the squall was coming, which had gathered strength from the brief repose that nature had given herself.

Lieutenant Heartwell stood in the centre of the cabin floor, his position was a crouching one, for he was compelled to accommodate himself to the heaving and tossing of the vessel. He knew too what was coming as well as the ablest and most experienced seaman that ever trod its planks.

Now he heard the moaning sound of the wind. Nearer—nearer it came, and increased in volume.

"Down with the helm!" he shouted. "Fly—fly before the wind, or you are lost! It comes—it comes!"

There was a roaring, rushing sound, and, for a moment, Heartwell thought the vessel was capsized, for she lay nearly flat upon the bosom of the sea.

"Gone—gone!" he cried. "This is death! No—no, she rights—we're saved! That crash—too well I know its signification."

There was a frightful crash on deck—a strong noise, and a shout of despair! The mainmast had gone by the board, bringing down all its standing rigging, and smashing everything before it. The sails and tackle trailed in the sea, and the appearance of the vessel was a complete wreck.

It was then that Heartwell's cabin door was dashed open, and several of the crew called upon him, kindly, by name.

"Save us—save us, Mr. Heartwell. The second lieutenant is washed overboard, and the sailing-master is killed by the fall of the mast! Come on deck, for God's sake, sir, and save us!"

How he got upon deck Lieutenant Heartwell never knew; but somehow or another he found himself, without any appreciable lapse of time, standing on the quarter-deck in the very midst of the storm.

His practised eye in a moment ran over the vessel, and ascertained the precise state of affairs upon deck. With a voice that sounded far above the roar of the winds, or the dash of the waves, he cried,—

"All hands to clear the wreck."

The seamen flew to execute the order with alacrity, for they had an abundant faith in the man who gave it.

"Heave all overboard, my men," he shouted; "the king has plenty of spars and rigging to spare."

"Ay, ay, sir," cried three or four cheerful voices; and in a few moments the mast, and all that appertained to it, were thrown into the sea.

The ship righted wonderfully in a moment; but some of the heavy guns had got clear of their fastenings, and had run out upon the decks.

"Run home the guns, and secure all," cried Heartwell. "Throw over anything that can't be made fast; keep her head to the wind, and she'll do yet."

The storm seemed to be abating, the wind blew steadier, although it was still a gale; but disencumbered as the ship was of a great mass of material and weight, she danced over the waves lightly.

A ship's carpenter came up to him, and proclaimed seven feet of water in the hold.

"Has she shipped it, or is it a leak?"

"I don't know, sir."

"You can find it out by sounding in a moment or two. Let me know instantly that you have made the discovery."

A few moments sufficed to satisfy those who went to make the inquiry that the ship was perfectly seaworthy, but had shipped a vast quantity of water during the early progress of the storm. Half-a-dozen hands at the pumps soon materially lightened her of this extra load; and although the weather was rough and tempestuous, and the vessel had suffered considerable loss by the springing of her mainmast, there was no danger of her becoming a complete wreck, as she answered the helm well, and scudded along easily some few points off nearest shore.

It was then, and not till then, that Lieutenant Heartwell looked around with wonder to know what could have become of Captain Harding.

"You have saved us, sir," said the third lieutenant, coming up to him. "The men were paralyzed, and had faith in nobody but you."

"Where is the captain?"

"I really don't know. He may have been struck by some of the wreck; but the last I saw of him was his going through the skylight to the state cabin stern foremost."

"Indeed!"

" Look, Mr. Heartwell—look! He comes."

Pale, ghastly, and staggering, Harding appeared from the hatchway of his own cabin. He was grasping at everything he came near for support. His hair was dishevelled, and his brain disordered.

" Is the storm over?" he said ; " is the worst over ?"

" Yes, sir," said the gunner ; " you needn't be afeard now, sir."

" D——!" said Harding ; " what do you mean by that ?"

At this moment his eyes fell upon Lieutenant Heartwell, who happened likewise to see something that required alteration in the rigging, and in a clear voice he shouted the necessary order, just as Captain Harding, who at the sight of him seemed to have recovered some of his strength and energy, strode up to where he stood, and with a face, on which were depicted the most demoniac passions, glared in his face, as if he questioned his very right to existence.

CHAPTER XXVI.

THE FURIOUS QUARREL AND ITS RESULTS.—THE NEUTRAL GROUND AND THE DUEL.

WITH all the pride that a consciousness of innocence and high desert could give to his conduct and appearance did Heartwell face the man who had done him so much injury, and but for him might even now have been food for worms at the bottom of the sea.

There was no quailing before the glance of deep concentrated hatred which Captain Harding bent upon him, and it was not likely that Harding could for long keep up such an appearance of steadiness of gaze upon a man whom he knew he had so greatly injured.

He turned aside after a moment or two, and then he spoke, for the silence became painful to him—ten times more painful to him than it was to Heartwell, and the latter did not seem at all inclined to break it by the slightest remark.

" Sir," he said, " it is something new on board a ship of war to see all discipline so set on one side, that an officer under arrest treads its quarterdeck, and assumes a command."

" I assumed no command," said Heartwell. " I was called upon to take the place of one who had deserted his post."

" Dare you insinuate ?"

" I insinuate nothing. I was called upon in the hour of peril to do my best to save the ship, and have done so."

" You are a villain !"

" Villain in your teeth. A greater villain than you never trod the earth, and you know, Captain Harding, you are a scoundrel, and a paltry one, too—a coward in danger—a poltroon, when the real courage of a man is required, but great in petty intrigue and lying."

Harding's passion would have prompted him to rush upon Heartwell, and make an effort to execute summary vengeance upon him, but even at that moment of passion his prudence whispered to him that he was no match for Heartwell, and he paused. Then turning suddenly, he dived down the hatchway into his own cabin, from whence he returned, in an incredibly short space of time, with a drawn sword in his hand.

Short, however, as had been the period of his absence, there was time for a friendly officer of marines, who had seen the whole affair, to dart to the side of Heartwell, and hand to him a cutlass, as he whispered,—

" Lieutenant Heartwell, the captain has gone below for his sword. I cannot see a brave man without the means of defending himself from the assaults of a ruffian."

Heartwell had the same impression—that is to say, that Harding had gone to fetch some weapon ; and when he saw him emerge from his cabin with a drawn sword in his hand, he was thankful, indeed, that a friendly hand had furnished him with the means of defending his life.

Of the fact that Heartwell was armed Harding could have no conception. He knew that when placed under arrest his arms had been taken from him as a matter of course ; and there can be no doubt but that, in the uncalculating passion of the moment, he would have inflicted some serious injury upon Heartwell, which he would have afterwards endeavoured to justify himself in doing, by averring that Heartwell was guilty of such mutinous conduct as to render some instant step absolutely necessary ; and that his zeal for the service had at the moment prompted him to act personally, instead of deputing the proceeding to others.

He was terribly disappointed, however, when he found that Heartwell had a sword, and felt the sharp ring of its blade against his own.

"Now, villain!" exclaimed Heartwell, "you have yourself sought this conflict, and you shall receive the reward of your treacherous and dastardly conduct towards me."

Harding appeared paralysed. He retreated backwards step by step, and called loudly for assistance, and then the combatants were immediately separated, for there was no excuse on the parts of those close at hand for non-interference, although they would gladly have allowed it to go on to its natural termination, which evidently would have resulted in the utter defeat of Harding, if not in his actual death.

We are well pleased that for Heartwell's sake the combat was prevented from proceeding any further, for, bad as was his present position, it would have been a thousand times worse with the death of his captain to answer for. Nothing whatever could then have saved Heartwell from destruction. The death of Harding would have sanctified his errors, and the whole affair would have assumed an aspect of so much danger to the service, that an example would, most assuredly, have been made of Heartwell.

The combat, however, was instantly stopped, and Heartwell, by the orders of Harding, was re-conducted to his cabin.

No doubt upon reflection Captain Harding felt that he had very foolishly committed himself, and that he ought, when he found Heartwell at liberty, to have simply again ordered him under arrest, and throw the blame of his temporary liberation upon the sentinel, whose duty it was to have resisted, under any circumstances, and at any risk, his escape from the precincts of his cabin.

However, he had committed himself so far, that there was now no excuse but to make the most of it and the best of it; so he made up his mind to adhere to the original charge against Heartwell, and to say nothing whatever, unless it should perforce come out in evidence, concerning the proceedings contingent upon the storm, in which Heartwell had performed so very important a part.

And that these circumstances would not come out at all, or if they did, that they would not be represented greatly to his prejudice, he was induced to believe, because he was aware that his connexion with one of the Lords of the Admiralty must be well known; and from that fact he concluded, that few who were seeking promotion in the service would like to make an enemy of him.

He was further encouraged in this course by the sycophancy of his spy, the surgeon, who went sneaking after him into his cabin, and offered to swear anything he, Harding, pleased, with respect to the proceedings of the night.

Upon the whole, therefore, Harding rather felt pleased that he had been prevented from doing a deadly injury to Heartwell, since his ruin and degradation in the profession he so much loved, was a state of things to be considered as quite certain.

And yet this feeling by no means hindered him from determining to take the first opportunity of being revenged upon the officer of marines who had provided Heartwell with the cutlass, and of which he, Harding, was duly informed by the surgeon, who had witnessed it, although he was not near enough to hear what words had accompanied the action.

CHAPTER XXVII.

THE LETTER.—THE ENFORCED DUEL AT GIBRALTAR.

WHILE Captain Harding was indulging in these reflections, we must not suppose that Heartwell was mentally idle.

On the contrary, he was the prey of a thousand uncomfortable reflections, which harassed him almost beyond the bounds of human patience. He could not but feel that such was the unfortunate fatality which seemed to have come over him, his situation was now worse than it had been before the storm had occurred.

He had now openly reviled and defied his captain in the presence of a number of witnesses, whose testimony could not be shaken; and the example had been, perhaps for the first time in the history of the service, an act of a personal contest on the quarter-deck of a vessel of war, between the captain and one of his officers.

The result of an inquiry into such a circumstance could be foreseen by any one at all acquainted with naval discipline. Had it been a period of profound peace instead of one of active war as it was, there might have been a hope that a thorough investigation of the circumstances might have ended in the exculpation of Heartwell. But now, when war was raging round our coasts, whatever opinion the authorities might entertain with regard to the conduct of the captain, and however he might eventually suffer professionally in consequence of that opinion, the punishment of the inferior officer was sure to be immediate and decisive.

See page 120.

Heartwell knew well that this would be the case, as a matter of policy, in order to keep up that sort of *prestige* in the service which it was wished should attach itself to the name of a superior officer, whenever he came in contact in any way with his inferior.

This conviction, however, as may be well imagined, was anything but likely to ameliorate the feelings of Heartwell. Indeed, it produced what was an extremely likely effect, namely, a perfect recklessness, as if it had driven him actually mad.

The more he brooded over his position, the more uncomfortable did it appear to him, and the less chance or hope did there seem of his ever emerging from it.

"In the royal navy," he told himself, "I am a ruined man. Let my justification be ever so perfect, no captain would like to have a lieutenant who has ever made out successfully a case against his superior in command."

Acting, then, under the impulse of this feeling, and knowing that now he could not by any possibility make his case worse than it really was, he made up his mind to have such satisfaction from Captain Harding as by any means he could goad that individual to give him.

It is just possible that, like all bold and brave men, Heartwell considerably underrated the services he had rendered to his country before the captain of the Eolus joined his vessel, as well as, in his mental calculations, placing too little stress upon his own conduct during the storm, as contrasted with that of Harding.

We say these circumstances might have enabled his judges to entertain such an opinion of the whole transaction, that, although for example's sake to the general service he might have been disgraced, some means would have been taken to make him feel that, individually, his conduct was looked upon in a different light.

Under this aspect of affairs, we regret that he wrote the following note to Captain Harding, inasmuch, as by so doing, he was only placing another weapon in the hands of his enemy, wherewith to do him more injury, and affect his interests.

The note was as follows, and dated from his own cabin :—

"TO CAPTAIN HARDING.

"SIR,—Although, feeling that all the circumstances of oppression under which I at present labour, are solely to be attributed to you, yet I am so far willing to overlook an infamy of behaviour, which should place you beyond the pale of honourable feeling, as to give you an opportunity of rendering to me that satisfaction which one honourable man may be called upon to give to another.

"I am quite aware that, at present, the rules of the service prevent an officer in actual commission from fighting with one his inferior in rank, likewise in commission; but, notwithstanding that state of things acting now as a bar to our meeting upon the first land we come to, I wish, on your word of honour as an officer, and one who would, I presume, wish to be called a gentleman, to have an assurance that, when these circumstances shall alter, you will meet me.

"Upon your assurance to this effect, I am willing, for the present, to seek no opportunity of coming in your way; but if, from any cowardly suggestion of your mind, you attempt to get out of the necessity of making me such a promise, I proclaim you a coward and a poltroon, and will do so at every opportunity that shall present itself to me to do so.   "I am, sir, with the courtesies due to myself,

"DAVID HEARTWELL."

As he was by no means denied the use of writing materials—for, indeed, the contents of his cabin were untouched, among which were arms, if he had chosen to use them, Heartwell found no difficulty in producing this letter, which he addressed to the captain, and handed to the sergeant of the guard that came to change the sentinel at the door of his cabin.

In vain, however, he waited in expectation of an answer to his note. None came, and, after a few hours, he was compelled to put up with the mortification of believing that Captain Harding was willing so studiously to insult him, that he would not even condescend to answer his note.

To regret having written such an epistle now was useless. There it was, and it only tended to add another drop to the cup of Heartwell's bitter feelings.

From his cabin windows, as the weather was now much calmer than before, and the day had dawned, he could see that the vessel was making considerable way; and, in the distance, he was surprised to see a line of fortifications and rocky-looking coast, which he did not at first at all recognise.

Upon a nearer approach, however, to the shore, he recognised the fortifications of Gibraltar, which he had once before visited, and much wondered now that he had not, at the first glance, known.

It was evident, from the course the vessel was taking, that it was intended to hold some communication with the garrison. A gun was fired, and a boat went on shore, after which the Eolus anchored in the roads under a salute of five guns, from one of the bastions.

What could be the motive for stopping at Gibraltar, Heartwell could not conceive, unless it were to deliver despatches to the governor; and, if that were their object, they would be under weigh again very shortly.

The whole day, however, elapsed, and the vessel remained stationary beneath the shadow of those frowning fortifications.

The captain went on shore, and on shore he remained so long, that it became evident that some political movement was on the tapis, and that the Eolus was to wait in the straits of Gibraltar for the issue of something which was not yet completed.

The night came, and while Heartwell, in quite an attitude of despair, was sitting ruminating in his dreary cabin, he heard some words passing between some one and the sentinel at his cabin-door.

After listening attentively, he knew that the person who was addressing the sentinel was no other than the officer of marines who had so generously handed him the cutlass with which to defend himself against the ferocious attack of Captain Harding.

"You will look vigilantly to your post," he heard the officer say.

"Yes, sir," was the reply.

"You have no report to make?"

"None, sir."

"Very good."

The officer then entered the cabin, and carefully closed the door behind him; and Heartwell felt convinced that his visit was a friendly one, and that the words of warning he had spoken to the sentinel were only in accordance with his duty.

"How are you by this time, Mr. Heartwell?" he said.

"Well enough in health," said Heartwell; "and all the better in mind for the sight of a friendly face."

"I am much concerned about you."

"Nay; I have, I believe, by my own impatience, brought the evil under which I suffer on my own head; but do you run no risk of censure by visiting me?"

"The captain is on shore; and, in truth, I don't care what he says. You understand —I consider you as committed to my custody, as I am commanding officer of the marines, and you are guarded by them, so I shall stand upon my right of visiting my prisoner, for whose safe keeping I am responsible, when I like."

"True; taking that view of the case, you are right."

"I know I am."

"I rejoice to hear you say so, for the sight of a friendly face is now the only alleviation I can hope for from the miseries of confinement."

"Nay, do not misunderstand me. I expect, when the captain comes on board again, he will soon take some means of preventing me from waiting upon you, so that I do really expect this is the only friendly visit I shall be able to pay to you."

"Indeed!"

"Yes; it is to ask you if I can do anything to give you satisfaction—if there is any one you would like communicated with in any way; and, in short, if I can, by any possibility, serve you?"

"You are kind and considerate. All I desire is, that Heaven may grant me the opportunity of coming face to face with Captain Harding, that I may force him to give me the satisfaction of a gentleman, or inflict upon him such punishment for his pusillanimity, as he deserves."

"There I cannot aid you."

"I know you cannot. Is he going to remain on shore?"

"I apprehend so."

"Would that I could reach it!"

"Do not think of anything so mad. You must be aware that no one can land without being challenged by the sentinels."

"I know—I know—except at one particular point, where, by a circuitous route, the piece of neutral ground, which neither belongs to Spain nor to England, is situated."

"But that is a morass."

"It is so, and hence its assumed safety."

"Do not, for Heaven's sake, my dear Heartwell engage in any mad scheme of escape. Captain Harding, I have reason to believe, will remain here some time—I think, for despatches, and, if possible, I will visit you often."

"A thousand thanks—a thousand thanks."

The officer of marines now left him, for a protracted visit could not be excused on the ground that it was for the purpose of seeing to the safety of his prisoner.

CHAPTER XXVIII.

THE HAZARDOUS ESCAPE.—THE MORASS.—THE FIGHT, AND THE BOAT AT SEA.

THE idea of escaping from what looked extremely likely to become a very protracted imprisonment on board the Eolus, had taken possession of Heartwell's mind, and each moment it grew stronger.

It was just such an idea as a man in his circumstances would brood over until it assumed a very gigantic aspect indeed, and thus, moment by moment, it gathered strength, until he became almost to consider it as one of those things which were fully concluded to be done, and the best means of accomplishing which only had to be considered.

The Eolus lay about half a mile from the shore, and Heartwell knew well that he could swim without any difficulty double that distance. He likewise considered that he could easily make his way through one of the cabin windows, which served for port-holes when any exigency of war required.

He had—as we before remarked, from a consciousness that in the inquiry which would be instituted into his conduct he would get no justice done him—become reckless and desperate.

His life he valued not, and he made up his mind to run any risk to reach the shore with the faint hope of falling in with Captain Harding; a very faint hope indeed, when we come to consider the probabilities and possibilities of the case.

Whenever, however, the image of Minna Woodward presented itself to his imagination, Heartwell became so frantic, that he seemed to be deprived of all power of accurate reasoning.

How fondly, at the last interview he had had with her, he pictured the joy of his return —his return, too, with honour, as one of those who had fought their country's battles, and fought them well.

But now all that was changed, and those blissful anticipations were scattered to the dust. He had no such hopes—no such anticipations; with a blasted name and a ruined reputation, he knew that he should now touch the British shore, and therefore what cared he for life?—what cared he now, in the agony and despair of his heart, if he never again saw the white cliffs of Albion above the ocean.

The future to him was worse than a blank, for he knew that it would be a period of suffering; and, therefore, any evils or chances of the present were most welcome. By the time the sun had fairly set, and the moon had risen, he had thoroughly made up his mind to leave the Eolus, and, watching his opportunity, when some clouds had swept over the moon's surface, he slipped through the cabin window into the calm sea.

Previous to taking this step, he had from his wardrobe selected several useful articles; likewise a pair of pistols he provided himself with, together with a flask of powder and bullets. These he carefully wrapped in a case of oil-cloth, to keep them dry; and, so provided, he struck out from the side of the Eolos for the shore.

He had slipped into the sea so gently, that it was quite impossible any one could have heard him: but when he had got some distance from the vessel, one of the crew on deck for the night-watch saw him, and gave an alarm, as it was his duty to do, upon seeing any one at such a time swimming so near the vessel.

He was challenged from the deck, but of course he returned no answer, the only effect the alarm had upon him being to induce him to redouble his exertions to get as far from the ship as possible.

The sentinel on deck fired his musket at him, and Heartwell heard the plash of the bullet in the water close at hand. On he sped, and he was soon now so far off, that even —which was not likely,—if the trouble had been taken to launch a boat in pursuit of him, he would have stood a good chance of reaching the shore before it could have come up with him.

His object was to gain the morass, a point which he knew was undefended, on account of the presumed difficulty of any one landing there. Heartwell, however, had seen how a landing could be effected on that spot, and he did not now forget the lesson.

The moment he got sufficiently near the shore to feel the bottom with his feet, he lay upon his back, and so went the remainder of the distance, until his head touched the treacherous sands. Then, by a vigorous exertion, he rolled himself at full length upon the shore, and continued to roll over and over, at full length, until he got upon firmer ground.

This was not a very agreeable process, and besides, it was dreadfully fatiguing; but it was the only one by which he could at all hope to get over the quicksands, which, had he attempted to wade through, would soon have enveloped him so deeply as to have prevented him advancing another step, in which case he must have died a painful and wretched death.

Now, however, he gained his feet, and as each step that he took brought him upon firmer land, he walked on with rapidity until he found himself upon what is called the neutral ground, immediately contiguous to the garrison, which, in the history of Europe, has occupied at various times so important a place.

It was strange that now, when he had accomplished thus much, and all immediate danger was over, an irresistible desire to sleep came over Heartwell; and, saturated with sea water as were all his clothes, he lay down in the most sheltered spot he could find, and in a few minutes was in sound repose.

It was, doubtless, the exertion of swimming so far which had induced this drowsy feeling, as well as the change of scene from that cabin—which had become frightfully dull and monotonous to him—to the free fresh air upon the rock. Certain it is, however, that he slept for hours, a long, quiet, dreamless sleep, such as might have settled upon the senses of an infant and lapped it in oblivion.

When he awakened he was surprised to find that the day was dawning, and, for a few moments, until memory returned and told him all that had happened, he thought himself labouring under the impulse of some more than ordinarily vivid dream.

Then, as he remembered his real position, he rose to his feet; but it was with difficulty he did so, for his limbs were terribly benumbed and stiffened by sleeping so long in his wet clothing in the open air. Some vigorous exercise recovered him from this condition, and he set about seriously thinking what he should do next.

Not for long was he allowed the undisturbed company of his reflections, for he heard the sound of footsteps approaching, and he had only time to hide himself close to the wall of a house, which seemed to be a sort of depot for stores appertaining to the garrison, when he saw the figures of two men approaching.

The voices struck familiar upon his ear. Good Heavens! was it possible—yes—yes. These two persons were none other than Captain Harding and his great friend, the surgeon, with whom he was in deep conversation, little dreaming of such a listener.

They passed and repassed the spot where Heartwell was concealed, and, as they did so, he heard almost the whole of their confidential remarks.

" You quite understand," said Harding, " I think, now, all that I would have you say when the court of inquiry is held upon Heartwell?"

" Oh, yes, sir. I see my way clearly, and it shall be no fault of mine, you may depend, if everything does not go according to your wishes."

" Good. You may look for your reward from me, to a certainty, the moment this cruise is over. You intend going into business on shore?"

" Yes, sir; and of course your patronage would be to me of great importance, as well as the sums of money you have had the kindness to say you would assist me with in setting up."

" You may depend upon both."

" A thousand thanks, sir; and if there should come across your mind any other little matters you would like me to depose to, you have but to mention them, and I will take care they shall not be forgotten."

" Very well—very well. I wish he would commit suicide in the cabin."

" Oh, sir, he is not the sort of person."

" I am afraid not."

" No. You may depend, Captain Harding, that he will not do that. I can see he is quite a different sort of man."

" Well—well; we must manage the best way we can, of course, with such a subject; that's all I can say about it. I think we may quite consider him as settled and ruined."

" Oh, dear yes. Most certainly, sir, most certainly."

" Then you can go on board when you please. I have made an early breakfast, and shall take a ramble about this place, which is completely new to me."

" If I might request leave of absence from the ship for to-day, sir, I should be much obliged."

" Very well—very well."

After a few more words of a very common-place character, these two worthies parted, the surgeon going towards the garrison, while Captain Harding started in a direction southerly from the fortifications.

Heartwell had had difficulty enough hitherto to restrain his impatience, but he had done so with the hope of hearing as much as possible of the villanous counsels which had for their object his destruction, without reference to the honour or honesty of the means by which it might be accomplished.

Now he suddenly stepped forward and said, in a loud, clear voice,—

" Captain Harding, well met!"

CHAPTER XXIX.

FOLLOWS THE FORTUNES OF MINNA WOODWARD.

MINNA was so alarmed at this sudden onslaught, and, at the same time, so more than gratified at the prospect of deliverance from those ruffians who, from a mistaken notion of her character and her behaviour, would, in the exasperation of the moment, scarcely hesitated to have taken her life, that it is not to be wondered at she should rush into the street far more precipitately than seemed consistent with gratitude towards her preserver.

Still, when we come to consider the ferocious passions of the men who were so enraged against her, we must conclude that even the calmest reflection would not have suggested a course more likely to be highly beneficial in preserving both him and herself, than the one she was now pursuing.

That course was not to remain, and uselessly lament over his fall, perchance involving herself in a similar fate, but to fly from the house as she did, calling aloud for aid against the murderous ruffians who had committed such an outrage.

"Help! help!" she shouted; "murder! murder!"

Although there were but few passengers in the streets, such cries as these were highly calculated to bring those few together, and she found herself surrounded, in a most incredibly short period of time, by somewhere about a dozen of persons, who eagerly inquired of her what had happened.

But this effort she had made to procure something like aid for him who had been of such eminent assistance to herself, had been rather a thing of impulse than of reflection; so that, in her frantic, headlong career, and when she found herself surrounded by those who appeared willing and anxious to assist her, she was so bewildered for a few moments, that she could not find out the house from which she had so recently emerged. She wrung her hands frantically, as she rushed to and fro, exclaiming,—

"It is here—it is here—it is somewhere here!"

The people began to think she was a maniac, and one by one dropped off on their various pursuits, some with remarks of pity, and some of derision, leaving her alone, friendless, and most desolate of heart, in a street to which she had turned, that she knew not the name or aspect of.

Exhausted alike in mind and body, she sat upon a door-step, and, covering her face with her hands, she wept abundantly, and, as the tears trickled between her fingers, there arose to her mind's eye, like the dim shadows of phantasmagoria, the various events of her past existence.

She knew not why at that moment all these various circumstances should march before her mental vision in such terrific array; but there are times and seasons when, without any apparent provocation whatever to such a mental action, the mind will appear to be thrown back completely upon memory's resources, and to forget for a brief space the gloom and the anxiety of the present, until it shall arrive, in its due order, through the dim and uncertain vista of the past.

She remembered when a happy girl, and all around her was sunshine and joy, at the old tavern, which within its ancient boundaries comprehended as much as sufficed for her simple ambition—she remembered how she scarcely ever had a thought of more ambitious moment than should enable her to please that father, who was now no more, and the mother whom, for all she knew, grief ere this might have carried to the tomb.

Then she remembered how Heartwell came and told her that he loved her, and how she listened with all the girlish excitement, and the feeling of the heart's first passion, to the youth's tale. Then, then it was that she remembered how the ambition to be something more than she was, in order that she might the better deserve such a heart's devotion, came across her. She remembered how she had sighed to mingle with the great and the noble.

And then came the tempter, Lady Clare—the serpent who stole into her paradise, and with words of evil corrupted the gentlest heart that ever beat. And yet, how trivial had been her first error! How trifling, and apparently slight, had been that first false step of hers, which had indeed been merely to attend an assembly far above herself in presumed importance and rank, dressed in the borrowed plumes of a woman, whose conduct, from the first, had been more than questionable, and such as ought to have excited her suspicions.

It was ambition by which she had fallen—the ambition to be something greater than she could ever hope to be—the sin of pride, which turned from Heaven that terrific being, who, even now, in his exaltation of more than earthly intellect, is

"Not less than archangel ruined."

Oh, blindness! oh, infatuation! Was it not enough for her that she had won one of the best and noblest of hearts? Was it not enough that, as she was, and in her own proper character, she had achieved a triumph to which nothing surely can add a lustre?

Men like Heartwell do not love comparatively; they love once, love truly, and they love for ever, with their whole hearts, and their whole souls. Oh, Minna! Minna! could you imagine for one moment that you would have been dearer to David Heartwell, decked in a world's wealth of diamonds, and flattered and smiled upon by all that is courtly and all that is great, than you were as the gentle smiling daughter of the burly landlord of the Gun Tavern at Wapping.

Oh, fatal, fatal error! she saw it now as we mostly see our errors, alas! too late. Experience and suffering came hand in hand, and poor Minna, unequal as her fault was to its consequences, was now reaping the bitter fruits of a folly, the seeds of which she had, in a moment of thoughtlessness, placed in her bosom.

But little account had she of late taken of time; but now, with a hurried mental calculation, and a trembling eagerness, she began to tell herself that the period could not be far distant when Heartwell would return.

Oh, with what different feelings might she have welcomed the approach of that happy day to those with which, in all the agony of despair, she contemplated it.

Truly, could she have said with the half-distracted Lear when this thought crossed her mind,—

"That way madness lies."

The memory of all her crushed and ruined hopes rose up gigantically before her, and once again the dreadful idea of suicide flashed across her mind as a refuge against despair.

"I can meet," she said, "the censure, tempered, as it will be, by justice and mercy, of Heaven, far better than I can endure the cruelties of a world in which I can now know no peace."

With this specious argument upon her lips, she rose from where she had been sitting, and muttering to herself,—

"The river; yes, the river!" she began to calculate in what direction she should go in order to meet it.

There was a fixed calmness now which bespoke a far more dangerous amount of resolution than that which primarily had been so nearly heralding her to a fearful and guilty death.

She seemed to contemplate the awful step she was about to take as almost a natural result of a combination of circumstances far beyond her own control.

And she told herself, too, with a kind of superstitious awe, how she had heard of those who were near the confines of the grave being, as it were, impelled, by some spell cast over them, to review their past life and actions, even as she had done as she sat in solitary wretchedness upon that door step.

"I ought not to live," she said, "I ought not to live, for I bring wretchedness upon all those who would befriend me, and who would love me, and turn aside from their path to do me a kindness. There is not one of all who have spoken a word of pity or of sympathy towards me who have not suffered. Wherefore should I live to be the bane of the best portions of humanity, while I am the sport and derision of the worst?"

Then again she asked herself if she should consent to linger a while upon the earth—what she was to do in order to gain even a scanty subsistence wherewith to prolong that existence which she thought so little worth preserving.

The answer came to her mind with a shudder. She shrank aghast, and well indeed she might, at the dreadful course of life to which her to impending fate seemed hurrying her, and to which death appeared a thousand times less terrible.

"Oh, welcome!" she said, "welcome the oblivion of the grave! and, oh, if I could be sure that all David Heartwell would hear of me should be that I was no more, I might, at these last lingering moments, feel a ray of ancient happiness."

She wandered from street to street; she knew not whither she went; she felt that she could not command her feelings sufficiently to venture upon making an inquiry concerning the nearest route to the river. She was certain that if she did so, whoever she might address, would see her dreadful intention depicted upon her countenance; and so it was that she hesitated to ask, wandering onward with a vague feeling that she must be going somewhere in the direction of the river, until, with a shudder of terror, and a scarcely suppressed shriek, she found herself in a neighbourhood, every spot of which she was but too familiar with.

Yes; she was within a short space of that home of her infancy which, but a short time before, had risen up to her imagination in all its early pleasures and delights—that home which she had pictured to herself as the happiest which she could ever know, and which she could never know again but as a dim resemblance of what once had been.

Now she trembled so excessively, and such an accession of faintness came over her, that, though her first impulse was to fly from the spot, she found that, by a terrible kind of fascination, she was rather drawn towards her own home, than able to fly from it.

"What fate," she said, "has brought me here? Is this another emanation of the dreadful destiny that has pursued me so long? Am I never to escape? Is there really no hope for me but in the oblivion of death? and is death oblivion, or but a change from evils that we know, to those of a worse character, that we know not of?"

Even as she spoke, she moved nearer and nearer to her own home. She shook like one afflicted with an ague, and she mournfully told herself that she could not look upon the ancient house.

Yet, by a strange fatality, she moved towards it. Surely, surely, she was impelled by some unseen and wondrous power to approach that place, which had become terrific in her imagination, but where a circumstance was to occur to her, that was calculated to make a great change in her views and prospects, notwithstanding even the unhappy condition in which she was placed.

With what a tearful recollection she looked upon the well-known ships and houses that, as she hurried onwards, met her gaze.

There was not a name that she was not familiar with; not a trade there carried on, but she knew the persons who followed the calling, together with much of her personal history.

She wondered that no one saw her, that no one spoke to her; she dreaded, and yet she felt surprised that no old familiar friend came up to her to say, "Minna Woodward, is this really you, whom we had lost so long, and so nearly forgotten; or are you some vision of the past, with the familiar countenance of one we knew, but never thought to see again?"

And now she stood for a moment at a corner; another step—it was but one—and the old inn met her gaze.

CHAPTER XXX.

MINNA'S VISIT TO THE OLD HOUSE.—THE RECEPTION.—THE MYSTERIOUS MAN AGAIN.

SHE leaned against the ancient portico of a well-known old wooden house, before which she had sported many a time in happy childhood; and for a few moments only before her eyes so filled with tears that she could see nothing, did she gaze upon her father's home, once so dear, now such a subject of painful recollection.

Perhaps it was well that she wept, as she thus stood. Those tears relieved the surcharged heart when nothing else could have done so. She let them fall freely; and then she felt much refreshed, and was able to look more scrutinisingly upon the Gun Tavern.

But what did she see? what dreadful truth now rushed upon her mind? Surely her excited fancy had done much, in exhibiting to her gaze the ancient structure; for all that really remained of it was a portion of the blackened, charred front, and the swinging signs, which, with all in common appertaining to the house, bore ample evidence of some destructive fire, which had only spared that portion, as if to mock at what it had destroyed, rather than as an exhibition that it might be merciful.

Then, and not till then, did the thought cross her agitated mind that, while rowing down the river with that man, who, whatever might have been his social offences, had behaved kindly and considerately to her, she had heard of a fire, and of the supposition that it was at the old Gun Tavern.

So rapid—so distressing—and of such a varied character had been the incidents that had occurred to her since that eventful night, short as had been the interval, that she had completely forgotten the boy's suggestion, until she saw it so fearfully confirmed, in the blackened timbers of that building which had bidden defiance to time, but, per force, yielded to a more rapidly destructive element of mutilation.

"And that is all," she said; "and that is all that remains of the home that I left. Oh, that I had but perished amid these ruins! Oh, that I had been in very centre of the conflagration, and fallen with that mass of timber, up piled upon that spot where once old and well remembered rooms spread out their fair proportions! I might then have been happy, and those who spoke of me would have done so with a sigh; while, perchance, a tear of regret would have fallen to my memory; while now, alas! the good may congratulate each other, when I am gone, that one who had walked from the path of light to one of darkness, has been swept into the shadow of the tomb."

She was not aware, for a few moments, that some idle boys had gathered round her, and were speculating upon her evident emotion and evidences of care and grief.

When she did observe them, she moved on towards the remains of the old tavern, but a little girl, who was compassionate, plucked her by the dress, and said,—

" Please, don't go near the ruins ; they say they'll come down one day."

" And fall upon any one," said Minna, mournfully.

" So they say, ma'am."

" Pray, child, that they may fall upon me."

The little girl shrank back, and Minna passed onwards, until, if there was danger, she was in a fair way to meet it, for she stood close beneath the front of the old building, which seemed in so tottering and uncertain a condition, that one would imagine the slightest wind sufficient to demolish it all.

" Yes, yes !" she said ; " and this is what remains of the home I loved. I have lived now to see the ruin of everything. I have lived now to see every sight I could possibly dread except one, and that one I will go to the grave to avoid—it is the face of Heartwell, when he shall know that I can no longer be his—that my vows were as unstable as if written on the sands of the seashore, and that I am lost for ever."

"Now, if you please," cried a man, "those walls are going to be shored up to day; what do you stand so near them for; do you want to be crushed to death?"

"Yes!" said Minna; and she passed through what had been the ancient doorway, and stood in what had been the passage of the old inn.

The chaos of confusion that everything presented baffles description; such had been the insecure state of the ruins that had been left, that no person as yet ventured in to clear away the burnt timbers, fragments of furniture, and other debris of the fire.

Indeed it had been hoped that the walls would have fallen of themselves, in which case the whole structure, having attained the extremity of ruin, might have been approached with perfect safety; but high winds had blown, and rains had fallen, without producing this result, so that at length, as the ruin became a scandal in the neighbourhood, and a reproach to the parish, it was resolved to move it, and on that very day some workmen were intending to set about the necessary piece of work.

Certainly the danger was not increased by the fact that the place was on that day going to be shored up, or pulled down, popular rumour said not which; but, by the great care with which it had been avoided, any one would really have supposed such to be the case.

The man, when he heard Minna's declaration, looked upon her as cracked; and, after a moment's hesitation, he muttered to himself,—

"Well, it's no use interfering; I don't want to be bothered about attending an inquest, and all that sort of rubbish, losing a day and a half's work. I'll be off and say nothing, and see nothing; that's my best plan. It can't make any difference to her; and, besides, if it did—but, however, it can't."

And away he walked.

Minna crept on like some spirit, with noiseless footstep, among the ruins; she had no fear; on the contrary, it was a dreadful hope that she might avoid the stigma of self-slaughter by her death, at all events, appearing to be the result of accident, even if it really was not so.

It would have been a ghastly thing for any one to have seen her looking up at those walls, and hoping that they would fall upon her and destroy her.

The space which was now left in consequence of the destruction of the building, was much larger than even the old house had seemed to occupy, and she could hardly believe it possible that it had been composed of such an enormous mass of material.

It was not likely she would be interrupted now in this visit to the ruins of the Gun Tavern. No one, not so weary of life as she was herself, would for one moment have ventured within its precincts. The raging element which had destroyed the building, had created for her a solitude such as she could not have found in a populous city under any other circumstances.

A strange sort of maddened feeling came across her. She sat down upon a large piece of charred timber, and, with a gloomy aspect of almost fanatical resignation, she seemed there inclined to resign herself to whatever fate might come across her.

"Why should I seek the river," she said, "that cold and melancholy grave of the unfortunate, when I can die here, at least, upon the spot, if not amid the well-known sights and sounds which greeted my earliest years? Who will pluck me from this melancholy ruin? What arm would be stretched forth at its own peril to save me from the destruction I court and covet? Why will not yon shaking wall now fall down upon me, and so end at once the miseries which I have for so long and so weary a time endured, until life has become a pilgrimage without an object, and I am full of awful wishes that my next step should be into my grave."

But as it was not to be that Minna Woodward would be long permitted to congratulate herself with such a horrible species of rejoicing upon being left to suffer where she was.

Even at that dilapidated and broken entrance which had afforded her admission to the scene of destruction, there appeared a human form.

It was that of a tall man closely enveloped in a cloak of ample dimensions; a hat with a peculiar broad brim was slouched over his eyes, a stout stick was in his hand, and his eyes were bent upon the ground, as if in anxious search for something which he hoped to find amid those ruins.

Entering as he did in this attitude, and crouching, from his extreme height, to avoid coming in contact with some loose pieces of wood-work, that, with burnt and blackened ends, projected from the wall immediately above the door-way, he did not see Minna Woodward until he was fairly within the area which had been occupied by the demolished house.

Suddenly his eyes fell upon her, and he recoiled a step or two, and plunged his hand into the breast of his apparel, as if he would there have clutched some weapon of defence, to save himself from the probability of an impending attack.

"A woman!" he said, as he withdrew his hand, and his sudden energy of manner deserted him; "it is but a woman; some wandering mendicant, I presume, allured by the prospect of a few faggots from the ruins for her fire at home. I must bribe her to leave me alone here, or, seeing me searching for that which I want, but which is not of intrinsic value, she may suppose some hidden treasure is hereabouts, and watch me closely."

Minna looked at him with listless eyes, and in mournful accents, as she shook her head to and fro, she said,—

"No peace, no peace, even here. Why cannot the world leave me alone even upon this spot, so full of danger as they say it is, but to me so full of recollections that rob it of its terrors?"

Slowly picking his way, and it required caution to do so, towards her, the man came onwards until he was sufficiently close to speak to her, when he said, in a tone by no means divested of kindliness,—

"My good woman, you will oblige me very much by leaving here—it's a dangerous place—here's a shilling for you—go home, go home."

She looked up, and their eyes met; he started back as if something had struck him, and exclaimed,—

"Good God! is this Minna Woodward!"

"Away, away!" she cried; "do not pronounce that name within this sacred place. It is a name I will not own; a name I dare not own—begone, begone—leave me, leave me be, you who you may!"

"Thank Heaven," he said, "for this chance. I have left no probable spot unsearched for you; and now I find you here, where least I should have expected to encounter you. Come away, Minna Woodward, come away; I have a tale to tell you which shall enable you to have more than ample revenge upon him who has brought you to these straits."

"Revenge!" said Minna; "what have I to do with such a passion now? I want no revenge. I have no one to be revenged upon—you mistake me. If you knew me in happier days, and had one feeling of respect, or kindly feeling for me, I pray you to leave me to myself, and to the fate I have marked out for myself."

"That will I not do, Minna Woodward; you talk like one disgusted with the world, because a succession of its bitterness have come upon you; but this may not be; it shall be my task to free you from the trammels that are around you, and to make for you a bright and a better destiny."

"Can you undo," she said, "that which is done? can you absolve me from the memory of the past, and teach me to forget? can you make me what I once was in innocence and in happiness?"

"No, Minna; but I can make you look upon the present with a better aspect. I can enable you to see the good which, under all circumstances, can be extracted from our condition, and which should go far towards reconciling us towards it."

"No, no, no," said Minna; "impossible."

"Nay, you fancy that I am preaching to you in the common-place cant phraseology of sympathetic consolation; but, believe me, Minna Woodward, I am not doing so; I wish to promise you revenge for the past, as well as more satisfaction for the future. Believe me that I am your good genius, and that I have not sought for you so long without an object."

"It matters not, it matters not," said Minna; "all this is too late."

"Too late, Minna Woodward! No; let me assure you, you are not what you seem."

"Yes, I am—yes, I am, to the full, what I seem."

"And that is ——"

"A wretched outcast; one tired of life, one who would be rejoiced to bid it a long, a last adieu; one who can never joy again, and who hopes that Heaven, in its mercy, will now cut short a life of misery and unmitigated despair."

"This is madness, girl; you are yet young, nay, you are yet beautiful; life and the world are yet before you. You owe it to yourself, and you owe it to that society of which you are a member, to exact what retribution you may for the past; while, at the same time, you make the best of the future."

"Vain thoughts—vain thoughts."

"Not so, Minna. I have day by day searched these ruins with the hope of finding yet additional evidence to that which I can already sufficiently prove to satisfy the most sceptical; but I will make assurance doubly sure, and therefore I came here again, little expecting that on this, my last visit, kind fortune would place one in my way whom I so ardently wished to see. Come with me, Minna, come with me—I have a tale to pour into your ear that will so deeply interest you that you shall live again, feeling that you have an interest in existence, and that it opens before you with new prospects."

"No, no, I will not; I will not stir from here."

"But, by Heaven, you shall. I will be cruel to be kind, and if you will not come by fair means, I have an arm that can force compliance."

"By violence!" said Minna.

'Nay, it will not be necessary—you will not enforce such an extremity. If your mind be fixed on death, surely, surely, before you do depart this life, and throw yourself upon Heaven's mercy, you would wish to know a secret, which only from my lips can you know—the secret of who you are."

"I know too well—I am the wretched Minna Woodward; you have yourself pronounced my name."

"I did so pronounce it, because it is one you are in the habit of answering to, and, as such, would understand to address me when I uttered it."

"And is not that my name?" said Minna, interested, despite herself, by the manner in which the stranger spoke, and the peculiarity of his words.

"It is not."

"Indeed!"

"No; and before you descend into the grave, it is fit that you should become acquainted with the name you ought to bear."

"It is—it is, indeed. If you will tell me briefly, and tell me here, I care not if——"

"No, not here—I cannot tell you here. Come with me; I am a friend—believe me, on my soul, I am. Minna, you may trust me—I can claim kindred with you."

"Kindred with me!"

"Yes; as Heaven is my judge, I speak the truth. I've no desire for further concealment; I have long sought you to tell you all, freely, frankly, and truly. I have been trying a great experiment, and it has failed. Had it succeeded, I should have shrunk back to an obscurity from which I have recently emerged; but it has failed, failed most signally, and the world shall now know who and what I am."

"You bewilder me," said Minna. "I know not what to say—I know not what to think."

"Come on—come on, then; you can walk well. Lean upon my arm, I will support you; fear not for your weight. Alas! Minna, you are wonderfully changed since last I looked upon you. I could weep, and play the woman, to see you thus. Come, come, you feel—you know now that I am your friend."

CHAPTER XXXI.

THE MYSTERIOUS COMMUNICATION OF THE MAN WITH THE BLUE FACE.

THERE was a kind of enthusiasm of tone and manner about the man which insensibly had its effect upon Minna, and she now rose obedient as a child at his bidding, and hung upon his arm. A change had been given to the current of her thoughts, and an undefined but powerful curiosity arose in her mind to know who and what he was that spoke to her so strangely, and appeared to be so deeply interested in her fate.

"What have you to tell me," she faltered; "what have you to tell me?"

"In good time, Minna, in good time; come on, I will take you to a place of security, and shelter you where you will be able to rest from your fatigues, and to feel that the season of your calamity has passed away."

"No, no; it can never pass away to me."

"It will; nay, it has. From the first moment that a happy chance brought me to the ruins of the old Gun Tavern to-day, fate had ceased to persecute you, and a happier, brighter era in your existence had commenced."

"Oh, if I could but think so; if I could but think so for a moment."

"You will soon feel, thoroughly feel, that it is so; there, there, you are already better; now that we are clear of these gloomy walls, and so soon as we can find a coach, you shall not have the fatigue of walking."

"Well, well," said Minna, mournfully; "it matters not; I am wretched, desolate, and so deserted, even by hope itself, that evil fortune has not another arrow in her quiver to launch against my breast, half so envenomed as the barbs she has already planted there."

"Ay, and this is just the state in which I should have found you," said the man, "because I can raise you at once from it, and from all its deep dejection to a far different condition; but here is a coach; we will talk more of this presently; let me assist you. Even already, Minna, you're looking wonderfully better. The dawn of a newer and a happier existence seems beaming upon your face; you will again live to be the admired of all observers."

"This is a dream," said Minna.

"It is one then so real, that you will not awake from it."

"Tell me all at once; at once tell me all."

"Nay, wait 'till we get to a more convenient spot. I'm taking you to a home which, from the first moment that you cross the threshold, you may call your own; a home in which there are servants waiting your command—a home full of all the realities of that splendour which, even to your imagination, bore so brilliant an aspect, and to obtain but a glimpse of which you ran so great a risk and endured such terrible tortures."

"Do not; oh, do not," said Minna, "recal the memory of that dreadful time."

"Nay, I will not; it is not a theme I wish to talk upon; let us banish it."

Minna looked in his face with a strange kind of curiosity, as if she could hardly believe the words he uttered were true. The thought did flash across her mind that he might be a madman, but then, again, there was a vehemency in what he said that contradicted that idea.

Moreover, now and then there was a tone and manner about him which seemed to come dimly upon her recollection, and she asked herself when, where, and under what circumstances he had before crossed her path.

Memory was treacherous towards her, and afforded her no clue whatever, but each moment, as he spoke, she felt more impressed with the conviction that they must have met at some time, although she could not define the circumstances under which the meeting had taken place, or recollect who he was.

"You do not know me," he said, in answer to her inquiring look. "It is in vain for you to rack your memory to discover who and what I am. The effort is in vain, and, besides, an useless one; because it is a piece of knowledge that you shall soon acquire from my own lips."

"I'm content," she said, "to wait your own time, and, at all events, I believe you have saved me from the sin of self-destruction. Before this, I think that I should have been no more, but for your interposition."

"Thank Heaven I came as I did; but here we are at home."

The coach stopped at the door of a handsome house, and the stranger alighted and knocked for admission.

The door was flung wide open, and some servants obsequiously welcomed Minna's mysterious companion.

There advanced, too, towards him, a man venerable by age, but who, with a look of the most cringing and hypocritical servility, seemed inclined to bow down to the very earth before him; and although he looked upon Minna, when she was handed from the coach, with a stare of astonishment, he took good care that her companion should not observe that look upon his face; but, whenever he turned towards him, his eyes were again bent to the ground, and his body assumed a curvilinear position.

Minna's companion stepped aside for a moment, and addressed this man. He could not have said to him above a few words, but this had a magical effect as regarded his behaviour towards Minna, and it was quite evident that he would have lain down and allowed her to walk over him, had such been her pleasure.

The handsome furniture even of the hall, the noble aspect of the house, the rich liveries of the servants, and everything connected with the establishment, struck Minna with amazement; the only person that appeared of a plain and unassuming aspect was the man who had brought her from the ruins of the tavern; and yet he seemed, to all appearance, the lord and master of all.

He led her up a richly-carpeted staircase, into which her feet sank as if she were treading upon snow, and thence into a drawing-room replete with everything which could charm the fancy and soothe the senses.

The place was literally crammed with articles of taste and *vertu;* statuary, pictures, and *bijouterie*, sparkled in all directions.

Oh! what a change was this for Minna Woodward, from the misery, the destitution, and the desolation of spirit which she had experienced while sitting amid the ruins of the house of her infancy, where she had expected, and, indeed, where she had wished to find a grave.

And when she heard her companion say, in tones of deep sincerity, "Minna, you're welcome," she thought she would have dropped upon the spot; lest, by some chance word or touch, she should awaken, and find all but "the baseless fabric of a vision," which would vanish from before her admiring gaze, and "leave not a wreck behind."

"Be seated," said the stranger; "you shall have rest and refreshment before I unfold to you the circumstances which have made me so joyous at finding you; and believe me to speak in all sincerity, when I tell you that you may look around you, and feel that all you see here you may freely enjoy as your own. But you look faint—the colour forsakes your cheeks."

He rang, and ordered wine. A glass of the generous liquid restored Minna to herself again. She became more composed, and declaring herself fully capable of hearing any tidings, however agitating they might be, the stranger rose, and closing the door of the apartment carefully, he said, in a lower voice than he had yet spoken in,—

"Did you ever hear of Sir Bulkley Harding being haunted?"

"Haunted!" exclaimed Minna, in surprise.

"Yes, it is true; he was haunted; and I thought you were just cognizant of the fact, and no more."

"I do remember his being scared, I think, by some one who they said had a blue face, and that is all."

"Improbable as it may appear, it is true. Let Harding be where he might for the last two years, a man, whose face was of a strange, deep, blue colour, has constantly crossed him, telling him of things that he thought locked up in the recesses of his own heart, urging him with a romantic earnestness, to acts of nobleness and honour, and imploring him to fly from that course of life, which would only end in degradation and contempt."

"But he did not heed the monitor?"

"He did not; he trembled while the mysterious being was present, but still the wine-cup went as often to his lips—still, at the beck of pleasure, he would outrage all that should make a man noble and honest—still would he give ear to the greedy sycophants that surrounded him, and who, because he lavished his gold freely amongst them, stirred heaven and earth to procure for him a variety of pleasures, all which he partook of, heedless how far he outraged social law or the commonest decencies of society."

"It was so. I have heard so much, and you know how I have suffered."

"Yes, yes! no more of that; the hour of suffering is past—that of vengeance is at hand."

"I want no vengeance."

"We shall see. Can you not guess, Minna, that when I talk to you as I have talked to you about this mysterious man that used to haunt Harding, that in me you see him?"

"I guessed as much."

"Yes; for two years I have followed him from place to place, until very lately, in the hope of finding some latent good in his nature. I have been grievously disappointed; there is nothing of such a description in him. If I had found but one spark of virtue that I could have fanned into a flame I could have been content, but there was not such a spark, it was not to be found; and, therefore, have I now concluded to do all that is in my power to do to bring him from the high estate he now occupies, and make him low indeed!"

"What power have you to do so?"

"The greatest; but in order that you should hear that which I have to relate to you in due order and sequence, let me not commence at this point, but at one which will bring us to it in more regular order. If, however, you desire rest before you hear more, there are no events at present which require hurry or precipitation. If you know that which I have to say to you to-morrow, instead of to-day, no evil of any kind will result from the postponement of the information."

"No," said Minna; "tell me now, I implore you to tell me now—let me hear all now at once. I should not sleep; I could not taste of repose, with a consciousness that such secrets were pending."

"Well, be it so; I will condense the narration, so that in a few words, comparatively speaking, you shall know all."

After a few moments' pause, during which a sad and serious expression crossed his countenance, he said,—

"Lord Saltoun was a man in whom, perhaps, the vices and the virtues of humanity were about equally balanced; but he lacked that spirit of determination which might have enabled him to become either a great good character or a sufficiently vehement bad one, to put society on its guard against him. What he wanted, however, in energy of character, Lady Saltoun amply possessed. She came of a family very far inferior in rank to his lordship, who, when but a few months past his majority, had become enamoured of her for her personal attractions, and elevated her to a rank in life which, doubtless, her wildest dreams of ambition had never aspired to.

"That he should have made so unequal a match, coming, as he did, from so honourable and ancient a family, I attribute principally to the foolish conduct of his father, who, during his minority, kept him in such needy circumstances, that he was compelled to seek for his pleasures and his society in a grade of life below that in which fortune had cast him.

"Of course, his marriage enraged the family; but it was a perfectly valid proceeding, and, consequently, let their rage be what it might, nothing could be done but repudiate the young man, or receive his wife.

"Now, as he was an only son, and heir presumptive to the title, and likely to live long as the head of the illustrious family whose name he bore, although it went sadly against the grain for his haughty relations to do any such thing, they chose the lesser of the two evils, and with great reluctance consented to receive the wife.

"But although they received him, it was not with a good spirit; and you understand, Minna, that in that class of society, to receive a person, and to appear to be upon the most friendly terms with them, is but sometimes a shallow pretence, put on for the purpose of inflicting upon them the most deadly injuries."

"I understand."

"I do not know that the male members of the Saltoun family would have gone out of their way to do any mischief to Lord Saltoun's wife, notwithstanding she was so far beneath them in social rank; but it so happened that there were some women so connected with that distinguished line, that all their petty pride and arrogance were at once roused to repel what they considered the intrusion of plebeian blood among their noble race.

"These women were not satisfied by merely treating Lady Saltoun with the coldness appertaining to the most frigid civility; but they at the same time set about, being idle, and having abundant means, contriving what they could to her disadvantage and ultimate unhappiness."

"Precisely."

"You are interested?"

"I am. Pray proceed."

"Lady Saltoun was not a woman long to remain in ignorance of the machinations which were being carried on against her. She repelled scorn by scorn, hatred by hatred, and, finally, insult by insult; so that, at length, the breach between her and Lord Saltoun's family was about as complete as anything of that kind could be."

"What an unhappy state of things!"

"It was, indeed; and most unhappy was it, likewise, for another branch of the family."

"Indeed!"

"Yes; he who is now Admiral Harding, and one of the lords of the admiralty, was the brother of the Lord Saltoun I speak of; and in order that you should fully understand my narrative as I proceed, I should inform you that that gentleman made an alliance in every way suitable to his rank, as the brother of a peer, with a lady of considerable accomplishments and personal attractions.

"Somehow or another, the Admiral Harding that is now, then a captain in the royal navy, and rapidly rising in that distinguished profession, was greatly attached to his brother Lord Saltoun, and deeply solicitous for his happiness in life."

"Harding, then, is the family name?" said Minna.

"Yes, and Saltoun the title of the family."

"I understand clearly, pray go on."

"Admiral Harding, then, far from joining in the persecutions to which Lady Saltoun was subjected, did all in his power to make her situation more desirable, and exerted himself to the utmost to procure for her a pleasant position among the members of his proud and arrogant family."

"He was surely much entitled to her gratitude."

"Yes; but she was one of those women, who, when once their passions are fairly aroused, think of nothing, and care for nothing, but their gratification. She knew that Admiral Harding had behaved extremely well to her; but if, in the prosecution of any of her schemes, it became necessary to sacrifice him, she was not the kind of woman to hesitate for a moment about doing so.

" The sequel will prove to you that when I talk thus of Lady Saltoun, I use an amount of candour which must be painful to myself, and which is quite sufficient to rescue me from the charge of exaggerating any of her faults."

" I do not believe, for a moment," said Minna, " from the manner in which you have spoken, that you are likely to exaggerate the faults of anybody."

" And, least of all, would I do so in that quarter ; probably, but for a circumstance, as sudden as it was unexpected, things might have gone on in the Saltoun family much as usual —a kind of civil war raging among its female members, which the men tried to keep out of as they could—had it not been that about two years after the union of Lord and Lady Saltoun, a dangerous illness seized upon the former, and seemed to baffle the skill of the most eminent persons of the medical profession.

" He was evidently fast approaching his end, and there seemed to be considerable anguish of mind attendant upon some circumstances, which pressed strongly upon him almost to the moment of his dissolution

" A son had been born to him and his lady, a healthy child, who seemed likely to perpetuate in himself the honour of his family, and effectually to mingle the inferior stream of his mother's blood with that of the illustrious and antiquated house, to which, by a strange freak of fortune, she had succeeded in allying herself.

" On his death bed, Lord Saltoun sent for his mother and two of his sisters, and what he then said, Minna, I will relate to you in as nearly the same language as it was told to me."

" Believe me," said Minna ; " I'm deeply interested ; I'm quite certain that you do not tell me this narration aimlessly."

" I do not, indeed."

" Then you admit it has some direct connection with my own fate ?"

" A connection so direct that you shall be astonished at its closeness."

" Then, indeed, am I all impatience to know more."

" Minna, tell me, before I proceed further, have you no vague recollection of some state of existence very different from that of the tavern of Wapping, as being yours in your very earliest years?"

" I cannot say. Sometimes, certainly, I have seen my father and my mother whispering together, and looking upon me strangely."

" Ay ; no doubt—no doubt."

" Then, again, when I was first introduced into the splendid drawing-room of Lady Clare, the spacious apartments, the lights, the music, and the gay forms, seemed to come across me like the remembrance of some early dream."

" No doubt, Minna—no doubt ; I can be the soothsayer that can translate for you that feeling. It was not the dim remembrance of a dream that made such scenes as those appear not so strange to you as they otherwise might."

" Say you so ?"

" I do, indeed. It was a reality that you remember ; for during some of the earliest years of your existence, you had encountered scenes far exceeding those in the very romance of richness and beauty."

" Oh ! tell me not of myself," said Minna ; " but let me know more of those in whose history I cannot help feeling that I am most deeply and largely interested."

" I will. Restrain your impatience for awhile, and let me proceed systematically ; so that when you hear a sudden result, you will not, in the abundance of your astonishment, be compelled to ask a multiplicity of questions, but you will feel yourself in a condition at once to understand your real position."

" Yes, yes," almost gasped Minna ; for a thousand strange surmises were chasing each other through her mind. Some of the wildest chimeras which the most active imagination could have conceived, now at times found a home in her brain.

She hoped and feared a thousand things, to which, in fact, she could give no form or adequate expression, and the resemblance of which to reality must all depend upon the continued communication which was being addressed to her by the mysterious stranger.

Every word of that communication that fell from his lips bore so strong and vivid an aspect of truthfulness, that she could not for one moment doubt the verity of every word he uttered, as well as that it was uttered with sufficient prudence and caution, to make it rather under than over the fact.

After a slight pause, he continued,—

" Lord Saltoun, then, upon his death bed, as I told you, summoned his mother and two

of his sisters.   His wife was not in the room at the moment; but a woman was there who had been her confidential domestic and friend before her marriage, and who, no doubt, knew every circumstance connected with her history.

"I am about," said the dying man; and he spoke with pain and difficulty—"I am about to ask of you, my mother, and of you, my two sisters, a favour.   It is one which to grant me takes nothing from you, while it gives to me, in these my last moments, what I most require upon earth—peace here—peace here."

He struck his breast as he spoke, and it was evident that, whatever might be the subject of his communication, it was one that affected him deeply and nearly.

"Are you aware," said his mother (she was a stern woman that mother)—"are you aware there is a domestic in the room?"

"Yes," said Lord Saltoun, "I am."

"Then, you do not wish her to hear the communication you have to make?"

"I do wish her to hear it; it will be no news to her, and she will be a witness to the promise I intend to exact from you, if you have one spark of affection for me in my dying moments."

The mother of his lordship looked with an evil eye upon the woman, but she no longer objected to her presence; in fact, she was not mistress in that house, and had no right to object.

As for the two sisters, they looked on coldly.   They were proud, arrogant women, with but little of the amenities of life in their composition, so that the death of their brother was an event which called but very little upon their sympathies, and perhaps, if it added to their circumstances in any way, they would have become easily and completely reconciled to it, as an event less to be deplored than desired.

Lord Saltoun spoke at this, his dying hour, with a firmness and a precision which in life he had scarce ever been able to pretend to.

He raised himself upon his arm, and fixing his lustrous eyes upon his relatives, for they looked large and lustrous, in consequence of the wasting of his flesh, he said,—

"At such a time as this, candour best befits him who speaks, and patience them who hear.   It is needless for me to seek for courtly phrases in which to trammel the truth. You have all of you then, been bitter and uncompromising enemies of my wife; you know it, and therefore it is no use denying a part which we are all perfectly cognizant of as a forgone conclusion."

The mother looked fidgetty and restless, but the daughters assumed cold and contemptuous aspects, as if—but for the occasion, and that they did not consider it worth their illustrious while so to do—they would and could have justified their heartless proceedings.

"That wife," continued Lord Saltoun, "of whom you have been so uncompromising an enemy, has been an amiable wife to me, whatever she may have appeared to the world."

"Indeed!" sneered one of the sisters.

"Peace!" cried his lordship; "at such a moment as this I will have no such speeches made.   Beware that I leave not behind me, at this solemn hour, some malediction which shall haunt her against whom it is launched even to the grave's brink."

This remark seemed to silence them for a moment, for with all their other qualities they were superstitious, and they seemed to have a dread of the dying curse which Lord Saltoun had hinted he might leave behind him as a fitting legacy for those who deserved at his hands no better treatment.

"Go on," said the mother, who seemed the most shaken by what was proceeding; "go on; if that which you ask be at all possible, it shall be done."

"It is very possible," he said.   "It asks you to do nothing but to abstain from doing that which, if in another world I have cognizance of the proceedings in this, will assuredly afflict me more than any other pangs which I could suffer."

"Speak, speak," said the mother, "speak your wishes."

"It is simply this," he replied; "I wish you to promise me, that, let what will occur of a suspicious, a doubtful, or an apparently conclusive nature, you will never, so help you Heaven, dispute, litigate, or affect to doubt the legitimacy of my son."

This communication, so sudden, so unexpected, and so startling, appeared for the moment to paralyse them all three.

"Do not misunderstand me," said Lord Saltoun, with increased energy; and he rose in the bed, stretching out his arms, as if he would appeal to Heaven to attest the truth of what he uttered.

"We cannot misunderstand you," said one of the sisters, eagerly.

"Hold!" he cried; "I can see by the triumphant glance upon that face that you do misunderstand me.   The child is perfectly legitimate; but there is room for litigation upon a matter which had better be numbered among the things that are past, and which I knew not of myself, as Heaven is my judge, until very, very lately."

"If there be room for litigation," said one of the sisters, "there is room for abundant doubt."

"Give me the promise," he cried.

"Not I."

"Nor I," said the other.

"My dying curse ——"

"No, no—I promise—we will all promise.   My dear children, at such a dreadful moment as this do not let me see you divided by animosities that may bring me with sorrow to the grave; give the desired promise he claims, and let your brother die happy."

"Never," they both cried, and then one added,—

"There could not be a more fitting opportunity for getting rid of all the consequences to our family which such an unequal marriage has produced."

"I promise—I promise," said the mother; "you hear me—I promise."

"I accept your promise, mother," he said; "and may the great God above ——"

She thought he was going to curse his sisters, and she interrupted him, imploring him, by all that was sacred, not at such a moment to utter any words but those of peace and good will to all.

Again he spoke, lifting up his arm as he did so, and his voice had all the solemnity of one already almost in the presence of his Creator.

"May the great God above ——" he cried.

"No—no!" shrieked the mother.

"Forgive," he added, "those who would wrong the innocent and the fatherless."

"Thank Heaven for this mercy!" said the mother; and she sank fainting upon the floor. Lord Saltoun fell back upon the bed a corpse.

CHAPTER XXXII.

THE STRANGER'S EMOTION. — MINNA'S QUESTIONS AND DEEP INTEREST IN THE NARRATIVE.

WHEN he who had been relating to Minna Woodward this narrative, and who had evidently, from the deep interest he himself took in it, given a graphic power to that narration, which otherwise could not aspire to it, came to this point, he seemed deeply affected. He shook with emotion, and the expression of his countenance was such that one could almost imagine he saw vividly before him the scene he had depicted, consisting of that dying man, with his last words of forgiveness hovering upon his lips; the mother, in whom at that moment a better feeling than had for a long time actuated her, exerted a benign influence; and the sisters, so cold, so heartless, and so callous, that even at that moment when death was in the apartment, they could not throw off their worldly mindedness, and that feeling of resentment, which surely should be left at the grave's brink, even if it be carried so far.

"You are much moved?" said Minna.

"I am, I am."

"You have a stronger interest in this narrative than you have avowed?"

"Yes, Minna—yes; I cannot say to you that I have not."

"Tell—tell me all, let me sympathise with you, and feel that by so doing I am at least attempting to make a return for the distinguished kindness with which you have treated me always since the few short hours that I have been in your company."

"Not quite yet," he said; "not quite yet."

"Nay—why keep me in suspense?"

"It is better; and besides, believe me, I grieve to think how sad it must have been to such a father at that moment, to be deprived of the society of his only child."

"Ah! was it so? I had forgotten the babe."

"Yes, it was far away; one of those temporary accessions of convalescence, which frequently occur after disease has made its most insidious progress, and nearly heralded its victim to the grave, had occurred a day or two previously; so, that Lord Saltoun had yielded to the advice of his physicians, and had his child removed from the atmosphere of a sick house to a beautiful and salubrious marine retreat, belonging to the family, near the coast of Dover."

"And was there not time to get him back?"

"No, no, no."

"That was sad, indeed; but, I did not hear you say that Lord Saltoun felt this strongly at the moment of his death."

"He spoke not of it."

"And, therefore, it is hoped he felt it not acutely."

"Nay, I cannot indulge in such a hope—I would if I could."

"Indeed! How is it you know so accurately what passed on the occasion?"

"Because I had it all word for word, exactly, related to me, as I now relate it to you, Minna Woodward, by that domestic, who was permitted by Lord Saltoun to be present during his communication to his mother and sister."

"I had forgotten her."

"It was from her lips that I heard the tale, but not till years and years had closed over the remains of him who was the principal actor in that fearful little episode of real life."

"And was the child's legitimacy disputed?"

"Wait awhile, in good time you shall hear."

"It would be very cruel."

"Ay, but no cruelty could surely come amiss to those who could look so calmly and so unmoved upon the death bed of one as nearly related to them as was the dying nobleman, who had only made to them so natural and so kindly a wish."

"Could such people be happy ?"

"No; the day of retribution for them would surely come. It did come, and in a manner, too, that affected them most closely and nearly: in their pride—that fell passion which no human beings possessed to a greater degree than they—were they doomed to suffer, and they did suffer most completely."

"It was just that they should."

"Ay, but that matters little; the suffering of the guilty can be but a poor subject of congratulation while the unmerited agony of the innocent awakens our tenderest sympathies, and calls strongly upon our best feelings for succour."

"But you will tell me more ?"

"Yes, I will tell you all. I have not commenced for the purpose of giving you an incomplete narrative."

"First, though, let me hear what Lady Saltoun said and did upon the death of the man who had raised her from so humble a station to one of power and influence; you have not painted her in favourable colours heretofore. Did she deserve, under these distressing circumstances, a better judgment ?"

"She did! she did!"

"I'm very glad of that."

The mysterious stranger rose, and, with agitated strides, paced the apartment. As he passed Minna in his excited walk, she heard him muttering to himself some words confusedly, but some sufficiently distinct for her to comprehend them, and catch much of the meaning which they conveyed.

"'Tis very strange," he said; "but surely, surely some hidden natural impulse of the mind—which is one of those things that baffles all inquirers of human motives—induces her to feel a gladness upon this subject, when she can have but no more real knowledge of the parties than what she can gather from the particulars of the narrative I have communicated to her. Call this sympathy nature or instinct, what we will, there it is, clear and palpable, and not to be mistaken."

"Why do you talk thus ?" said Minna; "you seem to be continually keeping me on the verge of some secret which, if told, would be deeply interesting to me; but which, from some motive that I cannot comprehend, you consider necessary to keep yet from me for a while."

"It is so; it is so," he said. "Now, listen."

"With all my soul I listen to you."

"The death of Lord Saltoun, although expected day by day, was yet sudden when it happened, or I am assured his wife would have been at his bed-side.

She was in the house, and it was not until the chamber had been deserted by all but the confidential domestic I have mentioned to you, that she came towards that apartment.

Much of the natural fervour of her disposition, partaking, as it did, of a passionate character, was gone, and grief sat heavily upon her eyes as, with a slow and solemn step, she came towards the apartment.

The servant whom I have mentioned heard her approach, and hurried to the door to stop her from receiving so sudden a shock as might be the case were she to enter abruptly, and look upon the dead form of him who was so nearly allied to her while living.

But the manner of the woman proclaimed at once to Lady Saltoun the fact which she, for a short time, had wished to conceal from her; the aspect of her countenance, and the way she sought to bar her ingress to the room, were more than sufficient to be convincing proofs that sympathy for the sick must now be exchanged for mourning for the dead.

She clasped her hands, and she looked her attendant in the face, as she said, with more real feeling than might have been expected from a person of her usual habits,—

"You need not put your news into words—your looks proclaim it—Lord Saltoun is no more."

"I cannot deny the fact, your ladyship," said the woman; "I pray you to be comforted."

"Comforted!" exclaimed Lady Saltoun; "comforted! stand out of my way, woman, and do not insult me by using such words of common-place consolation."

She pushed the attendant on one side, and entered the chamber of death. That domestic was a woman of considerable nerve; but yet she dreaded to follow her mistress for there was something in her appearance that deterred all communication at such a moment.

She listened, however, at the door, while her mistress remained in that chamber, which was for a period of time nearly reaching to half an hour.   More than once she felt tempted to interfere, and to persuade her to come away from the sad sight which was there presented to her; but a feeling of respect for the dead, as well as for the living, at such a moment, held her back.

"It was a natural feeling," said Minna.

"Yes," replied her informant; "and from her own lips I had the particulars of how anxiously she kept watch and ward at the chamber door, while Lady Saltoun was within.

She told me she heard her sobbing as if her heart would break.   She told me that then she heard her talking to herself, in accents apparently of rage and of defiance, and, after that, by the deep solemnity of her voice, the listening domestic thought that she was praying.

And thus the time passed away, until suddenly the door was opened, and, with a calm and almost stately demeanour, the Lady Saltoun emerged from it.

She spoke to the servant in a firm and collected voice.

"Harriet," she said, "you know where my child is?"

"Yes, my lady."

"There is money—go to it at once.   Keep watch and ward over it.   Lose not sight of him for a moment.   Remember who he is—you have a nobleman in your keeping!"

"A nobleman, my lady?"

"Yes!" cried Lady Saltoun, furiously; "Lord Saltoun is no more, and does not his son succeed to his title?"

The servant shrank back, for she was appalled at the manner of her mistress; and, at that moment, the door of another room opening on to the same corridor was opened, and the deceased lord's two sisters made their appearance.

There seemed no doubt that they had overheard the brief colloquy which had taken place between Lady Saltoun and her confidential domestic.   Something expressive sat upon both their countenances, and one of them, confronting the servant as she was about to go, said, with marked emphasis,—

"Yes; be sure you take care of the young nobleman, if you should chance to find one."

The servant left; but Lady Saltoun walked up, with a dignified air, to these arrogant sisters of her deceased husband.

Her manner daunted them, and they shrank instinctively.

"I know you both well," she said; "you have all the pride and all the malice that belongs to your race, without any of those respectable and dignified qualities which ennoble even nobility.   I know well, now that he is dead who stood between me and your malignity, that you will attempt to do something dangerous to my peace.   I do not for a moment doubt it.   But, beware! I warn you.   I know you well, and shall detect you, even let you act with all the cunning of which you can be the mistresses; and I am not one quietly to suffer a wrong.   My vengeance shall be ample and complete."

They were abashed.   There was a vehemence and truthfulness about her manner, which terrified even those cold-hearted women, who were brought up to habits of indifference, and to fancy that the height of dignity was to be callous and insensible to all the ordinary and better feelings of humanity,

Before either of them could reply to this sally of Lady Saltoun, she had walked from the corridor.

Then their anger induced them to make a movement to follow her; but, before they had got far, they spoke to each other, and deeper, if not better, counsels prevailed.

"This is well enough," said one; "she has warned us."

"Yes," replied the other; "and we must be all the more cautious."

"True.   In her rage she has done us a service.   Let us retire, and consult upon the singular communication."

"Communication!" remarked the other.   "He made no communication."

"Indeed! can you be so blind as not to feel that what he said to us was tantamount to a declaration of his child's illegitimacy?"

"It certainly looked like it."

"Can it be possible that, after all, we have been enduring the society of this woman for more than three years, and putting up with endless vexations and troubles on her account, when, after all, she may not be our brother's wife?"

"That would be a discovery, indeed, worth making."

" But not half so much worth making as it would have been had he lived."

" How dreadfully provoking !"

" If I were a man," said the eldest, " I should swear."

" Swear away," said the younger.   " I think nothing of it."

" Ladies," said the confidential servant, who had merely retired to an open chamber within a few paces, on the same floor—" ladies, if I were not engaged upon an errand for my mistress, which will admit of no delay, I might be amused by remaining and listening to what manner of oaths you would give utterance to ; but, as I must go, and as I do not like to leave you in any state of doubt about the legitimacy of Lord Saltoun's son and heir, I will communicate to you what I do know upon that subject."

" And, pray, what may that be," said she, " putting aside for an instant the unbounded insolence of your conduct in listening to our conversation ?"

" It is just this, ladies, that Lord and Lady Saltoun were married at the little church at Willesdon, in the neighbourhood of London ; that I was present at the ceremony ; and in the records there kept you will find an ample voucher of the fact."

The sisters looked at each other with a peculiar meaning in their faces.   From long habits of intimacy, they almost understood each other's thoughts at a glance.

They each nodded to the other ; and then one, advancing towards the domestic, said,—

" My good woman, of course, like the rest of the world, it behoves you to look to your ·self and to your own interests."

" Certainly, madame."

" Then, you heard what Lord Saltoun said upon his death-bed ?"

" I did."

" That there is some secret connected with the child, we cannot doubt ; and, moreover, we are inclined to believe that you know it."

" There is a secret."

"And you know it ?"

" I do."

" Then, what sum will induce you to reveal it to me ?   Think well upon the subject. Your interest is entirely with us, and not with Lady Saltoun, who will have very little in her power, as it will be a number of years before her son comes to his property and title, even if he should live so long, or not be dispossessed of both by legal means."

" Well, ladies, I have no objection to trust to your generosity, as regards payment for the secret which I shall communicate to you freely."

The sisters looked at each other with a contempt for the intellect of this woman, which they did not attempt to conceal.   No doubt, they were the best judges in the world of what poor reliance could be placed upon their generosity, after they had obtained possession of the secret, which they would, in the first instance, have handsomely paid for.

" Well, what is it ?" said one.

" Hush !" said the servant.   " Take care we are not overheard ; and as it is as much my fault as any one's else, I should not wish it to go further."

" No, no, it shall not."

" You give me your word of honour that you will not repeat it ?"

" Oh, decidedly, decidedly."

" Because to do so would create much mischief, and hurt my feelings."

" Oh, dear me !" said the youngest sister ; " we believe that servants and tradespeople may have feelings, just the same as anybody else—that is to say, to a certain extent in their way ; and I'm sure we don't wish to hurt yours."

" Well, then, ladies, listen.   The fact is ——"

" Yes, yes."

" That his lordship's son ——"

" Yes."

" Hush !"

" There's nobody here."

" Well, then, to out with it at once.   He—he has never ——"

" Never what ?"

" Don't blame me ; but he's never been vaccinated.   I was to have got it done ; and there was a nice, healthy child, Mrs. Bayles's baby, who had it fine ; and Mr. Simpson said ——"

" D—n Mr. Simpson !" said the eldest sister.

" And d—n Mrs. Bayles's baby !" said the other.

" Ladies, ladies !" said the domestic ; "I'm waiting for my reward.   I threw myself upon your generosity, you know, and I hope I shall not be deceived.   I assure you it's

THE FIRST FALSE STEP.

^a fact; he never was vaccinated, and the consequence may be, that he may have the small pox naturally. I don't say he will—he may, or he mayn't. I knew a Mrs. Golightly, that never vaccinated her children ——"

The haughty sisters turned upon her. They seemed for a moment as if they would have forgotten their dignity so far as even to strike her; but they got the better of the feeling, and, after a moment's hesitation, they, with as much dignity as they could for the moment assume, left the spot.

CHAPTER XXXIII.

MINNA'S ANXIOUS INQUIRIES.—THE CONTINUATION OF THE STRANGER'S NARRATIVE'

" Have you not arrived yet," said Minna, "to that part of your discourse which enables you to be candid with me, and tell me what relation all these circumstances bear to me ?"

" Not quite, Minna."

" But you admit they all do bear some relation to the events of my own existence; and you promise eventually to afford me a key to them all ?"

" I do, Minna; and that as shortly as possible; but you ought to hear more yet before you will be able to connect the narrative in such a manner, as to make anything tangible of it."

" Then I will have patience—such patience as I can command—and listen further. For its own sake I feel interested in what you have related to me, apart from feeling that it is of importance to myself, individually. I pray you, then, go on, and let me hear all."

" Be assured that I shall keep nothing from you. Attend to me as I proceed."

" Yes; with all the attention that a human being can give to the communication of another."

" It is impossible to say, then, but that Lady Saltoun felt considerable anxiety, almost amounting to fear, on account of the threats which had been used against her by her deceased husband's sister.

You will, however, be inclined to think that the remarks which fell from Lord Saltoun at the time of his decease could not be utterly pointless, or without some particular reason upon his part to give force and consistency to their utterance.

It was not likely that a man upon his death-bed, feeling all the affection that he unquestionably did for his child, would jeopardize its inheritance and its fair fame by making such remarks as those that had fallen from his lips.

And he must have felt that there was a likelihood that some circumstance, even without inquiry, would come to light, which, unless he received the promise which he endeavoured to extract from his sisters and his mother, might be used greatly to the disadvantage of his son.

You have perceived, Minna, that nature awakened the latent feelings of affection in his mother's breast, and that she made the promise which he at that awful moment required of her.

But the sisters, who were much more unfeeling, by no means so far committed themselves to mercy, but only felt that what had occurred gave them a hint which might possibly turn greatly to the advantage of their views.

It was not so much that the disinheriting of Lord Saltoun's son would be of any advantage to these imperious and haughty women, as an evident wish upon their parts to rid the family of the plebeian connection that, to their notions, had so far disgraced it.

They knew that the title, if Lord Saltoun's son were declared illegitimate by the proper authorities, would go to Admiral Harding, who, having no child but a daughter, presented no means of perpetuating the honours of the family in the male branch.

But this, to their idea, was far more desirable than allowing a child of Lady Saltoun's to become the head of the family, and thus they set up legally Admiral Harding and his daughter as opponents to Lady Saltoun and her son.

They spoke to him upon the subject, but it was in vain that he repudiated all idea of interference, and implored them to let the affair alone; they would not do so, and consequently he was placed in an extremely awkward and antagonistic position with persons whom he had always hitherto been on friendly terms with.

And now, by foul means and by fair, the ladies Harding set about inquiring into the early life of their brother's widow, in order to ascertain some things which would be grounds for action.

They employed a legal practitioner, who was directed to spare no time, trouble, or expense, in the prosecution of the inquiry.

With such an unlimited order as this, if there be anything to find out, a clever man is likely, sooner or later, to light upon it; and, after trying a number of expedients, this attorney hit upon one which procured him some information.

He caused an advertisement to be inserted in the public papers to the following effect :—

"If any one can claim to be descended from, or nearly connected with Elizabeth Gray, late of the parish of Willesden, and will call upon Anderson Knott, Esq., of Gray's-inn, they will hear of something to their advantage."

This advertisement produced a woman, a garrulous old woman, of the name of Gray, who claimed to be cousin, or some such thing, of Elizabeth Gray, of Willesden, and she insisted that the said Elizabeth Gray, such being the maiden name of Lady Saltoun, had married a man in London, who either was a brazier by trade, or whose name was Brazier.

Which of these two was the real state of the case, all the lawyer's ingenuity could not make out, and further information this old woman could not give, except that the brazier, or Mr. Brazier, was a good-looking man, with an open countenance, and remarkably like her first husband.

Mr. Knott was extremely anxious to get an accurate description of Brazier, and he said, with all the cunning of a weazle, to the woman,—

"Now, I dare say you have a more vivid perception of the personal appearance of your husband, than you have of this brazier?"

"Oh, of course, yes," she said; "uncommon."

"And what was he like, then?"

"Why, as like the postman, as one P is like another."

"What postman?"

"Him as died two years and a half ago."

After this Mr. Knott feared that his witness was quite intractable, and he gave it up as a bad job; that is to say, the idea of getting anything further out of her of importance.

A five pound note, however, satisfied her that she had reaped all the benefit of the something advantageous which was alluded to in the advertisement and promised her.

This new light upon the affair, with regard to the insisted upon marriage, with a, or the Brazier, however, was quite sufficient to set Mr. Knott's wits to work, and he advertised to parish children, and others, offering five pounds to any one who would produce the certificate of marriage between Elizabeth Gray and somebody Brazier; and, likewise, ten pounds more for any information concerning the said Brazier, living or dead.

This partially had the desired effect he got a certificate of the marriage with Brazier, or John Brazier, as the fates would have it, but he heard no news whatever whether he was dead or alive.

Being satisfied now that he had achieved as much as could be expected, until the affair attained a much further amount of publicity, he applied to his employers what they would choose to have done, and advising himself that counsel should be applied to on the subject.

The facts were of so meagre a character, that counsel found great difficulty in advising. The opinion given, however, was, that Admiral Harding, as the heir-at-law, provided the illegitimacy of Lord Saltoun's son was proved, was the proper person to take proceedings in the courts for the purpose of substantiating his own claim to the peerage.

Now, Admiral Harding, notwithstanding a disposition upon a broad principle of common justice to take the part of his brother's wife, yet had no idea of lending himself to the machinations of a woman who might, after all, turn out very far from standing in that honourable position, so he consented to the suit on this principle.

"It will either," he said, "beyond all cavil and dispute, substantiate the legitimacy of my brother's son, in which case it will do him no harm, or it will expose the deceit of his mother, who, if she have been deceitful, deserves the severest reprehension; and I," he added, "will take care that, in that event, for my brother's sake, his child shall suffer but little, if anything, beyond the mere loss of a title."

No one could find fault with this course of action. It was all that a noble, generous-minded man could do, under the circumstances; but when we say no one could find fault with it, we forget for the moment that when people's feeling and passions are strongly interested in any subject, they have not that accurate power of distinguishing right from wrong which they would have, were they but indifferent spectators of the scenes in which they are themselves acting a prominent part.

Lady Saltoun was an example of this, and she made a memorable speech upon the occasion.

"My enemies," she said, "are those who stir in this matter, be they where they may. I trust to none of them, be their professions as seemingly fair as possible; while, at the same time, I defy them all."

It was an unhappy thing that such a state of feeling should have taken possession of Lady Saltoun. She ought to have known better than to have set herself up in opposition to anybody who was at all inclined to befriend her; because she must have felt that she was in a position to require friends, rather than to lose them.

Had she but listened to the suggestion of Admiral Harding, who, with so much generosity and good feeling, was inclined to befriend her, she might have avoided a vas^t amount of misery and anxiety, which was eventually her portion ; but this her pride forbade her to do ; so that having once adopted the absurd principle, that all who did not go with her, must necessarily go against her, she shut the door against any conciliation, and dared the whole family of the Saltouns to do their worst.

This was either an extremely bold proceeding or an extremely hazardous one. She, better than any one else, must have known what grounds there existed for any legal proceedings that might be instituted for proving the illegitimacy of her son ; and that there were grounds which were quite a sufficient excuse for the Saltoun family, not only the dying declaration of Lord Saltoun himself proved, but the discovery which the solicitor had made—a discovery which could not take Lady Saltoun by surprise—went far to verify.

And thus was it that legal proceedings commenced, in the name of Admiral Harding, who claimed the Saltoun peerage, on the ground that his brother had died without lawful issue ; notwithstanding his son was put forward, and affected to be acknowledged as the successor to his title.

Lady Saltoun, as the nearest friend of the minor, took up the cause; and, at a vast expense, and with a world of trouble, these proceedings, of a doubtful and lasting character, commenced.

It was a rational-enough thing for the Saltoun family to believe that the publicity which was now being given to the whole affair would produce further evidence; and hence, if there was further evidence producible in any quarter, the indiscretion of Lady Saltoun, in forcing on proceedings, only became more manifest.

The public papers soon took up the affair—first with inuendoes and initials, and then more openly, when the affair was freely spoken of and canvassed, as a broad and open matter of judicial inquiry.

All this while, Lady Saltoun kept custody of her son—a custody which no one pretened to dispute with her ; and, during nearly a whole year and a half that this litigation dragged its slow progress along, he was unseen by any of the friends of the family.

I am not sufficiently versed in the technicalities of the law to explain how it was that a decision on some point was come to, that placed Lady Saltoun in a bad position, without settling the whole of the case ; but, in arriving at that decision, an eminent judge made some remarks about the complexity of the proceedings, and the enormous hazard there was of doing injustice to one side or the other, that Admiral Harding, through his solicitor, interfered to stay proceedings, and made an overture to Lady Saltoun.

He offered to drop the whole affair, and not to assume the title himself, provided it was not assumed by her son, with the care of whose future fortunes he charged himself.

This was what he could do so far as regarded his own lifetime, because no act of his, with regard to a non-assumption of the dignity to which he was entitled, could in any way prejudice the heir-at-law after him.

Lady Saltoun by this time was worn out, both in body and mind. She had by no means extensive funds at her disposal, and a sickness of a month or two's duration had sufficed to calm her down sufficiently to enable her to take a soberer view of her condition.

She acceded to the admiral's proposal; the law-suit was dropped; and, by appointment, she one day appeared at his house with her son in her arms.

"Here," she said to him, "is the heir of the Saltouns, your brother's son, who is not thought good enough by his imperious family to mingle with them."

The child looked tall and thin for its age ; but it was received kindly by the admiral, who not only promised to take care of it, but to educate it along with his own daughter, who, with a sigh, he remarked was in a more delicate state of health than the young Lord Saltoun appeared to be.

The Saltoun family were furious at this concession ; they exhausted their language in vituperation upon the admiral, and, with an affectation of thorough disgust at his conduct, they repudiated him completely, and would hold no sort of communication with him.

By common consent the property of the family fell into his hands—at least, that portion of it which would have gone with the title ; from it he made a handsome allowance to Lady Saltoun, and liberally educated her son; and thus the affair went on for nearly ten years, during which time the admiral's daughter had died, and at the end of which period he found himself the father of a female child, so that it was not likely, let the law-suit have terminated how it would, that he would have perpetuated the honours of the Saltoun family through his children.

It was then, when the whole affair seemed to have been forgotten, and one would have thought that public curiosity, private malevolence, and every species of wounded feeling —of pride had long slept, that a circumstance occurred which raked up again the embers of discord, and fanned them into a furious flame.

CHAPTER XXXIV.

A SUDDEN ARRIVAL. — ADMIRAL HARDING'S GRIEF, AND THE RENEWAL OF THE LAW-SUIT.

NOTWITHSTANDING the length of the stranger's narrative, Minna Woodward felt so deeply interested in the facts which he disclosed, and so anxious to hear its conclusion, that although he pressed her to restrain her curiosity and wait until the morrow before she heard the remainder, she begged him to proceed.

"No," she said, "I shall be devoured by anxiety. I am well convinced that all you have hitherto told me is as nothing to that which you have still to communicate; and I beg you to recollect that I am still in ignorance of the bearing of these circumstances on my own fortunes."

"If you're not wearied," said the stranger, "I am willing to proceed."

"I pray you do so."

"Be it so—be it so. You are right in your conjecture that what I have to relate is of far more importance than what has already fallen from my lips; but it was necessary, in order that you might comprehend what I have to tell you, that you should know what I have already related to you as briefly as possible."

"I can well believe that," said Minna. "I pray you to pardon my impatience, and proceed."

The stranger, after a slight pause of thought, resumed as follows :—

"I am enabled, Minna Woodward, to tell you of these circumstances with the greatest possible precision, because I made it my business most specially—I may indeed say the business of my very existence, to ascertain from the individual actors in the various scenes precisely what had passed. By such means I am enabled to tell the tale to you with clearness and precision."

"I have marked so much," said Minna; "and it will be more intelligible to me for you to continue as you have commenced."

"Agreed; the remarkable circumstance to which I have alluded, was this :—

Admiral Harding's child was about two months old, and he was still remaining at his town house, until his lady was quite in a state of convalescence, and able to remove to the country, when one day, as he sat in his library after dinner, a visitor was announced.

Upon asking the servant who brought him the intelligence that some one wished to see him, who it was, he was informed that the party would neither name himself nor his business, but had seated himself in the hall most pertinaciously, and said he would take no denial of an interview except from the admiral's own lips.

Now, Admiral Harding was then, as he is now, a man of extremely unaffected manners, and accessible to almost any one who chose to call upon him.

He did not like the idea of any one being repulsed from the hall, who asked merely to see him, and taking the chance of finding the visitor to be merely some importunate beggar, which was extremely likely; he said to the servant,

"Show him into a room, and say that I will come to him immediately."

This was done; the visitor was shown into a private apartment, and the admiral made his appearance, but he took with him a young gentleman who was his private secretary, from whom he kept no secrets, and to whom he intended to leave the task of showing the intruder out if that step should become necessary.

It is from this gentleman that I have obtained my information, because I succeeded in convincing him that I had a good right to know what passed on that occasion.

The man who had so insisted upon seeing Admiral Harding, appeared to be between fifty and sixty years of age; he was weatherbeaten, and looked like one who had led a rough existence for many years.

That he was anything but a gentleman, his appearance sufficiently testified, and upon his countenance there was an expression of cunning and ferocity which was anything but pleasing. He had seated himself, but he arose on the admiral's entrance and looked audaciously in his face; he then shifted his glance to the young man who accompanied him, saying,—

"I don't want any witnesses, and no more will you, when you know what I come about."

"I have no secrets," said the admiral, "and I don't intend to get up one for your convenience; state your errand, sir, as quickly as you can, or I shall regret that I have given way so far as to condescend to grant you an interview."

There was an air of dignified command about Admiral Harding, which awed the fellow for a few moments; and, in fact, had a sensible impression upon him, which, during the remainder of the interview, he could not shake off.

"Very good, sir," he said; "it makes no difference to me, if it makes none to you. You had a brother, sir."

"Well?"

"And he's dead, leaving a widow and a son."

"These facts are sufficiently notorious."

"So they are, only it's necessary I should say that I know them. You've been going to law about it, but that seems all arranged, now, and without consulting me."

"This must be some madman," said the admiral.

"Not a bit of it," said the stranger: "don't flatter yourself. I say, you stopped the lawsuit without consulting me. I wasn't in England; but now I am, I shall make a little change in the matter. I suppose you haven't the least idea who I am?"

"I certainly have not."

"Ha! that makes all the difference. Now I'll just tell you."

"It seems to me, my friend, that that circumstance should have come before."

"Does it? Very well; better late than never. My name's Brazier."

The admiral started, and turned pale. He saw in a moment the commencement, now, of a world of trouble and bitterness of spirit.

"You're surprised," said the man; "but you don't seem half so pleased as I thought you'd be. You've got the estates, I hear; but you wanted the title, and natural enough too. They tell me the lawsuit broke down, somehow, and that you found it best to compromise it. However, I can put you all square again. I tell you my name's Brazier, and I think that's about sufficient. I rather think that I'm about the best friend you've got at present. A nice-looking room this. Have you got anything good to eat?"

"You seem to imagine," said Admiral Harding, "that the news you bring me is of an extremely welcome character, inasmuch as it tends to place me in a position to assume the title of Lord Saltoun?"

"Rather," said the fellow. "You've hit it there."

"You never made a greater mistake in your life, my friend; but you will find that I am a better judge of human nature than you are. How much, now, did you expect me to give you for your intelligence and your testimony?"

"How much?"

"Yes; how much money. Name it in round numbers. Let me know the extent of your cupidity at once."

"Why, as to that, I—I—expected the matter of a couple of hundred pounds, or so."

"Which you would drink and squander away in a few weeks, and then be a beggar again, as you seem now, and without any further claim upon me at all."

"Ah! but I'd have a claim upon somebody else. She's got money."

"For the respect I bear my brother's memory, I would furnish her with the means of eluding you."

"The devil you would!"

"Yes; you perceive, my friend, that you've made a mistake, and that nobody's inclined to thank you for your news; but still you have got a better market than you expected. Prove to me that your name is Brazier—prove to me that you are the husband of her who is now called Lady Saltoun—promise me that you will never molest her or her child; that you will change your name, and keep this whole affair a profound secret, and you shall get from me a settled annuity, sufficient in amount to keep you above want. I make this offer to you because—because I have an affection for my brother's child, who has been some years under my roof."

"The devil! Well, d—n it! there's nothing like bringing one's pigs to the best market. I'll do it; only there's one little circumstance that may be a trouble."

"And what is that?"

"Why, the fact is, I've been to her first, to ask her what she'd give. She blowed me up, and told me she'd see me d—d first before she'd give me anything. It strikes me she's a little cracked, so I came to you. She says you keeps her son away from her."

"She is much mistaken. I have always courted her society here on his account."

" Well, she's a rum un' ; howsomever, I don't want to stand in the way."

" Be secret, then, and quiet, and call upon me to-morrow, when I will further arrange the affair."

The man left, and Admiral Harding returned to the library to ponder over this new circumstance, which might yet be a source of much uneasiness.

This visit caused Admiral Harding immense disquietude. He said nothing to his wife upon the subject, for she was not in a state of health to bear mental emotion ; besides, he knew that her feelings and predilections did not go with him in the transaction ; for although her affection for him prevented her making any disturbance about the subject, she rather, upon the whole, thought it would be a nice thing for him to be Lord Saltuon, carrying with it, as it did, the contingency of her being Lady Saltoun.

He passed nearly the whole night in consideration of the subject; and in the morning the first thing he did was to send for Lady Saltoun, his brother's widow.

This message was quite sufficient to convince her that Brazier had fulfilled his threat, which he had uttered to her at parting, of communicating who and what he was to the admiral.

She, it appears, then, mistrusting the object of the admiral's message to her, shrank from the interview, and sent him back an indignant as well as a highly offensive reply. This was sufficient to incence anybody ; but he loved the son more than he could possibly dislike the mother, so he took no notice of her bad conduct, but determined upon completing his arrangement with Brazier, just the same as if she had behaved as well as ill.

He kept the affair secret at home, and sat down in his study to make a memorandum of precisely what he wanted to agree with Brazier to perform. While there, his child was brought to him by his nurse, to be kissed by him previously to its being taken for a walk, according to custom. He pressed his lips tenderly to the infant's cheek, and watched it from the room. From that time to this he has never set eyes upon that child.

" Some dreadful accident ?" said Minna.

" No one knew. Nurse and child both disappeared. Weeks afterwards the body of a woman was found in the river, which was supposed to be the child's nurse ; but so decomposed was it, that no satisfactory identification could take place."

" And was no trace of the child discovered ?"

" Not the remotest."

" Oh, what must have been that father's feelings !"

" They were too terrible for description. After the first month of unremitting search was over, and he began to give way to the certainty of the fact that his only child was lost to him for ever, despair took possession of him, and he was confined for many months to a sick chamber.

The conditions with Brazier were carried out, it appears, fully, and he disappeared, to the great triumph of Lady Saltoun, who called upon the admiral, and jeeringly asked him if he would renew the law-suit against her, when he found his lost child ; for she seemed to imagine that it was the loss of that object of his affections which crushed his energies and prevented him doing so.

Some there were who suggested that she had a hand in the disappearance of the infant, but nothing could be brought home to her, and the police authorities gave it as their opinion that the nurse, who was believed to be fond of the child, had wandered with it in her walk to some unfrequented part of the Thames in Westminster, where the admiral resided, and had accidentally let it fall into the stream, perishing herself either in an effort to save it, or from an absolute dread of returning home with such a story in her mouth.

This seemed probable enough, notwithstanding that no traces of the infant were discovered. The admiral's despair changed to a gloomy sadness, and from that it became chastened into a melancholy demeanour, which at times even now manifests itself strongly in his actions.

" And was no news ever heard of the missing infant ?"

" None whatever. The admiral turned all his attention to his brother's son ; and it is one of his griefs that he has lived to see that attention ill-requited. Captain Harding is a reprobate, and a thoroughly bad man. The admiral knows he is such, although he knows not a tenth part of his delinquencies, and he will go to the grave without knowing them, for there is but another person in the world, beside Harding himself, who could tell him all, and he would not grieve the old man by the recital."

" That person is yourself," said Minna.

" It is so. I have for the last three years watched his career with pain and anxiety, but I have not found one redeeming trait in his character, although I declare that the object of my watching was with a hope to discover sufficient good in him to counterbalance some of the evil."

"And you found it not?"

"As you say, I found it not, and so I shall have a duty to perform, which, however it may make him suffer, he has merited."

"And how long since was it that these circumstances occurred?"

"It is now about twenty-one years since Admiral Harding looked in his child's face, which makes Captain Harding, his nephew, about thirty-two. My own age is thirty, so that you perceive he is my senior."

"Yes; but you do not mean to leave me lost in a sea of conjecture concerning that which you have related; you know more."

"I do; and the remainder that I know shall consist wholly and solely of explanation on explanation, which will enable you to put together the foregoing facts in a tangible shape, and to draw your own conclusions from them as to your future course of action."

"Then they do concern me?"

"Yes, most closely."

"And what became of Lady Saltoun—does she still live?"

"No."

"She was drowned by the foundering of a wherry on the Thames. Once, when she was proceeding to make a visit to a particular house situate upon its banks, whither she always went twice in each year, and only twice. A squall came on, and the lad, for he was a mere lad who rowed the boat, became alarmed. Instead of exerting himself to do the best he could for their mutual safety, he gave himself up to lamentation and despair. Before, then, any other boat could put off to their rescue, the wherry foundered, and they were both drowned; their bodies not being found until the next day."

"Alas! that was a dreadful death."

"It was," said the stanger; and he rose and walked to the window of the apartment, as if to hide some sudden emotion which came over him.

"You knew her?" said Minna.

"I did."

"And you respected her at least for something, or you would not betray this emotion in speaking of her death. She was not then entirely so bad as you have painted her?"

"Minna," he said, "you have much to learn. I thought that I could have commanded my feelings sufficiently to go through this day with the whole of my narrative, but I find that I cannot; you must spare me till to-morrow."

"Most certainly," said Minna; "Heaven forbid that I should press you."

*					*					*					*					*					*					*

Since the mysterious stranger finds his feelings so much acted upon by the narrative he is relating to Minna Woodward, as to require time for its conclusion, we shall take this opportunity of devoting some space to Lieutenant Heartwell, whom it will be recollected we left upon the rock of Gibraltar, after his escape from the cabin of the Eolus frigate, and at precisely the moment when he confronted Captain Harding with the fixed intention of forcing him to fight.

CHAPTER XXXV.

THE DUEL BETWEEN CAPTAIN HARDING AND HEARTWELL.

It will be recollected that Lieutenant Heartwell, when he reached the neutral ground at Gibraltar by swimming from his ship the Eolus, unexpectedly came upon Harding and the surgeon, between whom he overheard a conversation relating to himself. The surprise of Harding at the sudden appearance of Heartwell, when the surgeon quitted him, was inexpressible. The blood forsook his lips, as he stepped back a pace or two gasping; his lips moved, but no sound issued from them.

Heartwell gazed steadfastly in his face for some time, until Harding's presence of mind returned, and he said, in a tone of forced composure,—

"It is well, Lieutenant Heartwell, you have broken through your arrest. It is a piece with the rest of your conduct. For what purpose may you be lurking about here?"

"I will answer that question, Captain Harding, by telling you the object I have attained."

"It must be edifying."

"I have heard all that has passed between you and that scoundrel who has just left you; and you may make what distinction you please between the complaisant tool who, for a reward, will not hesitate to commit a crime, and he who instigates such a man to do a deed he would fear to do himself, or I should say it was an act such as only a treacherous nature could perform."

"You have been playing the eavesdropper, and now you give me a lecture upon morality. Oh, fie! Lieutenant Heartwell, of the Eolus, I thought you, at least, were a man of probity; but, alas! one crime follows another."

"It does," said Heartwell; "ask your own heart, Captain Harding, whether one falsehood don't require another to back it up, and can any character be more repugnant to that of a gentleman, than that of a poltroon and a liar?"

Harding bit his lip with malignity and rage, but he replied by saying,

"I am not compelled to answer your catechism, Lieutenant Heartwell, and it would be well if you immediately returned to the Eolus, and there wait your discharge by a court martial."

"I am fully aware of all you intend; but why I have incurred your hatred I know not; but it seems to have been planned with all the forethought and certainty of success, calculated upon by such minds as yours, and you have succeeded; but I am not so destitute of the means of satisfaction, as you imagine."

"And in what do they consist?"

"In that which one honourable man offers to another, the alternative of fighting."

"Fighting?"

"It may not be to your taste, Captain Harding, but you have maligned those who are dear to me."

"I have not."

"Do not compel me to utter the word I used before to you, for assuredly you deserve it, and added to that, I may add traitor and coward."

"You may add what you please; but at the same time, it is no more a fact, nor less a lie, because you choose to indulge in any choice brutality."

"I never injured man or woman. The weak or strong; my actions and my motives are alike—open."

"It is well your actions are open, sir, for those you will be called to account at a proper time."

"In the meantime," said Heartwell, "we will settle a difference we have upon a matter not connected with discipline."

"I do not understand you."

"You may affect not to do so: your conspiring with that man who has just left you is a sufficient ground of quarrel if I had no other, but I have another."

"Indeed! and what may that be? Some sweet, pot-house nymph, whom you seem to be more choice of than I am; but that may be accounted for ——."

"Captain Harding, say no more upon that subject, unless you would provoke me to do that which I might regret, but which you would most assuredly well deserve."

"Assassinate me! well, it's not improbable."

"I am no assassin either of reputation or of life. I malign no one, and I do not either perjure or league with those who do; nor suborn false witnesses to ruin a man; I dare not face; you, Captain Harding, are such an one."

"'Tis well," said Harding; "but you have wandered from your original intention."

"A little," said Heartwell. "But let me tell you again, Captain Harding, you have maligned those dearest to me. I have given you the lie, that's not enough; you must give me satisfaction."

"Indeed!"

"Yes; here are a brace of pistols, they are both surely loaded, and there is no time like the present."

Harding started back a pace, and said,—

"No, if I must fight, I will not fight like a ruffian and a butcher; it shall be according to the usages of gentlemen, and not in this style, Lieutenant Heartwell."

"You refuse?"

"I do; this is neither time, place, nor occasion; and were it likely I would fight you, I could not do it under such circumstances; you know very well what you desire is absurd."

"It is but just, and your objections are but those of a man who dare not face his enemy openly and fairly."

"I dare do both."

"And yet you dare not fight me."

" I dare, but I will not bandy words with you ; you know very well I have placed you under arrest ; and, though you have broken through your confinement, you are amenable for that, remember. I could not, consistent with my own honour and the rules of the service, consent to fight my own officer—it's contrary to custom."

" And yet you have not availed yourself, Captain Harding, of that excuse to abstain from maligning those whom I love."

" Whom you love ?"

" Yes."

" I have said but the truth."

" Liar !"

" It is well ; such gross conduct is a disgrace to your profession. You ought to know ere this that the coat should cover a gentleman, and not a blackguard."

" It may be very well, Sir Bulkley Harding ; but I need not retort upon you, but refer you to the man whom you have taken into your confidence."

" Into my confidence ?" said Harding, disdainfully.

" Yes."

" I have not."

" You plotted and planned between you for my destruction. You suborned him to give false evidence against me, and you offered him several rewards as inducements to him to do so. Tell me, what sort of man is that, and what the difference in point of mind and character is you can distinguish between yourselves."

Harding was enraged ; he had endeavoured to brave it off coolly, but the impetuous character of Heartwell was too much for him, and he seemed to have lost command of himself more than once by the bitter taunts of Heartwell. However, he once more paused before speaking, to gain a moment's reflection.

" Your insolence, Lieutenant Heartwell, shall not serve your purpose. I have said what you heard, and I will abide by it, till you can refute what I have said ; and if then you can come as a gentleman and a man of honour, both in my eyes and that of society in general, and there is no professional usage violated, then I will grant what you may be entitled to demand."

" You have fenced yourself about with conditions."

" They are necessary."

" They are used to save you from meeting me in this instance. You will neither fight nor make amends."

" Make amends !"

" Yes—retract the offensive words."

" What words ?"

" Those relating to Minna Woodward."

" No ; I will not be bullied into anything of the kind. I speak as I spoke then, in respect to her, what I said then ; I will abide by my own words, and make them good when I once more reach the old Gun Tavern."

" Liar !" cried the excited lieutenant, every vein of his face swelling up with emotion at thus hearing the fame of her he loved so well injured and aspersed.

So lately as he had seen her and parted from her, it must have been utterly impossible that she could thus have altered her very nature, and become what she abhorred.

No, no—there was no fear of that. It was the senseless boast of a silly man, whose pride was rather excited by a boast of having ruined a beautiful girl than he would have been had he been the victor in an encounter with the enemy.

" This is a gross falsehood, and only persisted in because it gives me offence ; it can have no other object."

" Allow the matter to stand in that light, if you please ; but you had better return to the ship, or I may be compelled to send a file of marines after you," said Harding, as he turned away from the enraged and almost maddened Heartwell.

" You go not so, Captain Harding," said Heartwell.

" I do go when and where I please."

" You cannot leave thus."

" Do you intend to become an assassin ?"

" No ; but here are two pistols."

" I see."

" Take one."

" No."

" You must."

" I will not."

"I say you must take one; measure your ground yourself, and give the word; as I do not wish to take any advantage of having the weapons, take one."

"This is impossible."

"I cannot see any obstacle but your own cowardice, and yet you must overcome that."

"I will not fight without witnesses."

"Will you retract and apologise for the use you have made of the name of Minna Woodward?"

"No; I will not."

"Well, take the alternative. I am sure I do you an undeserved favour in thus giving you a choice. Such a man as you deserves any death but that of a brave man."

As Heartwell spoke, he thrust the butts of the two pistols close to him; he looked at them for a moment, and then, if as making up his mind to something desperate, he suddenly seized one of them and cocked it, and then fired it in Heartwell's face.

By a miracle the bullet missed him, but so close that his face was scorched by the flash, and the bullet was almost felt by his temples. For a moment Heartwell was astonished, so sudden and unexpected had been this dastardly action.

Harding himself wavered, but seeing Heartwell did not fall, he concluded he had missed him; he turned completely round, and fled with the utmost precipitation.

As soon as Heartwell saw his enemy fly, he ran after him at a desperate pace, and called to him,—

"Coward—poltroon! turn, and face me like a man; you are a disgrace to your rank, country, and profession."

But nothing was sufficient to induce Harding to turn back, and although not really or absolutely a coward, yet, on this occasion, he seemed so panic-stricken, that fear lent him wings, and Heartwell saw he was in danger of losing him from two causes, speed, and his approach to the castle.

He therefore stopped, steadied himself, and levelling the pistol full beween Harding's shoulders, fired.

Harding fell huddled up in a heap on the earth.

The effect of this shot close to the ramparts was to cause an alarm; seeing this, Heartwell immediately betook himself to flight, and concealed himself among the places of concealment he could then find.

How long he remained here he knew not, but his reflections were none such as to render him a whit the more happy. True it was he had avenged the injuries he had received, but in what condition did it leave him? in one that would not permit him to show himself, for who would believe that Harding was otherwise than assassinated? they would not believe that he had committed the dastardly act he had been guilty of.

The sun soon set in gloom and clouds; the evening appeared rainy and squally, and he could hear certain indications from the castle that told him they intended searching round all that spot for the cause of the alarm.

He, under cover of the shadow of the castle, crept along towards a place where some fishing-boats lay anchored off, and some of them were near a kind of jetty, erected for some temporary purpose, and held there by a rope.

Into one of these he crept, and for some time remained watching for some quiet moment to slip the cable, and get out to sea unobserved.

He was compelled to take what he could find. It was a small vessel with one sail, which was furled; the wind blew off the shore. This was favourable.

He slipped the cable, and gently let fall a small part of the sail, merely a reef, but it gave an impetus to the vessel, for the wind was fresh, and she left her moorings, and slowly glided through the bay.

To evade suspicion, he let her pass close by the batteries, but it did not escape the vigilance of the sentries who were placed along the ramparts.

He was challenged, but no reply was returned, of course, and then a shot was fired at Heartwell.

In an instant David Heartwell let fall the whole canvas before a fresh breeze, and it filled in an instant, and, pushing the rudder up, sailed clear away from them, and though he was challenged and fired at from several batteries, yet he escaped without injury or hurt of any kind.

"I am safe," he muttered; "they may chase, but a stern chase is a long chase; and besides, this little craft sails well, and they will lose sight of me before they can get ready."

However, a long gun was suddenly brought to bear, a bright flash, a splash in the water, and then a loud booming sound came across the waters, but it did no harm; it told him, however, that the guns were served well, and, had there been more light, the smack, small as it was, would have been hit.

"Ah," he said to himself, as he saw the angry state of the heavens, "this will be a rough night, but, at the same time, the bark is sound, and if I can but keep her head before the wind, I may yet escape an ocean grave."

He partially furled his sail, and secured himself in the stern of his little vessel, and sat down to a long watch and a dangerous voyage. He was alone on the angry deep.

There is something sublime, and yet fearful, in such a situation; and to know that but a few very frail planks are between you and the waters, which are ever ready to become the grave of all who fall into them; less than the starting of a plank might destroy him. A sudden squall, or a sudden breaking of a heavy wave over the little barque, or a rock, or, indeed, any unforeseen circumstance, might carry him to the depths of the ocean.

CHAPTER XXXVI.

CONTINUES THE MYSTERIOUS STRANGER'S NARRATIVE, AND CONTAINS SOME
SURPRISING REVELATIONS.

FEELING as we do, that doubtless our readers are anxious to know in what mysterious manner Minna Woodward is connected with the singular and complicated narrative which the stranger is telling her of the Saltoun family, we once again request them to fancy themselves in the gorgeously decorated and furnished house, to which Minna had been taken, and to listen to what is passing between the unhappy girl and he who evidently takes so strong an interest in her past and future fate.

Minna passed a night of restless anxiety, during which, in various strange forms and groups, the people and the incidents of his narration, flitted before her mental vision.

At one moment she would fancy herself by the bed side of the dying Lord Saltoun, whose request to his sisters had been treated with so much heartlessness and cold indifference.

Then again she thought she was in a boat upon the river, and that she was by the force of some fatality, which could be by no mortal power resisted, compelled to witness the brief catastrophe of the death of Lady Saltoun, and of the boy who was rowing her to some house upon the river's bank, which by some combination of ideas she, in her dream, felt firmly convinced was the old Gun tavern, where she herself had passed so many years of her existence.

Thus the minor scenes in the drama of real life, which had been related to her by the stranger, passed in rapid review before her, so that although she slept or seemed to sleep the whole of the night, she arose in the morning without feeling at all refreshed.

When she met him at the breakfast table, he noticed her condition, for her eyes looked heavy, and as if she had been weeping.

"Minna," he said, "the night has not been one of refreshing slumber to you any more than it has been to me."

"Have you, too, had dreams?"

"I have passed a sad and restless night."

"But you knew all?"

"I did. The relation, however, of what I did know to you, and the necessity for the first time of putting the facts into appropriate language, has brought them all before me with a fulness as if they had but just occurred, or had, at all events, only just been made known to me."

"I can imagine that."

"I feel now," he added, "that it would have been better, if I could have commanded my feelings, to have told you all yesterday, because, by not doing so, I have not only harassed my own feelings by thoughts of what I had to tell you to-day, but I have left you to be tossed to and fro in a sea of wild conjecture, which might or might not hit upon the truth."

"Tell me now then, quickly, and at once."

"I will, and as I do so, I will endeavour so to control my own feelings, as that I shall be able to go on calmly to the close."

"Do so, I pray you."

"I have told you of the admiral's bereavement, and of the death, sudden and awful, of Lady Saltoun."

"Yes, yes."

"Under these circumstances, after he had recovered from the mental shock which a conviction of the loss of his child gave him, he turned all his attention to the nephew whom he had promised to behave as a father to.

"He had him educated with the utmost care. He did all that mortal man could do to make him a gentleman and a man of honour."

"And he failed?"

"He did most signally, adding one more to the numerous examples of the fact which some people are so loth to believe, namely, that no education, no association whatever, can infuse gentleness, honour, and integrity of thought and action into a nature unfitted to receive them."

"That is true."

"It is, Minna; and however ungracious a truth it sounds in the ears of those who for their own interested purposes endeavour to assert the contrary, it is one which, as the world advances in knowledge, will become day by day better appreciated and acknowledged.

But to proceed.

The admiral, no doubt, as soon as he was of an age to understand him, took an occasion to explain to Harding his real position, for he has never once made an attempt to assume the title of Lord Saltoun, and has always appeared thoroughly to feel and to acknowledge his dependence upon his uncle.

His way, however, of feeling and acknowledging such a dependence of course took the general complexion of his mind.

He did not endeavour by honourable conduct to merit the esteem of the old man, or by any meritorious actions to repay him for the kindness he had lavished on him ; but he, by every shift and manœuvre in the world, regardless of truth, honour, or honesty, endeavoured to keep him in ignorance of the vicious course of life he pursued.

This, to a certain extent, he succeeded in doing ; for although his uncle now knows that he is bad enough, he does not know how bad he is.

" And did the man Brazier entirely disappear ?"

" He did ; but his disappearance was a forced one. In obedience to the arrangement which the admiral made with him he changed his name, but he could not with that change his nature. He soon committed a crime for which he was transported for fourteen years, and therefore was it that he was never encountered by any one for so long."

" Is he living ?"

" He is ; and where and under what circumstances you shall soon now know. Let me now reveal to you the secret proceedings of the late Lady Saltoun."

" Do you really know them ?"

" I do."

" And from such authority as to enable you to vouch for their correctness ?"

" Most unquestionably."

" Then I shall indeed listen with an absorbed attention. I feel quite convinced that by some marvellous means you have become acquainted with particulars such as it rarely happens that any one individual knows of any set of circumstances whatever."

" I have made this the business of my life."

" You must have done so."

" The interest that I had in doing so was amply sufficient. Little as Bulkley Harding, as he is named, suspected that, go where he would, engage in what adventure he would, there was always one to watch him and to scan his motives, with a hope of finding some pure one for which he could really be given credit."

" And that hope was in vain ?"

" It was indeed."

" What would have been the consequence of your finding him a very different character to what he is ?"

" Most important to him ; for then I would have sought him out and made a friend and a confidant of him. He should then have known all that I am telling to you, and he should have found that, although there was the power, there was not the will to alter his position in life."

" He is indeed a bad man."

" As bad as can be."

" But heed him not. Tell me of Lady Saltoun."

" I will. You must not be surprised, Minna, that, to a certain extent, I shrink from the subject, because, before I have finished my revelations to you, you will be supplied with an amply sufficient reason why I should so shrink."

" No doubt—no doubt."

" Now then for the private thoughts and actions of Lady Saltoun. She knew that she had committed a wrong by wedding Lord Saltoun in the way she did ; but the splendour of the alliance dazzled her and blinded her to all consequences, except those of a pleasant nature.

With, therefore, the full knowledge that she ought, even if her former husband were dead, to marry again by his name, and not her maiden one, she chose the latter.

That the man Brazier, who was as great a scoundrel as ever stepped, was dead before she contracted the marriage with Lord Saltoun, she had every reason to believe, from evidence which she considered to be of a conclusive nature.

But she was deceived, as the sequel showed. However, such a state of things takes much from the amount of moral guilt which we should otherwise be disposed to lay at Lady Saltoun's door.

" Most certainly."

" Then, again, we may excuse some of her actions, on account of the acerbity of disposition which was induced in her by the marked hostility towards her of Lord Saltoun's family—a hostility which she was not of a disposition to bend to, so long as there was the least chance of retaliating.

She conceived, therefore, the most violent hatred, particularly against the sisters of her husband; so that, when he was no more, and his feelings could not be compromised, she thought of little else but how to be avenged upon them.

Now, she had borne a child to Brazier—a sickly infant, whose life seemed to be held upon the most precarious tenure in the world, and the death of whom she made up her mind so completely to, that she scarcely considered she was keeping any secret by never hinting at its existence.

There was but one person, besides herself, who knew of these matters, and that was the same confidential domestic of whom I have spoken who had witnessed the last moments of Lord Saltoun.

With a sister of this person's Lady Saltoun's first child was at nurse, and, contrary to all expectation, it lived, gradually shaking off the weakness of its earlier years, but still being so far from robust or strong, that, although two years the senior of Lord Saltoun's son, the one looked as strong and as old as the other.

It happened, too, that the general complexion of these two children was the same, and, when Lord Saltoun's family went to war with Lady Saltoun about the illegitimacy of her son, she had the two children nursed together for the year and a half that, if you recollect, I told you was consumed in litigation.

When, however, at the end of that time, Admiral Harding abruptly put an end to such a state of things, she, Lady Saltoun, no doubt, at the period, mistook his conciliatory overtures for some sort of confession of a weak cause; and, although she knew that the cause against her was strong enough, if the opposite party could get all the necessary proofs, she concluded they had failed in so doing.

But, although such a failure might then have taken place, that was no reason why it should continue; and, therefore, she was well enough pleased to accept of compromise, rather than go on.

A demonaic spirit of revenge, however, still actuated her against the whole family, and as she knew that their pride had been terribly hurt at the idea of a son of her's, notwithstanding it was likewise a son of Lord Saltoun's, to mingle with what they conceived their purer race, she determined to play them a trick.

This was no other than to change the children. It was her son by Brazier that she placed in the arms of Admiral Harding, while she kept his real nephew still at nurse, where he had been for some time.

It was strange how such a thing as this could give her the intense satisfaction which I am told it did. She gloried in the deceit she had practised; and, although she lavished much real tenderness upon the boy whom she had retained so wrongfully, she never thought of placing him in his true position.

" Then Captain Harding is, after all," exclaimed Minna, " not the son of Lord Saltoun, and the nephew of Admiral Harding !"

" Certainly not."

" How strange a tale !"

" It is, indeed; but, by listening further, you will find that the revenge of Lady Saltoun did not end here."

" Indeed! One would have thought she had done enough."

" Yes: and so, perhaps, did she, until the man Brazier made his appearance again upon the scene.

This man, whose sole object, from first to last, in the affair, was to obtain as much money as possible from all parties, had, it appeared, no doubt fancying that the secret of his existence was of more importance to Lady Saltoun than to any one else, called first upon her.

Now, in that visit, he behaved himself too peremptorily and triumphantly; the consequence of which was a famous quarrel between them, and his going from her house to that of Admiral Harding, as, with his last words, he threatened her he would.

This, when she got calmer, awakened, as may well be supposed, in her mind the most serious apprehensions. She became half maddened to think that now the only link in the chain of evidence against her which had been wanting, and which she had thought would for ever be wanting, was suddenly found; and feeling, or fearing that now the Saltoun family would undoubtedly triumph over her, she did not make the least attempt to struggle against defeat; but she turned her whole attention to the question of how she was to obtain revenge.

She knew that the infant daughter of the admiral was not only by him much thought of, but that by the whole family she was considered as a very unexceptionable little personage, inasmuch as her mother came of an ancient race.

In a few hours, then, she concocted the terrible scheme of robbing the admiral of his child. This was a plan, the execution of which she entrusted to no one. She herself set about it; and on the following morning she dogged the footsteps of the nurse, until she was in a desolate part of the park.

Lady Saltoun rushed upon her, and struck her on the brow. The woman was stunned for a few moments, and when she recovered, she found that the child was gone.

How she then came to drown herself, no one can tell. Probably some dread of going home with the story of her loss, as well as some amount of mental confusion, incidental to the blow she had received, induced the act; but that she did commit suicide there can be no doubt.

Lady Saltoun took the child at once to the same confidential person who had had charge of the two boys, and telling her who it was, she promised her so large a sum to keep the secret and maintain the infant, that she at once took the charge.

When, however, which was very shortly indeed, Lady Saltoun found that her fears were all groundless, and that nothing followed from this most unexpected appearance of the man Brazier, she would have restored the admiral his child; but the woman who had it to nurse said,—

"No. The sum you have promised me with it is of too much importance to my comforts. Take the child now away from me, and I will see what I can make by a disclosure of the whole of the proceedings, from first to last, to the Saltoun family."

This was no idle threat, and Lady Saltoun felt all its force. She gave up the idea of restoring the admiral his child. Perhaps the desire to do so was never a very strong one, and thus affairs again went on for a long time, until the death of Lady Saltoun, and then the person who had charge of the child suddenly disappeared, leaving it in the hands of her sister, who was the domestic that had been in Lord Saltoun's room when he died, and who had married a decent man, in her own class of life, who had been a butler.

Now this woman, although she knew of the change of children which had placed Lady Saltoun's son by the man Brazier in the station which ought to have been occupied by the real son of Lord Saltoun, did not know whose child the girl was at all; but taking an attachment to the infant, she, after Lady Saltoun's death, and the departure of her sister, maintained it."

"And what became of the real son of Lord Saltoun?"

"Why, upon the disappearance of his mother in the waters of the Thames, he was destitute, and led a sad life of hardships for a long time, passing by his mother's maiden name, until one day chance, or providence, brought him to a lonely village situate in Hampshire.

In the only public-house which this little place afforded, a woman, who appeared to be in the last stage of poverty, was dying.

She had, she said, some revelations to make before she breathed her last; and she wished that what she had to say should be heard by as many people as possible.

In accordance with this request, he, the wandering son of Lord Saltoun, along with others, stood by the side of the couch on which she was lying, and she spoke these words,—

"If there be any kind person present, who, after hearing what I have to say, will utter a prayer for my forgiveness, it may do me much service, for Heaven knows I am in need of mercy."

At such a moment when her spirit seemed to be but just hovering on the verge of its earthly tenement, it was not likely any one would refuse to her so simple a request.

One proposed that the clergyman of the parish should be sent for, and he was, but, before he arrived, for he was out fox-hunting, she had ceased to breathe; before, however, this happened she made the following declaration,—

"I have for a long time kept a secret which I was sworn to keep, and which I have ever dreaded to utter. But now that I know that I am dying, I feel assured that Heaven will absolve me of my oath, and that I cannot resign my spirit to its mercy without making an endeavour to do some justice to the innocent."

Here she paused a moment, as if her strength failed her, and every one then present concluded that she was dying.

After a short time, however, she rallied again and proceeded.

"Do not fancy I shall die," she said, "before I have told all. No. I feel assured that I shall be permitted to live till then, and no longer. I will be as brief as I may, for I have no desire to linger longer in a world which can present to me no gratifications, and with which I feel that long since I have done for ever."

She then drew several long and laborious breaths, after which, in a slower tone of voice than she had yet spoken in, she said,—

"I had a sister, who was the confidential servant of a Lady Saltoun. She was trusted by her in everything, and indeed bore her trust well. Misfortunes came upon this Lady Saltoun after the death of Lord Saltoun, her husband.

"She had borne to him one son; but by a previous marriage she had a son likewise, and when, as was the case, the deceased Lord Saltoun's relations went to law with her to endeavour to prove that the son she had borne to him was not legitimate, in consequence of her having married him in her maiden name, instead of in the name of her former husband, who was believed to be dead, of course, the two children were nursed by me and my sister together.

"My sister got married, and I had the sole care of the two children. Lady Saltoun seemed to like such an arrangement better, for I was not so scrupulous as my sister, and she, the lady, soon found that I could, by money, be tempted to almost anything.

"She did tempt me. An arrangement of the lawsuit took place between her and the family of her late husband, Lord Saltoun; but she palmed off upon them her son by her first marriage, instead of Lord Saltoun's child, as the genuine young nobleman.

"The cheat was not discovered, and I swore a solemn oath of secresy.

"I never, in all my life, knew any human being so full of spite against others as this Lady Saltoun was against the family of her husband. Her whole thoughts, night and day, were, I feel convinced, for years bent upon a constant consideration as to how she could in some way make them suffer.

"She was not content with thinking merely; the most desperate deeds did not deter her.

"She at length did commit a very desperate one. She waylaid the nurse, who was out with an infant child, a girl, of Admiral Harding's, the brother of Lord Saltoun, and she took the child from her.

"She brought this child to me; she told me whose it was, and she offered me so large a sum to nurse it that I was tempted, and again I took an oath to keep this second secret.

"After a time, however, she would have restored this child, but I opposed her, for, although she said I should, I doubted, if, when the child was once gone, she would pay the money all the same. So she gave up the idea of restoring this child, and when I fell ill, which I did, and was unable to nurse it, or look to its safety, I, without telling her who it was, got my married sister to take care of it.

Lady Saltoun used to visit it. I believe my married sister thought it was a child of Lady Saltoun's, and so made no inquiries concerning it.

One day, in going to visit this child, Lady Saltoun was drowned on the Thames, by the upsetting of a wherry. This affected me so much, that I was laid up for a long time with a brain fever; and in, I fancy, a paroxysm of that complaint, I rose, and left my home.

"I never returned to it; and from that time to this I have been a wanderer from place to place, only always, with great care, avoiding London. I know not what became of the real Lord Saltoun; that is to say, the son of the deceased nobleman who was left in my care. There was an old cabinet, with a number of secret drawers in it, which was placed by Lady Saltoun in the house of my married sister, which I always believed contained papers which would give a full and clear account of all these transactions."

Here the woman paused, and it was evident to everybody present that her death was very near at hand, indeed.

Suddenly the wanderer, who knew from what he had heard that he was alluded to, stepped forward and confronted her, saying—

"I am here."

She knew the voice in a moment; and, with a loud shriek, she rose up to a sitting posture, and gazed in his face.

"It is! it is!" she said. "It is Lord Saltoun's son. Now I can die."

"No, no!" he exclaimed; "tell me more."

"What—what more?" she said faintly.

"All! You have related the tale clearly enough; but you have omitted, perhaps purposely, some particulars which I demand to know of you."

"Speak," she said; "I am bound to answer you."

"As you are a dying woman, then, and must soon stand in the presence of your Creator, tell me truly, what was the name of your sister after she married and left you?"

"Woodward."

"Where did she reside?"

"At the old Gun tavern, by the Gun-dock, at Wapping, in London, which house was kept by her husband, who bought it with money he had saved during a long period he had been in service as a butler."

"And by what name did Admiral Harding's child go?"

"They named her Minna, and passed her off as their own. They had much affection for her, and, after a time, dreaded that circumstances would occur to take her from them."

Minna, at this point of the narrative, clasped her hands and burst into tears as she exclaimed—

"God help me!—God help me!"

"You must find a father, Minna," said the stranger.

"And he! what will he find?"

"A daughter!"

"Yes, yes! but one who will be a disgrace to him and to his name. Better had I died a hundred deaths than this."

Her feelings completely overcame her. She paused; and then, but for the supporting arm of the stranger, she would have fallen to the floor, for her senses forsook her, and she lay as if dead in his hold.

CHAPTER XXXVII.

THE WRECK OF HEARTWELL'S BOAT.—THE ESCAPE FROM DEATH.—THE BEACH AND THE COAST.

NIGHT came on rapidly, for scarce had the sun sunk beneath the western waves when the clouds rose rapidly and overspread the whole hemisphere with a dull, dismal, leaden-coloured mass of vapour, that every here and there deepened almost to a black, and now and then seemed so low, that it kissed the waves.

Each moment, too, deepened in gloom, and the little light the clouds permitted to reach the ocean was fast diminishing, and the wind increased to almost a gale; the rain fell slightly at intervals; altogether it was as uncomfortable a night as could be imagined.

"Heaven above knows how I shall get through the night; it bids fair to be stormy and boisterous; quite enough for the Eolus to keep a good look-out; and how I am to weather it, I know not. It will be a rough night."

The wind came across the waters with an ominous sound—a continued roar; and every now and then the fierceness of the sound came suddenly upon the ear like the discharge of artillery.

The sound of the waves was incessant; no moment's rest was thought of, but the ocean's roar expended itself in one long murmuring breath, which brought itself out in a continued howl, that seemed as if it never would cease.

The little boat was quite out at sea in less than an hour, and with the last of the sun's light David Heartwell endeavoured to put his boat about, and steer her in a northerly direction.

"Right home," he said, "if she runs not smack upon some of the Portuguese islands, or, what is more likely, unless she get capsized or swamped by a sea. I must shorten sail, and then trust to her power to resist the waves. I fear a night in this will be but a sorry chance, and yet it is better than waiting in yon place or being disgraced by that cowardly assassin, Harding, for he is no better. May he live to see and bitterly repent the error of his ways."

He got up, and having secured the rudder by means of rope, he next proceeded to shorten sail, which he did with some difficulty, for the wind swept over the face of the ocean with such force and power, that made it difficult to do anything. But Heartwell was a seaman of the boldest and hardiest class, and what could be done he could do with his own hands; and this he accomplished, leaving but one reef to keep the vessel's head to sea, and to maintain his power over her course, and her obedience to the helm.

The next thing he did was to make all snug below and aloft, so that not a stray rope or anything should be about to offer the least impediment or check to the working of her; then he spread the tarpaulings, so that she would admit but a small quantity of

See page 157.

water to be thrown into it; and lastly, he spread some tarpaulins over himself as he lay in the stern of the little vessel ready to act as emergencies should require him.

"It will be a sorry night," he muttered. "I care not much now how it ends; but yet, oh! Minna Woodward, I would once again behold you, even though I the next moment breathed my last. Heaven pardon every fault; surely, as far as earthly justice and punishment go, they have been visited very severely.

"Oh! may Heaven deal tenderly with my Minna, and enable her to bear the misfortunes of David Heartwell more calmly than I think she can bear them. Alas! who knows, she may at this moment be motherless and unprotected, exposed to the insults beauty ever is when it is unsupported by a strong arm."

Many were the strange thoughts and fancies that flitted across his brain. Oh, well did he at that hour of peril remember the past. Not a thing, however minute it might have been, and unheeded at the time, but was now brought out in strong relief in his mind.

The scenes of joy and happiness he had gone through with Minna Woodward at the old Gun Tavern were to him at that moment as plain and as evident as they could well be even when in the process of being enacted; but there was a strange, wild accompaniment to the thoughts that were now so strangely recalled to his memory.

There is no place so appalling as the ocean at night, especially when, as it was then, bad weather—more especially as it was with David Heartwell when he was but poorly provided to meet the impending dangers; and the ocean was one scene of contention, turmoil, and foam, the wind blowing hard, and the rain falling at intervals.

This was indeed a night of peril, for Heartwell had no compass to steer by, nor had he even a star or the moon for his guidance; the sky was murky and black; no friendly hand was near him; not a hope could be found that had not some antagonistic fear or danger that overwhelmed it, and bore him down with the weight of immediate and future danger to himself.

He steered his little vessel so that she kept bounding over the waves like some fairy bark that floated on the surface of the storm. Away he went, though he had scarce sail enough to catch the wind, stiff as it was.

David Heartwell had gone through fatigue enough to have knocked up some men that day; but he had no desire for sleep; he lay, or rather reclined, in the stern of the boat he had set sail in. Some of the tarpaulin he had thrown over himself to secure him from as much of the wet as he could, as well as to prevent much water from lying at the bottom, and thus prevent the necessity of baling.

The night was pitchy dark, and the wind increased to a hurricane, and Heartwell found it necessary to have the least possible amount of canvass, for the wind strained the mast.

"This will be a sorry night on the ocean for better vessels than mine," muttered Heartwell. "If I live through the night I shall be more fortunate than I can yet hope with any prospect of success."

He listened to the roar of the hurricane, and it struck a chill to his heart. No human being was near; no sound that issued from any human being could be heard; nothing but the ceaseless roar of the ocean could be heard.

Sound came from afar off, as though thunder could be heard; but tossed as he was on the waves, and then buried in the trough of the ocean, he could see no flash of lightning, for at times he could not see farther than the top of the next wave.

Thus onward he went without any check, but also without any hope of being saved, for he deemed it almost certain that he should be struck by some sea or other, and then swamped or capsized, or the boat filled with water altogether.

Such a fate might well be his, for he ran every risk of it, and every probability was in its favour.

While he sat, well knowing the chances for and against him, he listened to the roar of the ocean, and to the ceaseless sound that knows no rest, he could hear at intervals the sound of thunder.

"There are horrors enough," he muttered, "without the superadded terrors of the elemental strife."

He thought of home, he thought of the Old Gun-deck, and the house where he had left all he loved and all he cared for. If he could but see her again, then indeed he would have thought he had lived to some purpose; but, alas! could he expect a miracle to be performed for him to save him from inevitable destruction.

Thus passed away many hours of the night, the storm growing slowly but gradually worse. The little vessel in which he sailed held its way, and floated like a nautilus upon the ocean's wave—now floating upon the mountain wave, and then into the deep abyss, that seemed yawning to swallow up the little vessel.

Onwards he sped—onwards flew the little bark—and, could any human eye have seen him, they would have said,—

"Yonder sails some fairy—some ocean-spirit—who fears not the deep; or, perchance, the spirit of the storm rises thus triumphantly on the surging waves, alike defying the wind and ocean depths—some enchanted bark, that cannot be engulphed beneath the angry foam, but which would ride upon the very wave-tops, did they reach the skies."

Oh! it would have been a delightful thing to have seen the little vessel thus tossed to and fro, apparently though at the mercy of the waves, braving all, and defying the utmost power of the storm.

"Home! home! home!" thought Heartwell. "How that one word strikes a chord in one's heart; and yet, what place is there that I am not less likely to visit, now that I am at the mercy of the winds and waves? What if I escape the perils of the night—what should I do for food? There is neither water nor food aboard. I am a doomed man, but I will steer and sail on while I can. I will not despair though death stare me in the face."

" Oh, Minna !" he exclaimed, after a time, " what would you think if you knew the state of your lover ? Your kind heart would bleed to see him thus disgraced, and now a fugitive, without almost even the prospect of escape from the angry waves."

Heartwell was a bold sailor, and knew, as well as any man could, the danger he ran; but he was used to dangers, and looked at them with comparative indifference.

He was accustomed to conflicts in which dangers of the most imminent character were frequent, and he looked on them with an unblanched cheek; but yet, now, he considered there was neither honour to himself, nor utility to his country, to be won; and, above all, now that this heavy misfortune came across him, he was more than ever anxious to see Minna Woodward again.

This desire seemed to cling to him the stronger, as the probability seemed to be less and less; and, when despair had fairly taken possession of his soul, the clinging hope to see her whom he so tenderly loved was painfully strong.

" Heaven's own will be done," he said. " I have fought for it, and if I cannot attain this one desire, it will not be because I have not deserved it, but because chance wills it otherwise. Hope and desire may be one way, but, when fate and Heaven decree another, the utmost mortal can do is to perform his allotted task, and die conscious he has not deserved the fate that has befallen him."

Many hours had elapsed since he put to sea, and he judged it must be past midnight, and the night must be making rapid strides towards the morning.

He thought he heard a gun come booming across the ocean, but he was uncertain. The sounds of wind, waves, and occasional bursts of thunder, intermingled with each other as he sat alone, almost rendered it impossible to distinguish accurately between any one of these sounds.

Suddenly the sound of a gun reached his ear in a partial lull. It was the sound of distress—a sound that, he well knew, came from a ship in danger. Again it came.

" God help the poor fellows," he said, " if I am to see them sink. I have it not in my power to aid them by any means. They may bring danger to me, for, if we meet, my fate is certain, and they not bettered."

The thunder now became more distinct than heretofore.

" Ah !" thought Heartwell, " I have not felt the storm yet; it is blowing up from some place in the south. I shall have it soon, and then comes the moment of danger."

Indeed it was a moment of danger, for the fury of the sea seemed to increase each moment, and the billows rose and fell in rapid and tremendous succession. The sea was one boiling, surging mass of tempestuous motion, and the little boat with difficulty sped its way through the troubled waters.

Thus he went on for another hour, dripping wet, and the rain coming down very fast. It was a most uncomfortable situation, danger apart; but, all things considered, a worse could scarce be conceived than the one in which he was placed.

Again the gun sounded over the bosom of the ocean. He could now hear it distinctly. It was near at hand, and the gun sounded at shorter intervals than before.

" The danger thickens," he said, as he listened to the sounds, " and yet, poor wretches, there is no help from this quarter. I cannot aid, and shall want it soon, for my little vessel owes its safety more to its lightness, and the little there is of it to be acted upon by the wind and the waves. It floats lightly upon the water, and, while the tempest is not too strong, so as to capsize it, I have a chance. But here it comes."

In truth it did come. The wind came like a hurricane bringing with it a sheet of spray and rain that seemed more like a sea washing over the boat.

" In another minute, Heartwell had taken in all sail, and nothing but the bare mast stood up, and even that was straining its cordage, and the little vessel heaved to and fro on the waves, as they lifted her up and then let her down again. Yet onward she sped, to the surprise and admiration of Heartwell.

" Upon my life," he thought, " I could not have believed such a vessel could have lived in such a sea."

Again the gun was fired, but this time the flash came across the head of his boat, and in the excitement Heartwell stood up expecting that the next moment would be his last, and that the sea would receive him, for a collision seemed inevitable."

" Ship, ahoy !" shouted Heartwell.

A pause ensued.

" Ahoy !" was returned, but Heartwell could not tell if it were only the echo of his own voice.

"Ship, ahoy!" he shouted, in a yet higher key.

"Ahoy!" was returned in a higher key also.

"It is merely the echo of my own voice," he said; "the shout could not reach them; the wind would have carried it away."

Another gun now boomed over the water; but it was not from the same quarter; it was still out of his course, and he had now room enough, without fear of collision.

"Poor things, if they heard my voice it must have given them a gleam of hope; but to suffer the pangs of disappointment, how wretched they must be."

He now thought it must be near day break, and he looked towards the quarter where he expected the light to appear, but could see no signs of it as yet.

"The night wears slowly," he said; "slowly, indeed, each moment spent in it is an age of danger, one moment of which may prove fatal."

He had scarcely muttered these words, when a wave carried his little bark high up in the air, and then a gun flashed close by him, and he heard the report at the same instant.

"By heavens!" he said, aloud, "the vessel is close along side of me; Heaven help them!"

Another flash and report.

"Ship, ahoy!" he shouted, more from impulse than reason, for had he done as he most wished, he would not have allowed the poor creatures to have heard his voice, seeing it would give them false hopes and expectations of relief; but the impulse was irresistible.

"What ship?" shouted a hoarse voice.

Before he could reply, a flash of light illumined the sky, and he could see the vessel rolling in the sea at some distance from him, and the sound of the waves and winds, and now the rattling peal of thunder, as it broke over head, rendered any voice communication impossible.

Heartwell's experience at once told him, that the vessel was almost dismasted, they were in great distress.

The lightning now played away, and sometimes for nearly a minute the whole ocean seemed illumined by the vividness of the flash, and he could see, when his vessel was on the crest of the wave, some miles of water; but no vessel, save his own, met his sight.

What a view that was when he caught a momentary, but sudden sight of such an extent of trackless waste of waters. It seemed as though the waves were mad and furious, that kept rushing and tumbling about one after the other, in a desperate turmoil and foam; now rushing up to a great height, and then leaving great chasms; here all was white and foam, and there a deep pit, black and angry, and fearful to look at.

The storm was at its height, and surprised, indeed, was Heartwell, that he had as yet escaped from the danger of the deep, but he owed it to his not having been struck by any of the numerous and heavy waves, that would at once have beaten him to pieces and swamped him in a moment.

So light was his little vessel, and so little acted upon by the wind, that it was carried forward as much by the waves, and impulse of the waves, as the wind; thus she rose and fell and rose again, as the waves broke and left by turns; and thus, carried on and with them, she escaped destruction.

Heartwell saw this, and well understood how it was he had succeeded in securing himself an impunity from the effects of the storm.

"If she should hold out, thus till day," he muttered, "all may yet be well. I must be somewhere near the coast of Portugal, and though not famous for goodness of heart, the people will not I dare say refuse me food and shelter. I can run into some harbour or creek, or on to the shore of some fishing village or other, there I may obtain all I want from men exposed to such calamities."

He looked towards the east, and saw a broad streak of light, the sun was rising and would soon appear; day was breaking, and now he would have some chance of being saved from his perilous and unhappy state, and he might be able to shape his course.

"Morning is now at hand," he muttered, "and Heaven be thanked for such a mercy. I have been singularly preserved during such a night, nothing but the hand of Providence could have carried me through so many dangers as those I have been through this night."

Each moment added to the lighting up of the scene; great care was requisite in steering the boat, for the sea seemed to have some new impetus and a different direction of its current, and this caused him a new danger.

Surely he thought I must be near some shallow part of the ocean, which causes this change of current, perhaps breakers, or possibly nearer shore, than I imagined.

He looked around and could see nothing but the wide tumultuous sea, not a vestige of anything save water.

Water! water! water! was around him on every side. He could see nothing but this element, save the one above him, which was now a close assimilation to the one below him, for the rain fell in deluging masses, so thick and so heavy that it was almost impossible to see more than a few yards.

The sky darkened again, and though the sun must have been above the horizon, yet he was not now seen through this state of falling water; it was perfectly tremendous.

The flashing of the lightning was in fact a vivid sheet glare, or forked masses of light, that were seen playing about on all sides of him.

Heartwell felt assured that he was in the very thick of the storm, and to add to his disasters, a wind came howling along that seemed as though it would have annihilated the very waves; it was of such force that the waters below were made smooth beneath its presence and the crested wave-tops were blown along with the rain.

Heartwell saw it coming, gave one look upward, and then bent beneath the protecting bulwark of the boat, expecting some disaster to follow.

A disaster did follow, for scarcely had the wind reached his little vessel, than it caused her to pitch so much forward that her keel was nearly dry, but it was but for a moment, the mast gave way, and she righted.

"Thank Heaven!" he said; "I thought all had been lost."

The vessel righted; yes, but she no longer sailed along as she had done; she was no more than a barge without sails and masts, urged onwards by any impulse of the waves, but under no control whatever; she was carried forwards sometimes broadside first, and sometimes stern forward, and then, again, she would come head forwards.

Thus she went for some time, the waves breaking over her, and Heartwell now expected every wave would send her to pieces, and a watery grave was, after all, in store for him.

"Well, well," he muttered, "I am a seaman, and must expect and calmly meet the fate I am so soon about to meet."

He had scarcely uttered the words, when another sea came and struck her on the stern. The effect of this was, that the vessel, which was an old one, suddenly gave way, and she instantly filled, and sank in a moment. Heartwell had not seen exactly how it was done, but he found himself floating in the waves, tossed up and down he knew not where.

David Heartwell was a strong, powerful man, and a good swimmer, but he found that it would be impossible to long maintain himself afloat on the waves; a few more brief struggles, and his life was over; for each moment he was buried beneath a world of waters and foam.

Luckily, at that moment, a plank was washed close up to him; he seized it with a nervous grasp, but what was his horror and astonishment when he perceived a dead body lashed to it!

For more than a moment Heartwell looked at the ghastly object in silence; he could not even think, so much was he amazed at the occurrence, and so unexpected was it.

"Good Heavens!" he muttered, "he must have lashed himself here for safety, and has perished in the waves. Poor wretch; he is a type of what I shall be; heaven help me!"

He paused for awhile, and looked around him, but nothing could he see, nothing but waves and foam.

The plank he was on, and to which the dead man was lashed, was under water by the weight of both of them. The dead man's was a dead weight, he being a mere log, and not like a living man who had breath in his body, and helped himself by swimming stoutly with the aid of the timber.

"I must unlash him. It can be of no use to him," said Heartwell; "he is dead."

He unlashed the dead man in a moment, and the timber immediately became more buoyant, and Heartwell had some trouble to hold on at that moment, for it became more easily tossed about by the waves hither and thither.

He now lashed himself to the timber, and trusted himself to the mercy of the waves.

The light of day was now spread over every part of the hemisphere, for the sun had risen high; but he could not be seen, only his influence was felt.

No hope did this bring Heartwell, for to his mind there was no hope beyond prolonging his life a few hours at most; for there could be no prospect in making land, and the prospect of meeting a ship was almost hopeless, and, had he done so, he could not expect that it would avail him, for no ship could lay to, neither could they lower a boat, for it would be swamped in an instant.

The wind had certainly moderated much after the tremendous rush of wind that knocked over his mast, and destroyed his boat.

He had not seen this, but it was so; because while he was hidden in the trough of the sea, now immersed in foam and spray, he could scarcely tell what weather was actually in existence.

True it was, he endeavoured now and then to catch a hasty glance around on the ocean, to see if aught was near him; but he could see nothing.

Hope, which had buoyed him up, seemed now to desert him. He had now been for thirty hours without food of any kind, and this, and his constant immersion in the water, tended to render him hopeless; he had, indeed, arrived at the last stage of despair.

"Heaven bless her!" he murmured—"Heaven bless her! and save her from any calamity, and render her future life a happy one. Mine has been short, and now is brought to an unhappy termination."

He had almost an insensibility creeping over him, and then he seemed to give over any further effort to save his life.

He was sinking backward, when he thought he saw the tall masts of a vessel close at hand. It was but a momentary glance, and yet he could not have been mistaken.

Hope again took possession of his mind, and reanimated him. He again renewed the struggle for life, and kept himself as erect out of the water as he could.

He was rewarded; and when the next wave lifted him up, he saw the same vessel, as if she were bearing down upon him, at a rapid rate.

He secured himself to the timber, and placed himself so as he could best be seen, as well as that could be done under such circumstances as these under which he was placed.

When he was again lifted up he saw the vessel went much faster than he did, though she had no sail spread, and it was with a wild feeling, between hope and joy, that he saw she bore down straight upon him.

"Ship ahoy!" shouted Heartwell, as he rose on his plank, about a hundred and fifty yards from the vessel.

No answer was returned; and he again shouted. He must have been heard, for some one came forward, and stood on her bulwarks and looked over the ocean.

"Ship ahoy," he shouted.

"Ahoy!" was the answer returned; but from whence the ship was hailed the seaman could not conceive.

"Where is she?" inquired the captain.

"Don't know," said the seaman; "it must be Davy Jones surely, that's been hailing on us in this manner."

"There," said the captain, "did you hear that?"

At that moment Heartwell again shouted, for the vessel was within thirty yards of him, and he feared she would pass him; and he shouted, in a clear strong voice, lent him by despair,—

"Ship ahoy!"

"Ahoy! Where are you?" shouted the captain, in reply. "What are you, and what do you want?"

"Here on the starboard-bow, in the sea. I'm drowning—throw a rope—save me!"

"There he is," said the seaman, pointing to a black spot in the waves, "there he is!"

"I see him," said another; "he's lashed to a plank."

"Keep a good heart," he shouted, "look out!"

Then seizing a rope, he drew it near him.

"Lower a boat, boys—lower away, while I give him a chance with the rope," and then coiling up a rope in his hands, he took a good view of the spot, and threw it out with all his force.

He was a strong burly man, but the wind was very strong, and it required all his skill and strength to reach the spot intended, but he did reach it.

Heartwell saw the rope—it lay a few yards beyond him, and with the timber he could not reach it—he unlashed himself, and swam to it and secured it.

When he had secured the rope round his body, he then shouted out to the men on board—

"Haul away—haul in."

"Haul in boys!" exclaimed the captain; "he's got it."

Away they began to haul, as rapidly as they could, and they soon found that Heartwell had it safely enough. The ship did not stop in its course, but went on as before, and by this time Heartwell was trailing in the ship's wake.

"There, that will do, men," said the captain; "now, some of ye go aft with your hitchers and draw him up, and the rope also."

"Ay, ay, sir."

The men went aft, and taking some boat-hooks, they drew up the rope, and then, after hauling Heartwell up a short distance, secured him further by catching him with their hitchers by the clothes.

"All right," said Heartwell.

"All right," said the men.

In a few moments more he was seized by the arms of the sailors, and he was laid upon deck, a mass of weeds and water.

"Hilloa, mate, you have a little water."

"A little!" said Heartwell, "why, I have had a whole ocean; thank Heaven for sending me aid. I have just escaped death—I am not strong enough to thank you."

"Nor need you be so, lad," said the good-natured captain, "you wanted it I'll be sworn."

"I did."

"Take him below, and let him have some coffee royal, that will be the best thing he can have; strip these things off and place him in a hammock; but here, take a drop of brandy, to begin with; you must be soaked in brine."

Heartwell could not stand, but sat on the knee of one of the men who held him, and took the brandy, but he could not carry it to his mouth, and was compelled to suffer it to be poured down his throat by the sailors.

Then he was carried down the ladder by the seamen, and by their aid he was stretched in a hammock.

Once in there, the change was so great, and the fatigue also, that he fell into a sound sleep, and would probably have slept until death had closed his career; but by the captain's orders one of the men went down to wake him.

The man was unsuccessful for some time, but by dint of violent shaking and shouting, Heartwell opened his eyes in stupid wonder and amazement, and looked about him.

"Hilloa, mate!"

Heartwell only looked at the speaker.

"Are you dead or alive—better or worse?"

No answer.

"Well, you are a rum customer, anyhow. What do you want? Will you get up, and have a mess along with the captain?"

"Eh?" inquired Heartwell.

"Well, I thought if anything would do, it must be the mention of something to eat. I am sure of it."

"Where am I?" inquired Heartwell.

"On board the Mary Ann."

"On board the Mary Ann!" repeated Heartwell to himself, pondering, as if he were not quite sure he heard aright, or that he correctly understood the words in their full meaning.

"Yes; and a good ship she is."

"Yes, yes—a good ship—a very good ship; and her commander?"

"Oh! the skipper—yes, that is Captain Jones."

"Captain Jones!"

"Yes; and as good a man as ever rode over salt water, and as good and kind-hearted a man as ever broke biscuit or drank grog. There's plenty of everything where he is."

"I'm glad of it," said Heartwell. "I can hardly tell where I am or anything about it; but I begin to remember what I have gone through."

"Ay, ay; you have had a bad time of it, no doubt; but will you do it?"

"Do what?"

"Accept the captain's invitation."

"I didn't hear it," said Heartwell.

"Why, he wants to know if you'll mess with him in his cabin—he's going to dinner."

"I will accept of his invitation with pleasure; but ——"

"What?"

"Why, I haven't my uniform."

"Your uniform!"

"Yes; my clothes, I mean."

"Oh! I see. By Jove, he's wandering. Here are some clothes, in which you can get up, till your's are fit to put on."

"Thank you."

"We should have left you to yourself, but the captain feared you would hurt yourself."

"Thank you," said Heartwell; and he attempted to dress himself; but in so doing he found himself weak in the extreme. Hunger, too, now crept over him, and he felt the want of food very badly; and, drowsy as he was, his sense of hunger was very great; and when he had dressed himself, he felt as if he were unable to stand, but reeled about like a child.

"I'll help you to the cabin," said the sailor, as he watched him; "I'll help you."

"Thank you, friend."

"Nay, you are welcome. I never saw a man so nigh done up before. Why, how long have you been in the water?"

"I cannot tell, but soon after daylight."

"About six?"

"And now?"

"About three, or nearly four."

"I must have been out some hours."

"You must have been in about six hours. Well, that is a pretty spell for once, at all events. It would cure me of any desire to taste cold water for evermore."

"Yes; I'm pretty well soaked and soddened."

"Come along, then."

As he spoke he took hold of Heartwell, and led him towards the cabin, in which the captain was now waiting to receive him.

"I am quite helpless," he said, in an apologetic tone.

"Do not speak of it. I judge you have been put to extremes both as to danger and to privations."

"Indeed I have."

"How long had you been in the water?"

"About six hours."

"How long since you had any food?"

"This must be about or over the second day," repeated Heartwell in a faint tone.

The captain shrugged his shoulders, and pushing some food towards Heartwell, he said,—

"Take of what you will, and as much as you will; but for your own sake let me advise you to be careful of what you take, and how you do so, lest you suffer for it."

"I am well aware of my state," said Heartwell, "too well; and I am too ill to take very much."

The captain gave him some chicken, which he had cooked on purpose for him, being light and delicate. Then he had some coffee; he refused ale, stout and spirit; save a little he had put into his coffee, and when this feast was over, for such it was, he could with great difficulty keep awake; but by the captain's advice he refused to return into the cabin.

"Sit back and sleep if you will—you will awake soon; and if you turn into your hammock you will sleep too much, I am afraid, at once."

"It is perhaps for the best," muttered Heartwell, as he sank back in the chair, which he'd been placed in by the captain, and was asleep in a minute or two.

"I may as well take a nap myself," said the captain; "I have not slept since the night before last, and am fatigued enough. My turn has come now; but I'll go outside first and see all is right and then turn in for a couple of hours."

This he did, and left the deck believing the storm was abated, and then he returned to his own hammock.

In about two hours after this he awoke, and entered the cabin, and saw Heartwell again asleep.

"Ah! poor fellow he's having a long spell of it, but he wants it, and he shall not be waked yet until the coffee is ready, and then he shall have some, and if he be not awake why then we can awake him."

The coffee soon came round, and then the captain shook Heartwell by the shoulder and shouted at the same time in his ear.

"Hilloa, hilloa!"

"Hilloa!" said Heartwell, as he started up in a hurry, not knowing what was the matter.

"Nothing wrong, nothing wrong," said the captain, seeing Heartwell's flurry and bewilderment.

"I see what it is," said Heartwell; "I have not got used to my change of situation."

"It is a change for the better at present."

"It is so, from death to life."

"Yes, I hope it will be for your good."

"I hope it will," returned Heartwell, and he could hardly repress a sigh as he spoke.
" What vessel do you belong to ?"
" The Eolus. I was washed overboard."
" Ah, well," added the captain, " it can't be helped. I recollect being, not many years
ago, in almost as bad a situation as yourself."
" Indeed ; I should like to hear it."

See page, 162.

" The truth is, at the time I speak of I was but a foremastman on board a small fruit
vessel trading between London and Seville. The captain treated me very badly, and so
I made up my mind to give the vessel the slip the first opportunity. A boat had been
towing astern of the ship, into which I got, and cut myself adrift. Like you I floated at
the mercy of the waves for some time, but was at length thrown ashore on the Spanish coast.
We were then at war with the Spaniards, and I was made prisoner the instant I landed,

and thrown into a miserable dungeon. How many days I remained there I don't know, for I couldn't keep any reckoning, but I know when I regained my liberty, my beard had grown an enormous length, and my hair hung in ragged masses round my face. I had been in this sad situation a long time, seeing no human being but my gaoler, when, one evening, I was aroused from the bed of straw on which I had thrown myself, for I was so weak that I was scarcely able to keep my feet, by the noise of artillery, and the loud shouts of combatants. This continued for some time, and then it as suddenly ceased; then, after the lapse of a short period, hurried footsteps were heard close to my cell, the door was thrown open, and a man entered. He raised me from the ground, and, seeing my weak condition, he called assistance, and had me conveyed from the place of my captivity. I then learned the cause of my unexpected release. The English had bombarded and taken the town, and then I had been released by one of the parties who were despatched to free all English prisoners."

As he concluded, he perceived that Heartwell, overcome with exhaustion, had fallen fast asleep; and, drawing on his pea-jacket, he went on deck, to see to the state of and the vessel.

*   *   *   *   *   *   *

The vessel sailed against contrary winds, and a variety of untoward circumstances occurred to render their voyage longer than was agreeable or pleasant, and they encountered such a succession of gales and storms, that when they entered the English Channel they were in a very distressed condition indeed, with several feet of water in the hold, and the vessel in a very leaky condition.

There was another storm, and they were three days in making from Land's End to the North Foreland, and then, to the joy of all hearts, she entered the mouth of the Thames.

Heartwell was quite recovered and well; he was of essential service in preserving the safety of the ship; but when they rounded the Foreland it was dark, and they could only observe where they were by the lights at a distance.

The sea was tempestuous, and the waves ran high, while the wind blew furiously, and all on board expected a rough night of it; but as they were so close home, and sheltered, they only kept a sharp look out and proceeded up the river.

It was somewhere about midnight, when the wind and rain were at their height, that a sudden shake brought them all on deck, for nobody on two legs could stand, and those in their berths were thrown out. Up they came, for they knew that the ship had struck upon some of the sands.

It was true they were upon the Goodwin Sands, and the vessel, before leaky, was now fast going to pieces. They took to their boats; but being in the dark, and unable to tell where they had got to, they were all lost, save David Heartwell, who, having secured a plank, was again saved from the watery element, and thrown, more dead than alive, upon the coast of Kent.

CHAPTER XXXVIII.

MINNA'S NEW PROSPECTS.—ANOTHER DISCOVERY.—THE CONSULTATION.

WELL might Minna feel confounded at this wonderful change in her fortunes; well might she ask herself if all indeed could be real, so like a dream did it appear that she should be plucked from such a depth of misery and degradation to such a height, of what would have been felicity, could she but have told herself that the continued love of the brave and gallant Heartwell would be her ultimate reward; but, alas! she could not promise herself so much. Between her and him there was now a dreary gulf—a gulf so impassable that it was not to be considered for a moment he would make the attempt to leap it.

But Minna felt that yet there was something to be disclosed to her, and she became proportionately anxious to be made acquainted with it. She was certain that, although she knew the main features of the tale concerning her family history, there were some matters of which she was yet ignorant, and she longed for the re-appearance of the stranger, in order that she might ask him these questions which naturally arose in her mind.

She was not long kept in a state of suspense, and when he came to her he seemed more composed and cheerful than he had been before.

"Minna," he said, "I can imagine that you are impatient now to hear the sequel of those adventures, which you must feel have so strong a relation to yourself."

"I am, indeed," she said, "most impatient."

"You shall hear all, then, and that shortly," he said. "You now know, Minna, that you are the child of Admiral Harding, stolen by Lady Saltoun in the height of her vindictive rage, placed under the care of that confidential domestic whose sister became the wife of Woodward, the innkeeper at Wapping."

"Yes, yes, already have I gathered so much from your narration."

"You know likewise of the death of Lady Saltoun, by which let us hope that she expiated some of her offences against her Creator, and the social laws which bind humanity together. You are aware, likewise, of all the events which preceded those circumstances, and you have but now to hear some of the sequences upon them. Have you no surmises, Minna, with regard to me?"

"With regard to you?"

"Yes; surely you have not heard all that I have related, and you have not seen how I have related it, without believing that I had more than a common interest in it?"

"No, no! I have not been unmindful of your emotion when you have come to certain portions of your narrative. You are the son of Lady Saltoun, and that heir of Lord Saltoun who was repudiated by his haughty family."

"I am, am! and Harding, who has done you so much injury, fills partially the place in society which of right belongs to me. You, Minna, as the daughter of my uncle, Admiral Harding, are my cousin; and I trust that we may both live long, to be to each other tender, attached, and affectionate relatives and the very best of friends."

He took her hand, as he spoke, and pressed it to his; but Minna burst into tears, and, with accents of the greatest anguish, she said—

"Oh! grant me now but one request, and I will bless your name."

"Certainly, Minna; what is it that you can ask of me, that is in my power to grant, which you could imagine for one moment I would refuse to you?"

"It is that you would give me some small pittance, so that I might leave England for ever; and, in some foreign land, where my name and my disgrace are unknown, live out my allotted space of existence."

"Minna, Minna! you know not what you ask."

"Nay, you have promised to comply with my request."

"No; without the least quibble, Minna, I have not made a promise which can for one moment commit me to such a course as this that you mention. I promised you whatever it was within my power to grant, and this is not within my power. Have you forgotten again that you have a father; and that surely something is due to him in such an affair as this? Think better of yourself, Minna Harding, for such is your real name, and yet live to be the solace of the old age of one who has never ceased to mourn for you, and never would, until the grave had closed over all his human hopes and feelings."

"You are right, you are right!" said Minna. "My judgment tells me that you are right; although feeling goes completely opposite to such a conviction. But have you sufficient proofs of my birth?"

"I have; I have the declaration of the dying woman of the whole affair connected with the loss of the daughter of Admiral Harding, perfectly witnessed and attested. I have likewise, from the escritoir which was kept in the bed-room of Mr. Woodward, at the Old Gun Tavern, all the papers of the late Lady Saltoun, in which mention is made of the fact of her marriage to Brazier, and a variety of other circumstances connected with her history."

"Repeated attempts were made to rob that escritoir."

"Yes; by me. I was the person who, on more than one occasion, made efforts, not unaided, to find some of the secret drawers in it after the death of Mr. Woodward."

"And you succeeded."

"Yes; to a certain extent. I ascertained who you were, beyond dispute, but too late, for you were gone from the tavern; and my last visit to the scene of the conflagration of the old house was yet to hunt among the ruins for more documents upon the subject."

"But how is the question of the disputed succession to be settled?"

"That I settled with myself long ago. I found out that Brazier had a wife living before he married her who became afterwards Lady Saltoun, so that you perceive that in law her marriage with him was a complete nullity, and she was quite correct in wedding Lord Saltoun in her maiden name."

"I understand."

"I found out Brazier, and got this fact from him, and have all the particulars under his own hand, and have found likewise all the necessary documents confirming them."

"Then Captain Harding is his son?"

" Yes, his illegitimate son, and I look forward with some curiosity to introducing the father and son together."

" Then Brazier is not dead?"

" Certainly not. Admiral Harding thinks he is dead, but he is actually in London, and living upon my bounty."

" Have you means to do all this without making yourself known to the family."

" Yes, when I had all my documentary evidence in such a state that I could at any time prove who and what I was, I went to a respectable and wealthy firm of solicitors, and they, after an attentive examination of my claim, found it undeniable, and so supplied me with whatever funds I wanted. I regret that Captain Harding's conduct has been such that I can show him no sort of consideration whatever. Disguised as a man with a blue face, I have repeatedly tried to make him do one good action, but he would not, and therefore all shall be wrested from him; so that, at all events, he shall have no power to do bad ones."

" This is indeed retaliation."

" Yes, but not more ample than it is deserved. The rank which he dare not keep up of Lord Saltoun, I can and will; so that now, Minna, you know all, and if there be any point in my narrative which appears obscure to you, ask me what questions you please, and I will answer them."

" No, no, no, I see it all now as far as you have told me. What has become of the sisters of the late Lord Saltoun?"

" They are still living; but this affair will be a mortification to them, no doubt, since it will wrest from them a large portion of the family property of which I shall take possession, for I owe them no affection or good will, for my mother's sake."

" As heir-at-law you claim everything."

" I do, and now what I am at once, and most particularly anxious about, is to introduce you to your father, Minna."

She trembled, and it was some moments before she spoke, saying,—

" It must be so; but tell him all first. Let him, after he sees me have nothing to learn of my history. Tell him that I do not and cannot aspire to his affections, and that all I can ask of him is his forgiveness, and his leave to go far away for ever."

" I will take especial care that your feelings, Minna, shall be properly represented to him. I intend to-day visiting him, and procuring a final interview, at which I shall detail to him the whole of the particulars with which I have made you acquainted. I know that he is one of the most noble-hearted and generous of men, and that you have everything to hope from his affection, and nothing to fear from any ordinary prejudices, for he is far, very far above them. Be composed, I will return to you in the course of a few hours."

CHAPTER XXXIX.

HEARTWELL'S RETURN TO LONDON.—HIS PLEASANT ANTICIPATIONS AND VISIT TO LONDON.

WE left our friend Heartwell in a situation of comparative safety to what he had gone through since that time when he made his escape from the rock of Gibraltar.

Our readers will recollect that he had been thrown upon the British coast, after the complete wreck which had taken place, and that he was more dead than alive when that wreck took place.

He lay for some time perfectly insensible, but was at length picked up by some fishermen, who conducted or rather carried him to a cottage, where such means, as long experience had taught them was effectual, soon succeeded in restoring him to consciousness.

They accommodated him to the best of their ability with a bed, and he slept for nearly twenty-four hours, a long, dreamless sleep which they were especially careful not by any means to disturb, as they knew that exhausted nature required abundant repose, and that he would of himself awaken when his energies were sufficiently refreshed by slumber.

He felt, when he did again open his eyes, quite a new being, so wonderfully recruited was he by the long sleep he had had; and moreover he had an enormous appetite, which the kind-hearted people, among whom he had been thrown, made haste to gratify, at the same time advising him to eat sparingly and often, rather than to consult his inclinations in a hearty meal at once.

He found that he was not above half a dozen miles from a port from whence regular packets left daily for London, which was only distant about one hundred and thirty miles from the fishing village close to which he had been cast ashore.

Without any hesitation he made up his mind to proceed to the metropolis, and, being informed that in the immediate neighbourhood there was a preventive station, commanded by a lieutenant of the Royal Navy, he determined upon throwing himself upon the consideration of that officer to provide him with the necessary means of getting to London.

What was his pleasure and surprise, however, upon reaching the preventive station, and being ushered into the presence of its commander, to find in him an old and valued comrade, whom he had once sailed with in a frigate, and lost sight of for many years!

From him he obtained the assistance he required, and early on the following morning, provided with sufficient funds, and followed by the best wishes of his old friend, Lieutenant Heartwell, after amply compensating the fisherman and his family, beyond all their expectations for the service they had rendered him, took his way to the sea port in the neighbourhood, where he found a packet ready to start.

He, at once, stepped on board of her, and in the course of a quarter of an hour he was *en route* for the metropolis.

Little suspecting what a bitter and terrific disappointment he was likely to endure upon reaching London, he strove, as the ship sped on its way, to arrange in his mind all he should say to his own dearest Minna, when he should meet her, as now in a few short hours he expected to do.

The voyage was an average one, and by about ten o'clock at night, the vessel reached the mouth of the Thames, where the captain determined to cast anchor for the night.

Our readers will recollect that those were not the days of steam-boats, when a hundred miles are traversed in about eight hours, in spite of wind and weather.

By the earliest dawn, however, the ship was again put into motion, and steered slowly but steadily up the Thames. Oh, with what a world of expectation did Heartwell keep to that side of the vessel which was next to the house of his beloved Minna, and how tedious to him appeared the many tortuous windings of the river.

At length, the wished-for haven of his hopes was near at hand, and his eye ran eagerly over the mass of houses in search of the Woodwards' house.

"What," he exclaimed, "has become of the Old Gun Tavern?"

"The Old Gun Tavern?" said a man, who was close to him. "Oh, the Woodwards are dead, and the house has been burnt to the ground."

"And—and Minna Woodward?"

"The daughter. Oh! ah; she went off into keeping with some fellow or another. They do say she has been seen since starving in the streets."

All objects seemed to swim before the eyes of Heartwell. "God help me!" he exclaimed, and fell insensible upon the deck.

CHAPTER XL.

HARDING'S RECOVERY FROM HIS WOUND AND RETURN TO ENGLAND.

LET us now, since our tale is so very near to its conclusion, once more conduct our readers to the rock of Gibraltar.

It will be recollected that Captain Harding, after having in so dastardly a manner endeavoured to take the life of Heartwell, was himself shot in the desperate attempt he made to escape from the consequences of his meditated, but foiled, crime.

The bullet caught him about the shoulder, and he fell instantly and fainted, believing himself at the moment to be mortally wounded.

Some part of this affair was seen from the batteries of the fort, and a party from the garrison was immediately sent out to bring in the dead man, as he seemed to be. He was carried on a temporary bier by the soldiers to the hospital, and there it was found that he was not dead, although at first, from a great difficulty in tracing the progress of the bullet, the surgeons considered his wound a very dangerous one.

When he recovered his senses, this opinion was, at his own request, communicated to him, and he shewed at once, by his conduct, that death had for him many terrors.

He requested to see the governor of the fort, and, as his rank in the navy was known, that officer at once repaired to his bedside, and proffered his services in any way to the suffering man.

"I wish to declare to you," said Harding, "who it is that has been my murderer. It is a Lieutenant Heartwell, who was already under arrest in my ship for mutinous acts, but who escaped; and, meeting me upon the rock, murdered me."

"I fear," said the governor, "that, in spite of all we could do, he has escaped."

"Escaped!—escaped from here?"

"Yes, he has put to sea in an open boat, but, as the weather is each moment getting rougher, it is certain that he will be swamped and lost."

"Curses on him!—curses! I would have given worlds to see him hung. He will, after all, escape my vengeance, while I lie dying here."

"I think," said the governor, "that at such a time as this, when your life hangs, as it were, upon a thread, you ought to turn your attention to far different matters than invoking curses on the head of any one whatever."

"But he has been my deadliest foe."

"If he has, you can now feel assured that he is not only a doomed man in this world, but likewise for what amount of evil he has done, assuredly will he suffer in that world which is to come. You may safely leave your case in the hands of Heaven."

The governor, finding that Harding had really nothing to say but upon the subject of having vengeance upon Heartwell, did not choose to listen to such tirades, but left him shortly.

When he was gone, Harding trembled as he repeated the last words which had been spoken to him, and he asked himself,—

"Is there such another world as he speaks of? for, if there be, it is I, and not Heartwell, that may be made to suffer."

It so happened that just as he was in this frame of mind, a clergyman who had resided long in the garrison, and who was anything but a fanatic, and, in reality, a man of the most enlarged and comprehensive views, visited Harding, understanding from the surgeon the danger he was in.

This gentleman apologised for his visit on these grounds.

"And have they told you that I cannot live?" said Harding.

"No, they have not gone so far as that, but what they state is, that, in consequence of, as yet, not being able to extract the bullet from the integuments among which it is lodged, they consider the case a very troublesome one, and attended with great danger. Indeed, that unless the bullet be extracted to-morrow, it must end fatally."

Harding gave a deep groan, partly of bodily pain and partly of mental anguish.

"I do hope," said the clergyman, that you will not go out of the world without making a strictly true statement of all the particulars connected with the transaction which has placed you in your present very awful condition."

"I have," said Harding.

"Nay you have not," was the reply. "This is not a time to stand upon the punctilios of society. An officer from the garrison, who saw through a telescope part of what occurred, says that you fired at him—who ran after you and shot you—first."

Harding was silent.

"This is a much more serious affair to you," added the clergyman, "than it is to him, probably, whom you accuse of giving you your death wound."

"How so?"

"Because he, at the great tribunal of God, may be able to plead some justification for his act. I do not say that you cannot; but most solemnly, and in the most friendly spirit towards you, knowing nothing of either you or your opponent, I do implore you not to leave this world with falsehood in your heart."

"I have nothing to say to you," remarked Harding, gloomily, after a pause. "I have nothing to add to what I have said; but that the governor knows well who is my murderer. I will take care to have an accurate account of the transaction taken to England."

"As you please—as you please. I have no wish to press you in the matter."

So saying, the clergyman left him.

The symptoms attendant upon his wound grew worse, and as he was very particular, when the surgeons visited him, in questioning them with regard to his condition, they frankly told him that he was getting worse every hour.

"Then you mean," he said, "that I am dying?"

"Another attempt," was the reply, "will be made to-morrow morning to extract the ball. If that fail, there will be no hope for you."

It was at twelve o'clock that night, after a short and disturbed slumber, that Harding inquired for the clergyman who had visited him in the day time.

That gentleman was at once sent for, and when he came he found Harding in a terrible state of nervous trepidation. This the clergyman, under the circumstances, very properly took advantage of, and urged him, by every argument in his power, to tell the whole simple and unadorned truth, as regarded the circumstances attendant upon his wound.

Acted upon by the solemnity of the hour, the clever exhortations of the clergyman—who was that rarity, in the church, a man of intellect—and, more than all, by a sense of his own danger, the effrontery of Captain Harding deserted him.

He not only admitted the precise manner in which he received the wound, of which he believed himself to be dying, but he told the whole story of the betrayal of Minna Woodward, and how he had appointed Heartwell to be the first lieutenant of the Eolus for no other purpose than to take advantage of their relative positions to effect his total ruin.

All this the clergyman, as shortly as he could, reduced to writing; and, taking full advantage of the moment, he got Harding to affix his signature to it.

"Now," he said, "Captain Harding, you have made the only reparation in your power for the injuries you have inflicted upon the innocent people you have named. It is not, as you well know, doubtless, the province of the ministers of the religion to which I belong, to promise a remission of sins; but the mercy of Heaven is infinite, and may be appealed to by those who have even done much worse deeds than you."

"I feel more contented," said Harding, "now that I have told you all."

"That was sure to ensue. Such poor effect as my prayers may have, offered up, as they will be in singleness of spirit and purity of purpose, you shall have. Endeavour now, to sleep, for however the exertion you have undergone may be for the benefit of your eternal welfare, you cannot but, in your weak state, feel it."

"I will," said Harding. "I am weary; but I feel composed."

The clergyman left him, and he almost immediately sunk into a profound repose, from which he did not awaken until the morning was advanced.

He was really, or he fancied himself, much better, and, strange to say, from that time he prospered. The bullet was extracted from his shoulder with far less difficulty than had been anticipated, and day by day he rapidly recovered, so that, at the end of about another fortnight, he was declared to be completely out of danger, and almost in a perfect state of convalescence.

Now it was that the remembrance of the confession which he had made began to rankle in his mind, and he felt all the anxiety in the world to regain possession of a document which, to him, was of such a truly damnatory character, if produced.

He sought an interview with Mr. Russell, the clergyman, on the evening before he was about to rejoin his ship, having received orders to repair to England direct.

"Sir," he said, "when I was believed to be dying, you came to me."

"Yes; I perfectly remember."

"And, while I was in that state, I made a sort of statement to you, which, although very proper indeed for a man to make who was in such a condition, yet, when he is in different circumstances, is altogether, as you must be aware, out of the question."

"Is it not true, sir?"

"Yes, yes; but still ——"

"Still what? I am ready to hear any arguments, if there be such, which can be brought forward in favour of a suppression of the truth."

"In plain language, sir, I, as a living man, and one likely to live, demand of you back the confession which, as a dying man, I made to you."

"That is a request I cannot accede to."

"You cannot?"

"Certainly not. It is sacred. I received it in my official character, and I cannot think of giving it up."

"If it be sacred, then you will, I presume, give me your word to keep it so. You will not I presume, communicate its contents to any one?"

"Certainly not for the purpose of gratifying curiosity; but if you attempt to commit any injustice, which the contents of that statement, signed by yourself, will prevent, I shall feel then that it becomes one of my first and most sacred duties to produce it in the cause of justice."

"What do you allude to?"

"I allude to any persecution on your part of Lieutenant Heartwell. You must endeavour to do him justice, and to exonerate him from all that may in any manner affect him unjustly. Do this, and your written confession never meets a human eye, save mine."

Captain Harding looked awfully vexed at this piece of information, which, of all others, was about the most uncomfortable he could possibly have received. To be, after all his endeavours to achieve such a result, at last thwarted in his wish to accomplish some most complete revenge against Heartwell, was certainly one of the bitterest mental conclusions he could come to.

Captain Harding saw that there was really nothing to be made out of so thoroughly untractable a character as this man, and after uttering some more angry expressions, which totally failed in producing the least disturbance of the equanimity of the clergyman, he at once left the apartment, in which the conversation had taken place.

He thought, until thought became a positive pain, over how he could do something to counteract the effects of the confession which he had so imprudently signed.

At one time he considered, that the best way would be to deny altogether its authenticity; but then, when he came to consider how high in integrity of character he had heard this clergyman stood, he gave up that attempt in despair.

He was compelled to return to England, for the most peremptory orders had reached him so to do; therefore, on the evening of the day on which he had held this, to him, most unsatisfactory conversation, he set sail in the Eolus, with a fresh gale, from Gibraltar to England.

The passage was made swiftly, and without meeting anything in the shape of an enemy all the way; so that in less time than might have been expected, the Eolus once more appeared off Portsmouth.

The cruise had been a short one which this vessel had made; but it had not been an unproductive one, as we are aware, especially in its early stages; so that, upon the whole, Captain Harding went on shore with far more reputation than he deserved.

He had a prisoner on board his vessel, although it was not the one he would have wished to have, inasmuch as it was only the unlucky novice who had stood guard over the cabin of Lieutenant Heartwell, and who was brought home most uncomfortably in irons all the way, for not looking sharper after his prisoner.

The readers will now understand that the whole of our characters still living are now in England; and as their relative positions are tolerably well, we hope, defined, we have but now to depict how they came into juxtaposition with each other, and what results were produced such means.

CHAPTER XLI.

THE RESTORATION OF MINNA TO HER FATHER.—THE INTERVIEW WITH HARDING AND THE PROPOSITION.

HE whom we ought now to call Lord Saltoun, inasmuch as it is his legitimate title, to which he is the claimant, who must, without a doubt, succeed in having it duly conferred upon him, was as good as his word to Minna, and proceeded on that same day on which he had so much enlightened her with regard to the latest particulars of her family history to Admiral Harding.

The old admiral for some years had seemed to be changing rapidly for the worse. He looked a thoroughly careworn man, and probably the disappointment which he had experienced as regarded Captain Harding, contributed not a little to depress all his energies, both mental and physical.

Lord Saltoun, who merely gave in the name of Smith, had some difficulty in procuring an interview with him, for latterly he had found himself unequal to the task of seeing everybody who chose to call upon him—a thing which he had once done quite as a matter of principle.

However, after sending a young man who was his secretary, to the visitor, in vain, for not to him, of course, would Lord Saltoun detail his business, Admiral Harding himself walked, with a slow and enfeebled step, towards the room where the visitor had been shown.

Lord Saltoun, when the old man, who he knew to be his father's brother, made his appearance, could scarcely restrain the emotion that came over him, and it was only in faltering accents that he managed to say,

"Sir, but that my object in coming to you was not only of an urgent nature, but likewise one which I considered would be deeply interesting to you, I should not have troubled you with this visit at all."

His voice shook so, that the admiral looked at him with surprise, as he replied,—

"Make no apologies, sir; I assure you, that my not seeing you at once did not arise from any disinclination so to do; the fact is, I am not well enough or strong enough to see any one, unless it be upon real business."

See page 164.

"Sir, I thank you for your courtesy; will you allow me in your own house to hand you a chair?"

"I should rather have behaved with so much courtesy to you, sir; pray be seated. You seem to be much affected."

"I am, admiral, much affected. Are you prepared to listen to something which will affect you much?"

"Affect me?"

"Yes; something which you least of all expect, and which will bring to your heart mingled feelings of joy and sorrow."

The old man exhibited a visible emotion.

"Who are you," he said, "and upon what subject is it, that you come to talk to me?"

"Who I am, sir, will very shortly appear, in the narrative which I have to say before you; and the object on which I come to speak, is one which nearly and intimately concerns you and your family connexions."

" Indeed, my family connexions !"

" Yes, admiral, such is the fact ; so pray, sir, prepare yourself for some surprises."

The admiral walked to the window, and drew up a blind which partially obscured the daylight that was fast drawing to a close, and then he looked for some few moments fixedly in the face of Lord Saltoun.

" I do not know you," he said, " and yet you are marvellously like one long since gone to the tomb. Speak, young man—speak."

" Like—like—who?" gasped Lord Saltoun, much affected.

" The voice, too. The voice !" exclaimed Admiral Harding. " The voice of him who is now no more, as I knew it, and have so often heard it in the springtide of his existence. Is this a dream—is this a dream ?"

" No uncle, no—no. Uncle, look upon me again ; I am your brother's son, I am Lord Saltoun, and your own nephew."

The shock of these words, and the mental confusion they produced in his brain, were too much for the old man's feeble energies, and for some moments he appeared to be upon the point of fainting. Such a circumstance, however, did not take place, and, waving his hand to prevent Lord Saltoun from ringing for assistance, which he had risen to do, he said,—

" Tell me all—tell me all ! Explain your words, before I give way further to feeling. Speak, and speak truly, I charge you !"

He sat down in a large library chair, and covering his face partially with his hands, he listened to the rectal of Lord Saltoun, which embraced all those details with which the reader is already sufficiently well acquainted.

He heard him to an end without interruption, and when he had concluded he arose, and tottering towards him, he held him for a few moments in his embrace.

" It is true," he said, " It wants no confirmation to my heart. Take me to my child, oh, take me to my child !"

" You believe me, dear uncle," said Lord Saltoun, while the tears gushed to his eyes.

" I do—I do, as Heaven is my judge. Oh, for what a long period I have fostered in my heart a serpent, which has stung me ! That bad man, Captain Harding, as he is called, has caused me the bitterest feelings of my life, save, those with which I thought ever of my long lost child. Take me to her, oh, take me to her !"

" But listen to me, admiral ; she almost dreads to see you."

" Dreads to see me !"

" Yes ; you have not forgotten what I have told you of her fallen state ?"

" She is my child still, be she what she may."

" Come, then ; I will, after these words, take you to her, or perhaps it would be better that I should bring her here to you, for no doubt here you would wish her to be."

" Be it so—be it so. Bring her to me with what speed you can. Each moment will seem to me an age until I can fold her in my arms."

Lord Saltoun at once proceeded back to the house where he had left Minna, and related to her his interview with her father. She wept abundantly, but no longer offered any opposition to seeing him.

We cannot attempt by any language to describe the interview which took place between the father and the daughter. Our readers, with their knowledge of the character of both parties, will be well able for themselves to judge what description of interview it was likely to be ; suffice it to say that Minna took up her abode at her father's house forthwith, but with an understanding that as soon as possible she was to remove to the continent, where she insisted upon spending the remainder of her days.

She had such a dread of being in England recognised by any one who knew some of the dreadful scenes she had gone through, that she could not with any amount of pleasure remain in the country.

The old admiral consented to the arrangement, and the more particularly as his physicians had recently advised him to travel, considering that change of scene would be of material benefit to him, and invigorate his system, so he intended to go with Minna.

Let us now take a glance at Heartwell, who, it will be recollected, upon hearing so direful an account of poor Minna, had not been able to stand the sudden shock which it had given to him, but had fainted on the deck of the vessel which had brought him from the marine town, on the Kentish coast, to London.

He was paid every attention to, and at once taken on shore and conveyed to a respectable inn. By the assistance of a medical man who was sent for, he soon recovered his consciousness, and then he eagerly demand of those around him news of the Woodwards.

In that neighbourhood the affairs of the family were, so far as they presented themselves superficially to the public eye, well known, and from the people of the inn he had the story which had been so simply told to him on board the vessel fully confirmed.

This produced such an accession of profound despair that he at once wrote to the admiralty, stating who he was, and that he had deserted from his ship.

So singular a communication could not but produce some result. He was apprehended at once, and recognised, the impression being that he was most decidedly mad, so that when Harding arrived in London and reported himself at the Admiralty the first news he got was of the self-accusation of Lieutenant Heartwell.

In his exultation at that circumstance he forgot all caution, and boldly accused Heartwell of absolute mutiny on board the Eolus frigate, and a day was appointed for a naval court of inquiry to sit upon the subject.

" I have him now," thought Harding, as he walked from the Admiralty towards the house of Admiral Harding. " He has given himself up, so that I cannot be said to have gone out of my way to prosecute him, and that confounded clergyman, at Gibraltar, can by his own showing now have no excuse for producing my confession."

Little, indeed, did Harding dream of what had taken place in his absence. In the first place the clergyman had actually sent by one of the officers of the Eolus a letter to Admiral Harding, in which he placed a copy of the confession of his nephew and concluded the observations which accompanied it by these words,—

" Sir, it is contrary to my nature, as well as to the character of my sacred calling, to see any one wrongfully ill-treated; therefore, I enclose you this paper, not that you may do any injury to Captain Harding with it, but that you may prevent any injustice being done to Lieutenant Heartwell. I have pledged my honour that if Harding attempt nothing against Heartwell, this matter shall be kept secret; and I place my honour so pledged in your keeping."

The admiral had now, therefore, abundant additional reason for congratulating himself upon the circumstances which had dissolved all ties between him and Harding, whom we really now ought to call by his proper name of Brazier.

When he reached the admiral's house, he sent in his name, but instead of being introduced to the old man, a message was sent out for him to call again at twelve o'clock on the following morning.

" What new freak is this?" thought Harding, as he walked away. " Of all the stupid old fools, I do think he is the most. The sooner he dies and leaves me all his property the better; I have no patience with old fools living so long."

As the reader is aware, Admiral Harding had a seat at the board of the Admiralty, and the undaunted courage he had in early life exhibited in fighting the battles of his country, as well as the high character he had obtained for the nicest sense of honour, gave him immense influence with his colleagues.

He called upon every one of them privately, and told the story of Heartwell, so that not only was all idea of prosecuting him abandoned, but Admiral Harding got him the absolute command of the Eolus.

How the old man proceeded to release and inform Heartwell of these matters will be seen.

Minna had made up her mind that she would not see Heartwell.

" No," she said; " there's a gulph now between us which, if love would induce him to cross, I ought not to permit him to do so; I never can now, and I never will be his."

She spoke these words in a tone of voice which admitted of no doubt concerning her sincerity, so that no one pressed the subject, and it was arranged that she should write a letter to Heartwell, telling him that she was alive and well, and requesting that he would forget her for ever, as there was an unsuperable bar to their union.

We are inclined ourselves to think that in adopting this course, Minna adopted the wisest as well as the most feeling one, which she could; it spared Heartwell all the pangs of suspense regarding her fate, at the same time that it left him with a conviction that she wished him happiness—that happiness which, if he could ever forget his first love, she hoped sincerely he might feel with another.

<hr>

CHAPTER XLII.

THE CONCLUSION.

THE eventful morning arrived on which so much was to occur, and when the house of Admiral Harding was to be the scene of so many strange surprises.

Notwithstanding the old man, himself, had been abundantly satisfied with the word of

Lord Saltoun, to the truth of the events which he had related, yet the latter had laid before him the whole of the documentary evidence, which established the facts legally and beyond all possibility of cavil.

The solicitors who had assisted Lord Saltoun hitherto, were invited to be present on the occasion, and, as well, Admiral Harding had sent notes requesting the presence of the late Lord Saltoun's two sisters, who had been so unfeeling when he was on his death bed.

The mother had been dead now some years.

All these persons then were assembled at the house of Admiral Harding, and in the larger of the two drawing rooms, the one of which opened by folding doors into the other.

Minna had gone to a country seat of the admiral for that day.

Cupidity brought the two sisters of the late Lord Saltoun to the admiral's house, in compliance with the request contained in his note, for they had no doubt that he was about to make his will, and that they should come into some share of his large fortune.

This idea was confirmed, when they found themselves ushered into a drawing-room where there were two gentlemen, Lord Saltoun's lawyers, who appeared to be busy with papers.   Indeed, one of the ladies said,—

" Are you professional gentlemen ?"

" Yes madam, we are," was the reply; " and quite at your service."

" Oh ! then probably the admiral is going to make a will ?"

" We think it very probable indeed, madam," said the attorney, who knew very well who his questioner was, and wished to throw her as wide of the mark as possible.

This quite satisfied them, and they waited with the most exemplary patience the admiral's appearance, to commence proceedings.

Captain Harding, with all his effrontery, did not choose to do anything which would look like disrespect towards the admiral; and consequently he was at his house not later than a quarter of an hour after twelve.

He was shown into a small room, which formed a third room on the same floor where were the two drawing-rooms, one of which was already occupied by the attorneys and the two ladies of rank and fashion as they considered themselves, decidedly on the shady side of fifty.

In this small room he found his uncle, to whom he advanced with an affectation of the most affectionate warmth; but the old man waved him off, saying,—

" Stop.   Before we proceed to any other business whatever, I want to know if you are inclined to do an act of justice."

" Of justice, uncle ! can you doubt me ?"

" Well, I am glad to hear you talk so confidently about it.   It is a very simple matter. You have, I understand, in the most dishonourable and distardly manner possible, effected the seduction of a young and innocent girl."

Harding's cheek grew pale.

" And then you deserted her."

" You—you must have been misinformed, uncle.   Some enemy has been maligning me behind my back, I am certain."

" Do you then deny the fact ?" said the old man, sternly.

Harding was silent for a few moments, and then he said—

" Why, I may have been engaged in some such transactions, but what I meant to say was, that it by no means wears the bad aspect your words, uncle, would put upon it."

" Indeed!   Do you know a Lady Clare ?"

Harding now felt certain that all was known, and, in faltering accents, he said—

" Uncle, I have to confess an error of youth, but I have done what I could to repair it."

" That is well.   What have you done ?"

" I have sent the girl plenty of money.   I assure you that I will provide for her so that she shall never want all the comforts of life; therefore, uncle, let so ungracious a subject drop between us.   We all have our errors."

" We all have, God knows; but I cannot let the subject drop.   She denies that you have ever sent to her one farthing.   Sir, you are a villain."

" A villain !"

" Yes, a black-hearted and most desperate villain.   Your only chance whatever of future favour from me is to marry the girl."

" That I cannot think of, sir."

" You positively refuse to marry her ?"

" I cannot think of wedding with a person so far beneath me in rank.   I will provide for her, and that handsomely, too."

"But where are your means?"

"I think, sir, it is high time I asserted my own independence."

"Is it? Well, you know your family history?"

"I do."

"Then I can add something to it. You are aware that the difficulty which has been placed in the way of your claiming the title of Lord Saltoun vanished in the ascertained fact that your mother was previously married to a man named Brazier?"

"Well, sir?"

"And that, concealing that fact, she allowed your father to make her his wife in her maiden name, thus vitiating the marriage, and making you illegitimate?"

"I know not, sir, what motive you can have in bringing forward these facts now. I know them well. They have pressed heavy upon me, and I cannot help thinking that I have been unjustly treated. I have, indeed, some thoughts of going to law for my inheritance."

"Have you really?"

"Yes; and I think you ought to assist me."

"Well, we shall see. Perhaps I may take means to restore you to your proper condition, and place your proper inheritance in your hands. But I have a fact to add to what you know of the family affairs, which you do not now know."

"And what is that, sir?"

"Why, simply this, that the man named Brazier was alive when your mother married Lord Saltoun."

"Ahem! D——n!"

"Yes; it's an awkward circumstance; but swearing will not mend it."

"And are you sure of this?"

"I have seen him."

"Then thus vanish my hopes."

"Not so. Listen yet further. I made the most diligent inquiries into the history of that man Brazier, and the result, far from being such as compels you to bid farewell to your hopes, confirms them all."

"What—what do you mean?"

"I mean that I have discovered that Brazier committed bigamy in marrying your mother, so that his marriage with her being, in law, null and void, her marriage with Lord Saltoun in her maiden name was a correct proceeding."

"And makes me legitimate!" said Harding, springing from his chair.

"Ah! it looks like it to you, no doubt."

"I am Lord Saltoun, then, after all. Admiral Harding, I shake off the trammels in which you have held me, and defy you. You called me a villain, sir. Villain in your teeth! I defy you now, say your worst, and do your worst, old man. I am your superior, and will let you know it, too, to the full extent."

"Very well," said Admiral Harding, calmly; "and now, I presume, you will act liberally?"

"To whom?"

"The young girl you seduced."

"I'll see her d——d! Not a halfpenny she gets from me."

"Heartless ruffian!"

"Come, come, sir, no abuse. I throw up my commission in the navy, so that you are no longer my superior officer; and, if you are abusive, I challenge you."

"You are already superseded in your command and cashiered. There is the document."

The admiral threw a written paper on the table before Harding, who, as he took it up, said,—

"This is a piece of malice. Ha! what—Heartwell appointed to the command of the Eolus!"

"Yes. The brave man whom you did your best to injure, but have signally failed in harming. You are a coward as well as a scoundrel."

"A coward?"

"Yes; I know all. Your denials are now useless."

"Well," said Harding, drawing himself up, "what care I! I am Lord Saltoun, and shall now claim my title as well as my large possessions. I will exact a most rigorous account of everything, you may depend. And now, old man, I leave you, and shall henceforward think of you with the contempt you merit."

" Do so. All the contempt I merit I am content to suffer. But, before you go, there are in this house some persons to whom I wish to introduce you. Step this way."

Harding followed him into the drawing-room, where the persons we have previously mentioned were assembled, and said, as he entered,—

" Ladies and gentlemen, allow me to introduce to you Bulkely Brazier."

" Bulkely what ?" said Harding.

" Brazier. I am sure it is a very euphonious name. Now, Mr. Blunt, will you be so good as to read the document you have prepared."

One of the solicitors immediately stepped forward and commenced reading as follows, while so intense was the silence, that the suppressed breathing of Harding was plainly audible,—

" A statement of circumstances proven by documents, and other creditable evidence, relating to the peerage of Saltoun."

We need not pursue the document. Suffice it, that it clearly detailed all that we know of the history of the Saltoun family, and convinced Harding that, after all, he was but the illegitimate son of the convict Brazier.

At the conclusion of the reading of the document, the admiral called out with a loud voice,—

" Come in."

The folding doors opened, and an old miserable-looking beggar-man made his appearance.

" There," added the Admiral, " Bulkely Brazier, that is your father; you were christened Bulkeley, you know, and have a right to that name."

He, the discomfited and defeated villain, waited for no more, but rushed from the room and the house with a howl of despair and rage.

*　　*　　*　　*　　*　　*　　*

He was found the next morning lifeless in his lodgings. He had poisoned himself during the night.

The real Lord Saltoun found no difficulty in stepping into his ancestral honours and estates. He made the Ladies Saltoun refund all they had appropriated, and one of them —the one who always swore so—died of vexation.

Heartwell had a long interview with Admiral Harding, and then took the command of the Æolus frigate, with which he achieved some of the most brilliant exploits which characterised our war with France.

Minna, in the society of her father and her cousin, Lord Saltoun, was serene and at ease, if she could not be said to enjoy any great extent of happiness—a possession which human nature makes too many false steps long to retain.

THE END.

PUBLISHED BY E. LLOYD, 12, SALISBURY-SQUARE, FLEET-STREET.

www.ingramcontent.com/pod-product-compliance
Lightning Source LLC
Chambersburg PA
CBHW080828250626
47160CB00008B/2873